Praise for April Smith and **WHITE SHOTGUN**

"A satisfying thriller, but what's even more impressive is the crisp, spare writing." —*Los Angeles Times*

"It left me hungry for more—more Italy, more fun and more drama." —Mark Davis, *Las Vegas Review-Journal*

"Smith tells one heck of a crime story with tightly woven, suspenseful plots and lovable but terribly mixed-up protagonists." —*USA Today*

"Smith is a writer with a laser eye that can record with cold precision the details of the daily life of her crime-solving subjects." —*Chicago Tribune*

"April Smith writes in the forceful style of a true literary maverick, someone who has earned the right to break a few rules." —*The New York Times*

"Smith has created a vibrant, intriguing cast of characters and has a superb eye for detail, as evidenced by her vivid descriptions of the Italian landscape....Her true forte is storytelling." —*Pittsburgh Tribune-Review*

"Ana Grey is a credible, fascinating heroine, both worldly and rueful about her unsettled life....Tight suspense and fascinating background." —*Booklist* (starred review)

APRIL SMITH

WHITE SHOTGUN

April Smith is the author of *North of Montana*; *Be the One*; *Good Morning, Killer*; *Judas Horse*; and *White Shotgun*. She is also a television screenwriter and producer, whose most recent work was a TNT original movie based on *Good Morning, Killer*. She lives in Santa Monica.

www.aprilsmith.net

WHITE SHOTGUN

APRIL SMITH

WHITE SHOTGUN

An FBI Special Agent Ana Grey Novel

POCKET BLACK LIZARD
Vintage Books
A Division of Random House, Inc.
New York

FIRST POCKET BLACK LIZARD EDITION, JULY 2012

The Library of Congress has cataloged the Knopf edition as follows:
Smith, April, [date]
White shotgun : an FBI special agent Ana Grey novel / by April Smith.
p. cm.
1. United States. Federal Bureau of Investigation—Fiction.
2. Undercover operations—Fiction. I. Title.
PS3569.M467W55 2011
813'.54—dc22
2011011385

Vintage ISBN: 978-0-307-39101-8

www.aprilsmith.net
www.weeklylizard.com

Printed in the United States of America
10 9 8 7 6 5 4 3 2 1

For Molly Friedrich
True friend, incomparable agent

In bosco nasce,
In prato pasce,
In città suona,
Il vivo porta il morto
E 'l morto suona.

In the woods it is born,
In the pasture it grazes,
In the city it plays,
The living carries the dead
And the dead plays.

"The Riddle of the Drum"
Folk poem from the Palio of Siena

MONTE SAN STEFANO, ITALY

PROLOGUE

THE CHEF drove easily in the dark, anticipating the turns with pleasure, having been in the woods often enough to know the road by heart. The playlist he'd made of his personal favorites was a mix of Italian pop music with interludes of a folksy mandolin. The feel was upbeat. He drove a well-kept silver van with the company name in red lettering on the side and plenty of room in back. The entwined rosaries hanging from the rearview mirror jostled softly, and the black and white Australian sheepdog beside him kept an alert watch through the windshield. It was a cozy drive for Il Capocuòco—the Head Chef—known for his ability to mix chemicals like a master.

When they passed the barn and turned onto the dirt track, the dog stood up in anticipation. When the Chef got out and unlocked the gate, the dog followed and then jumped back into the front seat to wait. The Chef paused to appreciate the stars. It was silent except for the idling engine. Exhaust fumes spoiled the scent of juniper.

They continued through dense trees until the headlights picked up a half-burned abandoned house and, behind it, a prefab shack where sacks of lye were stored. The Chef's day job was delivering chemicals along a busy route of Tuscan farms. He still wore the dirty jumpsuit that was his uniform.

The charred ruins of the old house came closer into view. The headlights cut out, the door opened, and the dog scrambled down into the pine mulch.

A steel vat encased in wood stood on a platform high off the ground. The odd hiker would have thought it a water tower. Underneath the vat was a row of burners, connected to a tank of propane. The Chef lit the gas fire and waited for the chemicals inside the vat to heat.

For the past hour he had been putting off his hunger, eager to get to the site. Now he unwrapped a stick of *salame sopressata*, sliced off the tip with a sharp folding knife, and methodically scored and peeled the outer casing, cutting off slivers of meat, which he shared with the dog. The smell of garlic made him even more ravenous, and he went through the potato chips, orange soda, and packaged cream puffs as well.

The Chef sat behind the wheel with both doors open to the night, counting his money by the dashboard glow, until his pleasantly full belly contracted with venom. Once again, the *pèzzo di merda* who delivered his pay had skimmed 10 percent off the top, and there was nothing he could do about it. They must consider him an idiot, he thought with rage, and threw the empty soda bottle into the bush. The dog's tail went up and he continued to bark at nothing, while the Chef stalked around the back of the van and lugged out a large plastic bin. This time it was the body of a woman, and it was light. *Facile.* Easy. He slipped on goggles and gloves. When the temperature was right it would not take long for the corpse to dissolve in *la minèstra*, the soup.

The woman, Lucia Vincenzo, beautiful, a player both in money laundering and drug dealing, had vanished on a trip to the local market. Her car was left in the parking lot, containing bags of groceries and no evidence of struggle. In the language of the mafias, a murder where the body is never found is called *lupara bianca*, or white shotgun. To disappear with no one knowing how they killed you is a warning to the enemy meant to echo in the most lasting way—in the stark silence of the imagination.

The Chef dragged the bin up the ramp that led to the vat. He drew off the tarp and backed away as toxic vapors rose from *la minèstra*. No one appreciated the quality of his work. How smooth, complete, undetectable.

LONDON

1

IT WAS only another good-bye. Sterling McCord was lying on his back, staring at the lace-curtained window that looked out on the sidewalk. I was up on an elbow, studying the green in his eyes. Rainy light floated around us like the aftertaste of a kiss.

"Hello, cupcake," he murmured.

"Don't go," I said.

We had been camping out in a borrowed flat in South Kensington while I was on vacation status from the Bureau. The place had belonged to the deceased relative of a friend—four rooms in the basement of a Georgian mews house just off Old Brompton Road. The air smelled of mildew and face powder, and we found frilly candy wrappers balled up on the dresser. Sterling called it "the old-lady hooch." We'd had to push two narrow cots together, along with their wobbly headboards of padded roses, but we managed. After a couple of weeks of coming and going, it was starting to feel less like a tomb and more like a place to live. Keys on the table. Eggs in the refrigerator. Then Sterling got the call.

"Do you want to do something interesting?"

That was the way it always began. The voice on the phone. A deep Welsh accent. Sly, as if the reason he was calling wasn't all *that* interesting. An hour later, Sterling would disappear on a mission he couldn't discuss.

Sterling McCord worked for a private security firm called Oryx. His gear was stowed in a corner of the bedroom, laid out for quick departure, the black rucksack hanging from a doorknob. He did not travel with a weapon, preferring to improvise when he arrived. His first stop would be to purchase a Leatherman multi-tool—he must have left dozens in the field. With not much more than a canteen, a poncho, and GPS, it would take less than five minutes to dump his stuff in the rucksack and be gone.

"Is there at least time for a good-bye drink?" I asked, drawing my toes along his leg. Even at rest, his calf muscle felt like a knot of hardwood.

He played with the bracelet on my wrist. "We'll have time."

Sterling liked to say the only thing that made sense in the world was horses. He grew up in Kerrville, Texas, and learned the cowboy arts from his dad—how to train a cutting horse and weave tack, like the fine leather bracelet he had made for me, an eternity knot that would never come off. I had no intention of taking it off. Things were different with Sterling. It was the peaceful way we went to sleep together; deep conversations at three in the morning, someone always willing to rub the kink out of someone's hip. I knew I had fallen in love when I woke up one morning in a white sun-drenched hotel room in Madrid to the scent of baking chocolate. Sterling had ordered his idea of breakfast in bed: two *cafés con leche* and one fresh, sweet-smelling dish of molten chocolate cake with powdered sugar on top. We laid against the pillows feeding each other spoonfuls of bittersweet chocolate. That was it.

Oryx is a type of antelope, but also a helicopter, and Sterling's aircraft of choice. He piloted an Oryx during the war in Sierra Leone, after he left Delta Force, where he learned how to blow a door open without waking the cat. But the most essential skill in the top echelon of Special Forces is the ability to work in absolute secrecy, below the radar of the Pentagon and the FBI. The invisible warrior without boundaries is essential to our security—and a pain in the ass if he happens to be your lover.

I didn't even know to which continent Oryx was sending him, but it was a familiar trek: the rucksack over his shoulder and my hand in his, the touch of our palms unable to deny the sweaty tension of leaving, as we walked the five blocks to Baciare, a neighborhood bistro where you could get a good plate of pasta after midnight; neither one of us expected anything more than a stiff drink to numb the coming separation.

London was on high alert. It had been an explosive spring. Two separate plots to blow up airliners were foiled at Heathrow. A Muslim student at the University of Nottingham was stopped for being in possession of an Al-Qaeda handbook he had downloaded at the library. He died in custody, stabbed by another inmate. University students clashed with gangs of teenage neocons, and dozens of cars were burned during three days of rioting in East London.

The Metropolitan Police were doing a good job of making the rest of the city seem jolly as ever to the tourists crushing the Embankment, but to the interested eye there was a remarkable number of foot patrols, even in the residential boroughs. Edgewater Crescent was a private square lined with redbrick town houses and cherry trees, a tiny oasis off the main drag, which was constantly jammed with posses of young men and women moving quickly, wave on wave of ethnicities and languages, unruly lines in front of the bars and gelato places. Even in this tranquil area, we saw two pairs of female police officers making the rounds beneath the Victorian streetlamps, hair pulled into scraggly ponytails, wearing bulletproof vests and boxy uniforms built for men.

Our trek was interrupted when the cell phone rang. Actually, it was a series of maddening electronic notes like a clown on crack playing an accordion.

After a moment I murmured irritably, "Why do you have such an unbelievably annoying ring?"

"Not my phone," Sterling said.

It was my U.S. cell phone. It hadn't rung in weeks, although out of a habitual sense of doom I always kept it charged. I dug it out of the bottom of my bag.

"Ana?" said a familiar voice. "It's Mike Donnato, calling from Los Ángeles."

"*Mike—?*"

Sterling let go of my hand.

"—it's great to hear from you!" I said.

It wasn't great. It was a disaster. Donnato had been my handler on a domestic terrorism case in Oregon, where Sterling and I had met; and where it was pretty obvious that my FBI partner and I still had feelings for each other. Donnato's intrusion into our last moments together in London was an unwelcome surprise.

"Where are you?" I asked.

"At the office," Donnato said. "It's daytime in L.A."

"What's going on?"

"This is not official business, Ana; it's personal."

Oh God, I thought. *Now that I'm with Sterling, Donnato is finally going to say he's getting a divorce.*

"You need to check in with the legat in London," he said, meaning the legal attaché for the FBI. Although the Bureau has no jurisdiction abroad, we maintain a presence in foreign countries to serve American citizens.

"Did someone die?"

"No, but I can't talk about it on an unsecured phone."

"Am I in trouble?" I asked.

"Go to the American embassy. They're expecting you."

"Mike, why?"

"I'm only the messenger. Do it tomorrow."

I closed the phone. During the call, Sterling and I had not broken pace.

"What's that about?"

"Mike wouldn't tell me."

"Your good ole buddy?" Sterling gave it a Texas kick just to bother me.

"Don't be a dickhead. He's my best friend."

"Then why's he holdin' out on you?"

"It isn't him. It's the Bureau," I said grimly, feeling a gut clench, like when you pass your old school packed with bad memories. One day I'll have to return to the States to testify in that domestic terrorism case in Oregon, and possibly implicate a deputy director of the FBI. Meanwhile, I'm an active duty special agent on vacation—until they decide whether to hang me or give me a medal. Hearing the strain in Donnato's voice, I'm thinking they've made up their minds.

It was a relief to get to Baciare, our comfort zone in London, our signature place, where the owner knew to bring two Proseccos and a plate of *burrata* cheese the moment we sat down.

But not tonight. Our quiet hideaway had been invaded by a raucous birthday party, a long table of shiny-faced Italian men making toasts. Espresso cups and cake plates, bottles of Champagne and platters of biscotti littered the table. The object of the celebration was a sweetheart of a boy—dark-haired and red-cheeked—who had probably just turned twenty-one. His angelic face was filmed with sweat, and he looked completely stewed. Half the men seemed to be older relatives; the others were his age, laughing together uncontrollably from whatever they had smoked in the alley.

The owner of the restaurant, a lanky fellow named Martin, who wore wire-rimmed glasses and had long gray hair trailing from a bald spot, usually greeted us with a fawning smile, murmuring, *"Grazie mille!"* between each breath. Tonight he turned us away, apologizing that it was a private celebration, but a man from the party, fortyish, fleshy face and dark hair, intervened, putting an arm around Sterling and insisting that we accept two glasses of bubbly. Martin checked his watch and reluctantly waved us to a table in the back. We promised to be quick. Sterling was to be picked up by another operative in fifteen minutes, and Oryx people were precise.

"Sterling," I said with some urgency as we sat down, "are we all right?"

"Why wouldn't we be?"

"Just want to be sure," I said.

"You say that every time."

"It's no fun being the one who's left behind."

"We could try it the other way," he suggested wryly.

"You'd never move to L.A."

"Maybe I would, if you'd support my bad habits. You go to work, I lie by the pool. Fair?"

"Great, except who knows? Judging from Mike's call, I might not have a job when I get back."

"I was just playin' about Mike," Sterling said. "He's a good guy."

I started shredding a cocktail napkin. "This is not about Mike. That's in the past."

"Yeah, okay," Sterling said.

I squinted at him. "Okay, what?"

He stretched back in the chair, but his eyes held mine. His blond hair was greasy, and he hadn't shaved for the mission. My tender hooligan.

"What are you really trying to say?" he asked.

I blushed. Luckily, he had the grace not to point it out.

"I want us to be together, is all," I told him.

Sterling inclined his head with a tiny smile, and his eyes said, *I know you. I understand you.*

"I promise to be back as soon as I can." He glanced at the door, ready to move. "We ain't gonna work this out now."

I smiled and sprinkled napkin scraps into the ashtray. "That's what you always say."

It was how we kept going, I suppose. It's easy to avoid talking about the future when you tacitly agree there might not be one. He's leaving on a dangerous assignment. I'm on an ice floe of uncertainty concerning the Bureau. You don't want your last good-bye to be a fight.

Spoons were being tapped against wineglasses at the long birthday table and everyone was quieting down. A boy maybe fourteen years old waited to speak. He wore a yellow satin zip-up jacket, had spiked hair. Obviously they'd let him have some wine.

"I want to make a toast to my big brother, Marco," he said. "He's always been a wanker, but now he's an even bigger wanker. To Marco!"

Cheers and applause. Marco stood up and hugged his little brother, then got the kid in a headlock and pounded him until the father pulled them apart.

"*Basta!*" shouted the father, soft-bellied, workman's arms. "Happy birthday, Marco!"

From the back room someone who might have been an uncle appeared, grinning and rolling out a silver racing bike with wheels that seemed to twinkle.

"For real?" shouted Marco, and threw his arms around the dad.

Sterling's phone beeped. Time to go. He stood and slung the rucksack over his shoulder.

"Be safe," he said.

"You too, baby."

The party began to break up. Jackets were buttoned,

phone calls made. Waiters, abandoning decorum, quickly piled the dirty dishes into plastic bins. We walked the gauntlet of cheerfully inebriated men.

"*Ciao, bella!*"

"The party isn't over!"

"Come with us. Both of you. Come!"

We put on our neutral cop smiles, murmuring, "Thank you. Congratulations. Good night."

We pushed through the wooden door that mimicked a wine cask, relieved to be out of there and breathing the cool air. The cherry trees were in snowy pink blossom. Under the lamplight, the elegant street looked enchanting.

We kissed and separated without further words. I watched as Sterling walked away, trying to tamp down the phantoms of anxiety that always arose when he left. I thought about the empty basement flat, where it was damp as a cave.

The same gentleman who had invited us to the party came up behind me. I noticed his aftershave—ocean spray and menthol—and that he was wearing a linen suit the color of wheat.

"Aah, come on, don't look so sad! If he loves you, he'll come back."

I just smiled and kept on going. Others were emerging from the restaurant and hugging good night, lighting cigarettes and walking toward their cars. The boys were gathered around the bike, Marco demonstrating how light it was, and how balanced—you could pick it up with two fingers under the frame. I remember the linen suit because it reminded me of spring in Washington, D.C., and the cherry trees around the Tidal Basin, and the small stir of pride I always felt because somebody in the United States government had preserved them; someone was looking out for the trees.

A black Ford Focus rolled up. Peeling paint, dented doors. A taunting voice shouted, "Want a cigarette?"

I looked directly at the driver—twenties, dark skin,

baseball cap—thinking he was catcalling me. Another jerk, another hassle. And then the windows of the car exploded with orange fire from the muzzles of automatic weapons. I didn't hear the sound of gunfire, but could feel the hit of overpressure from the bullets around my head. The breath was snatched away from me, like being swept under a huge salt wave.

The car was gone. Sterling was lying on the ground fifteen feet away. There was screaming and the acrid stench of gun smoke, or at least it seemed that way as my sensory apparatus started coming back. I realized that the car had been moving when the shooters opened fire. An angle had opened up between us and the intended targets, and it had saved our lives.

Sterling got to his feet and helped me to stand. His face and arms were pockmarked with cuts. Stars swam through my vision and warm blood dribbled down my temples. I pressed a palm to my scalp. It came away crimson.

"You're okay," he told me.

Professionalism kicked in like anesthetic. I broke away and scanned the situation. Gutted storefronts. Two dozen bodies sprawled every which way. The victims who were still alive had sustained injuries only a trauma surgeon could address.

"Is anyone a doctor?" I shouted at the gawkers.

Sterling grabbed me and said, "Stop."

There was command in his voice I had never heard before.

"Leave the scene. The police can't know I was here. Deny you've seen me." He pushed me away. "*Go!*" he repeated, and disappeared around the corner.

Sirens were coming fast. People were running in all directions. Martin, the owner of the restaurant, seemed to be in a fugue state, sleepwalking across the sidewalk, sweeping the bloodstained broken glass aside with one foot.

An Englishwoman in her sixties took my arm. "We need

help," she said. She was hyperventilating. "Did you see that car? I never saw a car drive so fast around here." She pulled me toward a group that had surrounded two figures on the glittering sidewalk. When I saw what they were looking at, I was overcome with sadness, as if the twinge of abandonment at Sterling's departure had been just the foreshock of a complete cave-in.

Go! I thought. *Do not get tangled up with the British police.*

But Marco was sitting cross-legged, cradling his younger brother. Under the streetlamps the yellow satin jacket was black with blood. The boy's arms were around Marco's neck, and he was trying to pull himself up.

"Oh shit, I'm really hurt."

Several women of different ages were bending over them and saying calming things, although one could not help sobbing. The English lady looked at me with great intensity, as if we had a magic bond; as if we knew the truth. Her eyes were so close they seemed enormous. Exaggerated black equine eyes, shining with terror. The details engraved themselves: a silver chain interlinked with pearls and the collar of a pink crocheted sweater.

Marco's teeth were chattering. "Where's my dad?"

The lady bent down on one nyloned knee. "Your dad is coming," she promised.

"I can't feel my feet," his brother said.

The younger boy was hemorrhaging badly. He had life-threatening wounds to the chest and abdomen. I looked away, down the blurry, snow-laden street, willing the universe to give Sterling back; to see him trot out of the darkness with his rucksack of remedies and sanity. Now the patrol units and ambulances appeared. Sterling was gone, already in another country. The bike was resting on its side as if someone had laid it there, weightless, all its wondrous mechanisms intact. Citizens were rooting through the rubble, taking souvenirs.

2

TRAINING TELLS us a disaster is "anything that over-whelms you," and this qualified. So many bodies in unknown states of bleeding and shock, the clock ticking for those whose breathing was falling off. No latex gloves, tourni-quets, face masks, defibrillator.

"Anybody who can move, come to me!" I shouted.

Stunned residents who had left their flats lined up com-pliantly where directed, in front of a grocery store across the street, eager to obey anyone who seized authority. Once herded to safety, they raised their arms in unison to take pic-tures with their cell phones, staring at the tiny screens like invaders from another planet.

I began to triage the victims, tapping their heads and shouting, "Are you okay? I'm trained; I can help you," push-ing through the nausea and fear to focus on checking vital signs so I could direct the arriving paramedics. Marcos's little brother was an "Immediate" but later tagged "Dead," having succumbed to massive bleeding and a severed spine. I never found out what happened to the father, or to the man in the linen suit.

Despite Sterling's command to disassociate myself from the incident, the first thing I did was to let them know I was

FBI. This led to a clipped conversation with Inspector Ian Reilly from the Homicide and Serious Crime Command, a florid-faced dinosaur with a bad head cold, for whom I summarized my view of events: the taunting shout, the release of automatic weapon fire apparently aimed at the restaurant, the getaway north on Edgewater Crescent Road.

After making sure I was tended by a medic, Inspector Reilly sent me by squad car to Metropolitan Police headquarters at New Scotland Yard, a gray-windowed tower on Broadway, where I sat in a nondescript airless room with a female Pakistani sketch artist, collaborating on a composite drawing of the driver of the Ford. He ended up looking like every thug you've ever met—a long face, straight eyebrows, a prominent nose, dark curly hair, scowling eyes beneath a baseball cap.

When we sat down several hours later, Inspector Reilly wanted to know if I had ever met Clint Eastwood. I am based in Los Angeles, after all. I had to tell him that sadly, I had not, and asked what had been determined by the forensic team. Had they checked all the surveillance cameras in the area? Had they retrieved shell casings? Were there tire tracks? Who were the targets? What was the theory? A turf war? Random violence? Terrorists or organized crime?

Inspector Reilly was not eager to share. He did remark dryly that two witnesses reported that the driver had been wearing a turban. "No," I assured him. "A baseball cap." To his credit, he saw me not as a colleague but as a witness to the point-blank execution of seven people, who needed to be interviewed with sensitivity. Just as patiently, I went through the hoops.

When we were both satisfied that we had done our jobs, he said he would get me a ride back to South Kensington. It was seven in the morning and everyone in London seemed to be going in the opposite direction, toward the canyons of the financial center. My eyes burned with exhaustion as I stepped from the lobby of headquarters to find a glossy black Opel sedan waiting at the curb. It was too nice to be a Metropolitan Police car. A clean-cut driver hopped out, wearing a smartly tailored suit.

"Special Agent Ana Grey?"

He was American.

"I'm Ana Grey. Are you sure I'm the one you're waiting for?"

"Yes, ma'am."

He opened the rear door. Sitting in the impeccably clean backseat was a big-boned woman in her fifties wearing a nubby black suit and something I can never manage to get right: cream-colored sling-back heels. Her short blond hair was styled in waves that curled around gold shell earrings. Her cheeks were veined from what I imagined to be decades of Midwest winters. On her lap was a red leather business tote. You knew that all the accessories inside matched.

"Ana," she said warmly. "Good to meet you. I'm Audrey Kuser, the FBI legat in London. How are you doing?"

"Hanging in."

She inspected my face. "Rough night?"

"Better for me than for a lot of other people."

She saw that I was looking at the *Daily Telegraph* neatly folded beside her. The full-page headline said GUNFIRE IN S. KEN LEAVES 7 DEAD.

"You won't find your name in the paper. The Bureau isn't publicizing the fact that an American FBI agent was present at the attack."

"Not planning to write home about it."

"I'm sorry for what you went through. How are you feeling?"

"Dog tired, and disgusted with human nature. But I'm okay. If I weren't, I'd tell you."

"I want you to check in with a counselor."

"Sure thing."

Been there, done that.

"Excuse me while I just finish this." She was tapping the keys of a BlackBerry with the square corners of manicured nails. "Here we go. Your flight is confirmed. David?" she asked the driver. "Can we stop in South Kensington and make it to the airport by eight-thirty?"

"No worries."

He accelerated into traffic.

"Am I being deported to L.A.?" I asked, half joking.

She pressed a button, causing the glass divider to slide up so the driver couldn't hear our conversation. She was Bureau, all right.

"You're going to Rome."

"Rome," I repeated. Not a question, but a statement of astounding fact.

She nodded and removed a folder from the red tote. "You are now on official business. A couple of weeks ago, a call came in to the Los Angeles field office from a woman named Cecilia Maria Nicosa. Ring a bell?"

"Negative."

"She claims to be related to you. She says you two have never met."

"That's for sure. Where does she live?"

"Siena, Italy."

"I don't know anyone in Italy."

The legat stayed patiently on point.

"She's been trying to find you for a while. She hired a private investigator."

"I'm flattered, but why?"

"She claims to be holding a small inheritance for you from a family member in El Salvador. Besides, she wants to meet you."

"Why?" I repeated dumbly.

Ms. Kuser seemed amused. "That's often what people in families do."

"It's strange to me. I have no close relatives left."

"We know."

"Of course you know."

I stiffened in the seat, waking up to the hard-core nature of the inquiry. I would not be driving around London with the FBI legat if something weren't seriously up.

"This woman is from *Italy* and she's *Italian* and you think we're related? How is that possible?"

"I didn't say she's Italian," Audrey Kuser said with an edge. "I said she *lives* in Italy. She's originally from El Salvador. Just like your dad."

I had the sensation of ice cubes slipping down my neck.

Audrey Kuser was looking at the file. "Your father's name is Miguel Sanchez, is that right?"

"That's right."

I was shocked to hear her speak my father's name. He was an immigrant from El Salvador who married my American mother. He disappeared from my life when I was five years old, in a darkened yard in Santa Monica, California, bludgeoned to death because he had brown skin.

"How do you know about Miguel Sanchez?"

Audrey Kuser glanced at me over her reading glasses.

"You wrote your father's name on the application when you joined the Bureau," she explained. "We confirmed 'Sanchez' as belonging both to you and to this woman. Sanchez is her maiden name. She's claiming to be related to your father's family. She wrote several letters, in fact."

"Why did I never receive them?"

She narrowed her eyes mockingly. "Are you serious?"

I understood the implication. Personal mail from a foreign source to a special agent would have been sent to FBI HQ, where it was probably still being examined by umpteen layers of intel analysts.

"Here's what we've learned about your family member, and what we want you to do. Cecilia Maria Nicosa is married to Nicoli Nicosa, a wealthy coffee importer who made his money supplying the restaurant business. We believe the husband may be dirty. He was carrying on a very public affair with a woman called Lucia Vincenzo, a mafia operative who recently disappeared. Lucia Vincenzo had connections with international drug trafficking, and because of his history, we suspect Nicosa might, too. Ms. Vincenzo is not the only victim who has vanished in northern Italy in recent months; there has been a cluster of the 'disappeared.' Italian citizens are afraid the government cannot control the violence associated with global criminal networks—and in fact, the government has asked for our assistance. This case will give us the opportunity to help the Italians and also get intel on drug trafficking to the United States. We want you to check Mr. Nicosa out. We want to know if he's dangerous. You'll report to the legat in Rome. When you get there, he'll give you an official passport that says you're on U.S. government business."

We were pulling up to the Georgian mews house. The curtains were drawn over the basement window. I knew exactly what it would smell like inside.

"Palio starts next week," Audrey Kuser was saying. "Do you know what that is?"

"A horse race?"

"It's a festival in the city of Siena that draws huge crowds, ends with a big race. If you *were* a relative, and you *were* in

Europe right now, it is plausible that you would want to visit Cecilia Nicosa during Palio."

We got out of the car and she accompanied me down the basement steps. She would not leave my side until I was delivered safely to the plane to Rome.

As I turned the key, the borrowed flat seemed dead; whatever warmth and hopefulness Sterling and I had kindled was gone along with him. Audrey Kuser stood with feet planted, thumbing her BlackBerry, while I pulled out a suitcase. I could see from her aggressive stance the solid street agent she once had been.

"I'm sure you would rather take a shower and sleep for twelve hours," she observed.

"It sounds like a lot of planning went into this."

"The ball's been in play since we made the connection between you, your relative, and Nicoli Nicosa. We've been interested in him for a while, but with Italian-controlled crime syndicates, it's impossible to get inside unless you're trusted kin."

"I'm not exactly trusted kin."

"Not yet, but it could be a good fit. We had been looking at you going undercover, but last night's events pushed the time frame."

"Why is that?"

"The fact that you were on Edgewater Crescent Road. We had to ask ourselves, was it a coincidence you were there during the attack? Mike Donnato calls from Los Angeles to inform you of our interest, and an hour later our agent is caught in a hail of machine gun fire. Did someone overhear that conversation? Is someone out to eliminate Ana Grey— or the entire operation? The better part of valor is for you to leave London."

Vacation was definitely over. I'd been awake twenty-four hours and traumatized more than I knew, overwhelmed by manic exhaustion. The notion of putting up a front for some long-lost relative seemed beyond my capabilities. I found myself staring numbly at a jumbled drawer of T-shirts.

Audrey Kuser looked at her watch and began to fold each one and lay it flat in the suitcase.

"When you raise three boys, you get good at this," she said briskly. "Let me help."

ROME

3

ROME IS burning in the blaze of June. The heat comes at you in scorching puffs, like the fiery breath of seraphim, that eternal chorus of angels who do nothing but praise God. They must work extra hard in this fervent air, singing their adoring prayers in clashing discord with the earsplitting racket of motor scooters and jackhammers.

The ancient, toothless cabdriver has installed a navigation system in his vehicle, but not air-conditioning. We ride with the windows down, ripening by the minute, like olives. The summer crowds are global, colossal. As we come to a standstill in heavy traffic yet again, I am starting to feel as if I might evaporate along with my own sweat, leaving an empty black Brooks Brothers suit on the seat.

The taxi crawls up the Via Veneto. Every town in the U.S.A. has a "Via Veneto"—an Italian restaurant or shoe store named after the famous avenue lined with sycamore trees. Swank cafés have taken over the sidewalks in front of stately old hotels and apartment buildings, flaunting awnings and wicker chairs, tables separated by gauzy billowing curtains. I am not going there. I am going to an armed fortress.

The American embassy in Rome is housed in the Palazzo Margherita, which sounds grand, and probably was, until the threat of terrorism made it prudent to enclose the entire block in a web of concrete buttresses. We used to build embassies with walls of glass to demonstrate the pride of an open democratic society in a foreign land. Now the symbol of American diplomatic presence has been buried inside a depressing and impenetrable military stronghold.

I disembark on the Via Veneto at a confusing maze of stanchions, furnace-heated air gusting up my skirt. Somewhere close by is the disconcerting sound of fresh bubbling water. The driver has left the cab idling in the middle of the street in order to fill a water bottle from an archaic moss-covered fountain behind the barriers that has survived since God knows who was emperor. I would like to stick my head in it.

Young *carabinieri* are directing traffic while talking on cell phones. There are a lot of uniforms, but none seems to know the location of the main entrance, or how to interpret my paltry Italian. Why did I assume Americans would be guarding the American embassy? After several phone calls and three separate checks of credentials by three humorless Italian officers, I go through the gate and am met by a robust young lady from Virginia, who guides us through a blazing inner courtyard, zigzagging through a den of construction, until at last we come to the old chancery building, home of the ambassador and the site of sensitive consular activities, where I am relieved to be greeted by a pair of alert on-duty U.S. Marines.

We go through a gap in the scaffolding and enter a hundred-and-twenty-year-old palazzo, cross burgundy marble floors, and trudge up a stone staircase. It gets weirder.

Rome is not a solid city bound to granite like New York, but a fluid stratum of centuries of cities that seem to rise and fall and remake themselves by the hour. It exists in layers; layers of history, layers of paradox—visible and buried—all bound up in a modern hodgepodge. Nothing in Italy is *only* as it appears. The nice young woman describes two-thousand-year-old fresco paintings preserved in an underground passage beneath this very building. Maybe in Rome one should expect such juxtapositions, but after swishing down a mosaic-lined hallway with gold tiles, it is a bit of a shock to open a door to an exact replica of the same standard-issue FBI office that you would find in Omaha, Nebraska.

The air-conditioning is freezing, American-style, the tiny room jammed with steel filing cabinets; Old Glory droops in a corner. On the walls we have plaques and awards, and a display box of medals with the familiar caption, "Once a Marine, Always a Marine." Coming out with hand extended from behind a wooden desk identical to the one my boss has in L.A. is the FBI legat in Italy, Dennis Rizzio—a balding, moon-faced *paesano* from Brooklyn.

"Agent Grey! How ya doin'? Welcome to Rome."

The accent is unrepentant.

"What can I getcha?" He opens a small refrigerator. "How about a cold soda? Outside, you could fry eggs on the sidewalk."

"Tell me about it."

We sit across from each other in Bureau-issue high-backed leather chairs that always make me feel like a midget in a neck brace. They fit Dennis, however—a big man, easily six foot four—soft from too much gnocchi and nobody breathing down his neck to pass a fitness test. He's wearing the traditional white shirt, gray suit, and dull-ass blue tie. The wardrobe is deliberately neutral. The mind is like a diamond drill.

I press the icy can of soda to the back of my neck.

"Coming in, did you pass the Colosseum?"

"Yes, it was kind of a surprise. You're going through a slum covered with graffiti and then—wow. There it is."

"Did you know you could scuba dive underneath it?"

I must have stared blankly.

"Yeah. Under the Colosseum. They still have sewers from ancient times, underground rivers filled with statues and all kinds of crap. People go down there. Scientists. Oh, man, I thought I died and went to heaven."

"Swimming in crap?"

"*That* I could do in New York," he deadpans. "No, when I first saw the Colosseum. I always wanted to raise my girls in the old country. I wanted to hear them speak the language of my father. I can't tell you how many years I had to finagle and kiss ass in order to get over here."

"Special Agent in Charge Robert Galloway is from Brooklyn."

Dennis's sallow face almost lights up. "I just spoke to Bob on your behalf. About you coming on board. We worked the organized crime squad together in the early nineties. That sounds strange. 'The early nineties.' Like it was another *century*, which it was. How's he doin'? Still with the turtlenecks and the cigars?"

I nod. "He was my boss on a deep cover case. I had total confidence. Always knew he had my back."

Dennis grins. "Bob's got a gift for undercover. This was during the famous crack cocaine epidemic we had in New York City. We did good. Put a lot of creeps in jail. Bob and I, we were working out of the social clubs on Mulberry Street. I consider myself from Little Italy, even though I had to move to Brooklyn because the yuppies came. My entire family grew up in Little Italy, four generations. My great-grandparents came over from Napoli. There was this volcano called Vesuvius?" He looks at me with round, sad eyes. "You heard about it?"

I have learned, sitting in a room like this across from Robert Galloway, that you always answer New York irony with New York irony. Otherwise, they think you're a moron.

"I heard about it."

Without changing expression, Dennis goes on. "I got so good at communing with the mafiosi, the Bureau brought me here to oversee operations against drug trafficking by the mob. Excuse me, *tasked*. I was *tasked*—like taking out the garbage. And we don't say 'mob' anymore; that dates me. It's 'mafias,' to distinguish the fact that there's no single organization but—aren't we lucky?—*lots* of family-operated crime groups in Italy. So I hear you were in London and it was no picnic. Not exactly a cruise on the Thames."

"You saw the 302s?"

"London sent a priority alert. Whenever there's an agent involved in a shooting incident, they wake up the legats and tell us about it."

"Sorry to disturb your sleep."

"Sorry for the bullets whizzing by your head. Thank your lucky stars."

He knocks on the wooden desk. I knock on the coffee table.

"I have your debrief with Inspector Reilly from New Scotland Yard. You had a pretty good look at the gunman. What was it he said to you?"

"He said, 'Want a cigarette?,' but I'm not sure he meant me."

"Just the general public?"

"I don't know, Dennis! Do terrorists have a sense of humor? It's the kind of thing a lowlife jerk-off would say before he blows out a restaurant. Like, *Want a cigarette, asshole? Here's a match.*"

"Anything else come to mind that's not in the report?" Dennis asks.

"The attackers knew there was a party, and who was there."

"Why do you say that?"

"The street. A feeling I had." I am remembering the stillness of the cherry trees. "When we came out, it was quiet.

Deep quiet, the way it is past midnight on an upper-class street. The place was dead—I would have noticed something, but there were no lookouts. Nothing hinky. Then right on cue, a car speeds past. Twice as fast as you'd expect in that neighborhood. Doesn't stop, opens fire. Hits multiple targets."

"The Metropolitan Police are investigating the victims for links to terrorism or organized crime. The Italian government has asked for our assistance concerning the mafias, so we're into this on both accounts."

"Talk to the owner of the restaurant. His name is Martin." I surprise myself by saying this, as I had thought of Martin as a decent, if somewhat unctuous, guy. "He was nervous and didn't want to seat us. Interesting that he didn't turn out to be one of the victims."

"You think Martin was the tip-off?"

"The knuckleheads knew the targets were there. Somebody must have told them."

Dennis nods and jots a note.

"Got some new intel from the Met." He indicates the monitor of a massively outdated computer. "It was a Ford Focus, right? The attack vehicle? Kinda old? Bad paint job? Do you recognize the year?"

He shows me a group of Ford Focus photos. I can't reliably tell the difference between the models.

"London has more video cameras than God," I say. "They should check surveillance tapes of the nearby intersections. Interview everyone in every apartment building in Edgewater Crescent. I hope they understand that this is a boots on the ground operation."

"They're on it. What's your gut on the motivation?"

Dennis makes his face go slack. Open to whatever the subject wants to bring.

"It was a brazen act, meant to send a message."

"Not just random?"

"I can't believe it's random when you drive into an upscale neighborhood and shoot seven people with automatic weapons, with the city on high alert and cops patrolling the streets, in some tucked-away little square with not a lot of options for escape, unless you've got a compelling reason."

"Money?"

"Or you believe in something."

"Like radical Islam, you mean? I'm sure the British Counter Terrorism Command is looking very carefully at who the targets were—if there's a connection to the extremist attacks they've had the past few weeks, or similarities to other crimes."

"It's not necessarily the individuals who were targets. It could have been English society in general. It's a very tony area they hit. Diplomats, businesspeople. And a fourteen-year-old kid."

Dennis shrugs. "Collateral damage. What do they care? This is fun for them. Tell me again why you were there?"

The question is not as casual as it sounds. I had ducked it before, with Inspector Reilly, in order to protect Sterling. Now Dennis is watching me with an intensity I know very well.

"I stopped in at Baciare for a glass of wine."

"Just on your own?"

I give him a look. "I'm a big girl, Dennis."

"No doubt." He slaps a passport on the desk. "This is for you. Official government business."

"I feel like James Bond."

"Don't get cocky. We're dealing with 'Ndrangheta, not Dr. No," he says.

"Isn't 'Ndrangheta based in the south?"

He nods. "In Calabria, at the shit-caked bottom of Italy's boot, which they've turned into the distribution hub for cocaine in Europe. We're talking a multibillion-dollar crime syndicate made up of a hundred or so tribal families with strong blood ties, six thousand strong, holed up in remote mountain villages."

"Like Afghanistan."

"From a tactical point of view, it's the same. Just like the Taliban, 'Ndrangheta operates out of an inaccessible fortress, where they hook up with other transnational crime organizations, running heroin from the poppy fields in Afghanistan to the port of Napoli, and eventually, to Hometown, U.S.A. That's the FBI's interest, aside from helping our Italian friends. We want to know how and where these drugs are entering the United States."

"Where does Nicoli Nicosa fit in?"

"He could be a 'Ndrangheta affiliate, working behind a screen of respectability to run cocaine in the north. To do business at his level in society—believe me, nobody is clean. They all swim in the same swamp."

Dennis opens both hands like a book.

"Let me introduce you to your new family. Nicoli Nicosa is forty-eight years old. Drives a Ferrari, travels by private jet. He's made a fortune with a genetically engineered coffee bean—started out providing coffee to upscale restaurants, and now he's got his own chain of stores. Have you been inside a Caffè Nicosa?"

I shake my head.

"Did you ever take the train in Paris? Ever been to the Gare du Nord, where the Eurostar goes?"

"No."

"Ever taken a train in *London*? You don't take public transportation? What are you, a snob?"

He leans forward and puts his big paws on his knees. I can see him admonishing his little girls in Brooklyn. *Whatareya, stupid? How could you not know this?*

"If you were ever *on* a train, or spent *two minutes* walking around Rome, you would know that Caffè Nicosa is the Starbucks of Europe. You don't get your cafés into major train stations without heavy-duty connections and bribes, and that's just the beginning."

"What about the wife, Cecilia? My relative. The one who called the Bureau?"

"She's a medical doctor and a socialite on the Italian scene. Always in the magazines. She never contacted you before?"

"I didn't know she existed until the London legat told me on the way to the airport."

"So, why is Cecilia Nicosa calling you now?" Dennis asks rhetorically.

I consider the question. "Does she know her husband was cheating on her?"

"The world knows. It was in the papers."

"Does the world also know that his mistress, Lucia Vincenzo, disappeared?"

"The mafias make sure of that. Every so often someone who vanished after refusing to pay shows up in the ocean or as remains in a vat of lye. It keeps the little people on their toes."

"Cecilia could be afraid for her life."

Dennis presses the intercom, instructing the girl from Virginia to get Dr. Nicosa on the landline.

"If we really are related, am I supposed to spy on my own family?"

"Go and observe, then we'll decide. Don't bitch; this is a high-class assignment. Siena is a beautiful city. Plus, they have the best gelato *in your life*—at a hole-in-the-wall called Kopa Kabana. *And* you're there for Palio," he adds, his eyes taking on a rare sparkle.

"What's the big deal about a horse race?"

"It's not a horse race, it's '*a spectacular*,' as my father would say. Trust me, you've never seen anything like it—tens of thousands of people squeezed into a piazza, all going nuts."

"Security must be interesting."

He nods. "They have their hands full. Siena is made up of what they call *contrade*, like neighborhoods—actually little city-states, with their own seat of government and coat of arms—who have hated one another for centuries. Instead of killing one another, they have a race. It's the most dangerous, fastest horse race in the world. Ninety seconds, that's it, in the middle of town, on a track with *mattresses* stuck in the corners. The jockeys ride *bareback* and do anything to win— make deals, shove one another off the horse. The whips are made of the skins of calf penises. It's so crazy Italian."

"Calf penises?"

"They use them to whack the hell out of each other. It's a blood sport. Someone always gets hurt. God forbid the horse. The horse eats at the table. I kid you not. They have outdoor dinners, and *the horse eats at the table*. Kind of like Thanksgiving at my in-laws' house," he muses, screwing in an ear pod as the phone rings with my alleged new family member on the line.

"Oh, Ana!" exclaims Cecilia Nicosa when I've picked up and identified myself. "How beautiful to hear from you! I was hoping I would, but I was never certain that you got my letters."

Her accent would be hard to place. Latin, but not quite.

"I was on vacation in London when I got the call from Los Angeles that you were looking for me," I say, maintaining eye contact with Dennis.

"Where are you now?" she asks.

"At the FBI office in Rome."

"Rome! That is just two hours from us!" she says, and immediately invites me to come and stay with her husband and their teenage son, Giovanni, in their "little house on a hill." Dennis gives the thumbs-up. We settle on a train the following day.

"A car will take you back to your hotel," he says, "and drop you off tomorrow at Stazione Termini. Look for Caffè Nicosa, smack in the middle of the station. Get the prosciutto, goat cheese, and arugula *panino*. Trust me."

Despite the frigid air-conditioning, there are sweat stains under his arms. Had the interview been that stressful?

"I trust you," I say with a hollow laugh.

"We should be in good shape in Siena. No worries; I work closely with the locals. I'll be checking in."

He hands over a bound report issued by the U.S. Department of Justice, Federal Bureau of Investigation. "For Trusted Agents Only. PROFILE: NICOLI NICOSA."

"Reading material for the train."

"How long have you been keeping files on my relatives?" I ask lightly.

Dennis lays a big hand on my shoulder. "The city never sleeps."

4

AT STAZIONE Termini the next day, an impatient crowd is staring at a board where all the departure signs are rolling over to say, *"Soppresso."* Nearby, a group of exhausted teenagers lies in a pile on top of their rucksacks in the middle of the floor. I ask what's going on.

"It is a train strike," replies a girl with a Persian accent. "We've been waiting all night."

Everybody in Rome seems to know the trains aren't running, except the FBI's legal attaché. I wonder why this is. Has Dennis Rizzio been prisoner of the mock Bureau office so long he has forgotten that we are actually in Italy?

At least Caffè Nicosa is where he said it would be, a deftly lit island of elegance in the center of the hall. Brick dividers, aluminum moldings punched out with playful circles. Starbucks, it is not. Enviable customers are picking at tiny balls of mozzarella in nice white bowls. Floating like a golden leaf in a sea of sweaty, pissed-off commuters, Caffè Nicosa beckons you to come in and be civilized. I am dying to sit down with a cold glass of Pinot Grigio and bask in the irony of reading the FBI file on its owner, Mr. Nicosa, but every table is occupied and there's a long line.

Slowly I come to understand that the only way to get to

Siena in the foreseeable future is by bus. I text Cecilia the change in plans and haul my suitcase outside, where the devilish cobblestones break a wheel. The heat is laughable; the hot winds must blow directly from Algeria, because my face has dried out like a date. When I shout, *"Stazione d'autobus?"* over the car horns and swirling grit, a man in uniform directs me to a city bus, with instructions to get off at the last stop.

When I arrive at the bus terminal an hour later, there aren't many passengers left. It is the last point before the freeway in a run-down section of bleak, graffiti-covered apartment buildings that look as if they've taken one too many power punches to the midsection. I squeeze myself and the rebellious roller bag into a tiny cafeteria the size of a gas station convenience store, where skinhead families and black-shrouded *nonnas* have taken refuge from the hundred-degree heat. The mood is tense and incendiary, as if a harsh word could cause the place to combust. There are round signs dangling from the ceiling with Coca-Cola bottles riding rocket ships. I stare at the floor, meditating on the black and green diamond pattern of purgatory.

Hell is waiting. Hell is being unable to go forward or back, when your boyfriend is in parts unknown and home is a stack of cartons in a storage locker. What am I doing in this remote Roman ghetto, so far off the track that my sense of self has dissolved like the puddle of melted Popsicle at my feet? The language, the foreignness, the uncertainty, the heat, are percussive beats like the blood pounding in my head, urging me to flee. The exhilaration of being plucked out of London for a whirlwind trip to Rome now seems hideously misplaced. It's just another assignment. The arrows lined up and put me in the picture with Nicoli Nicosa, that's all.

Like Sterling, I am a soldier for hire, part of whose job is to soldier on alone. Every time I catch a TV monitor showing encounters in Iraq, Afghanistan, Pakistan, the

Philippines, I wonder if he's there, boosting my spirits by remembering that we both keep making the same choice. When I'm working, I don't question things. I feel whole. I know my world, and I'm confident there. As long as I respect the coach, I can be a good team player, but in this job, the best work is often done off the grid, on your own terms. You deal with the blowback later. Sterling and I are the same—happiest when we're acting solo. Or maybe it's the American way to go it alone. Looking around, I seem to be the only non-Italian packed into the Roman bus station; certainly the only woman not in the company of a mother or a sister.

There's no place like Italy to make you feel like an orphaned child.

I leave the cafeteria, dragging the suitcase toward an open lot backed by tenements that has been turned into a field of corn, a hopeful sign that somewhere in this degraded landscape the human spirit has prevailed. Ahead at the horizon is an elevated highway where cars are speeding out of the city.

Silhouetted against the setting sun is a woman, six feet tall with storklike legs, wearing nothing but a bikini and heels; obsidian-black skin, hair in a knot at the nape of her neck, languidly moving to a boom box playing African music. Curtains of laundry flutter from the windows above her. A car pulls off the ramp. A white businessman steps out. The woman extends her hand and leads him into the cornfield.

WHEN THE bus comes, it is new and air-conditioned. Despite the hordes at the station, there are not many going to Siena. The front seats are taken by two elderly nuns and a blind priest. When we pass the outer industrial rings of the city, the terrain becomes deeply green, broken by raked fields of mustard yellow, dappled with rolls of hay. As we enter the provinces of Umbria, and then Tuscany, there are no malls or subdivisions. The bus stops in few towns along the way. Soon the only sign of modernity is a power line going by in a hypnotic stripe.

I open the file Dennis gave me on Nicoli Nicosa. It describes a cagey player, adept at choosing the side in power, and apparently without political loyalty. He first came to the FBI's attention when he was observed by a surveillance team that had been following Lucia Vincenzo, forty-two, the widow of a crime boss who was executed in classic manner while he drove to the sweatshop he owned outside Naples, where he employed master tailors and seamstresses to make high-quality copies of designer clothing. He got behind on his extortion payments to 'Ndrangheta; they threatened to seize the business. He resisted; they took him out before breakfast.

After her husband's murder, 'Ndrangheta made Lucia a deal. She would continue to run the fake high-end clothing business, but now as a money-laundering scheme for their cocaine operation. Profitable for everyone. Her mistake was to hire Chinese immigrants, cheap labor, to work in the shop. It didn't matter that drug money flowed in and out as usual. By hiring the Chinese she had crossed the crime families who control the counterfeit merchandise trade—an unforgivable slap in the face that could unbalance the delicate truce between the clans. She was a wild card. 'Ndrangheta had to cut her off.

They called her La Leonessa, the Lioness, because she was remorseless and arrogant as a cat, and she obliged the nickname by sporting skintight animal prints, furs, and ropes of gold. From the photos and news clippings reproduced in the file, the Lioness looked like the cliché of a mistress: full-busted, with thick black hair and the size-two body of a teenager. She vanished from a supermarket parking lot in January of this year—punishment for dealing with the Chinese without permission.

That was the theory. But if the husband is always the prime suspect, the lover must be second in line. While the file details five trysts in luxury hotels in Como and Milan between Nicoli Nicosa and Lucia Vincenzo over the past year, it contains no hard evidence that they were in the cocaine business together—but why not? Lucia was an over-confident amateur and Nicosa a street-smart opportunist who might have been looking for a partner. Maybe he saw a way to prove himself to the big boys by aiding in her death.

Like the princes of the Italian city-states, Nicosa seems to possess a natural understanding of alliances. The son of a Sienese coffee roaster, he graduated from the Università degli Studi di Roma and studied in the United States at Harvard Business School. There he connected with the son of a member of the ruling class of El Salvador. In that deeply troubled country it was open season for ruthless young men. His classmate's father liked the charming, big-eyed Italian and treated him like another son; he gave him a postgraduate course in bribery and corruption that allowed Nicosa to buy out the indigenous farmers who were growing yucca, in order for him to plant coffee. The file notes that although the civil war had ended, "buy out" was often a euphemism for "disappeared."

Nicosa continued to profit from a cordial relationship with the right-wing power brokers. After a major earthquake, he was awarded a contract to build a water treatment system. Although the water project is still touted on the official government website as having revitalized a devastated area, it was never built. Nicosa and his behind-the-scenes benefactors pocketed millions.

It was in the aftermath of this earthquake that he met Cecilia Sanchez, a young doctor working in an emergency clinic set up near his plantation. There is a gap of three years before Cecilia immigrated to Italy, and they were married in Nicosa's hometown of Siena. It could not have been easy for a young woman to leave a poor extended Catholic family that depended on her income as a doctor. There isn't much in the file on Cecilia's side of the story, except copies of the letters she sent to FBI HQ in Washington, D.C., searching for an American relation named Ana Grey. She gives the reason as a small inheritance she is allegedly holding for me, but then the letters grow more desperate:

"...Since I was a little girl, I have held in my heart the name of Ana Grey, our relative who lived in America. I believe that we are meant to find each other. The discovery of her work for the American Federal Bureau of Investigation gives me hope. It is very important to my family that I can find her. Please reply as soon as possible..."

I can hear her voice as it was on the phone, with its unique blend of accents, like nutmeg and tamarind, speaking through the words on the dull photocopy. "Since I was a little girl, I have held in my heart the name of Ana Grey." As Dennis Rizzio had wondered, why make contact now? What is going on inside that "little house on a hill" that would cause the wife of a wealthy man in Europe to reach out to a stranger in America?

Glancing out the bus window, I see the landscape has changed. The yellow fields are gone; instead there is a cheesy strip mall with a discount shoe pavilion and outlets for tires and wine. As I observe families at tables outside a pizzeria, the image of the two young brothers at the London restaurant comes into my head. I watched as the younger boy expired in his brother's arms. I saw his body receive that decisive stillness. And Marco never once let go.

I hear the desperation in Cecilia's voice on the page and wonder if this is ultimately what she asks of me—the unconditional devotion of family. My heart stirs, but I deny the feeling. My grandfather Poppy's house, where I grew up, was a forbidding, unsafe place of locked-away love with no possibility of consolation. All my life I have held myself apart from family bonds because I never believed family could mean anything but cold disappointment. Yet now, under orders of my superiors at the FBI, I am speeding toward it.

SIENA, ITALY

5

THE COMMERCIAL sprawl continues until the bus swings around a corner, heading straight for a huge stone wall. At the last minute we swerve through a narrow gate topped by a statue of a wolf. Once inside the walls, we halt at the Siena bus station, a concrete island in a small piazza.

The driver waits as I bump along the aisle, impatient eyes meeting mine in the mirror. Out on the street, the air is baking and the spare trees are heavy in the stillness. The air brakes whoosh, and the bus is gone. I look hopefully for Cecilia Nicosa, but nobody approaches. I wait in the shade. The suitcase and rumpled shorts must immediately make me for American. I can't get a signal on my cell phone. After fifteen or twenty minutes, I set out to find a landline.

Straight ahead there is a fortress in a park. Turning the other way, you face a jumble of signs. Il Duomo, the main cathedral, is in that direction, which must lead to the city center. I seem to be near a school. College students are lounging on the steps of an apartment building, and there is a large outdoor café a few blocks farther on. I tick off the possibilities. Cecilia is late. Cecilia didn't get my text message. Cecilia is mistakenly waiting at the train station. I am starting to feel panicky, although there is no danger.

As I near the café, someone calls my name.

"Signorina Grey!"

A young man comes sprinting up from behind, waving. He wears baggy camouflage shorts and a T-shirt that says "Università di Siena." He has thick black curly hair and wraparound sunglasses on a loop, a beaded choker around his neck.

"I am very sorry. I apologize for being late. I am Giovanni. The son of Cecilia."

"*Ciao*, Giovanni!"

I laugh with pleasure and relief. He is one handsome dude. Half Salvadoran and half Italian is a hot combo plate. For a moment he hesitates, bouncing on his toes like a basketball player, then swiftly kisses me on each cheek. We hug. He smells like a boy.

"Sorry for the confusion," I say. "There was a train strike. I had to take a bus. I sent a text—"

"No, no, it is completely my fault. I was with a friend, studying for an exam."

"I was expecting to see your mom."

"My mother had to perform an emergency operation at the hospital. I am always late for everything." He smiles engagingly. "The car is over there," he says, taking the handle of the suitcase. "Your first time visiting? It is very amazing, you will see."

"You sound proud of your home."

"I love Siena. I would not live anywhere else."

"Not even Rome?"

He snorts. "What's great about Rome? They are covered by gypsies, like these. Look out."

A clutch of young Romanian mothers and children is coming toward us. The women carry nursing babies wrapped in shawls, like walking Madonnas, except their eyes are smoldering with want and hate. The little kids are trained to swarm the victims and pickpocket while they are distracted.

"Watch your purse," Giovanni warns loudly, all hyped up and seething with excitement.

"Not to worry. Got it covered."

Giovanni and I sidestep the situation, but instead of letting it be, he goes on the attack.

"*Vaffanculo!*" he shouts, with an obscene gesture.

The gypsies gather their ranks and move on with downcast eyes. Giovanni continues to shout at their backs. Nobody on the street pays attention.

"They steal your underpants," he says.

I just smile. "Giovanni, how old are you?"

"Sixteen."

"Sixteen, and you don't want to leave home? See the world?"

He fumbles. "What I'm saying, it comes from my heart. Forgive my English—"

"Your English is good."

"In Siena, we believe in the old things. Our blood, our DNA"—he pinches the flesh on his arm—"is pure. It is the same as the ancient Etruscans'. Science proves that we have lived here two thousand years. Right now we are inside the walls of the old medieval city. When you are inside the walls, everything is"—he searches for the word—"beautiful. Inside is life. What we love. Our history. Our church. Our family. Our *contrada*, which is the neighborhood where you grow up. In America," he adds self-assuredly, "you call it 'the hood.' Inside, we preserve the Republic of Siena. Don't worry, it's not like a museum; there are good shops and restaurants, and even an Australian bar where they speak English and have English beer!"

A Boddingtons right now would be awesome.

"Outside, there are only enemies. I know it sounds crazy."

He unlocks the smallest car I have ever seen, the size of a corner mailbox.

"Outside everything is bad," the boy continues, with complete sincerity. "Outside is death."

GIOVANNI TAKES a quick route out of Siena and the commercial zone, soon putting us on a deserted country road that undulates through dense forest before breaking out above scores of fields stitched with rows of green. He drives too fast, one hand on the wheel, windows down, constantly jabbering in cheerful tones on his cell phone.

It is hard to find anything remotely lethal in the verdant countryside of cadmium-yellow blocks of sunflowers, cultivated rows of grapes, the lofty Tuscan sky filled with pure white clouds. No wonder they paint clouds on church ceilings; they have unobstructed views of heaven. But for one so young and trendy, Giovanni's view of things is surprisingly entwined with morbid folklore.

What Cecilia described as "our little house on a hill" is a thirteenth-century compound built by Benedictine monks that later became a residence for a succession of cardinals. It even has a name—Abbazia di Santa Chiara, the Abbey of Saint Chiara—and the hand of the saint is preserved to this day in the sacristy of the abbey church, which is on the other side of the courtyard from the current family wing. Giovanni assures me the relic is a powerful blessing and an object of incalculable value, although a severed hand floating around does not sound to me like very good feng shui.

The road is banked by flimsy wooden poles lashed together. As the lane narrows, the cliff falls away. A hairpin curve reveals a panoramic view of the valley, and you can see the abbey in its entirety—the romantic twelve-sided tower, the two-story residential quarters, and the remains of the original tenth-century church, brutally exposed as if it had been cut in half, leaving nothing but crumbling buttresses and an empty arch.

We drive between rows of dark green cylindrical cypress trees, tips bending in the wind so they uncannily resemble a procession of monks with bowed heads. We turn into a gravel driveway that opens into an empty square big enough to hold a farmers' market. The engine stops. In the quiet, all you hear is birdsong. The abbey looms around us, rows of iron torches reaching out of sixty-foot pale stone walls that have been standing for over eight hundred years. The scents are pungent—oil of lavender, meat roasting over cedar chips. To the left is the entrance to the restored chapel, where the hand of the dead saint lies.

"I'll show you to your room and then I have to go." Giovanni punches the cell phone yet again. "My dad just texted. He says to make yourself comfortable."

I look around. Comfortable, where? The fortified palace, first an austere monastery, then a seat of power for rulers of the church, is no less commanding in its present role as a private residence. The open space is bounded by potted palms and urns filled with geraniums, carefully pruned, not a paper cup to mar the raked gravel yard. The clean perspective of shaded walkways and sun-washed tufa-stone walls creates a solemnity even deeper than the monks' devotion.

Who are these people who reside like old-fashioned royalty in a compound the size of a five-star resort? God may have lived here once, but the premises have since been vacated; this is about the ascending fortune of a single man. I feel more disoriented than ever, unable to imagine any connection to this foreign way of life, looking for a foothold to dig into for my work as an agent. The insistent beep of Giovanni's technology does nothing to dispel the eerie sense that when I entered the shadowed hush of this ancient courtyard, the curtain parted to a strange reality.

. . .

I LIE down briefly and wake up an hour later. The room floats in quietude. The bedspread is sage-green damask. At the foot of the bed is a folded cashmere throw. The cast-iron headboard is made to look like the tendrils of a sweet-pea vine. A strip of wallpaper with similar coils is set along the midline of eggshell plaster walls. There is one small arched window—no screen, no glass, just a pair of shutters over a grate that frames a grove of olive trees. I stick my face into the fresh air and listen to the regular splash of someone doing laps in a pool that is hidden from my sight. I am a pool rat. In Los Angeles I swim with a Masters team, a mile and a half every day. Nothing could make me happier than to work out right now. After the bus trip from Rome, my neck feels like a tangle of wire. I unpack eagerly, almost frantic from the nearby call of water.

My bedroom is on the second story of the monks' quarters. I walk along an exterior corridor laid with terra-cotta tile where archways look down on the courtyard. Apricot-colored draperies are gathered in the arches, the sun hitting them like golden chimes. Centuries of leather sandals and whisperings of prayer have softened the air and smoothed the stone.

I head down a marble staircase leading to the garden, carrying nothing but a towel and goggles, an old rayon dress thrown over my Speedo. Almost naked, the still hot air is now my friend. I come to a stand of pines. The scent of pitch is intoxicating, heavy and tinder-dry. Several cars are parked in the shade, engines hot and ticking. I wonder if these are guests, come to use the pool, but then sharp male voices cut through the torpor.

Peering over a gate, I see Nicoli Nicosa, wearing bathing trunks, holding back an angry group of hard-looking men—field-workers, judging from the size of their forearms and hands. They wear tracksuits, even in this heat. Nicosa has just climbed out of the pool, evidently surprised by their arrival. He is dark-chested, his longish hair slicked back, showing an aggressive profile. He has compact legs and a developed, hairy back; a street fighter.

He answers back, but they are like a pack of wolves stalking a lamb, going for the exposed soft belly of the rich man trapped in a corner of his own property, where nobody can see. The leader—gaunt, white-haired, in his seventies—is becoming more and more agitated, shouting and gesturing angrily.

The others join in the attack with rapid-fire Italian, repeating a word I have never heard—*"alfiere"*—all of them pointing at heaven, earth, and the dripping man in the bathing trunks. Nicosa has nowhere to go. To the right are a stone wall and a sloping hill of pine trees. Would he scale it and run? To the left is the pool. He might try for the cell phone gleaming on a towel thrown over a lounge chair. I know from the file that he is tenacious as a terrier; he would take a beating rather than surrender dominance. Yes, there it goes. The surge of adrenaline. The closed fists and challenging stance.

I push through the gate, calling, *"Buongiorno!* Is that Nicoli Nicosa? Hello! It's your relative from America, Ana Grey."

Dumbstruck, they all turn in my direction. Nicosa takes the moment to pull a pair of red sweatpants over the trunks and comes toward me with a tight smile. You can see Giovanni's resemblance to his dad, both in looks and the hotheaded willingness to attack.

"My God, you *must* be Ana!" he says in unaccented English. "You couldn't be anyone else. I am Nicoli, Cecilia's husband."

We kiss on both cheeks but do not hug, as he is still barechested and wet. Instead he holds me at arm's length and stares in wonder.

"You look just like my wife!"

"Do I?"

Nicosa's face is close enough that I can see the dark awareness in his eyes and the unspoken understanding that we are
both playing for time.

"This is wonderful!" He smiles handsomely. "Cecilia will
be home soon. You must be crazy to meet her!"

"I didn't mean to interrupt—"

"Not at all."

I face the group of angry peasant faces as if my heart isn't
going a mile a minute. Dry wind fingers the rayon dress. I
regard them amiably. *What are you going to do to us?*

They leave. But not without the same muttered word
Giovanni had thrown at the gypsies.

"Vaffanculo!"

When we hear the engines of their cars start up, I ask
Nicosa if everything is all right.

"No, but never mind." His voice is shaky; he has had a
serious scare.

"Who are they?"

"Oh, some people who are upset with me. Somebody
always is. But these are from my own *contrada*. Do you know
about that?"

"Yes; Giovanni explained. The neighborhood."

"Normally we have respect for other *contrada* members."
He falters. "I am embarrassed."

"Don't be. You handled it."

Barely. I wonder if he will thank me for intervening, but
that would mean acknowledging how close he came to having his butt kicked by his own neighbors, and clearly, he
would rather put the incident behind us.

"Can I get you something?" He lights a cigarette and
walks into the pool house. "You look like you're ready for a
swim."

"Would you mind?" I ask, tearing off the dress without waiting for an answer. "I'll be a much better person after I get in the water."

He smiles quizzically and gestures toward the pool.

Oh, what a soul-saving dive. Hitting a hard freestyle, I glimpse Nicosa through the crook of my arm, grimly pouring a drink. Catching my look, he changes his expression to one of forced amusement. Raising a glass, he calls, *"Brava!"*

6

THE WET swimsuit hangs over a chair in the sweet-pea bedroom. The mirrors of the mahogany armoire reflect a woman wearing white jeans and a black bra, frozen by indecision. My hair is as blow-dried as it will get in this humidity. I've put on eyeliner, eye shadow, and lipstick, which is a lot for me. Opening the doors of the armoire, the room revolves brightly in the polished glass, and then I'm staring into the despair of an empty closet. The sum total of my travel wardrobe rests on four lonely hangers.

This is when I miss Sterling, *a lot*. He would be lying on the sage-green bedspread wearing a Western-style shirt he ironed himself, jeans that have seen real horsehide, and soft R.M. Williams boots custom-made in Australia—completely oblivious to my pain. Getting dressed is easy for him: he is always himself.

"What should I wear?"

"Wear what feels comfortable."

That's just it. How do I present myself? As an FBI agent or as a long-lost relative? Girlie? Tough? There's the chocolate-brown wrap dress I splurged on in London, imagining Sterling and me in one of those minimalist restaurants where everybody looks like a piece of art, but it seems too special just for dinner. How dressy do you get in an abbey?

The hell with it. I pull on a stretchy black lace blouse, step into a pair of high-heeled sandals, open the door, and stop—fascinated by the play of air and light outside. So much vitality is contained inside the walls of the abbey. You could stand here all day, absorbed in silence, watching the sun creep through the spikes of lavender. Open a door in Los Angeles, and all you get is noise.

The iron latch falls into place behind me. Bands of light ricochet through the archways as I descend the worn travertine steps. The last warmth of day remains heavy in the courtyard, which is empty except for Nicosa, alone at a wooden table beneath one of the portals that frame the loggia. The sight of him texting on his phone is disconcerting. If he is a mafia associate, he represents a new breed: a global businessman who operates in the economic overworld. I can understand Dennis Rizzio's excitement. An ordinary FBI agent attempting to gain access to that elite brotherhood of power would be as effective as a peasant throwing pebbles at a castle. But here I am, already inside.

NOT SURPRISINGLY, Nicosa also possesses a brawnier-than-average sexuality. Powerful men have it—the kind of animal magnetism that must have kept the Rome-based surveillance team wide awake while they documented the affair with his counterpart sexpot, Lucia Vincenzo. It is impossible for him to simply sit in a chair in this theatrical setting and not look larger than life, simmering with operatic passions, especially when his artistically cut black and silver hair curls with just the right panache along the nape of the neck, and his expressive face gleams with a masculine hint of sweat.

"Sit."

He motions toward a cushioned wicker chair. On the table is salvation: a bottle of white wine in a silver bucket of ice.

"I'm glad we have some time to talk before my wife comes home."

Like that of the male guests at the London birthday party, the flirtatiousness is reflexive and without meaning, but he does have a way of making himself feel very close, as if his furrowed, animated face has become magnified with interest, following your every thought.

"How was your trip from Rome?"

"The train station was a nightmare," I tell him. "But you'll be happy to know that every spot at Caffè Nicosa was taken. Your company must be doing well."

"I have a secret weapon. His name is Sofri. He does not look like a secret weapon—he looks like Marcello Mastroianni with a white mustache—but he is an old friend and a brilliant biologist who cracked the genome of the coffee plant and created a new, genetically engineered bean. He is the reason for our success."

"In Italy, don't you also have to know the right people?"

Nicosa's eyes hold mine. Within the coarse stone walls, the early twilight softens our skin tones so we gaze at each other with frankness—there is no hiding in this sultry light.

"What do you mean, 'the right people'?" he inquires gently.

My cell phone rings. It is Dennis Rizzio.

"Sorry…"

"Go ahead," Nicosa says.

Dennis's voice is clipped. "Can you talk?"

"For a minute."

I look questioningly at Nicosa, and he reads it exactly. "I'll get some glasses," he says and politely leaves the table.

"Hi, Dennis. What's up?"

"I received a call from Inspector Reilly of the Homicide and Serious Crime Command, Metropolitan Police. He spoke to you on the scene."

"I remember." The dinosaur with the head cold.

"They recovered the Ford used in the attack."

"Where?"

"Aberdeen, Scotland. Pretty much burned to a crisp. Forensics has determined that the fire was deliberately set. Point of origin was the engine. Accelerant used was gasoline. They were trying to destroy the vehicle identification number on the engine block, but the team was able to recover another copy of it on the axel that the knucklebrains didn't know existed. They're using it to trace the original owner."

"Witnesses?"

"If there are any, they're under a rock. We're talking a poor section, infested with gangs. The Brits are canvassing the scene."

"You don't sound optimistic."

"Why Aberdeen?" Dennis wonders. "It bothers me."

"Scots nationalists?" I suggest. "They did hit a diplomat neighborhood."

Dennis mulls it over. "I dunno, but they drove way the hell to Scotland for a reason. It's likely they went there because they knew someone who would take them in after they dumped the car."

Nicosa is walking out the kitchen door with a corkscrew and two wineglasses.

"He's coming back. Tell me quickly, anything more on the London attack?"

"They used an Ingram MAC-10," Dennis reports. "A crap gun used by your basic street thug. I'm guessing the shooters were hired hands."

"I'll call you tomorrow," I promise Dennis as my host sits down.

"Everything okay?" Nicosa asks.

"Fine."

"*Va bène.*"

He flicks open a waiter's corkscrew, effortlessly withdraws the cork, and pours wine into two squat glasses, not of cut crystal as I might have imagined, but everyday tableware.

"You ask about knowing the right people," he muses. "I assume you mean the mafias? Italy, you will find, has always been a fairly lawless place. We have laws, of course, but nobody pays attention. We will always be a collection of dysfunctional tribal families ruled by old men who want to settle scores. But foreigners have the wrong impression. We are moving toward democratic capitalism; the old dons can't fix everything. *Salute.*"

We toast. The white wine is sweeter than what I am used to. Nicosa seems unfazed, so I venture deeper.

"It's not just Italy, Nicoli. Criminal networks rule the world—and that's no exaggeration."

I am about to add that they have become a main focus of intelligence efforts by the Bureau when he points to a red Ferrari parked near the gate.

"You see that car? I had another, just like that one. It was stolen in Rome in the morning, and they found it in Croatia the following afternoon. The collapse of communism has blessed us with a new breed of jailbeaks."

"Jailbirds?"

"Yes. *Allora*...what do you do in Los Angeles? I love it there. Some of it looks just like Italy."

"What do I *do*?"

I am about to explain that FBI agents do everything from bank robberies to counterterrorism when we are interrupted by the sound of tires on gravel, and a sporty green Alfa Romeo hatchback driven by Cecilia Maria Nicosa surfs through the gates to a space between two palm trees. There's a whirl of exhaust, and then the smell of leather settles briefly.

The door opens fast and she calls, "Hello!" an exuberant hand waving even before the car stops. Then she emerges— mountains of auburn hair, large sunglasses with jeweled frames. She's wearing a white lab coat over a tight-fitting silk sheath in vibrant shades of plum. She makes a diminutive figure in the solemn space of the sanctuary, but from her self-assured stride it is clear that she, like Nicosa, *owns* it.

We kiss back and forth in a fragrant blur, and next thing I know, her arms are around my neck. We hug wordlessly, tightly, for a long moment. Her body is heavier than mine, soft and voluptuous. The intensity seems a bit overwrought, considering we have never met.

Although Cecilia dresses like an Italian, she looks entirely Central American, like the Latinas I know in Los Angeles. The flat cheekbones, full lips, and broad nose show the African, Spanish, and Indian mix of our El Salvadoran background—the difference being that I received a dominant helping of Scots/Irish. She removes the sunglasses, revealing strong eyebrows and warm brown eyes, empathetic and searching, taking me in. We gaze into each other's souls and my thoughts come to a flat-out stop—I'm face-to-face with a brown-skinned woman from another part of the globe with whom I have nothing in common.

"Do I say *Buenas tardes* or *Ciao*?" I wonder.

"You say—*I am so happy!*"

We embrace again, awkwardly now, and when we step apart, the candid courtyard light permits no illusion.

She looks tired.

This is not a pampered social climber. This is a person in the real world, a doctor with a mind full of equations; a mother preoccupied with a teenage son; the wife of a man in the social spotlight, always under pressure to be fabulous.

As we walk, she murmurs, "I have a favor to ask. Please don't tell my husband you are FBI."

"Why not?" I whisper. "I thought he knew."

She shakes her head.

"God!" I gasp. "I almost spilled the beans!"

"But you didn't tell him?"

"No. What's the problem?" I ask. "Why can't your husband know?"

"Some people are upset by these things," she says evasively.

"He asked what kind of work I do. What should I say?"

"I don't know!"

"I'll think of something," I reply, pleased that she is reaching out to me, and wondering what she's hiding.

Nicosa comes toward us and takes both our hands.

"This is beautiful!" he cries. "Beautiful!"

"Do you think we resemble each other?" Cecilia asks innocently.

"Definitely," her husband affirms. "The same bone structure. The same wavy hair."

"My hair used to be Ana's color, but now I have to dye it. Too much gray." Cecilia shrugs. "Look. Our skin color is so different." She holds her arm up to mine. "Coffee and cream."

"Still, the family resemblance is unmistakable," Nicosa assures her. "Anyone could tell you two are related."

We grab the bottle in the ice bucket, and our wineglasses, and continue toward the southern wing, arms around one another's shoulders, an ungainly trio, not quite matching steps. Cecilia heads through the open door first. It is double-thick aged wood reinforced with square-head nails that could probably stop a battering ram, but the antique iron lock could be popped with a hairpin.

"I notice you don't have security."

Nicosa reacts as if he'd never considered it. "No security?"

"Do you have an alarm system? I don't see one." I gesture toward the cloistered yard, apparently unchanged since 1132. "You're isolated, with access from every direction. Forgive me." I smile. "You asked what I do in Los Angeles? I sell home security systems."

When making up a false identity on the spot, it is best to stick to something you know.

"We'll have to talk about that," he promises.

I exchange a look with Cecilia, expecting a conspiratorial smile in return for keeping my ties to the Bureau a secret, but she lowers her eyes, unwilling to connect.

Inside the family quarters is the layered smell of old fires. The floorboards creak as we enter what used to be a small chapel, with pale stone walls curving toward the ceiling like hands steepled in prayer. The room has been modernized with milk-white couches and a flat-screen TV. In a niche that must have once held a statue, someone has placed a miniature wine cask. High in the vaulted ceiling is a tiny six-paned window, the only source of natural light. I imagine that if the chrome lamps weren't shining, throwing a warm glow into the corners, it would be black as a closet in here.

We pass through a huge dining hall where naked plywood tables and folding chairs are stacked—before or after a party, or maybe always at the ready. The windows have been jazzed up with embroidered curtains, and one whole wall is a cupboard for china. The kitchen is cavernous, but it is the kitchen of a working family. A funnel-shaped brick fireplace dominates, with well-used iron grills. Do they actually cook over an open fire? There is also, of course, a gourmet range in stainless steel, and a pair of fancy refrigerators. Track lighting looks down on a ten-foot granite island with built-in sinks for preparing the baskets of tomatoes and baby zucchini, great bunches of sage and basil and loaves of bread that are making me faint with hunger.

Still in heels and the silk dress, Cecilia trades the doctor's coat for an apron, refusing offers of help.

"No, no. You relax. I hope your ride on the bus was okay. Giovanni picked you up?"

"Everything was fine. He said he had been studying— seems like a good kid."

"We are proud of him. He is going to carry the flag for our *contrada* during Palio. It's an honor. They always pick the most handsome young man." She caresses Nicosa's cheek. "It used to be his father. Still is."

Nicosa removes Cecilia's hand and kisses her palm with the passing intimacy of a long marriage. "Where is Giovanni?" he asks.

"He's at soccer. After school he practices the flag, and then soccer," she tells me with a smile. "Busy schedule."

"We had a nice talk." I describe our conversation about his love for Siena.

"That's more than we talk to Giovanni in a week," marvels Nicosa.

Cecilia says, "He likes to talk in the car."

"Or shopping. He'll quote Dante if you buy him a pair of tennis shoes."

Cecilia frowns, retrieving a melon from the window, swinging her hips around the kitchen in sensual display; just like Nicosa, she's sexual and distant at the same time.

"You're making him out to be a brat. He is not a brat," Cecilia says.

"I would never say that about my son! He's a good student

and stays out of trouble; what more can we ask? Do you need me to cut the prosciutto?"

"*Non ora. Fra un pò.*"

"*Voglio vedere Giovanni giocare.*"

"*Va bène.*"

Her husband leaves, and Cecilia lets out a sigh that probably says more than she would like me to know at this point. Her demeanor is guarded. Despite the excited welcome, she is hovering on the other side of the island and keeping her eyes on the food prep, as if to maintain a distance while evaluating the stranger in her kitchen.

"Nicoli wants to see a little of Giovanni's practice," she says. "We will have something to eat in a minute. I would have met you at the bus, but we had to perform an emergency C-section."

"Mom and baby okay?"

"The baby will have some problems," she says, ending the discussion.

I try to let things unwind as if I really were just a long-lost relation. There are moments of awkward silence. She takes a bowl from the refrigerator and starts dipping zucchini blossoms into a batter she must have prepared between surgeries. I thought *I* was efficient. But these are petty thoughts. This is an industrious woman who is also a publicly betrayed wife. Despite all that, she and her husband seem to be—wildly and improbably—in love. It makes me see that Sterling and I are still way at the beginning.

"Do you think Nicoli bought my story about selling security systems?"

"Sounded good to me," she says. "Do you really?"

"When I was on the robbery squad at the FBI, I used to collect the tapes from the surveillance cameras in banks. It's about as technical as popping out a CD."

"Don't worry; Nicoli wasn't paying attention."

"But you're still afraid to tell him I'm an agent."

"Not afraid. It's just not a good time. He's sensitive about politics."

"Is something wrong?"

"Not at all," Cecilia answers in a reserved tone, confirming my sense that we have taken several steps back from the warmth of our initial contact. "Tell me about you. Are you married? Do you have children?"

"No children, married to the job." *Don't push it. We have time.* "How did you find out about me in the first place?"

"I first heard your name when I was a child. My father told us that we had a relative in America named Ana, and if we ever wanted to meet her, we must work hard in school so we could visit. I never knew if you were real or something he invented so we'd get good grades. Who in your family came from El Salvador?"

A delicate aroma of dough sizzling in olive oil arises from a large copper skillet.

"My father. His name was Miguel Sanchez."

Cecilia freezes on the spot, still gripping a slotted spoon. "Your father was Miguel Sanchez? I didn't realize he was your *father*."

"What did you think?"

She fumbles. "I thought maybe he was an uncle or a cousin and that you and I were distantly related. But, Ana, he is my father, too."

I am not impressed. "Seriously, it's a common name."

"Yes, it *is* a common name," she snaps impatiently. "But for him to speak of a girl named Ana in America? That is too much of a coincidence. Did you know he was from the town of Cojutepueque?"

"I thought it was called La Palma, but that could be wrong."

Cecilia has put down the spoon and turned off the stove.

"It's in the mountains, thirty-five minutes from the capital, San Salvador. My mother was Eulalia. Together they owned a fish market. It started out as a space in the *mercado* but eventually they bought three stalls. She ended up running it because Papa wasn't always there. He was often in America."

"Where in America?"

"Nobody knew. At times he would send money, so maybe that's why she tolerated his absence. He would come and go. Then one day he never came back."

"Do you have a photo of him?"

"Somewhere."

"It doesn't matter. I don't remember what he looked like. He died when I was five, and my grandfather threw out all the pictures."

Cecilia is shocked. "He died?"

"Yes. I'm sorry."

"How?"

I hesitate. "Are you sure you want to know?" She nods. "He was murdered."

"Did they ever find the killer?"

"No. The case was never pursued. In fact, there never was a case."

"*Capito*. Because he was a Spanish man, in the country illegally."

I don't answer.

Cecilia brushes moist eyes. "We never knew what happened to him," she murmurs. "I was a teenager when he left for good."

"This is crazy."

"My mother told me that he had a wife in America."

I remember the day I found the marriage certificate in a bank vault in Santa Monica, California, after my own mother died, proving that she had been married to Miguel Sanchez. Her relationship with a brown-skinned immigrant was the cause of my California grandfather's lifelong rage at both of us (she, the whore; me, the half-breed), and why my mother and I stuck together, afraid of his explosive fits. I suppose I'm still fighting the bad guys because I couldn't fight Poppy. Now the sudden recollection of my mother—for some reason, that damn worn apron made of soiled, quilted squares that had seen a hundred meat loaves and pans of brownies, which she would never replace because it was good enough— makes me soften with longing for her comforting presence, taken away too soon.

"This woman in America," I press. "Did you know her name?"

"It was a strange name. Like a princess in a fairy tale."

"Was it Gwen?"

My mother's name. The recognition is instantaneous. Miguel Sanchez's other wife. We stare at each other.

Oh my God!

"We are half sisters!"

We embrace, embarrassed, giddy.

"What do we do?" Cecilia's brown eyes are wide.

"I don't know!" I laugh. "Make dinner?"

Cecilia throws a cold stare at the assemblage of dishes as if about to sweep it all aside.

"We should be making Salvadoran food!"

"What *is* Salvadoran food?"

"You've never had *pupusas*?" she cries. "Living in Los Angeles? Corn tortillas stuffed with pork? Next time I will cook them for you."

Our chatter becomes animated as we compare child-hoods—what we wore to school, friendships, crushes, restrictions, dating, church. I cut the melon and remove the rind. Cecilia takes a package from a cabinet near the cold stone floor. Sliding the burlap wrapping away, she reveals a dark pink hunk of prosciutto, which she slices with the practiced care of a surgeon. Moments later, crescents of bright orange melon and transparent feathers of prosciutto are arranged on a platter. We lay linen on the table, set the silverware and pasta bowls. She minces garlic, lemon zest, and parsley with precise, aware movements; not hurried, not dismissive, not just throwing something in the microwave, and I try to slow down and follow the rhythm of her lead.

Nicosa returns with Giovanni, who is fresh from the field of battle—pink-cheeked, with muddied legs and reddened knees, his hair as soaking wet as if it had just rained.

"*Cosa è sucesso?*" Nicosa asks, sensing that something is going on in the kitchen besides pasta with cherry tomatoes.

"We just found out we are sisters," Cecilia announces.

"*È vero?* Really?"

"Half sisters," I murmur awkwardly, still not used to the idea. "Same father, different mothers. Different countries."

"We are *sisters*!" Cecilia declares. "There are no halves."

Giovanni gives me a sweaty hug. "You are my aunt!" He grins.

"You understand why this happened?" Nicosa demands. "Because it is Palio."

Giovanni's cheeks flush. I expect a cynical teenage reply, but instead he cries, "It's true!"

"They say that in July and August the people of Siena go mad from the heat, and that is when they have the Palio. You must understand the Palio is not just a race," Nicosa explains, serious as a priest. "It is a time of analysis that arouses deep emotions. You abandon cowardice and embrace action. You defeat death and create life. The city is like a hole in time, every monument and painting in Siena possessing a symbol or a secret code that brings us back into the past. Show your aunt the famous Magic Square."

Obediently, Giovanni grabs a scratch pad and with dirt-stained fingers spells out the letters:

SATOR
AREPO
TENET
OPERA
ROTAS

"It's a Latin puzzle that can be read in every direction," Giovanni says, excitedly. "See how the word *tenet* forms a cross? This mystery"—he taps the pad—"is written on the wall of our own church, the Duomo."

Not for the first time since I have come to the abbey, I feel a chill.

"What does it mean?"

"'God holds the plow, but you turn the furrows,'" Giovanni says.

I look quizzically at my new sister, staring at the letters over my new nephew's shoulder. "What does *that* mean?"

"There are two types of fate," Cecilia replies. "The actions of God, and our own responsibility for our lives. Two kinds of fate have brought us together."

Nicosa pops the cork on a cold bottle of Prosecco. "Welcome to the family. *Salute.*"

We four touch glasses.

"Congratulations, Giovanni," I say.

"Why?"

"For holding the flag in the parade. Your mom says it's a big deal."

"Oh." He blushes. "*Grazie.*"

"It's not simply that he holds it"—Cecilia begins, but Nicosa stops her by encircling her waist and stage-whispering in her ear.

"Shhh. She will see."

"Okay, *caro*." Cecilia smiles and lifts her mouth to be kissed.

BUT NOW we have a problem.

I am leaning against the pillows on the sweet-pea bed, on the phone with Dennis Rizzio.

"She's not just a relative," I say, covering my legs with the cashmere throw. "She's my sister. Her son is my nephew. How can I do this?"

"Did you and Ms. Nicosa grow up together?" he demands, a crackling New York counterpunch. "Did you two share a crib? You know this lady less than twenty-four hours. You know nothing about her. She's a blank slate."

"I can tell you that she needs me. Why else would she want me here? She's clear about not letting her husband know I'm FBI—she's trying to walk some kind of a line. I don't know what it is, except there's fear and desperation that she thinks only someone close, like a sister, would understand. I feel a responsibility toward that. Also to the case." I'm worrying the fringes on the blanket. "I hope I can do both."

"Trust me, she's not a real sister. Your sister is the one who makes you drive three hours on the Long Island Expressway because it's Mother's Day and she doesn't want to come to *you*. She's a bossy pain in the ass you have to tolerate because she's your sister, because if you don't, your *brother*, who can't stand her either, is gonna get mad. You and Cecilia Nicosa have nothing like that. No obligations, which is good. So don't jump to conclusions."

"I think she's still testing me."

"Why do you suppose she doesn't want her husband to know you're Bureau? Because he's up to his neck in cocaine, and she knows it, and she wants her and the kid *out*. That's her agenda. Nothing has changed," Rizzio insists. "You're in an ideal position. She reached out to you, remember? Like you say, she wants your help."

I find myself relaxing back into the pillows. The tension escapes with a sigh—I am back inside my comfort zone. Dennis is right. Let me do what I'm good at: pretending to be who I'm not. Put aside these notions of what family is *supposed* to be and accomplish the task.

"You're more of a help to Cecilia as an agent who can get her out of there than as some bogus half sister. What does that mean, anyway? History. Words on paper."

Right, I think, wanting to be convinced. *My loyalty is to the mission.*

"Caught a break in the London attack," Dennis is saying. "Are you interested?"

"Sure."

In truth, I'm pretty well past the whole thing. It was literally another time in another country. Italy has absorbed my focus now.

"The Brits traced the vehicle identification number on the abandoned Ford in Aberdeen to Southall, West London. The original owner, Mr. Hafeez Khan, says he sold it to 'a foreign type' as a junker for five hundred pounds cash. It had almost ninety thousand kilometers on it. No paperwork; the buyer takes the keys and drives away. The seller doesn't even have a name."

I squirm underneath the covers.

"So there's no way to ID the guy?"

"Mr. Khan is sitting down with a police artist as we speak. It'll be interesting if he comes up with a description of the same guy you saw in South Kensington."

"How did he contact the buyer?"

"The car was sold on Craigslist. They met in a parking lot. Like I said, no paperwork, but Mr. Hafeez did keep one remnant of the transaction. He didn't remember at first, but he still had the buyer's phone number. Are you with me?"

"Barely."

"Mr. Khan is a butcher, so what does he do? He writes the phone number of the guy who wants to buy his car on a piece of paper and sticks it on that nail where they put the receipts. The Met Police search his shop and it's still there. You know that nail thing?"

"Yes, I do." My eyes are closing.

"Just like they have in every New York deli. They have them in London, too. And this entire case could turn on it. One nail. I thought that was something."

1

CECILIA DECIDES to give a party in my honor. It will be outdoors by torchlight at the abbey, in the ruins of the original church. I guess this is why she keeps banquet tables stacked up in the dining room, ready to roll. Someone else will do the cooking, but the key ingredients have to be assembled according to Cecilia's standards, from individual shopkeepers she's known for twenty years in the district of the noble *contrada* of Oca in the heart of Siena.

Oca district is clearly marked by green and white silk with a crowned white goose flying from every building—as opposed to Oca's blood enemy, Torre, the Tower, whose blue and burgundy banners, showing an elephant carrying a tower, warn that you are entering enemy territory. Just like gangland L.A., sporting the wrong colors in the wrong district during Palio is either a deliberate challenge or just plain stupid.

We are dutifully wearing Oca scarves, flowing capelike over the shoulders, as we haul string bags filled with groceries up the forty-five-degree incline of Arte della Lana; it's barely ten in the morning, and my neck is prickly with perspiration. We turn a corner and the street drops to S. Andrea Gallerani in a heartbeat. Ahead is another rise. If you graphed it, our little shopping trip would look like a killer hills workout on a treadmill.

And yet Cecilia is stepping doelike over the pavers in high heels and an Armani dress with tiny dots that she will later wear to the hospital, movie star sunglasses, and a buckle-encrusted marigold leather purse as big as a watermelon. I notice that the other women, young and old, all of them in Oca scarves like flocks of green and white hens, are also carrying handbags and wearing dresses—tailored cotton with belts, or splashy bosom-revealing rayon—going about their morning business with self-assured femininity. And here I am, dressed L.A.-style for a day in the sun: hiking shorts, adventure shoes, water bottle, and baseball cap, trudging behind.

Cecilia is so in charge of her world, you forget that it isn't her world. Passing a shop with eye-catching patterns of blush peaches and dark plums reminds her of helping her mother at the fish store in El Salvador when she was five years old. Her stories are told in clean, thought-out paragraphs. Reflexively running Cecilia through my FBI profiling machine, I assess her as a high-functioning, *fiercely* well-organized, extroverted personality. Which means it will not be easy to get past her defenses. When she feels secure, she will tell me her secrets; why she asked me here and what her husband is up to. I must be patient.

"I had to arrange the fishes on the ice so that they looked like flowers." She describes the design with a doctor's hand—long fingers, graceful and strong—gold bracelets jumping. "I was also working in the house. We had no housekeeper—no need for one since we didn't own things. We had coffee bushes growing everywhere, like weeds, and when I was little, I would pick the beans when they were red and sell them at the market. I would help with the laundry and take care of the pets. I had two dogs; they were my most beloved things in the world."

"I couldn't have pets," I say. "My grandfather wouldn't allow it. I used to talk to the worms in the backyard."

Cecilia laughs so hard she chokes and almost stumbles. "Playing with worms? That's very sad."

"I was happy when it rained and all my friends came out."

"Stop, you are making my makeup run!"

She dabs her eyes under the sunglasses. It pleases me to amuse her. Not everybody gets my jokes, especially at the Bureau.

"We had beautiful wild birds," she goes on. "We kept them in cages. I loved them, too. You know who was my favorite? That yellow one in the cartoon who is always making trouble, what is he called?"

"Tweety Bird?" I ask incredulously.

Cecilia laughs again and blushes. "Yes, that's him."

"You had one, a toy?"

"No, just a tiny room and a lamp. On the walls, I painted that little bird. I would spend hours painting him. It took me away from my homework or when I was overwhelmed and stressed out. My mother sent my brothers and me to private Catholic school, and then to the university—with no support from the government. My aunts and their husbands gave money to pitch in with my studies, so I had to do well."

"And our father? Miguel Sanchez?"

"He wasn't there," Cecilia reminds me quietly. "He was in America, remember? Married to *your* mother."

"Not for very long."

I am struck with a pang of envy. What if my absent father did spend more time with his El Salvadoran family? What difference can it make now?

"I guess we have that in common."

"What?"

She asks this kindly, as a question.

"It's funny, but we both grew up *without* the same father.

I have virtually no memory of him. Except for one blurry image…He's just not there. And you didn't get much of him, either."

"A little more, perhaps. I know his face. He was very friendly-looking. I'll find that picture. He was playful, and he enjoyed making jokes, like you."

"You and I, we each have pieces missing."

After a silence, Cecilia says, "True."

"And we're both half-and-half. You're from El Salvador, but you might as well be Italian."

"I am not one thing or another," Cecilia says.

Around the tourist attraction of the Church of Sant' Antonio Abate there are stores with bombastic windows crowded with cheeses, chocolates, sausage, and mountains of gorgeously wrapped *panforte*, the signature fruitcake of Siena, with seventeen ingredients—one for each *contrada*—and hard as the brick of the houses that surround us in an almond-colored maze. The old lanes tilt and curve, go uphill and down and return to the starting point, like the meandering talk between us.

"What made you search for me?" I venture. "Why now?"

"Didn't you read my letters?" Cecilia asks. "I thought you knew about the inheritance."

"Yes, you mentioned it, but I wasn't sure."

"You have an inheritance coming from the family. It's small—a couple of thousand euros. It came when we sold the fish market, after my mother died."

"Thank you," I say. "That's very honorable of you to seek me out."

"I did want to meet you, after all these years."

"You made a big effort."

"It was the right thing to do," she says. "The money belongs to you."

She sounds awfully matter-of-fact, compared to the

emotion in the letters, in which she begged for information about the American relation she had held in her heart for many years. Is she disappointed in what she found? Or, faced with it, has she reconsidered whatever bold moves she imagined?

As we walk, I'm figuring out how to go deeper. It is afternoon, and from the rows of houses, scores of green shutters have opened to the breeze. Old people are everywhere. And happy, too. They watch from doorways or perch on wooden fruit crates that they pick up and move as the sun moves. Cecilia introduces me to each and every *nonna*, it seems, and they respond with sweet attempts at English. "Hear you soon!"

Finally we come to a small square with a fountain and another church.

"Fontebranda is the oldest fountain in Siena. Here I was baptized into Oca when we got married. If I was not baptized to the *contrada*, the marriage would be impossible."

"Can sisters tell each other absolutely anything?" I ask.

"Yes, of course."

"I noticed that you and your husband are very affectionate—but you don't sleep in the same room."

"We do sleep together, but not every night," Cecilia replies tartly. "He starts snoring like a train and then I have to leave. I get emergency calls, I need my sleep."

"What does that do for your marriage?"

"Probably saves it."

We turn away from the fountain, down a steep side street.

"Did you want to be baptized into Oca?"

"It was a bit strange, but they consider it an honor."

"That's what I mean. You're obviously a smart, independent woman, but it seems like Nicoli runs your life."

"It only looks that way," she says, then smiles quickly.

"I'm not making any judgments—I've been there with

men—but I'm concerned. After we spoke at the embassy, I went on the Internet and read about the affair he had with this mafia person who disappeared."

"That was difficult, but we worked it out."

"You worked it out about the mistress?"

"Yes."

"But what about the mafias? Cecilia—do you know if he's involved?"

"Okay, stop."

"Here's why I'm asking. Do you feel like you're in any danger?"

She jerks her head in surprise. "That's ridiculous," she says. "Not at all." And she shoves me through a beaded curtain hanging in a doorway. Inside, a dank, cavelike store is presided over by a crone in black.

"I'm going to show you the best porcini mushrooms in Tuscany. I'm fine. Stop always being FBI."

BY THE time the guests arrive at the abbey it is night and the floodlit stone walls stand out in relief against the pitch-black sky. There is no roof above the half-dozen tables draped in white and laden with bowls of white roses. The women are glittering, in shoulder-length earrings, jackets woven with gold, long iridescent satin dresses, hammered bronze bracelets, and crystal-encrusted stiletto heels. The men look even more exotic; I have never before seen silk pajamas worn underneath a tuxedo jacket. They're shaven-headed with a tiny earring or—like Nicosa—breathtakingly tailored in dark pinstripes. And the faces! Filled with character and power.

They are the ruling class—bankers and industrialists, with a couple of hungry writers and art dealers prowling the edges—whose belief in themselves and in their accomplishments seems to make them untouchable by the facts:

uncollected garbage two stories high in Naples, human trafficking of eastern Europeans, reprisal murders in broad daylight, Chinese gangsters moving counterfeit goods at will,
even the time-honored kidnapping for ransom of executives
or their wives, are believed to be a "southern sickness," of
little consequence to the sophisticated north. The ruddy and
rouged faces are a smiling blur of civility. The business at
hand is to score points with their hosts in the high-stakes
tally of social influence, as volatile here as it is in Los Angeles.

Cecilia takes me around. I get a quick handshake, and she
gets a soulful exchange in Italian. I am the sidebar; she is the
star. Her hair is up in a loose tangle, which emphasizes the diamond hoop earrings and the square neckline of a black sheath
with spaghetti straps that turn into chains of gold snakes.

I have worked protection for celebrities who are addicted
to the spotlight and can't get enough, who will preen for
anyone who stops them in the street, but that is not Cecilia.
She is tense and keeps looking at her watch. I get the sense
that she plays this role for Nicosa—for their marriage—but
it does not come naturally, especially because she has been
preoccupied about Giovanni, who still has not shown up at
the party.

She had told me he would be there when we were in her
closet. She had tried to talk me out of the brown wrap dress
I bought in London with an invitation to enter her private
oasis (where I couldn't miss the price tag on the Roberto
Cavalli snake-strap dress—about two thousand U.S. dollars),
an enchanted forest of flirtatious fabrics, large enough to
have its own window with a writing desk beneath. She kept
plucking out hangers and murmuring, "This is your color,"
although I had no idea why it was my color. The dresses
scared me. I was afraid of ruining one just by putting it on.
They had intricate linings you had to pull down carefully, or
step into without catching a thread. I thought she was trying

awfully hard to make this experiment in couture work. Her clothes were too tight in the waist and too wide in the hips for me, pointing out the disparities in our figures—and that after all, this sister thing might just turn out to be a bad fit.

She had been inflated and boastful that unlike most teenagers, Giovanni is so reliable; her friends are envious of how grown up he is; and how she loves to show him off. She might have also expected to show off the guest of honor, but the brown dress was an embarrassment. Losing patience when in spite of her luxurious offerings I kept saying, "No thanks," she became the bossy pain in the ass sister Dennis had described, saying, "Never buy cheap things; it's a waste of money!" and "You should start wearing makeup and look like a woman!"

But now, in the sensuous candlelight of the outdoor party, as we chat with yet another diva with flat-ironed blond hair and blackened eyes, a white halter showing the crescents of her breasts (*"They all think they're Donatella Versace,"* according to Cecilia), I feel like a little brown squirrel in the cheap brown dress. Like everyone else, the wannabe Donatella is obsessed with Palio. Which horse is best? Which jockey will ride for Oca? What is Cecilia cooking for the *contrada* dinner, a preposterous-sounding undertaking where the women convene in the kitchen of their *contrada* headquarters and whip up dinner for *two thousand members*—and the horse— seated at tables set up in the street. From whose apartment in the Piazza del Campo will they watch the *tratta* and the *prova*? It's like listening to folks planning a tailgate party when you don't understand football.

Luckily, Sofri arrives to save me.

Nicosa's business partner, the brilliant scientist, turns out to be a white-haired, impeccable dandy with a hooked aristocratic nose and a folded square of green and white Oca silk in the pocket of a blue blazer.

"Sofri is the secret to our success," Cecilia says, kissing him on both cheeks.

He graces me with a luminous smile. "It is a delight to meet your beautiful sister. Has the *signorina* seen much of Siena?" he asks Cecilia. "It would be my pleasure to show her. You must please be my guest for Palio."

"I'd love to. Nicoli told me you invented a new coffee bean. How do you invent a coffee bean?"

He leans forward, speaking intimately. "The breakthrough came when I was able to decode the coffee genome. Then it was a matter of identifying the genes that produce characteristics of sweetness. But my passion is to create new recipes using coffee—*far beyond the usual*," he says, and his eyes grow big, as if he were describing a distant galaxy.

"Like what?"

"For example, rabbit loins stuffed with liver and coated in coffee. You will taste them tonight!"

It takes a moment to come up with a suitably Italian response: "Beautiful!"

He grasps my hand and leads me through the party, making introductions, replenishing my glass. Holding hands with an elderly gentleman feels very European.

"How is it to be the guest of honor inside the home of one of the greatest hostesses in Tuscany? I cannot imagine what it would be like if I, for example, discovered that I had a brother I had never met—and then found out he lives like this!"

I laugh. "It has been quite a ride."

"Not to insult you," he adds quickly. "Maybe you, too, live in an historic monument."

I am about to joke that I live in the Federal Building, but, remembering my promise to Cecilia, I put the brakes on just in time.

"I'm between addresses now," I say.

"What work do you do?"

"I'm in security," I reply, with what I hope looks like a sincere smile.

"I'm sorry—do you mean banking?"

"Protecting banks. Alarm systems."

His eyebrows rise. "*Interessante*. I would have thought fashion."

Involuntarily I look down at the brown dress. "Really?"

"Of course, *bella*! You know, you look just like your sister? Both of you are intelligent and lovely women. I adore her. And now I have the pleasure of knowing you!"

Sofri releases the pressure on my hand with a sigh of satisfaction, and I feel that I have met my prince—never mind that he is fifty years older than I am, and that I'm in love with Sterling. His courtliness makes me feel special. The other half of the equation, of course, is *my* appreciation of his masculine ability to charm. I am thrilled by the novelty of what promises to be an old-fashioned, chivalrous relationship; without the need to conquer, we are free to become great friends.

At one point, behind our wineglasses, we find ourselves watching Cecilia, who is standing alone in the smashing black dress and listening in dismay to a message on her cell phone.

"She looks worried," I say. "She hasn't heard from Giovanni."

"I know. I told her it is to be expected."

"Isn't it kind of a slap in the face to his parents not to show up?"

"Normally yes, but not during Palio."

"Because Giovanni's out partying?"

"Fighting."

"Fighting! For what? Defending the antipasti?"

Waiters have appeared with fried artichokes, marinated mushrooms, dried beef drizzled with olive oil, cured mussels, mozzarella and tomato and basil, plates stacked all the way up their arms.

"Each *contrada* has a blood rival. Our enemy is Torre, the Tower. If a young man enters the zone between Torre and Oca, it means a fight. Love for one's *contrada* is equal only to hatred for one's enemy," he says passionately. "You will find guests from different *contrade* here tonight, but never from Torre. Never."

Sofri removes the silk square from his breast pocket and pats the moisture at his temples. You have to love this guy. He takes everything seriously.

"Calm down, Sofri. It's only dinner."

We move toward our table, where six or eight well-dressed people gaily introduce themselves in an incomprehensible chatter of Italian. The mood is buoyant as the food is served. After the *primi* course of homemade ravioli stuffed with the porcini mushrooms we bought that morning, Sofri jumps up to pour more wine. "A big red," he explains grandly, "to accompany my latest recipe—*ròtolo di coniglio al caffè*, rabbit rolled with coffee!" Waiters are fanning out with plates of browned meat on skewers when I notice a figure crossing from the blackness beyond the ruin walls into the lights of the party. She is purposeful but respectful; a police detective wearing a skintight blue-skirted uniform, a white gun belt, and low heels. She taps the hostess on the shoulder. Obviously, they know each other. Cecilia looks up with recognition and joy, but the detective has her cop face on.

Sofri reacts immediately.

"Stay," he says. "This is not a problem," absurdly denying the presence of red lights pulsing on a cruiser parked nearby, and the grim policewoman. The guests are either in on the game or too absorbed to pay attention. My guess is they know the code: *Pretend to ignore this.*

Sofri excuses himself and joins Nicosa and Cecilia at a

serving station. The detective is holding Cecilia's hand. Cecilia breaks away for a brief hug from Sofri. After some conversation Nicosa, Cecilia, and the detective leave together, and Sofri returns to the table.

"What is going on?"

"There has been an accident."

"Giovanni?"

Sofri picks up his napkin. "He will be fine," he says.

8

ALONG THE Via Salicotto the flags of Torre were still, their colors of brilliant burgundy and blue at rest in the night like folded wings of mythological beasts.

Giovanni was found in an anonymous tunnel that turns off the main street and opens into one of a thousand tiny courtyards in the medieval part of the city, where buildings meet at random angles. The arched passageway of chalky brick is primitive, just high enough for a man seated on a wagon to pass underneath. By day it is as dark as an Etruscan tomb. By night it is lit by one fluorescent fixture. A street cleaner discovered the boy half dead in the fluttering light, in the heart of enemy territory.

If Torre was out for blood, they got it. His stab wounds made a trail of blood down the sloping pavers. We might have been able to recover footprint evidence from the attackers if the street cleaner hadn't sprayed the ground with water before—or possibly after—discovering the victim. The street cleaner's *contrada* affiliation was unknown; by then I knew enough about the cultural weirdness of Siena that it was the first question I asked.

The course the investigation should take sped through my mind—seal the crime scene, canvass the neighborhood,

interview witnesses. I was impatient to talk to the first respond-
ers. They had taken my nephew to Ospedale Santa Caterina,
twenty kilometers north of the city, because it is one of Cecilia's private clinics with a higher standard of care—a ques-
tionable decision that cost time. He was almost gone from
loss of blood. A knife to the chest had collapsed a lung.
Breathing must have been agony.

The priest of the Oratorio di Santa Caterina, the church of
the Oca district, had been a guest at the party. In his forties,
with thick black hair and gold-rimmed glasses, he wore the
green and white scarf with the Goose over his cassock. He
spoke at a gentle pace, a person of true contemplation—none
of the greedy egotism I expected in a religious leader. As a
hostess, Cecilia treated him with utmost respect, showing all
her sides—competent, obedient, and seductive—deeply desir-
ing to impress herself upon the quiet authority of this man.

So when Sofri and I saw that the priest had also gotten up from his table and was hurrying behind Cecilia and
Nicosa to the red Ferrari, we left the party immediately, and
drove thirty-five minutes on hair-raising jet-black roads to
the hospital, which was located in an industrial park. Like
my sister, it wasn't large, but inspired confidence. It had the
air of bold, forward-thinking modernity, with a waiting area
like an upbeat take on a sixties motel—turquoise sofas and
funky lamps like daisies that looked surreal in contrast to the
torchlit grandeur of the abbey, and the life-and-death struggle of a kid who was into something way over his head.

When we arrive, the waiting area is empty. Sofri disappears down a hallway to locate the family while I attempt to
engage the one police officer in sight—overweight, middle-
aged, with a big, bald, indented head. His front teeth are
yellow and pushed together as if he'd been attacked by a
mad dentist with a vise. When I ask for information about
Giovanni Nicosa, he shrugs as if he has never heard the

name. I try again, explaining that I am the boy's aunt from California, and I am very worried.

"California?" He understands "California" and slowly grins with recognition.

"TV?" says the officer.

"You watch TV?"

He nods.

"American TV?"

"*Sì.*"

"Really? What is your favorite TV show?"

He draws in the air. Tracing letters.

"*CSI*! You like *CSI*?"

He nods, pleased to have conveyed this important fact.

Once again, Sofri arrives to save the day. At his side is the woman police detective who appeared at the abbey, Inspector Francesca Martini, talking rapidly on a cell phone while clutching three unopened packs of cigarettes. Still talking, Inspector Martini manages to shake my hand.

"You are Giovanni's aunt," she says in English, then holds up a finger to signify the importance of her phone conversation, which is taking place with the head of the provincial police, her boss, "Il Commissario."

I give a nod. Her bangs go straight across, and the rest of her long, shiny black hair is efficiently pulled into a clip. The short-sleeved uniform reveals a set of muscular, beautifully sculpted arms. You could work out for a hundred hours and never have those arms—they are genetically authentic to the Roman goddess of war.

I ask Sofri how Giovanni is doing.

"Come outside," he says.

The red Ferrari is one of the few cars in the parking lot. The door is open and the interior lights are on so that Cecilia, bent over an appointment book, can read a number while punching it into her cell phone. She seems to be going down a list—the people you would trust in a crisis. Nicosa is also on the phone, pacing back and forth in the headlights. Sofri shrugs deeper inside his blazer. The temperature had dropped twenty degrees since the morning. The air is damp and there are halos around the streetlights.

"Giovanni will need emergency surgery," Sofri says. "They are waiting for the doctor to arrive from Montepulciano. I can't believe this."

The door slams shut and the car goes dark. Cecilia walks over to where we are standing. The black dress seems the one thing physically holding her together. Her hair is falling loose and her hands are clenched. Her face is white. I draw her aside.

"I can help you with this," I say gently.

"How?"

"Let me call the FBI in Rome. We can pressure them to kick-start the investigation."

"Right now I cannot think about that."

"I know. This is what I do. Let me take that burden off."

"I don't want you to call the FBI."

"Because of Nicoli? Whatever's going on with him, he'll want his son's attacker to be found—"

"Please, you don't understand. Just leave it to the provincial police."

Her eyes are glistening. She's on the edge of frantic. She needs to know she's still in charge of something.

"I'm here if you need me."

"Thank you, Ana," she murmurs, and my heart squeezes for her pain. "Sofri said you were inside, talking to the police officer. What did you find out?"

"His favorite TV show is *CSI*."

"Don't make a joke!"

"Forgive me; I'm not making a joke. The officer told me nothing."

Sofri is there. His fingers close soothingly around Cecilia's arm as Nicosa joins us.

"*Che succede?*" Nicosa asks.

Cecilia, tense, shakes Sofri off.

"I am telling Ana about Giovanni. He was stabbed several times." Her fear gives way to fury. "In the leg, chest, and abdomen. He has right now bleeding into the abdomen, with laceration of the iliac and femoral arteries, which means he could lose his left leg."

"Lose a leg?"

"The artery was severed; he lost the blood supply to the leg. There is the possibility of amputation." Her medical authority has returned to steady her. "Also his lung is collapsed from the knife wound to the chest, and he has a broken arm, probably from defending himself."

"What's the plan?"

"To get the best vascular surgeon I know to repair the artery and save the leg. He is on the way."

"What do they say about the assault?"

"Nothing," Nicosa interrupts bitterly. "It happened in Torre."

"Nothing? Because of a rivalry from the thirteenth century? No. I'm sorry, no. Modern police forces do not operate that way."

"Your brother-in-law is suggesting that the police are maybe a little bit slow tonight because the Commissario—the chief of the provincial police in Siena—is from Torre," Sofri explains.

I am astonished. "They're not going to investigate?"

"They'll investigate." Cecilia pulls out the clips and shakes her hair. "But we will never really know who did this. They'll say, *Cosa si può fare?* It is Palio," adding savagely, "when we all know it has nothing to do with Palio."

"This is ridiculous."

Sofri looks at his watch. "Where is the surgeon?"

I don't like the way Cecilia is refixing her hair with eyes lowered in resentful silence.

"What do you mean, *'Nothing to do with Palio?'*"

"I can tell from the wounds it was not a random stabbing, okay? Someone knew exactly what they were doing," she says. "If they wanted to kill him they would have cut his neck or shot him in the head. But no—they only come *this close*. Instead, they hurt him and leave him a cripple."

Sofri winces. "Please!"

"Why? It is the truth. They do it to send a message. This kind of attack is something we see in the emergency room in Napoli, not in Siena, when two *contrade* get into a fistfight."

"But it could happen," Nicosa says. "Between *contrade*."

"Why do you say that?" Cecilia snaps, venomous, as if the gold snakes on her dress have come to life. "If he went with friends, where are the friends? If they fought with Torre, why didn't anybody see?"

I cut in. "Is Via Salicotto a busy street?"

"Yes."

"Stores and cafés open?"

"Yes, of course. Summer is the busy season."

"If there *were* any witnesses, and if they were from Torre, what is the likelihood they would come forward to help someone from Oca?"

There is a pause as the three exchange glances, as if to decide just how crazy the Sienese might be.

"You have to believe not even the people of Torre, *sangue d'ebrei e Torraioli*," Sofri says, adding an ugly curse meaning that the enemy is as low as the Jews, "would be silent about something this serious."

"*Anybody* could have seen!" Cecilia cries, exasperated. "Thousands of tourists in the city—*someone* walking on Via

Salicotto had to notice if a boy was being stabbed almost to death."

Nicosa cocks his fist. "He will not die!"

"*Basta*," Sofri says. "We have to be together now."

"He acts like he has nothing to do with it," Cecilia murmurs.

"What is that tone in your voice?" her husband demands. "Are you saying this is my fault?"

"You have turned your head."

"Let's go inside." Sofri takes her hand. "The doctor is here."

As headlights swerve into the parking lot, Sofri steers Cecilia toward the hospital.

"I have turned my head?" Nicosa shouts. "You spoil him! You treat him like a baby! You don't allow him to grow up!"

Cecilia twists from Sofri's grasp. "He doesn't want to grow up. He doesn't want to be like his father—" But then she stops herself and her look becomes pleading. "*Mi dispiace, Nicoli. Sono spaventata così.*"

Nicosa relents and comes toward her. They embrace, long and hard and desperate; you can see in the fit of their bodies how the years have carved them together. They hold on until Sofri gently takes Cecilia's arm. The surgeon from Montepulciano has gotten out of his car. Nicosa watches as the three meet and the automatic doors swing open and swallow them inside.

"Giovanni is going to make it," I say.

Nicosa mutters, "Why don't you go home?" and walks toward the emergency entrance.

The chill from standing out there in the middle of the night has seeped into my skin. My head is throbbing from having consumed nothing but a couple of mushroom ravioli and some "big red" wine, and I would do anything to get out of the brown wrap dress and put on a pair of jeans. How can I fix this? I have none of my usual props. No weapon, no creds, no Nextel, no connection to a busy investigative team in a warm office with global reach to every foreign agency—I don't even have a sweater.

Out of the shadows a voice calls, "Signorina Grey?"

"Yes?"

"Over here."

The orange tip of a lighted cigarette moves in the darkness. Inspector Martini is leaning against the hospital wall, with a cop's instinct to stay out of the light.

9

INSPECTOR MARTINI says, *"Ciao,"* and offers a cigarette.

"No, grazie."

"You speak Italian?"

"Only enough to get on a train. Usually the wrong train."

"Tell me," she says, "how long have you worked for the FBI?"

"How do you know about that?"

"We know who you are. We were informed by your captain in Rome, Dennis Rizzio."

"When did you talk to Dennis?"

"Two days ago, *forse*? He told our department to expect you here."

"Why?"

She expels a funnel of smoke. "It is professional. We have a good relationship with the Americans."

"Nice if he would let me know."

She nods sympathetically. "I have the same problems with my boss."

"Does Signore Rizzio always call you when an FBI agent is in town?" I ask lightly.

"Usually only for tickets to Palio." She smiles and tosses

her head and then fixes me with a steely stare. "What do you do in the FBI?"

"I'm a field agent. My visit here is almost like being undercover," I say. "My sister has asked me not to tell her husband I am with the FBI. It's strange, because that's how she found me, through the Bureau. I wonder what else she's keeping from him."

Inspector Martini frowns. "I am of the same *contrada* as your family—Oca, the Goose. I know Cecilia well, but I don't understand what is in her head, keeping this secret from her husband."

"Could it have to do with Nicoli's relationship with Lucia Vincenzo?"

"We don't have the whole story there, except that she is most probably dead."

"Is there a connection between Vincenzo, the southern mafias, and Nicoli Nicosa?"

"I can't speak about that."

"I understand."

When you need to know.

"I could never go undercover like you," she reflects. "I have my baby."

"How are you able to make that work?"

"Around the time that she was born, a statue of Christ by a Renaissance master named Vecchietta was stolen from a church in Siena. A task force was formed to recover it. I have a degree in art history, and it was part-time, so I applied for a position. I went back full-time when she was one year old."

"Did you recover the statue?"

She shakes her head. "It is somewhere in the hands of a private collector. Now I'm back on the street, and I like it much better."

"Hard to go back to a desk job," I agree.

She hesitates. "You have experience with homicide?"

"I make trips to the crime lab and testify in court, just like you."

We give it a moment. Her arms are crossed. She grinds the concrete with a heel.

Finally she says, "I did not tell you this—"

"I never heard a thing."

I am becoming attuned to these disclaimers—*"This is not a problem,"* Sofri said when the police car arrived at the party flashing emergency lights.

"It is about the police report. On your nephew, Giovanni."

"What about it?"

Materializing as if from nowhere, the paparazzi appear out of the shadows of the parking lot—half a dozen athletic young men on the hunt, weaving and pointing the eyes of their cameras at everything in their path, like an assault unit of spiders.

"Cazzo!" grunts Inspector Martini, glancing at them, and then at her cell. "The boss must be here."

They had gotten here before the Commissario, grabbing whatever shots they could to feed the universal craving to see rich people suffer—no matter how pathetic the crumbs, like shots of Nicosa's Ferrari and the exterior of the hospital. They ferret out the two of us near the entrance, but Inspector Martini speaks sharply in Italian, and they back off with apologetic waves, signifying to me the ultimate control of the government over the press. Instinctively, she and I separate without a word as TV news vans swarm the parking lot.

A white car pulls up, doors open, and two plainclothes detectives spring out, positioning themselves for the exit of the chief. The Commissario is taller than everyone else, and extremely thin. Wisps of white hair flying in the backlight of the TV cameras show that he's balding. He walks like a marionette, lower legs extending stiffly on their own, as if badly in need of a double knee replacement. But the odd gait only adds to a kind of worldly elegance; at this late hour, wearing a well-tailored dark suit, he looks as if he has been called away from a state department dinner party behind locked gates.

Nobody stops anyone from entering the hospital, and I'm thinking the whole entourage is going to march right into the operating room, but in a country where politics is theater, Nicoli Nicosa recognizes the opportunity for an entrance and is waiting, with the priest in the background, for Il Commissario in the reception area, where they confer privately before facing the cameras. In the crowded space and overly bright lights, the Commissario speaks closely into the lens, and the speech looks smoky and intimate. On the flat-screens at home it will seem huge and crisp.

I imagine he is saying how shocked he is that an innocent boy was brutally attacked on the eve of Palio, promising the Nicosa family that the provincial police will bring these thugs to justice.

A grief-stricken embrace between the two men, and then they disappear down the hall together and the TV lights go out.

"*Il bastone ricco insieme,*" mutters a reporter.

The rich stick together.

For the next two hours I pace the visitors' lounge, picking up magazines I can't read, trying to get e-mail where there is no service. Finally Nicosa appears, exhausted from a long interview with the police while his son was in the operating room. He is still wearing evening clothes, but the tie is gone, and gray stubble shows on his hollow cheeks. He reports in a flat voice that Giovanni made it through the surgery and there is nothing for us to do but go home. Cecilia will stay at the hospital. The police will arrange for us to leave quietly through a back exit. As he is telling me this, Inspector Martini passes and catches my eye. I ask Nicosa to give me a minute, so I can surreptitiously join her in the ladies' room.

In the mirror over the sinks our reflections show a tall, olive-skinned police officer in a sexy blue uniform, and a shorter American in a brown party dress—two cops from opposite sides of the world who speak the same language. After making sure we are alone, Inspector Martini picks up where we left off when the paparazzi arrived.

"The police report," she says quietly, "will state that your nephew was attacked in the territory of Torre—you understand about the *contrade*, okay? He is of Oca, and he was found in Torre, and naturally there must have been a fight."

"But you don't think that's the way it happened?"

"His body was—changed places?"

"Moved?"

"Sorry for my English—yes," she continues urgently. "His car was found by the police *outside* the walls of the city."

"How far away from the district of Torre?"

"Two kilometers. There were bloodstains around his car. Not so many. I believe the worst took place in the tunnel at Via Salicotto."

"He was taken to the tunnel to make it *look* like he was attacked by Torre?"

She nods. "A nurse tells me she smelled ether on his clothes. It is commonly used in Italy for kidnappings, to subdue the victim. Probably they jumped him, he defended himself"—she raises a forearm to demonstrate—"they put a cloth over his face."

This is when I awaken from my romantic dream of Italy. My sister's analysis of the stab wounds was accurate. Giovanni was targeted by professionals who tracked him outside the walls, and dumped him in Torre—for a reason.

"But it wasn't a kidnapping, or a murder, although they could have killed him at any time. It was a warning. To whom?" I ask the inspector.

"Often it is to make an example for others. Witnesses. Informants. Anyone who resists."

"We are talking about the mafias?"

"I am afraid that is a foregone conclusion," she says soberly.

"Not necessarily," I say, and tell her about the confrontation that I witnessed by the pool with members of Oca.

"Why would they be angry with Nicosa?"

Inspector Martini shrugs. "I don't know. He is well respected. Director of the *contrada*. His son is *alfiere*, the flag bearer—"

"Yes, that's the word they were shouting. They seemed to be upset for some reason about Giovanni carrying the flag. Could they have been angry enough to teach him a lesson?"

"No. Never. No way. The *contrada* protects its own children. Everyone looks out for everyone else; that's why in general we don't have crime in Siena."

Still, how humiliating it must have been for Nicosa—the coffee king, whose son was *alfiere*—to be called into account on his own property by his own *contrada*.

I check the door. We are still alone.

"Is it possible Giovanni brought this on himself? Is he the type who gets into fights in school?"

"He is liked by everyone."

"Does he do drugs?"

"I would be surprised if he's never tried them. Marijuana and cocaine are everywhere. But he is not an addict, no."

She brushes aside her bangs, damp from the night. "I am of Oca. I want to know who did this to Giovanni, and then I will hang that person by his balls from a tree. But I have to be careful. It is possible that the bloodstains near the car will never be on the report. My boss, Il Commissario, may not allow it."

"Because he is of your enemy, Torre?" I ask incredulously.

"He doesn't want a crime investigation. It is Palio. The city is filled with tourists—you can see how the press is stalking him—and so at this time, simple answers are best. A fight occurred between the young men of two traditional rivals. *Perfetto.*"

The door swings open and I almost have a heart attack. It is Nicosa! What the hell is he doing in the ladies' room?

"Ana, we have to go," he says, matter-of-fact.

In the Bureau, the sanctum sanctorum for female agents, the only place where two women can talk in privacy, is the ladies' room. If two females close the office door they are accused of having a "knitting party." Men, of course, have "meetings." Italians don't make that distinction, at least when it comes to personal hygiene. Their public bathrooms are gender-neutral, where men and women share the sinks.

Nicoli Nicosa has every right to be staring at us impatiently with the door wide open.

"I am afraid I have no more information," Inspector Martini says, covering briskly. "Best wishes to your family." She offers a comradely handshake. In her palm is a scrap of paper, upon which is written an address.

ON THE ride back to the abbey Nicosa says little, but I can see his fingers tight on the wheel, and I imagine he must be scared to death—not only about Giovanni's survival, but also about the motive for the attack. He must understand that since two people close to him have been targeted so far, nobody in his family is safe.

"What do you think they want?" I ask.

"Who?"

"The people who attacked Giovanni."

"I couldn't possibly answer that question."

"Do you think they are the same criminals who took your friend Lucia Vincenzo?"

He gives me an accusatory stare.

"Why do you bring that up?"

"I'm sorry," I say. "It's all over the Internet."

"They are not the same. One is a fight between boys. The other—we may never know."

We drive in silence, then finally he asks, "Do you pray?"

"No. Do you?"

"Of course. I will open up the chapel later."

If he meant that as an invitation, it is declined. That night, unable to sleep, I walk out to the corridor, breathing in the scents of pine and cold. The chapel is dark, but by the light of the electric torches in the courtyard below I see Nicosa, alone, playing with the flag, a square of silk about a meter wide attached to a pole: white and green with bands of red, emblazoned with the symbol of Oca, a crowned white goose with the Cross of Savoy flying from a blue ribbon around its neck.

His starched shirt is open, his chest shining with sweat. His moves are worthy of an acrobat. Like a flag attached to a fencing foil, the banner of Oca follows a split-second pattern, first clockwise at Nicosa's waist, then tightly furled and thrown straight up, high enough to float by me on the second-story balcony, and then caught on one knee, behind his back. Unbound, it makes a figure eight, a butterfly of silk opening to glory—and then, unbelievably, it becomes a flashing green-and-white knot in the air, passes close to earth, and Nicosa leaps right over it, tossing it straight up again like a thunderbolt.

What is this? A private meditation? The rite of a man preparing for combat? Is he doing this practice for himself? For his youth? For his grievously wounded son? Does he see the visitor above the torchlight, watching breathlessly?

10

THE FOLLOWING day, thunderstorms are expected. The hammocks and laundry have to be taken in. There are predictions of powerful lightning strikes. In the morning the wind bucks and swirls, the unstable atmosphere trying to rid itself of electric charge. Then it rains, hard, like winter rain in Los Angeles. Alone in the abbey, the kitchen feels cavernous and damp.

Someone made coffee and left the espresso pot on the stove. Someone cut bread and left the crumbs on the board. Pieces of a meal have been left for me to put together: plums in a bowl, muesli in a cupboard, a wedge of local pecorino cheese wrapped in white paper in the refrigerator. Irish tea in a canister. I put on a kettle of water.

I zip my sweatshirt over my pj's and put up the hood—not so much from cold as unease. Cecilia came home at four o'clock that morning and said Giovanni's condition had become critical. They fixed the artery and gave him transfusions, but the blood pressure in the leg had not come up, and they couldn't figure out why. Today they will decide if it is necessary to amputate.

We spoke in the frank way of professionals, skipping the soft touch you'd use with a civilian, minimizing nothing.

"Is the medical information accurate?"

"You mean, do I want another opinion? It is straightforward, my colleagues agree. If the circulation in the leg is insufficient, the tissue dies, gangrene sets in, and you risk an overwhelming bacterial infection. I would rather have him alive in a wheelchair than dead of sepsis."

We were in her bedroom. She had torn off her dress and thrown it on the bed, done an efficient thirty-second sweep with a washcloth that covered all the bases.

"This is how we did it in medical school. Never enough time."

She disappeared into the cavernous closet. A moment later she was wearing a navy blue chemise.

I zipped it up for her. "They have good prosthetics now, don't they?"

"Yes, they do," she answered shortly.

She adjusted the straps on her black sling-backs, remembered earrings, grabbed the stethoscope, black doctor's bag, and purse off the bed, and then I followed down the stairs. Rain was already resounding loudly when she pulled the double-thick wooden door open. Outside it was cold and still dark. I held her stuff as she struggled into a raincoat. At the very last minute she spun around and gave me a quick hug.

"I am glad you're here," she said, and her heels dug into the gravel. Soon I could hear the engine catch.

But the professional talk is a ruse, just like my reason for being here in the first place. The moment Cecilia leaves I feel that I am losing traction, on the case as well as on my feelings. I can't let the attack on his son color the search for Nicosa's alleged connection with the mafias.

Sitting still at the long kitchen table, I let the cup of tea warm my hands. It reminds me of being stuck waiting for Sterling in Dublin for eight straight days of rain, in what I thought was a hotel, but which turned out to be a boardinghouse. Going crazy alone in the room one night, I went down to the parlor, a barren space with a linoleum floor and a heatless electric fireplace. Straight-backed chairs had been pushed against the walls and were occupied by dark-suited, middle-aged men drinking whiskey. Someone who lived in the boardinghouse had died, and they had gathered there. Nobody spoke to anyone else. The rain hammered. Then, as now, I was a foreign traveler wrapped up in someone else's crisis, with no place else to go.

In the kitchen I feel imprisoned by insurmountable great stone walls. I miss Sterling with a feeling of futility. How will we ever get from here to there? His absence has become an almost palpable thing, like the cold humidity in the kitchen. We haven't spoken since we said good-bye on the street in London, and the separation is becoming cruel. I could use his wisdom on the impossible position of being an agent of the law with no way to enforce it.

When I called Dennis Rizzio in Rome to tell him about the attack on Giovanni, as well as to chide him for alerting the provincial police of my presence without telling me, that's exactly what he said: "It's Italian on Italian. We have no jurisdiction; it's up to the local authorities," even if the local authority—Il Commissario—has conflicting loyalties, thanks to the gangland culture of Siena. And thanks to the convoluted double-talk of the Italian system, I'm beginning to wonder if I can trust the legat, either.

As if actually arguing with Dennis, alone in the kitchen I pose the question out loud: "What was Giovanni up to?" Why was he outside the walls? What made him a target? Was it his famous family, or was he up to shenanigans of his own?

On a table near the front entrance of the abbey there is a pile of guidebooks for the use of the guests. I search for a schedule of bus service to Siena, but then can't make heads or tails of it. Inside a binder of restaurant recommendations is a card for a taxi company. An hour later, when the driver arrives—receding hair, blue sunglasses despite the rain—we can't seem to understand each other, but that is not a problem. I show him the paper Inspector Martini passed me in the ladies' room, and we drive to that address, outside the walls of the city, where, she was covertly telling me, Giovanni's vehicle was found by the police.

THE LITTLE blue mailbox car is still in the same spot. It is a bad parking job, as if he stopped in a hurry and didn't plan to stay long. The two-story stucco apartment buildings in this low-rent suburb are painted in reckless colors of turquoise and tangerine. Sliding glass doors open to narrow balconies that seem about to slide off the walls, like tiers of a badly made cake. Huddling beneath a golf umbrella from the abbey, I take out a notebook and sketch a map of the crime scene. An old habit, it helps me to think.

The glossy wet street is deserted, bloodstains washed away by the rain. Whom did Giovanni come to see? I'm guessing it was a teenage friend. In America you can tell student apartments by the beer cans and Tibetan flags, but here there is nothing to indicate any kind of tenants other than working families. People are waiting for a bus; behind them is a sliver of stores, including an Internet spot that also sells Indian jewelry, a Laundromat with bright red washing machines, a grocery, and a store with a window full of nothing but espresso pots.

The Muslim guy in the Internet spot speaks English but has nothing to tell me, there's nobody in the Laundromat (who does laundry in the rain?), the coffeepot store is closed, and the grocery lady appears to have some form of dementia, but she's interested in having company, so I take what I can get.

She's wearing a dark flowered dress and a raggedy sweater,

stamping around the wooden floors with fiercely scattered energy. Her hair is white and her eyes are mad, unnatural blue—bright lights in the musty dark. The electricity is off except in the deli case containing cheeses and prosciutto, cartons of eggs, and antipasti materials such as roasted peppers and calamari salad. Behind the counter are shelves of yellowing school supplies. When I point to Giovanni's car across the street and display a photo of him that I lifted from Cecilia's bedroom, she bursts into smiles and grabs my hands, wringing the life out of them, urging over and over, in a bizarre segue, that I must have *torta di Pasqua*, a desiccated Easter cake lying in a chewed-up box, that by my calculations must be three months old.

Finally I buy the thing for a euro. Delighted to be rid of what the rats won't eat, she pulls a set of keys from the pocket of her apron and waves me through the back door. I have to laugh at myself: *There's always a deal.* Now she is happy to lead the way beneath a grape arbor that provides a pleasant shelter from the rain, to a staircase that goes up to an apartment over the grocery store. "*Fa presto!*" she keeps saying, and unlocks the door to what I believe must be her home, where her husband is no doubt sitting mummified in an armchair holding a piece of Easter cake, but no, we are in an artist's studio. An artist who, by the canvases stacked up against the walls, paints only clouds.

But they are wonderful, expressive clouds I recognize from the skies of Tuscany, captured in the midst of many ephemeral moods. This is a working painter whose mind is organized around neat rows of pigments in wire baskets, sketches pinned to walls, brushes in size order in clean tin cans, revolving sculptures of stones and twigs, shelves of art books and animal skulls. There is just a narrow cot for sleeping. This place is about disciplined work. A half-painted square of canvas, still showing ruled lines of perspective, is clipped to a large easel. The way it is positioned in the center of the room, underneath the skylight rattling with rain, makes you think of a big personality, always in the light.

Using hand gestures and my limited Italian, I manage to ask if the person who lives here is a friend of Giovanni.

"*Sì, sì,*" says the landlady. "*Visita sempre.*"

"He always comes here?"

"*Sì!*" Frowning, she mimes knocking on the door and walking in. Giovanni visits this place all the time, she seems to say. She knows because she sees him. He was here last night.

The old woman marches through the apartment, calling, "Mural?" and I expect to be presented with a wall-sized piece of art and bullied into buying it, but instead we enter the kitchen. Judging from the cot in the studio and the mess in here, Giovanni's friend does not care very much about sleeping or eating. The counter is nothing but a plank of wood lying across a pile of cinder blocks. The paint-splattered sink is jammed with dishes and teacups, a rusted water heater suspended above. The landlady doesn't react; she must snoop around up here all the time. Back in the room with the easel, I notice a pile of mail addressed to Muriel Barrett. Not "Mural," but "Muriel." The letters are postmarked London. The books around the house are in English.

"Where is Muriel?" I ask. "*Dov'è?*"

"*La sbarra Australiana,*" the landlady says.

I ask where Muriel is and she says Australia? I give her my notebook. Would she please write down the words? *Australiana.* Is she saying the painter is *from* Australia? With shaky fingers, the landlady draws a diagram with a crucifix in the middle, pointing emphatically—"*Il Duomo*"—and I understand she means the central cathedral in the old part of Siena, and *there,* where she makes a square and blackens it, is the location of the *Australian bar* that Giovanni told me about when we drove in from the bus station. *"They speak English and have English beer!"*

A special kind of excitement rises, as when pieces of an investigation start to fit. Hot damn. Six thousand miles away and I am back on home ground.

WITH A little push in the right direction from a bearded fellow at the English-language bookshop, I trot downhill on Via di Pantaneto until stopped by the words *Happy Hour!* chalked on a blackboard before a narrow doorway set into the stone-gray blocks of a nondescript building. A sign above says, WALKABOUT—AN AUSTRALIAN PUB. If you still had doubts such a thing could exist in the middle of Siena, Italy, the vestibule is stacked with placards for "Dundee Cocktail Hour."

The absolute darkness inside is like walking into a movie theater. A few groping steps, and then a gilded bar comes out of the gloom like a vision, a sparkling trove of golden beer taps and glistening glasses. There are strings of Foster's beer flags, and toward the back, a tattered map of Australia. All the lights in the Walkabout are crimson, the way a bar should be; the stools are hard; the booths are hung with drawings of kangaroos.

The bartender is on a cell phone.

"It's been sorted," he says in a monotone. "I've given them the good news."

The bartender is English, stern, in his late forties, with buzz-cut hair, hefty, wearing a white T-shirt and burnt-orange jeans. He closes the phone and in the same clipped accent asks what he can get me.

I ask if Muriel Barrett is around.

"That's her," he says, indicating an empty stool and two full shot glasses.

"What is she drinking?"

"*Rum e pera*. Rum and pear juice."

"Oh my Lord."

"Special of the house."

"Go for it," I say.

"You're American."

"I'm from L.A., and please don't tell me your favorite TV show."

"I don't watch TV," the bartender growls, putting two glasses before me. "First shoot the rum, then the pear."

I do it, and a few moments later, from approximately the third chakra, the Tuscan sun bursts forth.

The bartender goes back to washing glasses. In the rear, some guys are throwing darts. The stool beside me remains empty. I stare at an endless motorcar race on the flat-screen. Who is this doll, Muriel, alone at a bar doing shots in the afternoon? I'm imagining she's a solitary painter with a history of failed relationships, so she moves to Siena, a place so beautiful just walking out the door can give you an eye orgasm. She's rail-thin, worn-looking, a couple of years older—way too fast for a sixteen-year-old, but what does Giovanni know? The race cars go around another dozen laps, along with the rum in my brain.

A high-pitched female voice shrills at us: "Saved my spot?"

A short aging Englishwoman with kinky gray hair hauls herself up onto the stool. She is in her sixties, round like a barrel and eager as a toddler.

"Good man!" she cries, downing the rum and pear, one two.

The bartender says, "We thought you were a goner."

"I was in the loo," declares Muriel Barrett theatrically. "Having a nice bowel movement."

The bartender cracks a smile and offers another round. I am thinking it might be a good time to switch to Foster's.

"This lady has been waiting for you," he explains to Muriel.

Muriel, apparently playing the Queen of Rum, inquires imperiously, "*Who* is *she*?"

I introduce myself as Giovanni Nicosa's aunt and ask if she knows him.

"Yes, of course I know Giovanni. You're his *aunt*?"

And that kicks off the whole saga of how I came to be in Siena. I leave out the part about being an FBI agent.

Muriel Barrett has the face of a beagle, complete with errant whiskers, but she is not stupid. Her large brown eyes take in everything and hold it for future use. I ask how she knows Giovanni.

"Everybody knows everybody in Siena. Especially the English-speakers."

"Knows them, how?"

"Oh, the occasional game of darts."

"In a pub? He's sixteen years old. What's the drinking age in Italy?"

"I don't think there is one, is there, Chris?" the cloud-painter asks the bartender.

"The drinking age in Italy is when you're old enough to see over the counter," Chris replies.

"I'm his *aunt*."

Muriel watches with watery eyes. "You've explained the family history with stunning clarity. I do understand that you are his aunt."

"I'm concerned about Giovanni."

"Why? What's going on?"

Muriel's voice has dropped a key. Gone is the imperious bullshit. The eyes have adjusted to the line of questioning: cautious and indignant.

"He came to see you last night."

"Really? When was this?"

"Around ten-thirty. Were you home?"

"No, as a matter of fact, I was here. Wasn't I, Chris?"

Chris raises an eyebrow.

"His car is still outside your apartment."

Genuine surprise: "It is? I didn't notice." Then, "How do you know where I live?"

"Giovanni was attacked last night."

"Attacked!"

"He's in the hospital."

Muriel stares.

"What happened to him?"

"Tower on Goose," Chris pronounces flatly.

"Not necessarily."

"Really?" he mimics, sarcastic now. "Like the Sienese aren't all fucking nuts?"

"But—why did you come to my studio?"

"I wasn't looking for you, Muriel. I was looking for Giovanni's car. I asked around and met your landlady. She said he was there last night. He knocked on your door."

"I had no idea."

"His parents are at the hospital. I'm trying to help them understand what happened."

"Will he be all right?"

"We don't know. He was hurt pretty badly."

Chris is paying attention now. "This doesn't happen in Siena."

I look at my watch. "I should call the hospital."

"No worries; I'll take care of it," he says. "You don't want to deal with Italian phones."

Muriel uses a cocktail napkin to blot her tears. We wait in silence as Chris engages with someone at the hospital. He thrusts the phone at me. "Tell them you're a relative."

My mind stalls. I can't think of one word in Italian.

"How do you say it?"

Sono la zia di Giovanni."

I repeat the phrase like a dummy. Chris takes the phone

and listens deeply. Now he's thanking them. His tone has become polite. Muriel and I wait uneasily. He clicks off and speaks in that calm, eerie monotone.

"The boy is being taken to the operating room."

"For the leg?"

"Nothing regarding a leg. His heart is failing."

"Did he have a cardiac arrest?"

"Might have. She said it's critical."

"I'll drive. I'm perfectly able," Muriel announces crisply, and slips her purse beneath her arm.

11

EVEN BEFORE I get to Giovanni's room, there is a jam-up of nurses and technicians in the hall. As I peer at the huddle of green scrubs, listening to instructions ordered back and forth in Italian, the truth of being a foreigner has never been clearer. The huddle starts to move as one, and then the gurney shoots out the door, trailing IV stands and monitors. They veer left, and Giovanni passes right beneath my eyes. It is almost indecent to look at him, helpless and exposed, unconscious, pure white skin, his beautiful head in a blue paper cap lolling as they turn a corner. My jaw aches. I have been clenching my teeth.

Muriel, who has been arguing with someone at the nursing station, wobbles toward me looking flushed and unsteady.

"He has to have an operation on his heart. It's all I could get out of her, the cheeky little snit. And why does she *insist* on wearing that *God-awful* smock?"

Muriel sways on her feet. I grab her fleshy biceps and ease her into a chair, wondering if the *rum e peras* have finally hit.

"Are you okay?"

"I've been through several bouts of cancer with my partner, Sheila. As a result, I tend to have a hard time in hospitals."

In the car I learned that Sheila works for a bank in Piccadilly, and only comes to Italy for three weeks in spring. Nevertheless, their ten-year relationship has endured across the channel. Winters in Siena, Muriel is happy to roost like a hen among her cloud paintings. "It works out," Muriel assured me, while speeding to the hospital along a commercial shortcut through the sunflower fields, past storage silos and water treatment plants.

"How are you feeling?" I ask.

"Like what the bloody cat dragged in. Look, I'm sorry, but it's just too many bad memories. I've got to get out of here." She gets to her feet and totters toward the nearest exit, adding incongruously, "Give my best to Giovanni."

Crowded with immigrants from defunct communist nations, the hallway resembles a Balkan bazaar. Tough, shaven-headed Albanian janitors are pushing mops. A Yugoslav family argues over the slumped head of a matriarch in a wheelchair. Somehow I convince the cheeky little snit in the God-awful smock (dinosaurs) to page Dr. Cecilia Nicosa, and moments later she appears in a crisp white lab coat with a stethoscope in the pocket. Her eyes are shrunken and exhausted. We kiss each other's cheeks and sit side by side on a couch that matches the royal blue of the walls.

"Giovanni developed an irregular heartbeat," she reports. "He was going into hypotensive shock. Nobody could understand it. I told you Dr. Ciardi fixed the artery in the leg, but the blood pressure kept going down and the danger is that if the new blood supply continues to drop, he could lose the leg. We did two tests—an angiogram and echocardiogram—and they both showed that blood was extravasating from the heart."

"What does that mean?"

"There is a hole in the heart, and it is leaking blood."

"Was the hole there all along?"

"No," she snaps. "He was stabbed."

"I know that, but—"

"When we first examined the stab wounds, we did not realize that the tip of the knife had lacerated the pericardium. The sack around the heart. So now he will need a second surgery to sew up the tear."

"You were right. This is not about some boys fighting over a flag."

"All I care about now is that we have the best thoracic surgeon working on my son."

Despite fatigue, her eyes are defiant. Her composure is a skill that results from learning how to judge the degree of danger—not unlike our shoot/don't shoot scenario in the Bureau, where you have a split second to decide whether to fire at a figure on a video screen. In these moments you can only trust your training. Cecilia has no choice but to rely on the technology now in play beneath the surgical lights.

I ask if she knows the English painter, Muriel Barrett. She replies that you can hardly miss her.

"Muriel gave me a ride to the hospital, but then she felt squeamish and had to leave."

"Muriel? Squeamish?" Cecilia says skeptically. "She's a war hammer."

"Battle-ax?"

"*Sì.*"

"Why is she so upset about Giovanni? What is their relationship?"

"*Relationship*? She could be his grandmother, and besides, she's gay!"

"Then why does he hang out with her?"

"He doesn't. Why would he?"

"Last night Giovanni went to see Muriel Barrett. He was attacked in front of her apartment."

"How do you know?"

"The landlady saw him go up to Muriel's apartment. And the police found his car, along with bloodstains on the sidewalk."

"But he was found in the tunnel on Via Salicotto."

"The idea was to make it look like a war between the *contrade*. You were right—Giovanni was attacked as a warning. The police think it was a mob hit, Cecilia. They wanted to send a special message. The question is, to whom?"

Cecilia crosses her arms and her stare grows dark with suspicion.

"Ana, have you been talking to the provincial police?"

"Some."

"Stay out of it. You can't understand Italy."

"I understand that you're afraid—"

"I'm afraid of *you*. That you will step all over things with your FBI boots."

"I'll try not to do that."

Cecilia stands, eyes wet with rage. "My son is on the operating table, but I still have patients."

All I can do is watch her go.

AFTER THE second surgery, to sew up his heart, Giovanni slipped into a coma. They put him on a ventilator with a tube down his throat, taped to a bandage around his head. His face was pale from loss of blood. When I touched his hand, his skin felt clammy and cold.

Despite assurances from the doctors, after forty-eight hours Giovanni still had not woken up. Waiting became a vigil. The priest came every day, along with Sofri, who arrived precisely at ten a.m. and left at noon, as well as the extended Nicosa family, a flock of solemn-faced members of the *contrada*, and employees of the coffee company, all ritually paying their respects.

Day one of Palio was two days away, on Friday, June 29,

and visitors to the hospital talked compulsively about the uptick in retail sales, the full hotels, which horses looked fast, who had been chosen to bodyguard the jockeys, the health of the judges, and the direction of the wind. They spoke robustly, as if news of the outside world would distract the anguished parents. Not only would Giovanni not be *alfiere*, but also he might never walk again. They had not ruled out brain damage, and the doctors were saying he could still lose several toes from lack of blood to the leg. The prince was deathly ill and fighting for his life.

AROUND SEVEN on the Thursday night before Palio, Nicosa, Cecilia, and I simultaneously get the urge for soda and chips, available from machines in the basement lounge. We are in the elevator when she says casually, without shifting her eyes from the lighted floor numbers, "When Giovanni is well enough, I will take him to El Salvador."

"I suppose it is a good enough place to recover," Nicosa says.

"No, he will stay."

"Stay?" asks her husband. "For how long?"

"Until he is married," she answers grimly.

The elevator doors open. You could smell linty hot exhaust from the giant clothes dryers turning towels. We follow Cecilia's squared shoulders down a dim corridor. She is still wearing the white lab coat and heels. She opens the lock on a door with a security card.

"He will stay with my family, and he will be safe."

She turns on the lights. There are a few round tables and a microwave above an empty counter. Nicosa checks his cell, but there is no service in the basement.

"That will never happen," he says, addressing the cigarette machine.

"Are you going to stop me?"

"I don't have to. He will never choose to leave Siena."

"He will have no choice. I'm taking him. That's all."

"If you are trying to punish me by taking Giovanni away," Nicosa says slowly, "there is no need. I blame myself for what happened. I should have kept a closer eye. Not let him stay out all hours with people we don't know, like that boy he met on the Campo, the African punk who gave him his first joint—it was all downhill from there."

I recall Inspector Martini speculating that Giovanni most likely had tried drugs, and wondered how far down was "downhill."

"Does he still get high?" I ask.

"No," Cecilia answers. "Not anymore."

"It's in the past," Nicosa says irritably. "Right now he is very sick. He needs our prayers."

"I'm wondering if Giovanni's involvement with drugs has anything to do with the attack," I said.

"Giovanni is not involved with drugs!" Nicosa says. "Did you not hear me? I said I take the blame. Sometimes I am not as good a father as I should be or want to be, but right now I am going upstairs to be with my son. Don't even think about taking him to El Salvador," he tells his wife. "Now or ever."

"Infuriating man," Cecilia says when he's left.

The basement lounge is like a bunker, soundproofed from activity in the hospital above. With no cell service, we have no way of knowing that at that moment, Giovanni's condition has drastically changed. Instead, we slump in plastic chairs, mindlessly eating potato chips with packets of garlic mayonnaise Cecilia found in a drawer.

"I hid my pregnancy for seven months," she is saying. "At the beginning, Nicoli didn't know. We met in the aftermath of an earthquake on top of a civil war—everything was in confusion. You are young, you want to affirm life, you go to bed with a handsome stranger. We were madly in love, but we did not expect to be together again; it was too far-fetched. He went back to Italy. I studied for my medical degree. I felt the pregnancy was my responsibility. I was afraid to ask this man I hardly knew for help, so I went against everything and decided to have Giovanni on my own."

"Did your family support you?"

Cecilia snorts. "My mother said she wanted to die. I ruined all her hopes that I would be a doctor, and she had sacrificed so much for my education. After the birth I was very unhappy and in a deep depression, but all I could do was struggle and manage to work and do good in school. My aunts had to talk to my mother and say, 'You need to be stronger, and hold her, and don't let her sink, because if you let her go, what's going to happen to all these years of working so hard? Why give up now? For what people will say?' How can I put this to you? In the Latin culture it is not even your *choice* to have an abortion, because the idea is that to have this baby will be your punishment. You did it, and that will be the consequences. Of course, the moment he was born, Giovanni became my mother's joy.

"She urged me to contact Nicoli. I was terrified he would refuse to answer, but it was just the opposite. He cared more than I knew, and he was so proud to have a son. He was just starting out in the coffee business, but he did manage to send money. He insisted that we wait to get married in Italy, in the *contrada*, in the proper way. It took three years for him to make his way back to El Salvador. In the meantime I was a single mother.

"Giovanni was born before Christmas. In the New Year, when the next term started, I had to take this little tiny bundle to school. I fed him at midnight. I would come home so tired. I worked sometimes three days straight in the hospital. When he was older, I would come home half dead, and

Giovanni would say, 'Let's go paint!' and I would fall asleep on the table and Giovanni would say, 'Mama, wake up, you're not playing with me!' and sometimes I would cry because I felt I was not giving my baby enough. It was a rough and hard time in my life. It was like everything was crumbling. The only thing I held on to was the belief that Nicoli was coming back.

"He didn't see Giovanni until Giovanni was three. We left for Italy, and Nicoli and I were married immediately. Of course, I had to be baptized into Oca first, so Giovanni would be of Oca. I embraced everything my husband put before me. I learned to cook Italian food. I took care of Nicoli's mother, even though my heart was breaking because I had left my own mother behind. It was known that Nicoli had other women, and I was supposed to accept that as a way of life. He once had a mistress who disappeared in a supermarket parking lot; probably she's dead. It was a scandal. They said she was part of the mafias."

"Was she?" I ask.

"I did not hire a detective to find out," Cecilia says sarcastically. "Nicoli apologized a thousand times, offered to do anything to make it right. There were so many nights we both just cried. Once you go through something like that, no matter how much you try, the marriage is never the same. At one point I was going to leave him, take my son back to El Salvador, but that would have been too hard on Giovanni. We break apart, we heal, we continue. Nicoli pays for my clinics and pulls the political strings necessary to get the permits and paperwork and all the rest of it. Without his influence, we could not be of service to our poorest patients."

"Is that what Nicoli meant about not being a good father? Was he talking about his influence with the mafias?"

Cecilia shuts it down.

"Things are as they are."

. . .

WHEN WE get up to the surgical floor, an old man is standing in the hallway outside Giovanni's room. He wears discreetly checked trousers and a raincoat thrown over his shoulders. A young muscular fellow wearing a T-shirt and a jade disk on a leather thong around his neck helps the old man into his raincoat. He needs help because he has no hands. In place of his hands there are two black prostheses—medieval contraptions of polished stakes and wooden levers. Dressed, the old man nods politely at us and says *"Arrivederci,"* as they pass.

Cecilia's eyes widen. She bursts into Giovanni's room. Giovanni looks no different; a sixteen-year-old full of life who isn't moving. Eyes closed, the machine breathing for him. She swiftly checks the monitors that show his vital signs.

"Cecilia—what's wrong?"

"Do you think that man was inside this room?"

"Who? The old guy in the hall?"

I scan the place. The only sign of another's presence is the big chair where visitors sit. The shawls and pillows Cecilia brought for napping are in disarray on the floor, as if someone has thrown them off quickly.

"It looks like *someone* was here. Maybe Nicoli. Let's call his cell—"

"It doesn't matter," my sister interrupts quickly. "Giovanni's okay. He's okay," she says again, to reassure herself.

"You seem afraid."

"I'm fine."

"He scared you. Why? Who is he?"

She wets her lips. "Just a confused old man."

The door opens, startling Cecilia, but it is only the nurse, a squat, large-breasted woman speaking nonstop Italian. Cecilia listens, and stares at her son, who is apparently in a deep, drugged sleep.

"She says Giovanni is responsive. He squeezed her finger, just a few minutes ago!" Cecilia says. "She called my cell, but we were in the basement with no service. This is wonderful news! We can take him off the ventilator!"

The nurse smiles widely, showing gold teeth. Then she rams Cecilia with her bosom and crushes her in a euphoric hug.

12

"**HIS NAME** is Cosimo Umberto, but they call him Il Fantòccio, the Puppet," Dennis Rizzio says on the phone from Rome later that night. "Worked his way up to *capomandamento*, head of a district of mafia families."

"How did he lose his hands?"

"When he was a young *picciotto*, out to prove himself, he had the bright idea of blowing up Parliament. Unfortunately, all he's got is some half-assed ordnance from World War Two, so needless to say, the thing goes off while the schmuck is holding it. But they like his courage, so they make him a bag man for 'Ndrangheta."

"A bag man with no hands?"

"He scares the devil out of people. You own a falafel joint, and the Puppet shows up, wanting a protection bribe. You gonna argue? The guy is a success story; we should all be so blessed. What was he doing at the hospital? My guess? Putting the squeeze on Nicosa. They're telling him, 'We know where your son is at'—the implication being that anytime they want, they can pull the plug on his kid. Here's the thing. Cosimo Umberto is out of his territory. He should be working extortion for 'Ndrangheta, on his usual beat down south in Calabria. But suddenly we find one of their top *coglioni* pressuring Nicoli Nicosa, a major industrialist in Siena. Whatever was said in that room could change the picture of mob penetration of the north. You're in a unique position to know."

"Meaning what?"

"Talk to your sister. She knows exactly what's going down, or she wouldn't have freaked when she saw that guy."

"Now isn't the time. Her kid is still critical. Palio starts tomorrow and she's hyped about that—"

"Stop making excuses. You're in, and we want you to stay in."

I am talking to Rizzio from the far side of the pool, out of sight of the family. The underwater lights are on, heat still rises off the pine duff like a woodland sauna, while I pace the deck and consider betrayal. It's one hell of a postcard.

"You know what, Dennis? I shouldn't do this."

"You're the only one who can. You're in with the family; that's a tremendous plus."

"Let's do it right and bring the heat. Infiltrate with an undercover from the Bureau, someone fresh. I'll help them establish a cover, and then I'm gone. It doesn't feel right, and you know when that happens, it's time to go home."

There is a space of silence.

"'Home' is a relative concept," Dennis finally replies. "From what I understand, the door is not exactly open."

"Where? Los Angeles?"

"Like I told you, Bob Galloway and I are buddies from the old days. He filled me in on your situation, fingering Peter Abbott, deputy director of the FBI, for obstruction of justice."

"You have a problem with that?"

"Me? Not at all. Peter Abbott is a private-school prick like we used to beat up on the subway. But there's no way he's going to plead guilty and go away."

"You never know."

"You think Peter Abbott's just gonna roll over?" Rizzio

asks skeptically. "That's what family money and connections are *for*—obstruction of justice!"

He laughs.

"The Bureau is in for a tough battle in the courts. God forbid the trial goes south, and after a huge investment of time and money, it turns out the evidence *you* provided isn't all that solid. All I'm saying, Ana, is that it's easy enough to stay in their good graces."

I shake my head.

"I know how this investigation of Nicosa will proceed," I insist. "You'll want intel. Hard evidence. Pretty soon there are surveillance cameras planted inside the abbey, and I'm wearing a wire. Now we're involving family members. It's just too complicated for me."

"Are they really your family?"

"Kind of."

He hears my real hesitation. "Because I would never ask you to do something like that."

"I know."

"It seemed like since you never met these people, maybe it would fly," he goes on. "But say the word, and I'll send a new u.c. in tomorrow. If you have an emotional conflict, that's a nonstarter."

Dennis knows that admitting to an "emotional conflict" is a ticket to the community outreach squad, and that I've already gotten my teeth into this case. But part of his question is sincere. I can't call Cecilia my sister in the real sense. It hasn't been instant chemistry. Our lives are completely different. We've known each other for just a few tumultuous days. I entered her home with a role to play. She reached out precisely because I am an agent. I want to help, but we are more bound by circumstance than blood.

"There's no conflict," I say at last. "But I need you to take extra precautions."

"Fine. How long is your nephew in the hospital?"

"He's out of the coma, so hopefully not too much longer."

"I hear what you're saying. The safety of the family won't be compromised. I will personally make sure Giovanni has protection 24/7. I'll have Inspector Martini post a cop outside his room. No more creeps in the hall."

There's still something that feels out of joint. I slip off my shoes and swipe the water in the pool with a bare foot, kicking up a splash of frustration.

"Any news on the attack in London?"

"We had some progress," Dennis says. "The number for the guy who bought the Ford used in the assault turned out to be a disposable phone, so the Brits kicked the investigation up to the Counter Terrorism Command. They have the resources to trace calls received by that number. Four calls were placed from Calabria—the last one a few minutes before they assaulted the restaurant. It was a mafia-ordered hit, which explains why the car was dumped in Aberdeen."

"Funny, I thought Aberdeen was in Scotland."

"Don't be fresh," Dennis advises. "Aberdeen has become a landing point for the penetration of the mafias into the U.K. Go down to Sicily any day, and you'll see kids waiting at the docks, hoping to get on a boat with direct service to Scotland. For the up-and-comers, it's a promotion. The shooters dumped the car in Aberdeen because that's where they have protection. What I'm telling you is, these folks you came up against in London are well organized and connected to the Italian mafia syndicates. So be alert."

"I get it, but none of this has anything to do with me. The fact that I was there at that restaurant is totally random."

"Maybe," Dennis says. "Enjoy the Palio."

The surface of the pool has stilled. I'm looking at my reflection, not recognizable, just a play of darkness and light.

IL PALIO

13

PALIO, DAY 1—FRIDAY, JUNE 29, 5:45 A.M. The reflection of the empty ironwork bed slides around me as I open the doors of the mirrored armoire and pull out a linen skirt Cecilia has loaned me, wrapping it around my waist and slipping on a white T-shirt and leather sandals. I tie an Oca scarf around my neck, letting the point of the triangle hang down the back. Day by day, I seem to be losing my L.A. edge and looking more like Cecilia.

She and Nicosa were leaving at dawn for the *tratta*, or "choosing of the horses," that begins the festival, when I cornered her in the second-floor arcade. She was dressed with conservative elegance in an Oca-green suit with an opalescent sheen. I was still wearing pajamas with rockets on them.

"Cecilia, look. I know who he is."

"Who?"

"The man with no hands we saw outside Giovanni's room. He's mafia," I said quietly. "It's obvious."

She squinted at the soft light filling the archways.

"What are you trying to do?" she said at last.

"Protect you and Giovanni. Tell me I'm wrong. Tell me he wasn't the Puppet, a mob boss from the south."

She seemed very busy with the contents of her purse, so I went on.

"You don't think the idiots who attacked Giovanni aren't watching the abbey?"

"Giovanni is safe in the hospital under police security, is he not?" she said, making an inventory of her makeup case, sunglasses, keys, cell phone.

"Yes, but believe it—now they're watching you. They know every time you come and go. They are very capable of taking both you and your husband out in a heartbeat, and where would that leave Giovanni?"

"I know they are capable. Every day in my work I see people capable of the worst possible things." Her dark brown eyes, moist and troubled, met mine. "I will tell you the truth. When I started out to look for you it was because of my duty to honor my mother's wish—to make sure Miguel Sanchez's daughter had her rightful inheritance. When the detective found you in the FBI, I thought it was a sign from God. I know that my husband is under the thumb of the mafias, and I don't see how he will ever get out. I thought you could help me. Really, I am still a stranger here. I didn't know what to do. You see now why I have been desperate, especially now that this beast—" Her voice was trembling. "He comes to my son's hospital room—"

I wanted my notebook very badly to write down every word of her confession, but if I lost her, with Palio about to begin, it could be days before I got her back.

"Let's sit down," I said, indicating the carved wooden chairs along the terra-cotta-tiled corridor.

"I can't. The *tratta* is starting."

"Just tell me—how is Nicoli under their thumb?"

"I don't know for certain. It must be that he's paying bribes, like everybody else, and wants it to stop. He has tried to get out and they won't let him."

"How do you know?"

"That is my belief. When his mistress went white shotgun, he changed. He was very distant, even frightened. I see that today, but at the time I was so angry I could not see anything. And now, with Giovanni—I am afraid one day they will just kill us all."

"What does Nicoli say? Have you talked about this?"

"He won't speak about it. He says not to worry, that we are protected."

"By whom?"

She shrugged, holding back tears. "I don't know his connections."

"I can help you," I said firmly. "But you have to tell me everything you know about your husband's business. It's possible this all traces back to Lucia Vincenzo. You know she was laundering drug money for 'Ndrangheta? Maybe he is, too."

"Yes. Okay. I will tell you what I know. Maybe we can get inside his computer."

"We can do that," I say, almost choking with excitement.

"Will you go to the provincial police? You have to be careful. They are also in the pocket of the mafias."

"We'll take it step-by-step. But I need more information. When can we talk?"

"During the feast is impossible. Every hour is taken up with one ceremony or another, and Nicoli and I are always in the public eye. He is waiting for me now. I have to go."

"You need more protection than just his word. I'll go with you."

"It is not necessary. We could not be safer than to be in public, surrounded by *contrada* members."

Composure back, Cecilia struggled to look confident.

· · ·

AN HOUR later, Sofri pulls up in the courtyard, steamy exhaust wrapping around his little black Renault. Excitement has been building in town all week—kiosks festooned with brilliant colors, drummers in medieval costumes calling men to arms, the unfathomable buzz among the Sienese. As we leave the abbey, the flare of day is just striking the hills.

My elderly guide is all decked out in an Oca-green blazer with a white shirt and a red bow tie. The white mustache and flowing hair make him look like a yachtsman for the green team, but today he is *il professore*. We've scarcely said *"Buongiorno"* before he launches into a monologue about the *tratta*, the arcane system by which each *contrada* receives its horse by random draw—just three days, mind you, before the big race. A veterinarian is at this moment checking out all the horses entered in the pool, because the rules say a *contrada* cannot give back its fated animal, even if it turns out to be lame. However, attempting to poison the steed of your enemy is an honorable tradition.

We park outside the walls of the city and hurry past Ethiopian traders opening their stalls of Chinese-made contraband handbags. There aren't many tourists yet. It is barely 7:30 a.m. and the sun is already burning. We climb up hills, then down into the Piazza del Campo. Police are posted at the many entrances. After the empty streets, it is a shock to pass through the archways and discover a massive gathering of thousands of *contrade* members, as if the entire city had been herded into the plaza.

Sofri puts a hand at the small of my back, guiding us through the crowd to the doorway of one of the private palazzos that overlook the Campo. He unlocks a forbidding outer door, and then we enter a cool tiled lobby, climbing four stories to the top-floor apartment, a large open space dominated by an arch. Beyond is a fireplace with a window on either side from which you can see the square.

"Please. Be at home."

Home it is, with warm yellow walls, mismatched wing chairs, a red-and-white-peppermint-striped sofa for rainy afternoons leafing through the books and journals on the coffee table. A brass telescope stands in silhouette against the brash white light coming through the open shutters; there are stag horns on the mantelpiece, above which a Napoleonic portrait stares out.

"Take a good look," he calls from the kitchen.

The view is vertiginous and astonishing. The Piazza del Campo is shaped like a shell made of pink brick and gray travertine, rimmed with cafés at the foot of seven-story buildings that are joined together shoulder to shoulder. As the sun rises, their windows take on a glow like the amber eyes of the wolves that are the symbol of the city. Over the past few days, citizens have shoveled yellow earth off a truck and covered the outer ring of the Campo, transforming it into a racetrack. Sofri says it is good luck to touch *la tèrra*, the holy earth, which is as soft as powdered mustard.

"When you hold *la tèrra* in your hand, you hold the miracle of rebirth. Il Palio is about to begin. There is a saying, whenever we find ourselves fretting over something small and insignificant: 'Don't worry, because there will soon be *la tèrra in piazza*—earth in the piazza.' The cycle of life will go on."

I find myself staring down at thousands of men surging toward a small arena where ten unsaddled horses held by grooms are pulling nervously. The crowd seems young— average age thirty—ordinary men in short-sleeved polo shirts with cowls of their *contrada* scarves, excited to a fever pitch. I can see TV cameras and the flat white caps of local policemen. But from an FBI point of view, the Campo is a security nightmare.

You have a ring of ancient, unreinforced structures filled with windows. An enclosed, bowl-like space with narrow exits and roofs galore, creating the potential for a catastrophic number of casualties. They predict that on the evening of the decisive race, on day four of Palio, over sixty thousand people will jam shoulder to shoulder in the center of the ring, totally transfixed by violent men riding unpredictable animals. Nobody will be looking up.

"I hope a well-trained military unit is minding the store," I call back to Sofri. "Because this is an invitation to bad things happening."

"It is very emotional. There are always fights," Sofri answers. "It is expected."

I join him in the kitchen for the coffee ritual. With the most sophisticated apparatuses in the world available to him—some of which he invented—Sofri prefers the classic two-cup stovetop espresso maker, which produces a *crèma* (the delicate layer of foam) that is almost sweet. He talks about balance of taste in the espresso liquor as if it were fine brandy. It would be an unforgivable transgression to dilute the essence with steamed milk.

"I have been working on a new coffee recipe," Sofri says, pulling a plate from the refrigerator.

I hope it is not another species of wildlife rolled in coffee grounds. We escaped the coffee-roasted rabbit at the *contrada* dinner. This one I can handle: fresh dates covered with coffee cream made with egg yolks—sweet little bites to go with the espresso. Spearing seconds with a tiny fork, I ask if Sofri knows anything about a strange man who appeared outside Giovanni's hospital room.

"What strange man?"

"He didn't have any hands—"

"*Bleah*! That's terrible."

"—just weird old-fashioned wooden prostheses. He had a bodyguard who did everything for him. Well, hopefully not everything."

"You are making this up."

"I swear."

"You dreamt it, maybe."

"No, it's real."

"Then why are you laughing?" he asks.

"I'm not laughing," I say, quashing the smile reflex, which signifies deception. "It isn't funny, not to have any hands."

"Of course not," says Sofri, fussing with the gas flame, turning it up and then down. "It's a sad situation for anyone."

"I thought you might know him."

"Me?"

"Nicoli knows him."

"Why?"

"I don't know why. But we saw this man coming out of Giovanni's room."

Sofri shrugs. "It's a hospital. You are bound to see disturbing things," he says, pouring thick, slightly licorice-scented liquor into two tiny cups. "The old man must have had the wrong room."

I never said the intruder was old. Now I am fairly certain that Sofri knows exactly who the Puppet is, and what he was doing at my nephew's bedside.

A roar of exaltation goes up from the crowd, like the jubilant cry at the first strike in the first game of the World Series. We hurry from the kitchen to the windows. On the dignitary's platform a man wearing an ascot is picking numbered balls from an urn and announcing the results over a microphone.

"That is the mayor of Siena. A horse has been assigned to Torre! Wait, let's see . . ."

Another cry, and Sofri slaps his knee with delight. "*Aha!* Torre got a *brenna.*"

"What is that?"

"A bad horse. Hear it? That is Oca shouting."

I see a mass of green and white *contradaioli* braying, *"Beh! Beh!"*

"What are they saying?"

"Torre got a sheep instead of a horse! Look—there's the *commissario* of the police. He is a director of Torre. *Cornuto!"* he shouts gleefully.

The Commissario appears to be weeping and wiping his eyes.

"Is he *crying?"*

"I told you. Emotions."

The powerful *commissario*, who would go so far as to keep blood splatter evidence out of the police report in order to deny the attack on Giovanni, is *crying?*

"Ti faccio un culo così!" Sofri shouts deliriously out the window, making a ghetto move, fingers pointing down like pistols, which I guess means something like, "Die, asshole!"

I don't see what's wrong with the poor horse of Torre, to be jeered at like a nerd on the schoolyard. All the horses look beautiful, with long delicate legs and lean hindquarters; mixed breeds with thoroughbred lineage who comport themselves like aristocracy, compared with the down-to-earth, spiritually attuned wild mustangs I saw on the terrorism case in Oregon. But when Oca's horse is assigned—a gorgeous white one—Sofri reacts as if he has been pierced with a javelin. His hand slams his forehead and he drops dramatically to his knees—like just about everybody else down there in Oca, moaning and praying in a state of suicidal despair.

"What's the matter? Did we get a bad horse?"

"No," he moans. "Worse! A *good* horse!"

"What is bad about a good horse?"

"If you lose with a good horse, it's much worse than if you lose with a bad horse."

His cell phone rings and it turns out to be Cecilia, sharing this agonizing moment of having won the best horse in the Palio. After much crazed Italian back and forth, Sofri hangs up.

"She says everybody's losing their minds!" He thrusts a pair of binoculars in my hand. "Look at the stand for dignitaries, and you will see your sister."

The torrential screaming of the crowd, the braying of horns and popping of unknown small explosions, maybe firecrackers, maybe guns, make it hard to hear the person next to you.

"Where?" I shout.

"In front of the Mangia Tower!"

Panning the crowd, I find Cecilia and Nicosa standing on a platform with a group of officials at the foot of a square bell tower. The tower is several hundred feet high, tall enough to cast a shadow across the Campo to the fountain in the center, where Cecilia and I had stopped during a hot afternoon, on one of our first walks in the city, when we were still utter strangers. We sat on the edge in the cool mist, watching a pigeon drink from a braid of water pouring from the mouth of a she-wolf.

"This is historic."

"It is called Fonte Gaia, the Fountain of Joy," Cecilia said.

I laughed. "No, I mean us. The first time we're together."

"You're not what I expected," she admitted.

"In what way?"

"You're easier to talk to. I was afraid you would be cold and buttoned-up, like they are in the FBI."

I smiled. "You're different from what I expected, too. How can you live in high heels?"

"My back hurts all the time."

"Why don't you just take them off?"

"I'm used to it. You have a boyfriend? Doesn't he want you to dress up?"

"Sure, but you look amazing just going to the market."

She liked that. "Can I ask you something?" She seemed almost shy. "Do you carry a gun?"

"Yes."

"Even if you're not on duty?"

I nodded. "It's not required, but if you didn't, that's the one time something would happen, and you'd get in trouble because you didn't have your weapon."

She eyed me suspiciously. "I hope you don't have a gun right now."

"No worries, I left it home. I do have a boyfriend. I want you to see him."

I showed her the wallpaper on my cell phone, which is a photo of Sterling on a horse, all decked out in western gear, lassoing a calf. She looked shocked.

"Your boyfriend is a *cowboy*?"

"In his spare time. That's in Texas, where he's from. That's Wizzy."

"Wizzy?"

"The horse. My boyfriend's name is Sterling."

She raised her eyebrows skeptically, and we both started laughing.

"Does this seem ridiculous?" I asked. "Like, if you're American, of course you would date a cowboy?"

"It might be fun to date a cowboy."

"Trust me."

"*Scusi.*"

Her cell phone rang, and she answered with enthusiasm. A toddler ran in spirals in the middle of the Campo, trailing the white-and-black-striped flag of Istrice, the Porcupine. I found myself enthralled by the fountain, as if the sound had been turned up. The smell of damp stone took me back to winter rain outside my grandfather's house, looking through the screen door and feeling oddly safe.

"I'm sorry," said Cecilia, slipping the phone into her bag. "That was my husband's business partner, Sofri."

"The scientist?"

"He's more like the family adviser. The 'secretary of state.' I rely on him for everything. He's very charming," she confided. "A bachelor who *loves* the ladies. He'll love you. Should we go?"

"How are your feet?" I asked.

"Fine," she sniffed. "There was never any problem."

Now, as I look through the binoculars, Sofri leans in close.

"Are you able to see Cecilia?" he asks.

"She's right there. Near the tower."

"That tower has always reminded me of her," he says thoughtfully.

"Why?"

"Do you think I am right? Does it resemble her?"

I move the glasses along the graceful column of brick and examine the details of the white travertine belfry.

"It looks like a lily."

He is delighted. "Your sister *is* a devoted Catholic. A believer to the core. I can see it, the white Easter lily," he muses. "The resurrection. A wonderful analysis; she would like that."

"Why do you think it resembles Cecilia?"

He takes a moment. "It stands alone," he replies at last.

"It's lonely?"

He shrugs. "Lonely, maybe, but look how it dominates the square."

"She's not totally alone. Cecilia told me she depends on you."

"I love her like a daughter, but—you will see—it takes time to gain her trust."

"What do you think she wants from me?" I ask curiously.

"That's a funny question. Wave!" he urges. "She knows we're here."

I wave the Oca scarf, calling, "Cecilia! We're up at Sofri's. Look!"

Even through the binoculars she is small and far away, the space between us large. She idly scans the buildings but doesn't seem to pick us out in the mass of banners and faces in the windows. Eventually, she turns away.

14

SINCE THE last time I saw Giovanni he looked like a corpse in a wax museum, it is a wonderful relief to find him sitting up in bed in the hospital. He is on painkillers, making him glassy-eyed and carefree.

"Did you hear?" he babbles. "I won the lotto!"

"Yes, you were lucky. Do you know what happened to you?"

He shrugs. *"Boh."*

"You were jumped outside of Muriel Barrett's apartment."

He tries to process this.

"And then you were taken to a tunnel off Via Salicotto."

"The police said that, but I don't remember."

"What *do* you remember?"

He gestures toward a glass of water, and when I give it to him, he drinks with gusto through a straw.

"Did you see who attacked you, Giovanni?"

He lies back on the pillows and looks up at the fluorescent lights. Just drinking has exhausted him.

"Never mind. You rest."

He is quiet, and I think he might doze, but then a tear rolls down his cheek. I stroke his hair, thick and unwashed.

"What's the matter, baby?"

He tries to raise the broken arm, but he is too weak to lift the cast. "I kick their ass."

Tears are streaming now, but his eyes remain uplifted, as if by looking elsewhere he will not have to see something awful.

"My father all the time tells me, 'If they hit you, you kick them in the nuts.' No. You kick them *first* in the nuts—*first*."

"You're a fighter like your dad."

"He comes into my room."

"Who? Your dad?"

Giovanni rolls his head to one side, slowly. The tears hit the pillow.

I prompt him. "Who came in here? Was it a strange old guy without any hands?"

His eyes go empty. I find a tissue and wipe his cheek. He is fading fast as winter light.

"Why did you go to Muriel Barrett's apartment?"

He does not respond.

"You drove outside the walls to see Muriel. You went for a reason."

"*Non lo so*," he whispers. "The police already ask."

With the police guard outside the open door there is no privacy, so I sit on the bed and lean in close.

"Giovanni, listen. I have no agenda except to protect you and your family. You've been targeted by the mafias, and these people do not fool around. What's going on? Are you involved with drugs? Stolen property? You can tell me. I have friends who will help."

"*Sbagliato*," he answers heavily. An involuntary grin crosses his face—that sign of deception—but it probably doesn't count if you're high on Percodan. "Wrong. You are fucked up."

"Who's fucked up?" I ask gently. "Who's in the hospital because he was jumped by professional hit men?"

"I don't sell drugs." His head relaxes back and he sighs. *"Sono di merda."*

He falls silent.

I NOW have custody of Giovanni's mailbox car, which gets me to the Walkabout Pub. Chris, the dour Englishman behind the bar, is wearing rainbow-colored suspenders over a black shirt, adding a note of frivolity to the dull red atmosphere.

"Enjoying the Palio?" I ask.

"The party has barely begun," he replies ambiguously, putting a Foster's under my nose.

"What happens tomorrow?"

"I don't keep up with it," he says. "I just pour the beer."

"Why do you live here?"

"I enjoy the expat community."

"And the Italian girls?"

He blows through his lips. "I stay away from the Italian girls. I value my equipment, if you take my meaning."

Muriel comes in through the door, but instead of her usual oversized pop art tunics and wild tights, bare feet in splintering old Dr. Scholl's, she is wearing city clothes: a long brown skirt and a beige crocheted jacket.

"You look nice," I say. "Where are you off to?"

She is edgy, and does not sit down. "London."

"For how long?"

"I don't know. Sheila's taken ill again. The tumor's back. They want her to do another round of chemo. We'll just have to go from there."

"When are you leaving?"

"The taxi is outside."

"Anything we can do?"

"No worries. Madame Defarge"—meaning her demented landlady—"has everything in hand."

Chris puts up a *rum e pera*. "One for the road?"

Muriel turns away, as if the sight makes her queasy. She looks as flushed and panicky as she did in the hospital corridor, when we learned Giovanni had gone into cardiac arrest.

"No, I couldn't. I'm just too upset."

"Sorry, love," he says, disappearing the drinks. "What's that you've got? Going-away present for me?"

She's clutching a rectangular package about seventeen by twelve inches, tightly wrapped with brown paper and twine.

"No, dear; it's a painting for Giovanni, to wish him a speedy recovery."

"Very cool. I'll give it to him." I take the package.

She seems rattled. "I was going to leave it with Chris."

"No worries," I assure her.

"Well, all right. Give him my best. *Ciao*, everyone," she calls, and turns away, wiggling her fingers good-bye over her shoulder as she pulls the door open. We watch the taxi maneuver down the street.

"Did she say when she's coming back?" I wonder.

"In the meantime," Chris says, "let's not allow those shots to go to waste."

Chris places the untouched *rum e pera* back on the bar. He does one and I do the other. We do a couple more, until the alcohol makes the world a cheerful place, with pleasant surprises around each corner. By the time I climb a bit unsteadily out of the mailbox car in the abbey courtyard, faithfully clutching the painting, I'm not at all concerned that it is meant for Giovanni. Like a greedy child, I can't wait to see what's inside.

Veering into the kitchen, I turn on the lights and locate a knife. In a wink I have popped the twine and ripped through the brown paper and protective layers of newsprint. *What the hell; I'll fix it later.* I let the wrapping drop and lift out the painting. Another image of high-flying clouds, nicely done.

Admiring the delicate wash of blues, I notice that a puff of white powder has accumulated on my fingers. I flip the canvas over and slice off the rest of the backing. Hidden inside the painting is a plastic bag, spilling cocaine where it was pierced by the blade.

15

PALIO, DAY 2—SATURDAY, JUNE 30, 7:00 A.M. To ensure the highest level of security, a private ambulance and an unmarked police car leave the hospital early in the morning and arrive at the abbey before the city wakes. The former chapel on the ground floor has been emptied of white sofas and turned into a hospital room, where two nurses are at the ready alongside state-of-the-art medical equipment. Officers will be posted there around the clock. Giovanni, strength and youth on his side, is expected to make a good recovery. The optimism floating through the household like an errant butterfly matches the celebratory mood of the second day of Palio, when traditionally the banner is joyfully carried through the streets, to be blessed by all in church.

And here I come, with my plastic grocery bag of cocaine.

Having settled Giovanni and given instructions to the nurses, my sister is in the garden, cutting flowers.

"Are you ready?" she asks. "We are leaving for church."

She looks me up and down—surprised that I have agreed to wear one of the Ungaro dresses she offered, gray silk chiffon gathered at the waist, with transparent sleeves that button at the cuff.

"Fantastico!" she cries approvingly. "How do you like it?"

"It feels like nothing on."

She laughs. "That's what you pay for. A lot of money to walk around naked."

Cecilia is wearing another shimmery million-dollar Oca-green suit, low-cut, with multiple strands of solid gold necklaces. She has positioned her feet carefully on a paving stone so as not to ruin her hot-pink heels. Picking up a basket of roses, she pivots carefully on the stone.

"These are for Giovanni, because he must miss the blessing of the Palio. What do you have there?" she asks of the canvas in my hand.

"It's a painting by the English lady, Muriel Barrett. She left it for Giovanni on her way out of town."

"She is going for good?" Cecilia asks, in a tone that suggests she wouldn't mind.

"Unclear. Her partner in London is sick."

Cecilia examines the work. "*Che bella*," she says admiringly. "But why is the back ripped off?"

"I wasn't looking for it, but this is what I found."

I open the grocery bag. Inside is the broken sack of cocaine.

"It was hidden inside the painting. This woman is passing drugs to your son."

Cecilia twists her lips together. "What do you mean? Passing drugs?"

"They're both dealing, or she's selling and Giovanni is using. Either way, the load was meant for him."

"I find that hard to believe."

"She left it for Giovanni at the Walkabout Pub. I was there."

Cecilia stares off, trying to get her bearings. The morning sun has grown exponentially hotter; if we stay out here a moment longer, the two of us in our phantasmagorical dresses will air-dry like beef jerky.

"I'd like to talk to him," I say.

"He's just had a sedative."

"When we get back?"

Cecilia nods, striding ahead. "Without a doubt."

"And you'll tell me about your husband's business?"

I follow her into the cool of the kitchen, where she angrily fills a bucket and throws the roses in. Her rage is about to explode—at me, at everything.

"Don't worry, Ana; I am not going through this again."

"Going through what?"

Nicosa comes into the kitchen. He's wearing a finely sculpted dark suit, his hair still wet and tousled from the shower.

"Ready, ladies?"

Cecilia thrusts the plastic bag at her husband. "Cocaine."

He peers inside with the revulsion of a man looking at a dead animal.

"Giovanni is selling drugs. That Englishwoman hooked him back into it."

"Tenerlo! Fermata! Di chi parli?"

Cecilia explains, half-shouting in high-pitched Italian that the drugs were found in a painting given to their son by Muriel Barrett.

"Where is Muriel Barrett now?" Nicosa demands. "I will break her neck."

"Where is she, Ana?"

"Somewhere in the U.K."

"But the FBI can find her and have her arrested, right?" Cecilia says.

I'm stammering. "I don't know—"

Does she realize what she's saying?

Cecilia cries, "I want her to pay!"

"We can call the authorities in London," I say mollifyingly.

Cecilia's gold-laden chest is heaving with emotion. I am

watching the epitome of the Italian ruling class becoming undone.

"I insist that you arrest her!" she says.

"Arrest her?" Nicosa says.

"Yes, Ana can arrest her! Ana works for the FBI."

Nicosa regards me with astonishment. "You are with the FBI?"

There it goes. My cover. The case. One thing I learned in undercover school: it's a game that changes by the minute.

Make an adjustment.

I affect neutrality, as if there is nothing to hide. "It's true."

Nicosa rubs his temples. "I think I am still sleeping. I have not woken up to the new world order. Explain this to me."

"When we hired the investigator to find my sister, he found her in the Los Angeles FBI," Cecilia says.

"It doesn't mean anything over here. I can't arrest Muriel Barrett," I interject quickly. "But I can call Scotland Yard."

"Why did I never know this?"

Cecilia says, "I didn't think you would like my sister if you knew."

We exchange looks. She knows that she has blown it, and she doesn't care.

Nicosa shakes his head and laughs. "I am spinning!"

"Never mind about Muriel Barrett," I say. "The point is that whatever your son is into has to be stopped. Now."

He turns on me. "You have no place in this."

"I'm trying to help."

"I don't see how that is possible," he says dismissively.

"You didn't object when I showed up at the pool and saved you from a possible beating."

"What are you talking about?" Cecilia wants to know.

"When I first got here. Now I understand why the *contrada* members who confronted you at the pool were upset.

They did not want Giovanni to be *alfiere* because he was selling drugs to their kids. Does that make sense to you?"

Nicosa coolly lights a cigarette.

"You didn't understand the Italian."

"Translate for me."

Nicosa shrugs and smoothes his wet hair. "They're jealous. Who is *alfiere* is an important thing."

"Can we stop playing games?"

Cecilia breaks allegiance with her husband by making a confession: "Giovanni did at one time have a problem with marijuana."

"Welcome to the world," I say. "But now he's involved with hard drugs."

"Not at all," scoffs Nicosa. "He was smoking a little weed, but not anymore."

"Kids lie, I am sorry to say."

"Tests don't lie," Cecilia says. "We test his urine randomly, here at home. He made a contract with his drug counselor, and he's kept it. He's been through a program, Ana. He's clean."

I hold up the bag. "What about this?"

Cecilia slips on her sunglasses. "I don't know about that. We will ask Giovanni when we get back from church."

"I mean, this is evidence. Do you have a safe?"

Nicosa opens the bottom cabinet where the prosciutto is stored. "Put it here," he says.

I believe he is 100 percent serious.

Instead, we lock the bag of cocaine in the trunk of Cecilia's car, and after checking again on the sleeping boy, and the policeman reading a newspaper outside his door, the three of us jam into the Ferrari.

"I'm glad you will see the blessing," my sister says stiffly. "The ceremony is very beautiful."

Winding down the mountain in the open car, Nicosa

in glamorous Prada sunglasses and Cecilia and I with Oca scarves tied over our hair, we look like we should be in an Audrey Hepburn movie, but the tension is far from romantic.

"So now we have a spy in our house," Nicosa says.

"I'm sorry if it looks that way."

"Things went bad the minute you arrived," he decides, and then, essentially, invites me to leave. *"Vatene!"* is the command.

Cecilia snaps, *"Non parlare a mia sorella in quella maniera." Don't talk to my sister that way!*

"I'm curious about *tua sorella*." Nicosa's voice becomes louder as he goes on. "Is she here to report on us? Does she carry some kind of list in her pocket, and when she sees someone America doesn't like she calls the FBI? Because I don't understand. Explain to *me*." He catches my eyes in the mirror. "What are you doing here?"

"I'm trying to protect your family from people like the mafia boss I saw in the hospital. It did not start out that way. I was invited by my sister," I say, and the taste of the lie is sour on my tongue.

"How do you know this man you saw in the hospital?" Nicosa asks.

Cecilia cuts in quickly, "I never spoke his name."

"He had a bodyguard, and he looked like a crook," I say, covering. "I'm trained to know."

Nicosa bears down on the accelerator.

"He looks at you crooked so you make a terrible and false accusation?" The anxiety in the car ratchets up with the rpms. The curves come and vanish. We are rigid in our seats.

"Can you tell me what this man was doing there?" I say.

"I am delighted to tell you. He is a friend of the family," Nicosa replies. "He came to express his concern for our boy."

I imagine Cecilia rolling her eyes behind the dark glasses.

"How do you know him? What does he do?"

"He is a businessman," Nicosa says.

"Fine." I'm getting used to the Italian game of deny-what-we-both-know. "The important one here is Giovanni. As I told Cecilia, your son is in danger."

"Leave it to us to protect our son."

He hits the gas and we suck in the silence until we screech up outside the walls and stride without speaking to Oca head-quarters, where the procession to bless the banner is about to begin. Nicosa gets out, lobbing something in Italian that makes Cecilia flinch, and joins a group of men. She and I are left standing in the sun, filled with malevolent adrenaline.

"What did Nicoli say just now?"

"You don't want to know."

"Did he threaten you?"

She doesn't answer. I try to read her face, but all I get are fireballs reflected in the dark glasses. She glimmers and glitters with evasion. What is she still protecting?

"Don't worry about us," she says finally. "We will be okay. It is like the civil war in my country. You get used to it. You learn how to survive."

The *tamburino* drowns her out, banging a commanding pulse. People are chanting a poem about it—"*In vivo porta il morto / E 'l morto suona*"—how the living drum brings the dead to life. The cycle of Palio goes on. Lines of men and women are forming. And now, this is it. We truly *are* going to war, marching with an animated throng of Oca *contradaioli* through the sinuous streets, behind the drummer and *alfieri* carrying the flags of the crowned white Noble Goose. The boy substituting for Giovanni must have been practicing all year as well, because the two flag bearers are perfectly matched.

The soldiers at arms are dressed in pewter helmets and shoulder armor, leather tunics with mail skirts, carrying spears. The costumes are impeccable, down to the embroidery and finely turned swords. There are more men in tights than a Russian ballet, and it's no joke. Their faces are dead serious—no smirking or waving back at tourists, no awareness of them—as if the authentic Sienese among us have truly been transported back to the fifteenth century.

"Come with me and walk with Oca," says Cecilia.

"Am I allowed to?"

"You're wearing the colors; it is fine."

We are part of a long procession that includes all seventeen *contrade*. I feel like an imposter, walking with the Oca women—young girls, arm in arm, singing boastful victory songs, then mamas and *nonnas* in sleeveless dresses with pocketbooks hanging over their flaccid wrists. Ahead of us are teenage boys in baggy shorts, and men in business suits, including Nicosa and Sofri, way up front.

"What happens if you marry someone from a different *contrada*?"

"You will not see him. During Palio he will go back to his parents' house."

"Is that true?"

"Wives and husbands often separate for the week of the feast." Cecilia gives a rueful laugh, still smarting from Nicosa's parting shot. "Sounds like a good idea, doesn't it?" she says.

It is disorienting to be *inside* a parade instead of protecting it, to be the focus of dazed tourists backed into doorways, nobody understanding what in hell is going on. It's the folks in modern dress who look out of place, because the *contrada* procession dominates the streets, sweeping forward with the force of absolute commitment that carries the tall, elongated Palio banner through history to the church. A new one is commissioned each year from a local artist. This one is a bright abstract of the virgin, with multicolored garlands trailing like the tails of fanciful horses.

There are a couple of relaxed-looking provincial cops in

light blue shirts with epaulets—and, if worst came to worst, those guys with the spears. Is it possible there is one spot on earth where there is no need for security or suspicion of petty thievery, kidnapping, or terrorist attack? If so it must be here and now, at eleven in the morning, along this sun-kissed stone passageway thronged with believers, where the smells of deeply cooked complex sauces for the celebration lunch are beginning to drift through the aqua shutters of kitchen windows, where ghosts of ancient arches are still visible in the brickwork, and where plants grow arrogantly out of the walls.

Finally, giving in to the spirit, I march downhill to the rhythm of the drums, ending up in Piazza Provenzano, a small square facing the white façade of Santa Maria church. The doors are wide open and the procession keeps pushing inside, a giant traffic jam, as the parishes of each *contrada* enter behind their *alfieri* and *tamburinos*.

The church has simple smooth white walls and is filled with light. In the apse, a golden altar is topped with mosaics and covered with flowers. The moment we enter, a change comes over Cecilia. Never mind that the pews are overflowing, and the atmosphere is as rowdy as a ball game—this is a sacred space that is obviously a deep comfort. It seems natural for her to make the transition from the outside world, murmuring prayers without the slightest self-consciousness.

Sensing my curiosity, she tries to explain. "I am asking for help. I believe it will come."

"Me, too," I say, although I have no idea what I'm talking about. Help? From where? To do what? Make all of it just go away?

Cecilia and I stay close, but we have lost sight of Nicosa and Sofri in the multitude. I can't help snapping pictures on my phone. It's like being inside a wedding cake—round pillars of butterscotch marble topped with creamy rosettes, framing giant oil paintings of lessons and miracles. As more and more people crowd in, Cecilia and I are crushed beside a rack of gowns where altar boys are suiting up. It is touching to see their young faces full of self-importance, but my eye is caught by a single nun in white—older, head bowed, a point of stillness in the pressing crowd.

At last the Palio banner enters and the church erupts with shouts and drums.

Cecilia cries, "Touch it for luck. Go! Go!"

Pushing toward the center aisle as the banner is slogged through, reaching with mad ardor like everybody else—shouldering past gray-haired ladies and wide-eyed children, all of us greedy for a touch of magic—I cannot stretch my fingers far enough to reach the cloth, but then I am an outsider; why should I share in their good fortune? The banner continues toward the altar, where it will be blessed by an archbishop dressed in red and white lace. I snap a photo of the nun, a quiet eddy in the current, fingers curled against her fuzzy chin, eyes peering through smudged glasses. I envy her tranquillity.

"Is it too late to become a nun?" I whisper to Cecilia. But Cecilia doesn't answer, because she is no longer there.

16

EXPELLED FROM the church into the steamy square, the crush disperses slowly, *contradaioli* gathering in knots of animated conversation. It is easy to spot Sofri standing with a group of older men, also wearing Oca scarves, all of them smoking and talking at once.

Sofri says something that causes the others to nod with approving smiles.

"I told them you are my niece from America," he says.

I feel a blush of pleasure. "I'm touched. Do I call you *zio*?" I say, dragging up the word for "uncle."

"*Zio*, sure." Sofri grins. "*Molto bène!*"

"Where is Cecilia?"

"I don't know. You don't see her?"

We gaze over the crowd fanning out along the many streets leading out of the piazza. Tourists are still gathered, watching the spectacle of citizens in soft velvet hats and suede tunics chatting in front of motorbikes and smart cars.

"She was standing right next to me in church."

"Maybe she got a call and went outside to hear better," Sofri says, pointing helpfully to his ear.

Looking more closely at the clusters of ladies (the men and women have separated themselves like iron filings on a magnet) I see nobody in an emerald suit with a mountain of auburn hair.

"Maybe the call was about Giovanni? Maybe something happened."

Sofri speed-dials the abbey and speaks to the nurse.

"The nurse says they did not call her. It is still possible Cecilia went home."

"Is Giovanni all right?"

"He has a slight fever. The nurse is not concerned."

"How could Cecilia go home?" I wonder. "We have the car."

Nicosa, looking confident and at ease, is shaking hands with the archbishop, whose vibrant crimson and lace just knock you out in the sunshine. When His Excellency moves away, Sofri calls Nicosa over, asking questions in Italian, to which Nicosa shakes his head and shows his car keys, indicating that his wife could not have driven away. The square outside Santa Maria church is now empty. The tide has gone out, and there is no trace of Cecilia. Scanning the roofs and windows, I see only a Jack Russell terrier on a balcony, lustily pulling the leaves off a potted basil plant.

Squinting through the smoke of a cigarette, Nicosa tries her cell. No answer. He looks at his watch.

I ask, "What was the plan?"

"Meet outside the church," he replies impatiently. "Have lunch at the café. They are expecting us."

"She must already be there," Sofri decides. "Or at the *contrada* headquarters, cooking up a masterpiece for tomorrow night. Wait until you see the food these women put out."

She wouldn't be cooking, not in that suit.

"She's punishing me for the unpleasantness in the car," Nicosa says. "It's all Ana's fault." He smiles and squeezes my shoulder. "I am kidding. We are friends, right?"

"Of course."

"*Mangiamo!* Let's eat!"

I go with the men of Nicosa's circle, trooping back to Oca territory, where all the stores are bustling. Frequently they stop en masse to shake hands and kiss their brethren, everyone reciting hopes for a good outcome in Monday's race.

Finally we come to a small square with a church and a fountain—the fountain where Cecilia was baptized into the *contrada* for life. Unlike the flashy store in the Rome train station, the original Caffè Nicosa, where Nicosa's father started out as a coffee roaster, is a hole-in-the-wall—chipped plaster peeling away from the brick, a potted tree by the entrance, no sign, no menu, just a framed picture from Italian *Vogue* showing Nicosa and Cecilia looking very glam in the courtyard of the abbey. I picture her inside with her jacket off, wearing just the sexy chemise she had on under the suit, chatting and holding a glass of wine, a shrewd look aimed at the beaded curtain at the door, sights fixed and ready for her husband's entrance.

But the crowd has overflowed the street, and we can barely get inside. It is impossible to hear in the din of talk and laughter, or to move in any direction without the herculean effort of asking people to suck it in and step aside. *"Mi scusi,"* I keep breathing, wedging sideways, looking for Cecilia by randomly working my way in and out of the pack, blind as a worm. The place has that deep divine coffee smell, not just the brew of it, but the layered heart and soul of it, blackberry and chocolate. In view is the original roaster, an iron contraption of drums, ovens, pipes, and gauges painted bright red. They still roast here, every day, and the concentrated aroma rising off the tarry mountains of beans is as cool and seductive as tones off Coltrane's sax.

Pinned against the bar, where oval platters of antipasto seem to appear and disappear every few seconds, I figure what the hell, I'm famished, and start loading up on bruschetta and crostini with porcini mushrooms or fresh mozzarella. A glass of *vino rosso* restores my equilibrium and good spirits, which are impossible to resist in this tiny room jammed with people high in a communal delirium, on the crest of what promises to be a long party.

Besides, nobody else is concerned about Cecilia's absence. "I saw her a minute ago" or "Did you ask Nicoli?" are typical responses, when I can get the attention of someone I recognize. Then a quick smile and a back turned. Stymied and needing air, I push outside.

The afternoon sun is kinder, although the temperature is still sultry. The Fontebranda fountain is swarming with Oca teenagers. Some are singing rousing hymns like high school fight songs; many suck on baby pacifiers—a symbol that if Oca wins, everyone in the *contrada* will be considered to have been reborn, pure as a newborn baby.

Nicosa comes outside with a group of waiters who have been hired for the occasion, older men in black aprons, directing them to pick up the glasses and trash left in the street.

"We should call the hospital about Cecilia," I say.

"Why?"

"Maybe she's there, on an emergency."

"Don't worry about Cecilia; she takes care of herself," he says with irritation.

"Has she ever disappeared without telling anyone?"

Nicosa gives me a look from the corner of his eye. "You don't know everything about your sister. There are two sides to the story. Or maybe in the FBI, you don't think so."

"We keep an open mind."

"Do you?"

"Yes, but why would she go anywhere—willingly—when she's frantic about her son?"

He takes a step backward and lights a cigarette, attempting a softer tone.

"You must understand, this business with Giovanni is not new. I once found him passed out in the shower from taking pills."

"I'm sorry to hear that."

"The reason I may appear calm is that the drugs are locked up in his mother's car, the bitch Englishwoman has left the country, and he is sick in bed—guarded by a policeman!" He gives a bitter laugh. "As safe as he'll ever be. We'll all sit down and discuss this...whenever your sister decides it is time to come home."

17

PALIO, DAY 3—SUNDAY, JULY 1, 12:00 P.M. When there is still no sign of Cecilia by noon the following day, I call Dennis Rizzio in Rome.

"Do me favor? Check and see if Cecilia Nicosa left the country in the last twenty-four hours."

"Why would she do that?"

"Domestic dispute."

"Where would she be likely to go?"

"El Salvador."

"She had a fight with her husband, so she goes to El Salvador?" Dennis asks rhetorically.

"She's feeling a lot of pressure." I explain the illicit delivery of drugs in the painting. "She also confessed that Nicosa is 'under the thumb' of the mafias."

"Meaning what?"

"In her mind he's paying bribes, and she wants it to stop. It's why she reached out to me. Nicosa exploded at her yesterday in the car, just before she disappeared."

"Women have been known to abandon their families when they can't cope, although El Salvador is kind of far to go. And during Palio?" He thinks some more. "You really believe she'd leave her kid, who just got out of the hospital?"

"Honestly, Dennis...no. I don't believe that for a second."

"This worries me. It follows the recent pattern of the 'disappeared' in Italy. You have a high-profile lady married to someone with whom, let's say, the mafias have a beef. They take the wife."

"For money?"

"Could be for money. Kidnaps for money are a national sport. You can usually negotiate your way out, but if it's personal with Nicosa—if he got crossed-up with the clans—in that case, she never comes back."

I swallow hard. "What's the plan?"

"Sit tight. We don't know enough. Don't let it distract you; we still have a mission. I'll make some calls."

"You promised to protect the family—"

"I will. Trust me. Like I said, I'm as concerned as you are."

AT SUNSET, the *contrada* dinners begin. Long tables snake down the street, end to end, like a river of gold. Candlelight plays over the joyful faces of the people of Oca. Loud talk and spontaneous singing echo through the canyons of the old city, where each territory has become a raucous block party. Just before darkness, bamboo barriers ten feet high were unrolled across the streets, sealing off the ancient boundaries of each neighborhood, keeping enemies and tourists out.

Inside the barricade, the light is rosy and emotions are high. Tomorrow is the race, and anything can happen. Today we are with friends, floating in a bubble of hope. Nicosa and Sofri are radiant, exchanging toasts and laughter with everyone around them. Cecilia's place is empty, but Nicosa brushes inquiries aside; she will be here any moment.

At the far end, all the kids are swooning over the *fantino*— the jockey hired to ride Oca's horse. He's a swarthy thug from Sardinia, festooned with gold chains, with the long-legged body you need to race bareback and a conceited grin, making the most of his celebrity moment, as well he should. If he loses, he will be dragged off the horse and beaten by the very *contradaioli* who are feverishly toasting him tonight.

I cannot follow the Italian zinging around me, so I isolate myself in a safe cocoon of paranoia, surreptitiously holding my cell phone beneath the table and replaying again the images I had taken yesterday, looking for the moment Cecilia vanished.

The shots in the church are random. Mostly I was holding the cell phone up over the crowd; there are a lot of backs of heads, and shoulders with purse straps. Everyone is turned toward the silver helmets and spears just visible in the honor guard that accompanies the Palio banner down the aisle. Cecilia is out of range, behind me, but there are no suspicious faces in view. A couple of cops, unconcerned, are going the opposite way. There's the solo nun in white.

Afterward, in Piazza Provenzano, I took a picture of the banner being carried up the street, past a dark indistinguishable array of spectators. Two fellows in black tunics with gold trim are chatting in front of an ambulance at a paramedic station.

I feel Cecilia's absence in my body, which would be a ridiculous thing to say to Nicosa or Sofri, who seem to be putting on a show of nonchalance about the nonattendance of a major socialite at the biggest party of the year. Nicosa has a big responsibility tonight. It is his job to meet with the directors of the other *contrade* to negotiate *partiti*, a complicated system of bets that results in big payouts. Another Sienese contradiction: the night before Palio, blood enemies sit down and negotiate.

At the moment, Nicosa is conferring in whispers with two middle-aged balding men squatting by his chair—spies,

Sofri explains—who report on the other jockeys and horses, factors that could change the odds. He also says that at the starting line, up until the shot from the *mortaretto* that begins the race, the jockeys will be making deals among themselves.

"You mean the whole thing is fixed?"

"Let's just say there are two kinds of fate," Sofri says. "Chance, and money."

Is Cecilia angry enough to humiliate Nicosa by staying away at this crtitical event? Is Nicosa angry enough to have done her harm? Someone appears to be waving at me. Down at the curve in the street, where the tables turn and disappear from sight like a glittering toy Christmas train, a woman I don't recognize seems to be trying to get my attention.

Edging along the sidewalk, past the endless chain of tables, is like being inside one of those unbroken three-minute tracking shots in an epic movie, where they pan along a battlefield, ending at the eyes of an innocent child, a waif held by its mother, staring at the carnage of war with huge questioning eyes.

Inspector Martini and her baby.

Martini looks totally different all dressed up, smoking a cigarette, hair loose, wearing makeup and a low-cut, sensuous dress. Yes, she had been waving. We shake hands firmly, then relent and kiss on both cheeks. We are Oca sisters, not at the police station now. She pivots the child on her lap—a wispy-haired, tiny thing—eager to show off her daughter's English.

"Tell Ana your name."

"Sylvana," says the girl.

"Tell her how old you are."

She holds up two delicate fingers.

"Do you like Oca?"

Sylvana nods solemnly.

Martini asks, "What about Torre?"

The little girl sticks out her tongue and blows a raspberry.

The mother laughs with pride, exhaling smoke, and rewarding the girl with biscotti dipped in coffee.

I smile at the child. *"Brava!"*

In America we call it brainwashing.

"Have you seen Cecilia?"

"No," says Martini, looking around. "Isn't she here?"

"She disappeared yesterday in church. There's been no communication."

"Did she and Nicoli have an argument?"

"Yes, but this feels different. After what happened to Giovanni—and Lucia Vincenzo—we have to consider that she has come into harm's way."

Martini presses the baby's head against her chest, as if to shield her from the very possibility.

"You are saying someone took Cecilia?" she asks softly. "Kidnapped her?"

"That's Dennis Rizzio's feeling."

She crushes the cigarette, her expression serious. "It's common now, and on the rise. We have hundreds of incidents each year. Sometimes it's for money, but in that case they usually take a child. The mafias will also take someone to humiliate an enemy."

"What's the rate of safe return of the hostages?"

She twists her lips. "Not good. Less than half? I'm guessing."

"You can't know because you don't have the bodies."

"Esattamente. In this game of disappearances, they are winning. They deprive us of two weapons—evidence of the murder, and witnesses to the crime. Nobody will talk."

A man's hand closes around my wrist. Nicosa was quick to follow me along the tables. Inspector Martini's eyes rise inquisitively above my head.

"Ana," says Nicosa. "We are missing you!"

"I was just talking to—"

He cuts me off. "Come back. You must taste the pasta; tonight it is very special. Ravioli stuffed with squash and Gorgonzola cheese."

You could make him for unconcerned, holding a glass of wine and a cigarette, but his grip on my wrist is tightening, hard. I choose not to flinch. Remaining silent, accepting the pain, communicates my resistance.

"Come, be with the family."

"See you later," I manage.

Martini nods, but her large eyes take everything in.

My fingers are swollen and numb. I fear they will burst, like water balloons, until Nicosa releases my wrist. We walk back up the street, past hundreds of animated *contrada* members in folding chairs.

"Why are you talking to the police?"

"I was just saying hello." I stop the march to face him. "Where is Cecilia?"

"Always the same question. What do you think?" he says with anguish. "I took her? I kidnapped my own wife and hid her in the woods?"

I wish he hadn't said that. The husband is always the prime suspect, especially when he makes statements before he has been accused.

"I'm worried that she was taken."

"You may be right," he says grimly. "It wouldn't be surprising. But now is not the time. It is too soon to involve the police; that is not how the system works here. If someone does have my wife, I will handle it."

"How?"

"If it's ransom, pay the money."

"They haven't asked for money."

"Whatever it is, I will get her back."

"Really?" I say skeptically.

"I love her. What do you think?"

"I think you're up against a pack of ruthless criminals. Forgive me if I don't stay for dessert."

EVENTUALLY I find my way out of Oca territory, through darkened streets throbbing with laughter behind lighted bamboo walls, arriving at the Walkabout to find it empty. Chris, the Englishman, is actually sitting down and reading a book. He seems surprised to see me.

"Why aren't you in Oca?"

"It was time to go."

"Another outcast at life's feast," he says, automatically drawing a Foster's. "Frankly, I'd rather be in a civilized pub."

"I'm looking for Cecilia."

"Why? Where is she?"

"If I knew, I wouldn't ask. She wasn't at the *contrada* dinner."

Chris raises his eyebrows with mock concern. "Ooooh," he says. "Juicy! I'll bet she and the hubby are having *issues* again."

"Again?"

"Well, she had that revenge fuck with the Commissario, the old fascist. How could she?"

"Cecilia and the Commissario? From Torre?"

Is this what Nicosa meant by "Whenever your sister decides it is time to come home"? Does he seriously suspect that at this moment she is having an assignation with his enemy, the chief of police?

"You could have heard your sister and her husband screaming at each other all the way from the abbey. She even went back to wherever it is she came from."

"El Salvador?"

"For a while, yeah. Can't hardly blame her in a way. All the dirty stuff with the mistress all over the press."

"The one who went white shotgun?"

"Best not to say that too loudly," Chris advises, taking an order from some drunks who have just come in, wearing the colors of Leocorno, the Unicorn, orange and white.

18

THERE IS nothing to do but stare at the fat man with the gun. *Uno graso que repugna puerco*, Cecilia thinks hatefully, retreating to the comfort of her native Spanish. She has been reduced to a shivering column of fear, while he is enormous. A brute wearing a U.S. basketball tunic. Deltoids matted with hair. Nothing in his pea brain except what he is going to eat next. The soldiers in El Salvador were the same. Hungry peasants—except this Italian thug is citified, swollen up with bad food and disease. The pistol all but disappears inside his fat mitt.

He loves that pistol. He never lets it go, sticking it with bravdo into the waistband of the ludicrous shiny red shorts, not at all worried about blowing off his balls—just one in a cascade of violent fantasies that obscure Cecilia's thinking as she watches him chew through a PowerBar while lounging on an old desk chair set in the cavernous basement of the massive apartment building squatting over them.

Stinking water collects in a black lake that seems to go on to infinite darkness, stretching beneath blocks of slum housing called the Little City, somewhere in Calabria. She knows they are in the south because of the incomprehensible dialect they speak, hard for even the Italian-born to understand.

Also, she knows that they are far away from the long drive in the ambulance in which she was abducted from Siena, after being chloroformed and carried from the church by the two *combinatos* like another fainting victim overcome by the heat.

Occasionally little boys will scamper past, eager to perform errands delegated by the guy in charge, whose nickname is "Fat Pasquale"—he's just as fat as the gunman, but differentiated by a curly head of hair, bracelets, and tattoos. The boys, many under the age of eight, deliver drugs and act as lookouts. A literal underground crime network. They don't seem to care what Cecilia sees, nor do they restrain her. The first endless block of time is passed on a plastic chair fifteen feet away from the goon in the red shorts, who occasionally tosses a bag of potato chips or a half-used bottle of water her way. She tries to keep her feet up on the chair because of the spiders.

Everyone understands how kidnappings work. They are in the news every day, like soccer scores. The mafias have two objectives: get the money and move on to the next victim. Getting the money is easy. Everybody knows the drill and everybody pays. It is simply a form of human *pizzo*. But the next one—and the next—are dependent on maintaining a level of intimidation that will encourage immediate payment by terrified relatives, with a detour around the police. So before they return the merchandise, to show that they are serious, they cut off a finger or an ear.

Cecilia spends a lot of time in the basement trying to remember what she knows about otoplasty. She has absurd conversations in her head, instructing the goon, when the time comes, how to cut off her ear. *"Please swab three times with alcohol, and leave enough tissue for reconstructive surgery."* It is not easy to build a human ear from scratch, because it is such a complex three-dimensional form. Often cartilage is taken from a rib, but you need to be a craftsman. Luckily, because of the increase in kidnappings, both in Italy and Latin America, there are now world-class specialists in the field of ear replacement.

It is roasting down there, and the steaming bundle of pipes overhead radiates warmth like a heat lamp. Cecilia can feel her scalp start to burn, and tries to communicate that she wishes to move. The goon barks obscenities and warns her not to speak. But while he urinates into the black lake, she inches the chair out from under the heat, feeling such triumph she almost cries. Her heart beats with insane hope. If she can do this, she can fly right out of there and escape.

Then everything changes. Fat Pasquale comes out of the darkness to take her upstairs. She can barely walk after all those hours in the chair, but, carried away by euphoric delusion, she is only too happy to go. She never had any doubt Nicosa would pay quickly and naturally assumes she is being released.

19

PALIO, DAY 4—MONDAY, JULY 2, 3:30 P.M.   Another day has passed with the wretched slowness only possible in the heat of summer, in a Mediterranean country where time is measured in centuries. There has been no word from Cecilia in almost forty-eight hours, which, in America, would have already kicked off a missing person report. In Siena, during Palio, it gets you a shrug.

Last night's fervor at the *contrada* dinner has given way to a mood of lugubrious devotion as the people of Oca force themselves to put on the brakes for the last religious moment before the race: the blessing of the horse by the priest.

A grim, quiet pool of humanity is gathering in front of Santa Caterina, the *contrada* church on Fontebranda. Nobody is smiling. The quality of tension matches the overcast skies and the oppressive layer of heat trapped close to the ground. Even the press photographers behave with deference, willing to wait with endless patience for the star of the show.

"Sofri, I have to talk to you."

We have found a spot near the front portal of the church. He looks very much the distinguished elder, wearing a beautifully tailored dark gray suit with a green Oca pocket silk, his long white hair artfully swept back, emphasizing the unapologetically noble nose.

"What is it, *bella*?"

"Now I understand why you said my sister is like the Mangia bell tower. Why she is lonely in her marriage."

"Why is that?"

He is looking straight ahead, chin lifted and eyes narrowed with the emotion of the day. Before us, in the lane of pinkish houses, the crowned white goose flies from every window. The street is narrow as a stream and choked with people, but little boys still find a way to jump across it, doorstep to doorstep.

"I want to be careful how I say this." I check for eavesdroppers. There is nothing at our backs but the church. The group in front of us is speaking German. "I've been told that in the past, Cecilia has been a special friend of the police."

Sofri doesn't answer.

"Do you know what I'm talking about?"

"We may become separated after the blessing," he replies, instead of addressing the question of Cecilia's affair with the chief. "The mood will change, you'll see. Everyone is meeting at my palazzo. There will be plenty to eat and drink. It is the best spot in Il Campo to watch the race."

"But Cecilia won't be there. Will she?"

"I don't see why not."

"Sofri, she's been gone forty-eight hours. We should notify the police."

"That's up to her husband."

"Nicoli seems to think he can handle it without the police. I think he's wrong. They need to be involved."

The crowd has begun to stir. We can hear the pattern of the approaching drum.

"Not today. Impossible. Look what's going on here."

"It has to be today," I hiss. "If she's been kidnapped, every hour that goes by means less of a chance of finding her and now we're in the red zone."

"Maybe in America. In Italy, these things take longer to become clear."

The church doors open, and the bespectacled priest who was at the party at the abbey appears, wearing plain white robes and an Oca scarf. He shakes hands with Sofri and then descends the steps, so that we are in a position to look over the top of his pomaded head, at the upturned faces expecting a sign; but the priest just rests in patience, hands folded.

"They are coming now," Sofri says tersely. "The *comparsa*."

A cry goes up from the crowd and all heads turn toward the drummer and flag bearers appearing at the top of the street, followed by the *duce* and his men at arms, who are dressed in luxurious dark green velvet tunics embroidered with gold. Their tights are made of one red leg and one green, and there are lace cuffs at their wrists. I am impressed by the authenticity of the weapons—the lances, small swords at the belt, the large two-handed *spadone* carried by the *duce* with a blade that could chop off your head with one whack.

The *alfieri* spin the flags with confidence and finesse, just like Nicosa that night in the darkness of the abbey courtyard—the flags are rolled up, tossed into the air, caught behind the back. These two young men are the same age and height, and heartbreakingly good-looking. It would have been Giovanni, marching ahead of his proud father, who follows now with a group of other powerful *contrada* men, looking as beleaguered as the president of a country in wartime.

The soft white horse appears in the piebald medley of the human crowd. In place of a saddle, an Oca banner hangs over its back. It is wearing just a halter with a tufted pouf between the ears. The horse is calm and relaxed, led by a burly fellow in a beret with tobacco-colored skin and dark circles under his eyes, as if this awesome responsibility has kept him up for days. The horse is surrounded by its own bodyguards. The jockey, also protected by a security detail, is wearing an Oca tunic and jeans, considerably less dressed up than the horse. Clapping and cheering rise steadily from the crowd until the priest walks down the steps to where the horse has stopped, and then the people of Oca become so silent you can hear the clicking of camera shutters. The priest lays a palm on the forehead of the horse and speaks in Latin.

Sofri becomes utterly absorbed, transported by the prayer. It is hopeless trying to get his attention. The cell phone in my pocket vibrates silently. It is Dennis Rizzio, calling from Rome.

I text him back: *Urgent?*

Yes.

"See you at your apartment," I whisper to Sofri and slip out before he can answer, weaving between the rapt parishioners and onto the street.

Dennis texts: *Need to talk.*

Not secure.

Where r u?

Oca district.

Via dei Rossi 63 in 15 minutes.

THE GPS on my phone takes me to Via di Città, where I join a flood of humanity coursing down all eleven streets that lead into the Campo. I feel my heartbeat synching up with those caught in the race to claim a good spot near the track. There are three minutes left to get to the address on Via dei Rossi, where I assume Dennis Rizzio or one of his agents is waiting, and will evaporate if I'm not there.

Something has escalated. The Bureau must have gotten word of Cecilia. Jogging, I pass speed-walkers dragging their children, who curse the rudeness of Americans. Turning breathlessly onto Via dei Rossi, I almost run into a giant ice cream cone and realize with a start that Dennis's directions have led to Kopa Kabana, described by him as having the best gelato in Italy.

Is this a joke? Number 63 is actually a few doors down— an open alcove without a door. It looks like a white-tiled Laundromat, until you enter, to the overwhelming stench of urine, and discover that it is a bank of red pay phones. Graffiti crawls up the walls, and the floor is strewn with trash. A phone in the far corner is ringing. I use a tissue to pick it up.

"Dennis? What the hell?"

"Welcome to the monkey house."

"Smells like it."

"First off, we have no evidence that Cecilia has left Italy or crossed an international border. We checked airports, boats, and trains, but you and I know there are a million ways she could have been spirited out. Has there been a demand for ransom?"

"Negative."

"What's the mood up there?"

"It's insane. Today is the Palio race."

"No shit. Are we still secure?"

The phone bank remains deserted. Outside the open doorway, stragglers stream by at intervals. Dennis has chosen a side street that foreigners wouldn't normally favor.

"Clear."

"When we ran a search for your sister's movements through Interpol, something else came up. There was a no-fly alert at the Glasgow airport, with a name attached that sounded familiar. On closer look, I realized why. The incident was concerning you."

"Me? I've never been to Glasgow."

"That's not the point. The officer on the Interpol request was our friend Inspector Reilly of Scotland Yard."

"What was he looking for in Glasgow?"

"He got an ID on some suspects in the attack. The ones who left the getaway car in Aberdeen. The Brits worked some local boys and got them to flip. The geniuses gave up a couple of Italian nationals who had been staying with their lowlife Sicilian cousins in Aberdeen. The names were put on Interpol, and the Italians were picked up at the Glasgow airport, attempting to leave Scotland, booked on a flight through Cairo to Rome."

"Sounds good. Do they need me to confirm the ID?"

"Might. The suspects are being interrogated. Let's go back to family matters," Dennis says. "How has your brother-in-law reacted to his wife's disappearance?"

"Hostile and defensive. He thinks he can handle whatever happens himself."

Dennis clears his throat. "You've only been in Italy a short while, Ana. You haven't had a chance to really get to know your sister. Not like we do."

"You 'know' my sister? What does that mean?"

"When she wrote to the Bureau looking for you because of the inheritance money, we saw a connection between you two, and an opportunity."

"What kind of opportunity?"

"For you to get close to her. SAC Galloway put you on official business so we could see where it went. See if you and your sister could find some common ground. Build up trust."

"Galloway was in on this?"

"Take it easy. It's for her own protection."

"Always is."

I'm grinding a needle dropped by some crack addict with the heel of my shoe.

"And why would *she* need protection, Dennis?"

"Cecilia Nicosa owns three private medical clinics in

northern Italy and one in the south. Her husband's money built the facilities."

"She told me that was the trade-off. Her clinics, his women."

"Italy has a good health-care system," Dennis goes on, "but there's always a need for private hospitals. Your sister's clinics cater to the rich, but they also help poor people who need certain types of operations. They do good things, and she's a hero, okay? But the only reason they stay open—and do what they do outside the system—is because the mafias have given Cecilia their blessing. The reason for that is simple: she pays them off."

"Cecilia has been paying protection bribes? Does Nicosa know?"

"Everybody knows how it works."

"Dennis, you led me to believe my sister's husband was the dirty one."

"He is still the focus of our investigation."

"That's what Audrey Kuser, the legat, said in London. Nobody said Cecilia was part of it."

"Don't worry; we're not interested in criminal prosecution of your sister."

"Thank God," I say sarcastically.

"Cecilia looked to us like a way into the mafias—a good citizen caught in the evil machine. We were hoping somewhere along the line we might be able to turn her. She was on our radar, but we had no idea you two were related, until she reached out to the Bureau to find you. Like I said, we saw the connection and took the opportunity."

"But you intentionally denied me the information that she's involved with the mob. The whole damn family is involved with the mob! Don't you think that's a crucial thing for me to know?"

"Your supervisors recommended against it."

"Why?"

"Because you are a perversely moral person, Ana. They were afraid knowing she was doing business with the bad guys would prejudice you against Cecilia and screw up the whole shebang."

Instead they let that piece of information hang, hoping I would fall in love with her and have a stake in the outcome. I shouldn't be surprised. This is how recruitment works. They get you hooked so they have something to manipulate.

"Right now your sister has been taken, in all likelihood kidnapped by the mafias because, like that dame Vincenzo who went missing, she stupidly fucked them over somehow."

"Which means Cecilia is no longer useful to you."

"We are committed to getting her back. She is the sister of an American national; it's part of our mission."

"Also a convenient way to keep me close to Nicosa."

"I won't lie. Absolutely it is. The wife being gone is scary stuff. He might let down his guard."

"Damn it, Dennis."

"I know," he says with sympathy that is almost real. "It's just the way things worked out."

20

KIDNAPPINGS ARE a unique crime because they unfold in real time, simultaneously with the investigation. You never know which way they will go, but certain events are likely: if the suspects don't want money, they're in it for the torture and the kill. There has been no ransom demand, which bolsters Rizzio's theory that Cecilia was taken by her own mafia bosses as retribution for some misstep. Which means they are not overly interested in keeping her alive.

Neither is the FBI legat, despite the "sister of an American national" speech. His agenda is still to use my proximity to Cecilia to get intel on the mafias. He's got a hard-on for her disappearance because I am already established inside the abbey, where I can observe Nicosa make his moves, pick up on who he's talking to. Rizzio sees this as an organized crime case first, a kidnapping second. Even if he believes Cecilia is already dead, playing it out could present "an opportunity." Anything he can bring back on 'Ndrangheta will mean a bigger piece of the pie for the Bureau, and for him.

Leaving the phone bank from hell, I feel like a disembodied soul among the living, still trying to absorb the fact that earnest Cecilia has been paying protection bribes. The soft whoop of a siren parts the throng going to the Campo. A police car slowly plows along Via di Città, plainclothes detectives trotting on either side. Pedestrians attempt to move out of the way, people tripping over one another. Excited shopgirls are pouring from the stores.

A sophisticated-looking young woman wearing a black suit and pearls is watching coolly from the doorway of an expensive jeweler. I suspect that she speaks English.

"Who's inside the car?" I ask.

She names an American movie star.

"Wow. You get some famous people during Palio."

"Oh, *molti.*"

"Who is that with him?"

Beside the actor I can just make out another gentleman. Older and leaner.

"That is our Commissario of police."

Without hesitation, I shoulder through the wall of humanity. It makes sense that Nicosa would not go for help to a police chief who had an affair with his wife. But what if the chief still has feelings for Cecilia? What if he would throw his weight behind an investigation?

In trying to get a look, I have drifted too close to the car.

"Get lost," says one of the detectives in English, and I do, but not before snagging a close-up view of the Commissario. He looks like a tidy, underweight, middle-aged banker. The car turns into the Campo, where it is immediately swamped by military police. These soldiers are the real deal. They wear riot gear and carry automatic weapons. You'd need an armored personnel vehicle just to get their attention. I watch as the Commissario and his celebrity guest are absorbed into their ranks.

Somehow I have been spit into the dead center of Il Campo. The genius of the design is hard to comprehend. How did they do it? The shell shape and the slope of the brickwork is exactly right to hold a crowd. The walls of one palazzo adjoin the next in a crescent that overlooks the bowl of the Campo, which is quickly filling from all eleven entrances with spectators from all over the world. They didn't have sixty thousand people in Siena in the fourteenth century. How did they know? Turning in circles, I take in the maroon-draped balconies, *contradaioli* waving colors in the stands, clusters of medics in aqua scrubs, seas of law-enforcement blue, all simultaneously present inside the Campo for this one electrifying moment.

The afternoon is sultry, but at least the sun is hidden by clouds. I can pick out Sofri's windows. Behind them is that red-and-white-striped couch. Iced aperitifs. Moist slices of melon, bruschetta covered with olive paste, and, no doubt, coffee-flavored gelato. Here there is a popcorn stand. I am almost in the same spot as Cecilia was during the choosing of the horses.

I will never get to Sofri's; I am stuck. The density of population is multiplying by the minute. I see a sliver of space right up against the rail and make for it. A big man moves six inches to the right, enough for me to slip in beside him. I say, "*Grazie,*" and he says, "You're welcome."

He is American. In his forties and balding, with red artistic glasses, greasy slicked-back hair, and a graying goatee. At his feet is a plastic milk crate and a bag of cameras. Professional.

His name is Chuck. Chuck from Findlay, Ohio—a photographer, he says, for the Associated Press.

"How long have you been here?"

"Since eight this morning," he replies. "Hope you like the heat. This is going to take a while. You know what that scarf you're wearing means?" he asks.

"It's Oca, the Goose," I answer wearily. "I like the colors."

WE WAIT. Mountain ranges are formed and destroyed. There is no wind. The claws of the sun flash out from its striking place behind the clouds. I distract myself by observing the paramedic station. Every few minutes someone with heatstroke is brought in on a stretcher. Now there seems to be an asthma attack. I feel like I've known our boring neighbors all my life: an American family—Dave and Heather Bunyon, two kids, and a grandma playing cards—and the Japanese family with a fat toddler in a striped shirt who looks dazed with heat. Pairs of lovers are the only ones who seem to be having a good time.

Chuck offers his copy of the *International Herald Tribune*. We have already had the stranger-on-a-train conversation— that weird intimacy that springs up on a long journey, which this afternoon promises to be. He asks where I am staying, and I tell him about the abbey and the reliquary of the sainted hand. He knows the property well; he shot a wedding there, before Nicosa bought it, when it was briefly a hotel. He has lived in Milan eight years, and this is the second Palio he has covered for AP. He staked out this spot because it is at San Martino, the most hazardous curve in the track, where jockeys are thrown and horses crash. Padding has been placed against the walls. The pads look homemade and thin.

"How can those work?" I wonder.

"They don't. They want to see blood. Italy is a brutal society." He points to the paper. "See that?"

"What happened?"

"The Rome police found a girl who was murdered. African immigrant, sixteen years old. The lips of her vagina were sewn together."

"Why?"

"She was a prostitute. Turf war," the photographer explains. "Albanians and the Italian mafias, fighting over the sex trade."

I remember the willowy African woman wearing nothing but a bikini in the cornfield near the bus station. And the white man getting out of the car. No doubt she answered to the same type of criminal sociopaths who are holding Cecilia.

Seeing my reaction, Chuck says, "What's the matter? Do you find the word *vagina* embarrassing? Some women say it's a turn-on."

"What?"

His cell phone rings. I try to move away, but it is impossible. People who had claimed a space with blankets on the brick are now forced to stand. The Japanese toddler is picked up and placed over his father's shoulder. The Bunyons pack up the card game and squeeze into a nervous cluster. My abdomen is being pushed up against the rail, as the remaining space is squeezed out by the pressure of spectators continuing to push inside. People are literally hanging from the palazzos on overloaded balconies and stone outcrops. When everyone is finally jammed together it will be impossible to even turn around. A bunch of humanity the size of a small city—upright as asparagus, packed together, and tied with a bow—for anyone intent on doing harm.

Chuck jumps up on the milk crate, swinging an enormous telephoto lens over my head. I duck as the motor drive fires.

Stepping down, he grins, very pleased with himself.

"I just got a tip worth five grand. My buddy called me to say there's a famous actor in the VIP lounge."

"Where?"

"Up there, in the temporary police headquarters."

He points toward the palazzo to our left. We can see figures in the windows.

"Take a look," the photographer offers, holding up the viewfinder.

I see the actor and the Commissario. Clear as day.

"I can introduce you later," Chuck whispers moistly in my ear.

"Good-bye, Chuck."

"Did I offend you?"

"Yes."

"You'll never find a better spot!" he warns, cursing after me in Italian. Associated Press, my ass. I should have recognized a lowlife paparazzo.

The folks nearby are thrilled to step aside in order to suck up my space, not so the walls of anxious onlookers. Head down, shoulder in, there's nothing for it but to charge, holding my position by the black and white flag of Istrice, the Porcupine, flying from the VIP palazzo.

The commanding officer of the military police is a hunk in his sixties, with broad shoulders and a thick gray mustache standing out against dark skin; with medals on his chest and on his berèt, he looks like he just invaded Greece. He flicks me off like a fly, and none of the grim *carabinieri*, whose cold eyes sweep the crowd, pay attention to my garbled entreaties in Italian, so I sneak inside by following in the slipstream of a French TV crew, through heavy brass doors to a cavernous lobby bustling with cops and members of the press. We go up the staircase, where I recognize the light blue uniforms of Inspector Martini's provincial police, who have taken over an apartment on the second story.

Paintings are still on the walls and vases on the mantel, but folding tables and chairs have replaced the furniture along with a minefield of wires supporting laptops. Everyone's wearing ID tags and radios. I feel like the old guy in the park with his fingers curled around the chain link, watching the hot high school pitcher, longing to get back in the game that used to be his.

I'd better make a move before someone throws me out. The lumpy-bodied, melon-headed officer I met when Giovanni was in the hospital is sitting at a nearby terminal.

"*Ciao*," I say heartily, like we're old friends. He looks puzzled until I give the universal password: "*CSI!*"

He breaks into a grin with those twisted teeth. "*CSI!*"

"*Dov'è* Inspector Martini?" I ask, but before he can answer, she's right there: a Madonna in a tight blue uniform with a white gun belt, cradling a carton of cigarettes.

"What are you doing here?" she asks.

I take her aside and lower my voice.

"I have to see the Commissario."

"You can't. The race is about to start."

"I need his help. My sister is still missing. There's been no note. No demands. What you said last night is true. She's been taken. I know Cecilia was once a special friend of the police—"

Inspector Martini doesn't flinch. *Oh, God, is she sleeping with him, too?*

"I'm hoping the Commissario will start an investigation—"

A polished wooden door opens and the Commissario steps out of an adjoining room, along with two senior commanders with creased faces and crisp suits. The slender chief of police has flat brown eyes and hollow cheeks, like a cipher. Inspector Martini grabs my wrist and hauls me into his line of sight, talking rapidly in Italian. He shakes my hand and his long soft fingers linger. The five of us keep walking past the computer tables, aiming for the door. Inspector Martini has ten seconds to tell him my story, before they are faced with a coliseum's worth of spectators pumped to the gills at the most dangerous horse race in the world. Does it register with him who was taken? That it's *Cecilia Nicosa*?

He utters five words, like the crack of a whip, affirming what Martini has told him: "You are from the FBI?"

"Yes, but that is not why I'm here. She's my *sister*. They almost killed my nephew. The FBI's hands are tied. The only one who can find her is you."

"It seems the Nicosas are a marked family." From beneath the fixed hooded eyes comes a piercing stare. He gives me his card. "I promise we will do everything possible to locate Signora Nicosa," he says, and the entourage, including Martini, disappears through the door.

BY THE start of the race, I have inched and squeezed back through the spectators to almost where I was. Now points of sunlight crown the roofs of the palazzos, a moment that must be significant to the Sienese celestial calendar, because a heightened alertness has come over the multitude, the way a flock of birds will settle down, the body language of one individual passed to the next. When the corona of the sun spikes at a certain angle, sixty thousand bodies become absolutely still in the golden bowl of the Campo.

A *crack!* explodes with a puff of white smoke from the *mortaretto* cannon, calling the horses to the starting area between two ropes. Now you can see the dirty business. The jockeys, riding bareback, wear the colors of their *contrada*, painted helmets, and white running shoes. Their long legs hang over the heaving ribs of the horses, which are fired up on amphetamines. Round and round go the colors, as the jockeys circle in an unruly pack, negotiating deals and making lightning-fast alliances, menacing one another with long whips made from the phalluses of calves. There is more than one false start. And then the rope is dropped—the race begins—and a roar comes up like the explosion of a wind-whipped forest fire.

They gallop full-out, three times around the track, ninety seconds total. With each turn there seems to be another horse that has lost its rider. A jockey is thrown right in front of me and trampled. The whole bunch skids sideways in front of the San Marino curve. Dust flies, the jockeys trade whip smacks and try to shove one another off, the horses stretch, manic spectators cannot be stopped from running across the track, something happens at the far end that I cannot see, and then a banner unfurls from a window in the Mangia Tower, declaring Leocorno, Unicorn, orange and white, to be the winner.

Hand-to-hand combat breaks out everywhere. The losing *contrade* rush their horses, pulling off their own jockeys and pummeling them in the holy dirt. Young men stampeding blindly in all directions push me, spin me. Faces are contorted with rage and tears and joy. People are ripping at their own shirts. Someone running by smacks a little girl across the face with a flailing arm. They've breached the rails and are rioting in the center of the Campo—men are hugging, men are throwing punches. Women clutch one another, sobbing and screaming, in a wild blur of anarchy. I see the knife. I see the Torre scarf in burgundy and blue. The lips drawn back over the teeth of the man who is charging us. He shoves the American grandmother aside, and she hits the ground. The arm holding the knife is raised. I block it. The blade slices my hand. He keeps on running. If there is a coordinated police response, I can't find it in the pandemonium.

SIENA

21

AMONG THE crowd of passengers getting off the morning train in Siena, FBI legat Dennis Rizzio is easy to spot. Wearing a boxy charcoal plaid suit, a light blue tie, and Ray-Bans, he's a head taller and a hundred pounds heavier than the Europeans in summer clothes. The bulky, scarred-up briefcase is a hint that all he really cares about is the business it contains. And you can bet he's carried the grim look on his face all the way from Rome.

As soon as he has folded himself into Giovanni's mailbox car, he demands to know if I am certain of the way to the police station. He has to draw his knees up to his chin and rest the briefcase on top of them since there is no room at his feet.

"Our appointment with the Commissario is at ten," he reminds me testily.

"Under control."

"How's the hand? Lemme see."

I display the gauze bandage that was wrapped around my palm yesterday by the paramedic.

"You've had a tetanus shot, I hope?"

"Yep."

"How bad is it?"

"Kind of like when you're cutting an onion, and you look

up to watch the game?" I indicate a slice through the base of the thumb.

"Lucky he didn't cut your finger off."

"Stupid move on my part, getting into the middle of that."

"You're gonna let him attack an American grandmother? So the idiot was what? A guy from Torre?"

"He was wearing a Torre scarf, but he could have bought it on the street."

The mailbox car stalls as we are climbing the hill from the train station. The stick shift is tall and spindly, and I've been having trouble keeping the car in gear.

"Who taught you to drive?" Dennis asks.

"My sainted grandfather," I reply between gritted teeth, as Poppy's voice lashes out, *You're gonna kill us! What's the matter with you?*

"I hope you're going to kick butt with the Commissario," I say.

"When you saw him, what did he tell you?"

"He gave me his card and promised to be on the case."

The engine stalls again. I stomp on the brake, jam it into park, and restart the car. Traffic is backed up and everyone is leaning on the horn. In the rearview mirror is a row of sun-blinding windshields. The pain pill I took is wearing off, and I'm dying of the heat in my black FBI suit.

"You're doing great," Dennis says dryly. "Just don't crash into that van behind us."

It's a battered "airport van" driven by an unshaven, wild-haired psycho with a sweat rag around his gritty neck. What dummy would get off a plane and into *that* vehicle? Changing gears, I roll back and kiss his bumper, then we lurch forward. He leans out the window and yells, *"Vaffanculo!"*

"What does that mean?" I ask Dennis impatiently. "Everyone keeps saying it."

"Yeah, like all the time in Brooklyn. 'Fuck you.'"

"Excuse me?"

"That's what it means."

It is now five minutes before ten and my colleague's fingers are drumming the briefcase. You couldn't find the police station if you were looking for it, but it can see you. In an alley leading to the Piazza del Duomo, just wide enough for one small car to pass, a shaft is formed that is open to the sky. The walls are made of three-foot blocks of stone layered with ebony marble, like the gothic Cathedral of Santa Maria that dominates the plaza. Tourists in shorts and cowboy hats walk spellbound through this pocket of light. A few steps farther and they will emerge to a vista of the cathedral that will knock their socks off, but meanwhile the morning sun plays softly over the black-and-white stone, and they never see the surveillance cameras hidden in the corners.

Nor would they notice the nondescript *questura*, whose worn steps seem to lead to another of those tired postwar European buildings smelling of fresh paint and cooked cereal that have been converted to tiny condominiums at huge prices—which at one time it was. I park alongside a row of cruisers in the shade of a neighboring art museum. Sophisticated older couples with shorn silver hair and Swedish walking shoes are calmly buying tickets. Every day another gallery. Pastries in the afternoon.

Inside the vestibule of the *questura*, we are stopped by an officer who is embarrassingly deferential to Dennis, shaking hands with a flattering smile. Without a weapons check or even asking for ID, he leads us through an ordinary wooden door into the cop shop. Dennis and I exchange a look at the astonishing lack of security.

Palio is over, but the bullpen is still chaotic. It has the crammed-full industrial look of a carpeting wholesaler who expanded too quickly. Messy partitions and hulking old computers. There is a locked cage for stolen property and a vault for guns; good-looking male inspectors in natty shirts and ties, and *polizia* who carry 9mm Berettas and wear navy shirts with epaulets and military berets. The universal accessory, I notice, is the rubber stamp. There must be three dozen old-fashioned wood-handled rubber stamps in revolving holders on every desk, testament to a bureaucracy in which the right mark by the right hand still has more power than all the computers in the world.

Sitting in a row on a bench are the Bunyons. Mom, dad, brother, sister, and grandma.

"Who are they?" Dennis asks without moving his lips.

"That's the family. The Americans in the dustup yesterday."

The moment they see us, all five Bunyons get to their feet.

"Hello, Ana," says the somber dad. He's all showered up in a clean white polo shirt and travel shorts.

The mother stares at my bandage. "That looks awful. Are you okay?"

"Fine," I say. "Was anybody else hurt?"

The children shake their heads.

"Then why are you here?" I wonder.

"My mother was pushed to the ground," the dad says indignantly. "She's eighty-three years old! She could have broken her hip!"

The grandma, thin and muscular, with rakish white hair and sharp blue eyes, looks more resilient than any of them.

"We're gonna sue 'em!" she croaks.

"We're filing a complaint," says the dad. "We've never had such a terrible experience. Nobody told us they had riots in Italy."

"Those young men were crazy. Out-and-out dangerous," exclaims the wife.

The dad introduces himself to Dennis, taking in the suit and the briefcase.

"You must be Ana's lawyer. I gotta say, she saved my mother's life."

"I believe it." Dennis hands over his card. "Dennis Rizzio. I'm with the FBI."

Mr. Bunyon stares at the golden seal with the eagle and his eyes pop. Then they fill with tears.

"God bless America," he tells his wife with reverence. "They sent the FBI!"

Inspector Martini is coming. I make a break for it. She is in uniform, clutching her talismanic packs of cigarettes. I introduce Dennis and explain the plight of the Bunyons.

"*Civilians,*" I whisper, and she gets it immediately, handing them off to the obsequious officer, who leads them to a faraway corner, and, I'm sure, a morning of complete confusion on both sides.

We take off the opposite way, following Martini through the wooden door, across the vestibule, down a flight of steps, and through another door to a smaller secretarial office, which seems to have once been a barn. The old wooden gate, secured against a wall, has been replaced by a massive steel door that seals the entrance. There are remnants of a hayloft. Not exactly the boss's office. Two or three female civilians sit at computers, working-class divas with dyed hair, wearing silky bosom-revealing blouses, tight slacks, and heels. Why not? Through that door there are a hundred horny men. Martini drags over some chairs and we squeeze around a desk.

"The Commissario sends his apologies. He cannot see you today."

I am about to blow my stack, but Dennis handles it.

"We have an appointment. Ten o'clock."

"I apologize for the Commissario. He is in a meeting."

"We'll wait."

"The meeting is in Florence."

"When will the Commissario be back?"

"He won't be back today."

Dennis is steamed now, too, and showing it. "He's there now? *And I just got off a train?* You couldn't call? You don't have phones in the police department?"

The Commissario is not in Florence, and we both know it.

But Martini is a professional who has to answer for her boss. She sits up and tightens her shiny black ponytail. Crosses her legs and settles a legal pad on her blue lap. The skirt is taut as a drum.

"I am here to help you. I will do my best. Agent Grey, what goes on with your hand?"

"After the race, a man armed with a knife came running through the crowd. He tried to push past the Americans you met outside. I intervened, he took a swipe at me and ran. In the process, the grandmother took a pretty bad fall."

"Can you describe this man?"

"Twenties, Italian, dark curly hair, Levi's, running shoes, clean shaven, silver bracelets. And he was wearing a Torre scarf."

Martini stops writing.

"Like the men who alledgedly attacked your nephew?"

Dennis nods. "Exactly right. We're looking for a connection. This could have been your ordinary crazed Torre guy out to get Oca—Ana had on Oca colors—or a mob assailant with a deliberate target."

Martini raises large, black-rimmed eyes. "Who is this target?"

"Probably not Grandma Bunyon," Dennis suggests.

Martini waits, not understanding.

"We think it might be Agent Grey."

"*Ma*, why Ana?"

"She must have something they want. Isn't that the way it goes?"

Martini looks doubtful. "That makes no sense to me. He could find you out of so many people?"

"He could if he were following me."

"No, no," Martini says, shaking her head. "If we are to have an incident at Palio—and it's very, very rare—it is a result of high emotion and too much wine and no sleeping. No one stops to think, to plan this out. You were unlucky and got in front of the train."

Dennis sits forward in the plastic seat, elbows on knees, his face in hers.

"I am here to represent the United States government in an official capacity. We understand the FBI is in this country at the invitation of the Italian government, and we can't do anything without your permission. That is why we must ask for the Commissario's help. One of our federal agents has been attacked in your town. Maybe it *was* random. But her nephew was stabbed, and three days ago her sister was abducted right out of a church. That's bold, don't you think, Inspector Martini?"

"I agree, and I am sorry that it happened in the beautiful city of Siena."

Dennis shrugs. "It happens in Milan, it happens in Calabria . . . We are disturbed about what happened to our agent, Inspector, just as you would be if a police officer from Siena was attacked in New York City. Listen, I myself am Italian American."

He smacks himself in the chest and says something in their language that makes Martini relax a bit and nod.

"Family doesn't stop at the ocean. Agent Grey, *an American citizen*, is worried about her family living in Italy, and rightfully so." He inches closer to make a point: "Our concern is that Agent Grey could be the intended victim of a multiple kidnap scheme, in which her sister was the first to be taken."

Martini considers this and makes a decision. "You should

know the Commissario considers the abduction a priority. I am authorized to tell you that we have started an investigation to find Cecilia Nicosa."

"*Brava!*" Dennis leans back. I can see that he's sweating. "That's great."

She reads from the pad, translating unevenly from her notes: "'The following effects will take place in the disappearance of Cecilia Nicosa. One. To check all video cameras in Siena, most important, near the church of Santa Maria di Provenzano especially. Two. To interview any people who see her in the church or afterward, especially the church officials and the police officers.'"

"What have you gotten so far?"

She folds her hands. "We start this afternoon."

"You haven't even begun? She's been gone three days."

"During Palio, we have no police to spare. But now we will put our full strength behind this."

"*Va bène*," says Dennis, suddenly cheerful. "I expect you'll make good progress." He looks at his watch. "I believe I can still catch the eleven-fifteen train back to Rome. Do I have your word you will tell the Commissario what I said, about our fears for our agent?"

"Yes, you have my word," Inspector Martini answers solemnly, and they shake hands.

WE ARE down the worn front steps and striding past the museum to the car. It is heading toward noon, and the heat is scorching. Disappointment sweeps over us like a hot wind off a garbage dump.

"Explain that to me," I say.

We stand on opposite sides of the car. The roof is so low even I can look over it.

"They blew us off!" I go on. "First of all, the Commissario is not in Florence, he's ducking us, and second, why did you run out of there?"

"The meeting was over," Dennis says. "Do you want me to drive?"

"No!"

I have unlocked the car, but you can't touch anything inside. We leave the doors open to let it air out. I have a pounding headache, and the wound in my hand is on fire. The pills are in my bag, but I don't want to take one in front of Dennis. Three thousand miles away from Bureau head-quarters, the rules are the same: *Never show weakness.*

"It's how it works," he says, as we each remove our suit jackets. "You've worked undercover; you've dealt with intrigue and deception. Well, in Italy you'll get your mas-ter's degree. Nothing is what you think it is, or are trained to perceive from an American analog. You think you have the point of view, but you end up a hundred and eighty degrees wrong. What people are saying is decided by a person behind them. Martini was the eyes and ears for the chief. When she opened up about the investigation, that was the give." He snaps his fingers. "They're on it."

"A six-year-old could come up with a better plan."

We get in the car.

"This morning's exercise had nothing to do with finding Cecilia. We propose a meeting. The purpose is to get their cooperation. They agree. But it's not the Commissario tell-ing us what he thinks about finding Cecilia. It's to see *if he wants to sit down for a meeting.* It's high school politics."

"We don't have time for this. Seventy-two hours, Dennis. That's the cutoff point, when the trail goes cold."

"You can't apply your normal experience over here. We just have to let it unwind. Are we going to make the train?"

"Yes, we will make the train."

We are cruising downhill. It's a lot easier, with all the

traffic heading the other way. I want to unload the headache and everything else I've been keeping inside.

"Dennis, I have to tell you something. Cecilia and the Commissario had an affair. Apparently in retaliation for Nicosa's fucking around."

"Did she tell you this?"

"Town gossip."

Dennis squints through the Ray-Bans. "What's the source?"

"An expat British bartender. Does that change the picture?"

"The picture is the picture. She's still gone."

We pull up at the station with two minutes to spare. Dennis gets out of the car and lifts his briefcase.

"I believe the threat to you is real. Two to one the bad guys know you're Bureau, which makes you valuable. You'd be a major chip."

"Nicosa knows I'm Bureau."

"He made you?" Dennis asks.

"He didn't make me."

"Then how did he find out?"

"Cecilia told him. They were having a fight about Giovanni, and she let it drop."

Dennis stares at me through the aviator glasses. His entire face is red.

"Do you think the man who attacked you in the Campo *might* have been hired by your brother-in-law because you are FBI, and he would rather you didn't find out what he's up to?" Dennis says.

"I don't know! How could I know?"

"Do you think you can continue in your present role?"

"Yes, I do. We play it openly, that's all. I'm inside the house. I can still be valuable."

"Turn around and drive to the abbey. Take all precautions with Nicosa. Do not leave again until I call you. Got it?"

He slams the door. The train is coming.

. . .

AS SOON as Dennis is gone I swallow two pain pills with water from a bottle that has been in the car an hour and is therefore hot enough to brew tea, and call Mike Donnato in Los Angeles. After one ring I remember it is three in the morning in Los Angeles, but he has already picked up.

"I'm sorry, Mike. Go back to sleep."

"What's up?"

"Are you awake?"

"Just tell me."

"My sister disappeared. Vanished out of a church when she was standing right behind me. No leads, no witnesses, and I don't believe she left of her own volition."

"What's her psychological state?"

"Not depressed, suicidal, or crazy. Busy. Coping, like anybody else. She's been having problems with her husband, but her son just got out of the hospital and she adores him—she'd never just take off."

"Why was your nephew in the hospital?"

"He was knifed and beaten over a drug deal. He denies he's been using, but we know he's in possession of cocaine."

"Could Cecilia's disappearance be related?"

"Here everything seems to be related. Scorpions in a bottle. The north is fighting an incursion from 'Ndrangheta—the Calabrian mafia—from the south. The Bureau believes my brother-in-law is lined up with the bad guys. The question is whether he would do harm to his own wife."

"Sounds more like a kidnap for ransom."

"But there's been no demand for ransom. And there's a complication: I recently learned from the legat, Dennis Rizzio, that my sister's been paying protection money to keep her clinics open. If she somehow messed up with the clans, forget it."

"How can I help?"

"I'm just so frustrated, Mike! The Italian police are respond-ing, but slowly, and Rizzio goes along with their game."

"He's got a larger agenda."

"Exactly."

"Screw these people," Mike Donnato says. "You and I can find her faster than they can, even from Los Angeles. Let's do what we do. Start from square one. Make a timeline of her activities, find out who her enemies are—you know the drill. Anything you need, call me, and I'll throw the resources of the Bureau behind it, officially or otherwise."

"Thanks. I'll keep you posted. Tell Rochelle I'm sorry to wake up the boys."

He snorts. "Not a problem. They're teenagers. It's three in the morning, they're not home, and we don't have a clue where they are. Situation normal."

I FOLLOW Muriel's truck route back to the abbey. At first there is nobody on the country road. It is lunchtime in the clusters of working-class apartments, and everyone is behind the beaded curtains of their open doors, eating *nonna's* rice soup with bitter greens.

The turnoff is ahead when the white van shows up in the rearview mirror. Without hesitation he gets right on my tail. It could be the asshole with the dirty neck and wild hair I backed into, who has recognized the mailbox car or—and now alarms go off—it could be Chuck, the sleazoid photog-rapher from Ohio, miffed because I didn't respond to his come-on. For an FBI agent, it is not considered paranoid to assume, at any hour of the day or night, that someone is stalking you. The guy knows where the abbey is, having photographed it for a wedding. The last thing he hurled at me in the Campo was a string of curses. The van pulls up alongside and hangs in the opposite lane, playing chicken until another car appears coming toward us, then swerves in front of me at the last minute and takes off, middle finger wagging out the window. No good view of the driver and no license plate.

NICOSA AND Giovanni are in the kitchen at either end of the counter, the air between them palpably roiling. Giovanni is in a wheelchair, leg elevated with an ice pack. His hair is unwashed, his sallow face turned toward his cell phone with an expression of deep concentration, as if he's texting the Rosetta stone. Nicosa's sleeves are rolled, and his shirt is half opened.

"What's up?" I say, going for the refrigerator.

"He won't talk." Nicosa gestures toward his son with a glass of vodka. There's a bottle on the counter and an attractive white dish of lemon wedges and olives. Style is the best revenge. "He sits there and doesn't answer."

I pour some cold wine. The pills are kicking in, and I'm feeling kindly toward my fellow man.

"Why are you giving your dad a hard time?"

"He's giving me a hard time," answers Giovanni.

"What about?"

Giovanni's eyes rise toward his father. "Ask him."

"He's up all night on the computer," Nicosa says. "And now he decides he's not going back to school. All he wants is to play video games all day. He's depressed, which is understandable—"

"He thinks I should be doing homework!" Giovanni cries incredulously.

"You'll fall behind," warns Nicosa.

"My father thinks everything is a race. Be first or die."

I pour more wine. "I might have been followed here."

Nicosa's eyes widen. "When?"

"Just now."

"Followed from where? By who?"

"From the police station, by a thug in a white van."

I straddle a stool and toss back a few olives.

Nicosa frowns. "What does this mean, that you were followed?"

"Beats the hell out of me."

"Did you call the police?"

"I told you. I was just *at* the police station. The Commissario refused to see us. He instructed the inspector to lie and say he was out of town. Maybe he's the one who sent the guy in the van."

"Are you drunk?"

"I'm taking pain pills. Knife wounds tend to sting."

Nicosa puts down his glass. "I think it is best if you go back to the United States."

"You've said that."

"You make everything worse."

"I'm trying my best to help. We can help each other, Nicoli, but we can't be in denial about Cecilia."

Giovanni looks up. "What are you saying about Mama?"

"Nothing," says his father.

"Doesn't he know?"

"Know what?" Giovanni asks.

"Your mother is missing," Nicosa says at last.

"Why didn't you tell me?"

"It was Palio. You were sick—"

"Where is she?"

"We're not sure what happened," I say. "But she disappeared two days ago, during the blessing of the Palio. Do you have any idea where she might have gone?"

"No!" says Giovanni angrily. "Papa? What is going on?"

I want to confront my nephew. Right now. I want to thrust

the bag of cocaine in his face and ask *him* what's going on, but he is still too weak.

"Where's Mama?" he cries.

"See what you have done?" Nicosa demands.

"I'm sorry. I promise we will find your mom."

I take my wine and leave the kitchen. My eyes are drifting closed. By the time I've climbed the endless marble steps to my room, it seems to have become so late in the day that all the reptiles have come out, and the balcony is alive with snakes of sunlight and shadow, whipping across the tile and up the walls, and the only way to escape them is to quickly get inside and climb on board the bed, which is rocking like a raft in the ocean.

I WAKE up in the middle of the night with the heart-stopping knowledge that there is a man in my room. The shutters are open and cool air is pouring in, along with monochrome brightness that shows the shape of someone near the door. Seconds go by. I don't move. I still don't move. Can he see that my eyes are open? Sweat builds under my back. He has the advantage.

A silent contest of wills. He is lifeless. I am frozen. My eyes adjust to the half dark. No weapons. Attack first. Bad hand. *Let him come to you.* Grab his head, break his nose across your knee. I smell him before he gets close. Metal. Dirt. Heavy sweat. The sense of coarse fabric and leather. He steps from the shadows and the stench becomes awful. Excrement, earth, and decomposing bones. In the anti-light his face is stubbled and dark, his eyes colorless. The rucksack drops to the floor. It's what we call in the Bureau a WTF moment.

"Sterling? Is that you?"

He sits heavily on the bed.

A hoarse whisper. "Hello, cupcake."

22

STERLING UNTIES the bandanna around his head.

"Don't turn on the light."

My heart skips. I don't need light to see that the gorgeous blond hair has been shaved off, and the bare scalp is impacted with dirt. He unfastens the field jacket with trembling fingers. Dried flakes of mud that have been carried who knows how many miles, across how many time zones, scatter over the linen sheets. The smell of recent death is undeniable.

He unfolds a rain poncho, meticulously spreads it on the floor, then empties the contents of the rucksack.

"What are you doing?"

"Better wash this stuff out," he says slowly, as if in a dream, taking off his shirt and Under Armour.

"I'll take care of it."

Heeding the silent message, *Don't touch me*, I slip off the bed and retrieve a robe from the bathroom. He continues to face away, as if he doesn't want me to see his body. He used to eat breakfast in the nude, not give it a thought. Has he been wounded, a ladder of sutures up his chest?

Gently I slip the robe over his shoulders. I bend down, draw up the sides of the poncho and shoulder it, maybe too fast, because suddenly he is suspicious.

"Where're you going with that?"

"I'm going to the laundry room to wash your stuff," I reply patiently. "It's in the family quarters, in the main building. Are you hungry?"

"Yes, ma'am, I am hungry."

"I'll bring you something. There's soap and shampoo in the shower. Is it okay if I leave?"

"Go on."

"You'll be okay?"

"I just said so, didn't I?"

In the night, cold wind rakes through my hair. I carry Sterling's combat clothes in the poncho like contraband. I would rather burn them, but they are crucial to him, to his other self. As I cross the torch-lit courtyard, goose bumps rise at the thought of the silent monks who would have been at prayers in a few hours, shuffling through the dark to kneel on the unforgiving floorboards. The workings of the human mind haven't changed over the centuries: in the perilous hours just before dawn, everything our rational minds have been telling us flies up and away to the realm of the gargoyles.

Shoving rancid woolen socks and bloodstained camos into the washer, and later, assembling a he-man sandwich out of a kilo's worth of salami, mortadella, mozzarella, and roasted peppers on an entire loaf of bread, I try to draw the shredded realities of the present together. As relieved as I am to see him whole, I know something has happened to Sterling. I have no idea how deep it goes, or how he found me, why he came back, or how long he will stay. It could be overnight. He could have deserted and be on the run, or about to be reassigned. Putting all these unidentified conditions alongside my sister's disappearance makes my knees go weak. I sit down on a kitchen chair, immobilized.

I suppose it is something like panic. It makes no sense to start evaluating a relationship at four in the morning, when the man has shown up out of nowhere, hostile and disoriented and not himself, but that's where my stubborn mind keeps going. True, I had become impatient with his comings and goings, but there was something comforting, even pleasurable, in the delayed satisfaction of his return. Until tonight, his reappearances had been smooth and hearty—he had been as happy as I was to recharge with some robust sex, bittersweet chocolate cake for breakfast, the afternoon in a hotel bed, sleeping, reading newspapers, watching movies, staring idly into each other's eyes. From the glimpse of the bones poking through his back, it looks as if he has dropped ten pounds, which is a lot when you weigh one-fifty. From the deadness in his voice, it sounds as if he's not feeling the deprivation in his body—or very much at all.

I had a bad gut reaction when he took off the bandanna. He looked less like a warrior than a hardened killer. Security operatives are hired to protect, not fight—although it doesn't always work that way. Some of my best friends at the Bureau are snipers, but lord knows, they don't do it for the money. How well do I know Sterling McCord and what kind of assignments he will accept? How long and hard will I stand by? It is troubling to realize these are the same irksome questions I've been asking myself about Cecilia. She made a deal with the devil when she married Nicosa, and a deal with the mafias (same thing) to keep her clinics alive. Maybe she's escaped to a safe and happy place in the arms of 'Ndrangheta. How well do I know *her*? What makes me qualified to save her from her own life?

When I get back to the room with the food, Sterling is clean and showered and dead to the world, lying across the bed in the bathrobe as if he'd literally just dropped. Wedging into a valley at the edge of the mattress, I try to roll him over, but he kicks out, slashing my leg with a jagged toenail. I debark to the chaise. It isn't much of a sleep, awakening with the roosters and the light and filled with a million questions.

All of which will have to wait, because Sterling sleeps for the next sixteen hours. I dash to get his stuff out of the dryer before anyone else wakes up, and I keep the bedroom door locked. Finally, sometime around sunset, I return to find him fully dressed—and from the lavender vapor in the room, having showered again—wearing clean jeans that fit too loosely, a T-shirt, and a baseball cap, and buckling on his watch. The sandwich has evaporated. My laptop is open on the desk.

"Don't you get Internet in this hooch?"

"Depends on the time of day."

"It just cut out on me," he says sullenly. "We've gotta go."

"Where?"

"Meeting a buddy."

He slips on a pair of blue Oakleys the color of the Florida gulf. We exit the room into the billowing evening.

"Are you okay? Are you done with the mission?"

"Yes to both."

"I won't ask a lot of questions, but I'm curious to know how you found me," I say, as we hurry down the marble stairs.

"Word got through."

Instead of crossing the courtyard he grabs my arm, and we go the other way, ducking underneath the staircase and around the back of the family quarters where the pine forest comes down to the stone wall. Following in his careful footsteps over the scrub, it occurs to me that maybe Sterling believes we are on reconnaissance, that he has truly lost his mind. We pick up a deer trail that comes out into an olive grove on the neighboring farm. From here it is fifty meters to the road. This must be the way he gained entry in the middle of the night.

A well-used black Fiat is waiting on the shoulder. Sterling opens the door, and we climb in.

"You're late, you cunt," says the driver.

"Ana, this is Chris."

Seeing Chris is a shocker.

"I know Chris!"

Chris is the English bartender from the Walkabout Pub.

"And I know Ana!" he echoes mockingly as we take off.

"How do you know Sterling?"

"Never saw the lad before in me life," says Chris. "He was out there on the road, trying to pick me up."

"Fuck off."

Chris pulls a serious face and seeks me out in the rearview mirror.

"Everything green?" he asks Sterling.

"Good to go."

"Well then, no worries."

"Chris is former SAS," Sterling explains. "Now he's also an operative for Oryx."

I see it. The buff body. The detached observer who stays out of the limelight, placed in a job that positions him to know every English-speaker in town.

"Chris told you I was here?"

"I saw you were having troubles," the bartender says. "The missing sister and all."

"Thank you, sir. You could have also told me that you work with Sterling."

"Normally we're mum around the girlfriend—but now I discover you're not the girlfriend, you're FBI."

"*You're* the girlfriend," Sterling intones, folding his arms and hunkering down under the Oakleys.

This gets a tiny smile out of Chris.

"Just think," he says. "If an RPG hit this car right now with the three of us in it, what a total bummer for covert ops."

"Not for Oryx. We are a hundred percent deniable."

"The girlfriend isn't."

"According to the FBI," I say, "officially, I'm on vacation."

"Enough of that kind of talk," Sterling mutters. "Bad juju."

We are down off the mountain and turning onto the main road to Siena.

"Anyone care to say where we're headed?" I wonder.

"I'm going to my day job," Chris says. "Pouring drinks for alcoholics."

"We're going to the pub," Sterling interrupts. "To try to get on the damn Internet."

"What for?"

"There's an e-mail from Glasgow, which I couldn't open."

"About a job?"

"About you."

IN THE back room of the Walkabout, under the crude map of Australia, Sterling's gaunt face is lit by the glow of Chris's laptop. He is accessing a secure site referred to as the Circuit, available only to private military contractors—a cyber version of the old soldier-for-hire magazines—where buddies are located and private military companies are rated by operatives as places to work, the way consumers rank can openers on Amazon.

No worries, as Chris would say, since nobody posts under their real name. They use handles, just like in the field. Sterling's handle is Bullrider, but he'd kill me if I ever called him that, like the old superstition about never letting a woman board a sailing ship. Talk about bad juju.

While Sterling works the Internet, I am banished to the bar, to stare at another motorcar race on the flat-screen, interrupted by a news update describing the disappearance and suspected kidnapping of medical doctor and socialite Cecilia Nicosa, wife of the well-known coffee king. I stare with fascination at the inner and outer confluence of events:

at the moment her image appeared I was making a list of people who could tell me about Cecilia's associates and routines. This is how we do it in the big leagues: interview everyone who might have been in contact with the subject twenty-four hours before the abduction. The hospital staff. Giovanni's teachers. The parents of Giovanni's friends. The ladies I met at the party. The ladies she cooks with at *contrada* headquarters. Donnato's advice makes sense: skirting the authorities may be the most direct route to finding her.

Sterling calls me over. I take my *limonata*. He is eating a chocolate bar and drinking water.

"This is something you need to know," he says, very serious. "It comes from a solid source, a Scotsman I knew in Fallujah. He quit the private contracting business and he's back home, on an antiterrorist unit with the Glasgow police. He gave me a heads-up through the Circuit on the investigation into the attack in South Kensington. Being an honest cop, he first asked what in hell I was doing at a multiple homicide in London. When Oryx confirmed that I had been leaving on a mission, he e-mailed this photo. It was taken just before the shooters opened fire."

Sterling flips the computer around to display a blurry-but-discernable picture of me in front of the London restaurant, Baciare, staring at the camera and looking plenty annoyed for having been catcalled by a jerk in a Ford. You can see Sterling in the background, heading off, wearing the rucksack.

"Where did this come from?"

"The investigators got it off a cell phone belonging to one of the three men who were detained at the Glasgow airport, off an Interpol no-fly alert originating from the Met. Three Italian nationals, trying to get to Rome through Cairo."

"I'm aware of them. The FBI legat was here yesterday. He told me they had three suspects in custody."

"Did he say anything about the bad guys being in possession of a picture of you?"

"No. Maybe he didn't know," I say. The failure of different agencies to talk to each other is a given these days.

"Oh, honey. He knew."

To prove it, Sterling highlights the list of forwards on the screen. The Glasgow police had sent the photo to Inspector Reilly at the Metropolitan Police, who forwarded it to Dennis Rizzio. Sterling peers disconsolately over the bar of light rimming the laptop.

"That honcho in Rome is holdin' out on you. He's playin' you for something."

I do not reply.

"Why do you suppose that is?"

"It's SOP at the Bureau," I say bitterly. "Keep the field agent in the dark. Withhold information, so the Bureau maintains total control over everybody's actions."

I can barely speak. Why didn't Rizzio tell me about the photo? Or, earlier, that Cecilia was paying bribes?

"Meanwhile," Sterling says, "here's the puke that shot up those kids."

Mug shots appear on the screen. Three awfully young and stupid-looking men in their twenties. The names mean nothing, but I do recognize a face: the scowling eyes, long face, heavy and ruler-straight eyebrows. He looks remarkably like the drawing made by the sketch artist in Scotland Yard. Amazing how they can do that.

"That's one of them," I say. "The one I saw in the Ford."

Sterling leans back and pushes up his baseball cap.

"We're fucked."

"How so?"

"What you just did." He nods toward the screen. "Identified the bad guy."

"Why's that?"

"Security contractors have their own networks; you have yours, the criminal clans have theirs. According to my Scots friend, this picture went out on multiple servers that feed the terrorist networks. That means your face is on all the mafia websites, which also reach into Bulgaria, Turkey—basically wherever they do business, which is all of eastern Europe and North Africa, for a start. My contact says the Met thinks the attack in London was a reprisal shooting. The target was someone in the restaurant."

"Someone at the birthday party?"

"That's their theory. But the point is, the bad guys have your picture. You are not only a witness who can ID them, but also I'm sure that by now they know you're Bureau. They want you as a bargaining chip, or to take you out of the game. Which could explain the knife attack in the Campo."

He closes the laptop, leaving us in the ubiquitous red glow of the Walkabout Pub. We go out to the bar just as the TV news bulletin announcing the disappearance of Cecilia Nicosa comes up again.

"They've replayed that thing five times in the past half hour," I sigh. "Worse than a mattress commercial."

Sterling stares at Cecilia's picture on the flat-screen. "You look a helluva lot like her."

Long curly hair. Flat high cheekbones. Almond eyes. She has darker skin and definitely a different style—in the TV photo she's on a yacht, smiling and windblown, large black sunglasses on top of her head, wearing a multistrand gold choker woven with jewels, like Queen Nefertiti cruising the Nile.

"There's a resemblance," I admit.

"A strong resemblance."

"If you didn't know us."

"I'm sorry to say this."

I know where he's going. It's the look in his eyes. A lump rises in my throat.

"Say it."

"The mafia sees the cell phone picture. *This lady could identify the shooter; she's starin' straight at him.* So they put an APB out on their network. Every punk in Italy goes looking. And some lower-level dope says, *Hey, I found her, smack-dab in the middle of Siena.* They watch for a while. Yep, it sure looks like the lady in the photo. The bad guys, they're not from around here; they're from the south; they don't know who Cecilia Nicosa is. They think they've got the witness in the photo, so they nab her in the church. But they took the wrong girl."

"I was wearing Cecilia's clothes that day," I say softly. "She was always trying to get me to dress better." I wait. "What will happen when they figure out she isn't me?"

There is no need for him to answer.

Then comes the long, slow sigh of defeat. "Most of the time," I say, "the 'disappeared' are never found."

"Bad police work."

"No, it's because the bodies are dissolved in lye."

Sterling's eyes flare briefly. "Lye?"

I nod. "Nothing left to find."

He slides his fingers over mine for just an instant. It's the best he can do.

23

THEY BLINDFOLDED Cecilia and pushed her up a staircase. Thin metal stairs, leading up from the basement. She was between the two enormous men, a gun jammed into her ribs. They were moving fast, almost carrying her between them. Briefly outside, it smelled like night and hot winds. Hurrying up another staircase. Shouts, conversations, radios, the smells of coffee and spilled beer. As they turned abruptly she was able to put out one hand and feel a rough stucco corner—then she heard locks turning, murmuring voices, and she was pulled inside an apartment with a TV turned up, the scents of oilcloth and something in the oven—phyllo dough?—and shoved inside a room. The door was locked and immediately there was pounding on the other side by shrieking, taunting children.

She took off the rag that covered her eyes. The first thing she saw was a piece of foam on the floor, two feet by six feet. Grimy balled-up sheets. Who knew who had been sleeping there? A window. She lifted the blind and saw another window of another apartment less than five feet away. The window was the sliding type, secured with a lock. She noticed she was standing on a filthy remnant of gold carpet. It curled up at the edges, revealing a concrete floor. There was a plastic basket filled with clean folded laundry, as if someone had forgotten about it. Copies of the magazine *Oggi*, months old.

She sat on the foam pad and took off her heels. She was still wearing the shiny green suit she'd had on at the church in Piazza Provenzano where the Palio banner had been blessed. It was now so tight and uncomfortable she wanted to rip it to shreds. She peeked at the laundry. Kids' clothes. Male sweats.

She threw off the sheets, turned the foam pad over, and lay down. The vertebrae in her neck cracked, and she realized that her back was killing her. With the window closed, the room was stifling, like the room in El Salvador, in the outbuilding near the garden, where she sometimes hid to rest from the exhaustion of working while she was pregnant. There was no sleep. Roosters crowed and dogs barked all day long. Outside, her uncles and brothers lopped corn off the stalks with machetes. It was like an oven in that room. She felt the baby kick. She could only feel sorry for it, to be born to such a failure of a mother. Cecilia couldn't move in that room because of the heat of the afternoon and the weight of sadness. It was during the time her own mother had exiled her to work in the garden and grind the corn for tortillas, giving her study room with its unfinished mural of Tweety Bird to a younger brother, as punishment.

Now she was a lady of elegance, a doctor. What had those years of suffering come to? She saw her death outside the door. The fat man with the gun. She would be humiliated by these men, that was a given. They would take her dignity, but what did it matter? We are all naked in death. She could accept everything else, she thought, but not that she would never see her son again. Lying down, with tears running along her temples, she forced herself to prepare, to travel slowly through the tunnel of darkness, at the end of which, in a bright mist, was Giovanni.

The lock slid open and a woman entered. The woman was ordinary. Middle-aged and silent. She had a mass of black hair and wore a cheap print dress. She brought a small bowl of garbanzo beans in olive oil and a piece of bread. She didn't look at Cecilia but picked up the laundry basket and left. Cecilia knew better than to try to talk to her. Women can kill you, too.

24

EXUBERANT SHOUTS are coming from the court-yard—sounds I've never heard in the abbey before. Sterling had woken early, leaving the sweet-pea bed with quick and economical movements, so as not to wake me. He told me he's been dreaming about airplanes falling out of the sky, and I'm afraid that's what got him up—although maybe it was also to avoid the possibility of sex. He has been uncharacteristically indifferent. "I'm kinda all wore out," he said. Alone, the former monk's room seems even starker than before, somehow even threatening. Without the safe harbor of his warm, accepting body, I feel like I'm the one falling through space.

The morning sun lies in curtains across the inner space of the compound, warming the old stone. The electric torches are still burning, pale as the new day. Looking down from the second-story loggia, I see Sterling and Nicosa playing soccer, grunting and hooting. The taut leather ball sails off their feet with hard percussive pops. Giovanni, still on crutches, coaches from the sidelines. The sun plays golden notes in his dark curly hair, but his features are drawn.

Mom is gone, and the boys are out to play. Somehow they found each other this morning—Sterling, the uninvited guest, lean and buff, wearing camouflage shorts and a black

T-shirt with a dragon, and Nicosa, the host, in pajama bottoms and an undershirt. He is unshaven with unkempt hair, throwing sweat, not moving as fluidly as when he played with the flag, but with red-faced determination to stay in the game.

Sterling and Nicosa go at it with competitive abandon. Nicosa has superior control, is good at disguising his moves, but Sterling stays on him, stealing the ball with a sharp inside curve. It rolls toward Giovanni, who gives a feeble swipe with a crutch. His shirt rides up, exposing a pale sunken belly and sharp hip bones.

"Be careful," I murmur to myself.

Giovanni shouts at his father, *"Vai così!"*—*Go this way!*— but Sterling swings forward with a powerful strike squarely through the center of the ball and makes a goal between two potted palm trees. It's a good shot, and everyone high-fives and cheers.

"È uno spettacolo!"

I clap also, yelling, *"Bravi!"*

The result is that while the two men tussle over the next point, Giovanni's attention is drawn to the second floor, where I am standing; he looks up at the same moment his father boots the ball. It hits the boy in the chest, the crutches fly, and he collapses.

I run down the marble steps. Giovanni is lying on his back, gasping for air. Nicosa and Sterling squat beside him, talking rapidly and at cross-purposes in each other's language.

"Posso aiutare!" says Sterling. *"Sono addestrato come un paramedico."*

"My boy...he just had surgery, and he has a bad heart!"

I assure Nicosa we know what we're doing, and he steps back as I take the boy's pulse while Sterling checks the airways. We lift his shirt, inspect the surgical scars. Intact. No visible contusions from the soccer ball. A nod between us says, *All clear.* We count to three and gently roll my nephew onto his side. Soon his breathing returns to normal.

Nicosa has been watching with hands on hips, like the boss at a construction site. He smells of musty bedclothes and alcohol.

"How is he?"

"Had the wind knocked out of him is all," says Sterling. "Like falling out of a tree, right, son?"

"He's done that, too. *Sono così spiacente, mio figlio,*" he says, repentance in his voice.

"*È giusto, Babbo,*" Giovanni replies as we help him to his feet.

Nicosa hands his son a rucksack that has been lying in the grass, then slowly walks back into the abbey with his head down.

"*Tu sarai giusto; giusto riposa il minuto,*" Sterling tells Giovanni.

"I'm okay," Giovanni assures him. "Your Italian is very good."

"The army sent me to language school."

"Are those real army shorts?"

"Nah. They look cool, but they're not that cool. See this?" He pops a pocket in the waistband. "Yuppie iPod holder."

"Were you in *Special Ops*?" Giovanni asks, carefully pronouncing the words. "Is that why you learned Italian?"

"Why not learn something on the government's dime?" Sterling says genially. "I was just a ranch hand before," he adds, leaving out a lifelong career in Delta Force.

"He's a real cowboy," I point out. "Can't you tell by those bowed legs?"

Giovanni obediently looks at Sterling's legs. "Do you have guns?"

"Several."

"Is it true that everyone in America owns a gun?"

Sterling smiles easily. "Lots of people do have guns. Just like everyone in Italy grows olives; is that true?"

"Around here, yes."

"Where can we get some really fine olives?"

"Anywhere."

"I mean, not a store, but where they grow the fruit and cure it. We raise olives in Texas, just like you. My dad's a rancher, but he's got a good-sized olive grove."

"You never told me that," I say.

Sterling raises his eyebrows, mocking my surprise. "You never had a need to know."

"Oh, you can see our friend," Giovanni offers. "His name is Aleandro; he owns the farm next door. That's where we get our olive oil."

Honking the horn, a kid driving a small car like Giovanni's pulls into the driveway.

"Are you sure you're well enough to go to school?"

"I would rather be in school than *here*," he replies bitterly.

Slowly, he makes it to the car, and it is amazing how his manner changes the moment he comes within range of his friend. Suddenly he's a different person, all jokes and smiles, clownishly climbing inside, despite the weight of the pack pulling him backward, and the crutches awkwardly held in one hand.

"Giovanni," I call, "you're not ready."

"You're not my mother," he says sharply.

"If your mother were here, she would say you need to rest."

"You don't understand. My father is crazy, and my mother ran away."

"Is that what she did? She ran away?"

"Yes, of course, to get away from *him*. So why should I care what she thinks?"

They take off, spraying gravel.

Sterling is waiting alone in the courtyard.

"Giovanni has no idea what's going on with his mother," I tell him.

"Maybe it's better that way," he says as we head toward the front door. "Does Nicosa always look so wasted?"

"No, usually he's the king of cool."

"He still expects to get Cecilia back?"

"He believes he'll get a ransom call, and he's waiting. Just waiting."

"When're you gonna tell him the truth?"

"Which is?"

"If she was taken by the mob, they've most likely already killed her."

I let that one go by, like a wasp hanging in the air. If you don't move, it won't sting you.

"We have no proof one way or another. We don't have a big enough picture."

"What are we missing?" Sterling asks, just to humor me.

"Here's how I see it: there are three separate strands, one for each member of this messed-up family. The FBI believes Nicosa has ties to the mafias because he was sleeping with one of their players, who has disappeared and is believed to be dead. Mom pays bribes to the clans in order to keep her clinics open. And the son is caught receiving cocaine from a British expat who has since left the country. None of them has the slightest clue about what the others are up to—what makes them tick, or where they go at night."

"The part that braids it all together is the boy," Sterling muses. "Let's see what comes loose when we pull that thread."

WE FIND Nicosa in the kitchen, pouring a long shot of grappa into a short cup of espresso.

"Forgive me," he says. "I am an idiot."

"For what happened out there? It was an accident," Sterling tells him. "Could've been me, kicked that ball."

"It is unbearable to hurt your own child."

Nicosa's mouth is set in self-reproach. On the table is the morning paper from Rome. The photo of Cecilia on the yacht is on the front page with the headline, IL MISTERO DI PERSONA MONDANA MANCANTE IN SIENA!

"What does that mean?"

"'Mystery of missing socialite in Siena,'" Nicosa says, as if resigned to the media onslaught that has only begun.

I squeeze his arm in sympathy.

Sterling scans the story, translating as he goes: "'People are speculating about what happened to Dr. Cecilia Nicosa, wife of the well-known coffee entrepreneur. Rumors are that Dr. Nicosa has disappeared, like Signore Nicosa's mistress, Lucia Vincenzo, a mafia associate whose body was never found...People are afraid...Nobody feels safe...If Dr. Nicosa has been kidnapped, it will be a daring assault on the upper class—'"

"Enough," says Nicosa. "I've read it."

Sterling pushes the paper aside. "The family should issue a statement. Put a lid on information getting out."

"I'll see to it," Nicosa says.

He brews us two espressos, and we gather at the counter, hacking off pieces of yesterday's bread, spreading them with honey and slices of pecorino cheese.

"What do you do?" he asks Sterling, finally. "Are you also FBI?"

Sterling picks a pear from a ceramic bowl and quarters it with the blade of his Leatherman tool.

"I work for a security company called Oryx. I'm a private military contractor, Mr. Nicosa."

Nicosa's eyes refocus. Soldiering, the military hierarchy, is something he understands.

"I hired a company like yours in El Salvador to protect our coffee plantations."

"Did they do the job?"

"Yes, they did."

"Good." Sterling offers a crisp wedge of pear.

"Why are you here?" Nicosa asks.

"We completed the mission. I knew Ana was in the neighborhood, so I thought I'd stop by."

Nicosa eyes us back and forth, sniffing out the connection.

"Do you know what Ana does?"

"Yes, sir, I do. We've worked together before."

"Well, she lied about it to me. My sister-in-law, she sits at my table and tells me with a smile that she sells home alarms."

"I notice you still don't have one," I say pleasantly.

Sterling sighs. "That's the way they do it in the Bureau. You'll never meet such lying bastards."

"Why did you hide it from me?" Nicosa asks.

"Cecilia begged me not to tell you."

He is now pouring straight grappa. "*Cecilia* told you to lie? I find that hard to believe."

"She said you were 'under the thumb' of the mafias," I reply matter-of-factly. "She thought I could help you and the family to find a way out."

"I don't know where she got that idea." Nicosa waves dismissively.

"Maybe because the Puppet was in your son's room. Was he there to threaten you?"

"Not at all!"

My cover may be blown, but I'm still on assignment. Sterling senses I'm about to push it, and he steers us back to the line of inquiry most likely to engage Nicosa's cooperation: his son.

"Sir, it's Giovanni we're most worried about. With all due respect, I just got here, but anyone can see there're problems. Ana and I worked a case where young people came under bad influences, just like your son. I understand that you want to concentrate on your wife's situation, so why not let us help untangle this mess with the boy? What do you know about his relationship with the woman who passed him cocaine?"

Nicosa shrugs with his eyebrows, his shoulders, his whole body.

"She's just a local oddball. I don't know what's in Giovanni's head."

I ask if he knew how much the boy had been using at the time he was found passed out in the shower.

"He was buying painkillers from some little piece of trash who stole them from his grandparents."

"Giovanni told you that?"

"Of course not. We hired a private investigator. The same private investigator my wife used when she was looking for you. Pain pills were nothing compared to what Giovanni was into. Our son was hanging out with heroin addicts. Nice kids. University students. The detective said it was a matter of days—hours—before we lost him forever. We got him away from his 'friends,' the hardest thing we've ever had to do. The rehab people came and took our boy in the middle of the night. There was no other way he would go. We had to tell everyone he was trying out another school. Cecilia was the strong one. She sees addicts every day; she knows what has to be done. I thought, you know, lock him in his room. Beat the crap out of him, like my father would have done to me. I didn't know what we were up against. But three months later, they brought him back to us, and so far he's been clean. Now we will always walk on eggshells. It's my fault. You don't have to say it."

"I wasn't going to say that, because it isn't true. It's the mafias who control your lives," I tell him.

Nicosa shakes his head sadly. Hollow-eyed, he says, "The trouble is inside of us," and bangs his own heart.

"Be fair," Sterling advises. "You're up against a well-armed criminal organization. You live in a castle, but you're in the middle of a ground war."

"What you keep calling a kidnap—it's all for show, just a game," Nicosa interrupts impatiently. "They ask for ransom, you pay, they give her back. It's like a bank robbery. No one gets hurt."

This has been Nicosa's stance all along. Sterling remains silent, but his face conveys the message: *Let him have his little fantasy.*

Nicosa sees this, and it incites him to a fury.

"If I believed otherwise *for one minute*, I would be on the phone right now to the prime minister of Italy. You don't think so?"

"I don't doubt you, sir," Sterling assures him.

"One phone call to Rome and the military police would take over my wife's disappearance. But I agree to play their game, because unlike you, I have patience, and I do not like war."

"I didn't say I like it," Sterling says quietly.

"I am sending the clans a message. We are businessmen; we work it out." Nicosa wipes his forehead, adding, "The president of a company, who kicks a ball like an idiot and almost kills his son."

His voice cracks and his eyes redden. Mine fill up just watching.

"Let us talk to the private investigator who followed Giovanni," I suggest. "He can help us understand some things."

"You can't. The man is dead."

"How did he die?"

"I believe it was a stroke. He had a terrible headache, his wife took him to the hospital, and he didn't come out. He never finished the report," Nicosa says. "I have what he left on the computer in my office. I'll get it."

He seems relieved to have an excuse to leave. As the day breaks open, the kitchen is feeling more and more like a slow-motion hydrogen explosion. Sterling places both elbows on the table and digs his knuckles into his bare scalp.

"Wishing you were back in the field?"

"Not in that field, ma'am, no way. Texas. I'm wishing I was back in Texas, where at least they flat-out shoot you and put you out of your misery."

I laugh. "They're pretty good at that in Italy."

"Man, these folks are into the pain. Christ on a stick! All this bitchin' and moanin', until you can't see straight. He doesn't like war? Boo-hoo for him. I hate to tell him, but he's walking a freakin' minefield." Sterling stands up from the table with disgust. "First day of deployment, we tell the newbies, 'If you plan on coming home alive, remember this— there's a difference between a hard-ass and a dumb ass.' He truly believes he's the Man of Steel, the only one who can negotiate with the mafias."

"I believe Nicosa loves his son, and he's desperate to get Cecilia back. He needs to be contained, that's all."

Sterling shakes his head. "I'll say this, I'd hate for the guy to take a bullet the size of his ego."

25

THE DEAD investigator was at least a good dead investigator. His report included phone records, photographs, lists of my nephew's teachers, friends, and relations living in Siena. Family members alone took up two single-spaced pages. It could be days before we deciphered who was who, and we had no time for that. The surveillance section covered the boy's activities during ten days over two weeks in January of last year, detailing to the minute when he left the abbey for school and returned through the gates at night.

We looked for patterns. Soccer, practicing the flag for Palio, chilling at the Fontebranda fountain in Oca territory—that was the norm. Then we looked for the exceptions, always more interesting. One jumped out at us: a cluster of encounters with a young Italian woman named Zabrina Tursi. Her photo showed a goth, raven-haired, undernourished university student who worked part-time as a waitress. A copy of a police report showed one arrest for the sale of marijuana, but she was placed on probation because she was a minor at the time.

The dead investigator hired by Giovanni's parents had discovered his relationship with Zabrina after following him and two male friends to the wine bar where she worked, situated in the Medici fortress near the bus station on the outskirts of town. He observed the subject first being served by Zabrina Tursi and then engaging her in conversation on the patio after the place closed. Two nights later, the young woman appeared at the fountain in Oca territory and made contact with Giovanni. There is a photo of them with other students at a café in the square. At 1:05 a.m., Zabrina and Giovanni left the café and went to her residence, a ten-minute drive outside the walls, where he stayed until 3:45 a.m. Then he returned to the abbey.

The file details Giovanni visiting Zabrina's residence five times. It bothered me until I realized the association— five was also the number of assignations the FBI recorded between Nicosa and Lucia Vincenzo, La Leonessa, the disappeared drug dealer. Numerology aside, I wondered if Giovanni was subconsciously imitating his father's public transgressions by flaunting it with a woman who was also dangerous to his health.

Sterling and I drive to Zabrina's address. It is a decent apartment building in a quiet neighborhood shaded by oak trees. Stacks of terraces with hanging laundry and potted plants face the west. The entrance is down a hill, past the usual fleet of parked motorbikes. Inside the building we get no farther than the vestibule. You have to be buzzed in. "Tursi" is listed on a mailbox with "Kosta" and "Lawrence," but there is no answer to our ring. The vestibule smells of cigarette smoke and frying meatballs.

Sterling says, "Let's go."

"We should wait for the girl."

"Best bet is to come back later, when she's likely to be home."

"You have another idea?"

"I would like to see how his neighbors make that olive oil Giovanni was talking about," Sterling says.

"Why?"

"Brings me back to summers at home. When I was a kid, my job was snake wrangler. You want to cut the bottom branches of the olive trees to keep the ground clear of rattle-snakes, but they're crafty. My all-time record was shooting six in one week. Now my folks give ranch tours to tourists, but when we first started planting, it was us, some clay hills, and a couple of Mexicans. Good times. I'm curious how they do it in the old country."

It's the blazing hot middle of the day, and most people will be going nowhere, hunkered down behind the shutters. The last place I want to be is sitting in the mailbox car.

"Okay."

I agree to give it up for an hour. Climbing the hill from Zabrina's apartment house back to the car, I slip my arm around Sterling's waist, relieved that he's able to connect to something besides bad wars and bad dreams.

THE OLIVE farm is just past the abbey, beyond a grape arbor and some chicken coops. The house, a two-story stucco building with a red tile roof, would not be out of place in a Los Angeles subdivision, except it is not likely you would find the wife eviscerating chickens, which is what Antonella Calabrese is doing when we show up. She and her husband do not speak English, but her reaction to uninvited guests is nothing but warmth.

She is over sixty, with dry reddish hair and a pleasant face filmed with sweat from hard work in the small alcove in the back of the house. Although scraping entrails into a bucket, she displays that Italian feminine self-respect by wearing pearl stud earrings, a black camisole that bares her arms underneath an apron, and a circular diamond pendant. Three chickens—supermarket clean—are folded up in a roasting pan with three full-feathered bodies to go. "Why would anybody," she asks Sterling in Italian, "cook just one chicken at a time?"

Not wanting to leave the task unattended (flies are gathering), she calls for Aleandro and leads us to the basement, where he is plastering a wall. Her husband is hearty and weathered-looking, with dark skin and strong forearms, wearing a blue checked shirt splattered with white. His gray eyebrows peak like a horned owl's. He's got a broad fleshy nose and a wide smile. Side by side, he and Antonella look like brother and sister. Both radiate the grounded, earthbound simplicity we city folks associate with outdoor life.

But it wasn't always so. Aleandro, we discover, is retired from a long career as an electrical inspector for a government agency, which explains the pleasant home and sense of tranquillity. He is done with it. He has always kept chickens and rabbits, always had olive trees, an organic vegetable garden and grapes, but now, he is proud to say, he and his wife are self-sustaining.

Their olive operation may not be as grand as what Sterling had in mind—it consists of a single windowless basement room, away from light and heat, with sacks full of chemical pellets, curing barrels, and a stainless-steel tank in which they store the oil, which is pressed at a community mill. All of this is fascinating—especially the discussion in Italian of how the Spaniards brought olives to Texas—and I am more than ready to leave, but somehow, by mental telepathy, before she went to finish the chickens, Aleandro and Antonella have agreed that we are not going anywhere until we've had something to eat.

We are shepherded upstairs and seated at a heavy dining room table with a white lace runner. Behind us is a dark wood cupboard jammed with glassware. Antonella comes through the brick archway of the kitchen, carrying a welcome carafe of water. The kitchen has a vaulted wooden ceiling that mocks older Tuscan architecture. I am antsy and uncomfortable. They are talking a blue streak that I can't understand, and I am wondering if this will turn into a tedious lunch. I just want to get back to Zabrina, hoping she can shed light on Giovanni and his dealings, if she has anything to say that might factor into Nicosa's alleged drug connection and Cecilia's abduction.

No, it isn't lunch. Antonella returns with the coffee and then bread and preserves made with fruit from their orchard—the most fullbodied, jewel-like jelly I have ever tasted. Unknown to me, the conversation around the dining room table has taken a much darker turn than Spanish olives. Sterling has been asking questions, that much I can tell. After a point, Aleandro's powerful hand curls into a heavy fist. His wife's eyes are downcast. They can only be talking about the mafias.

When we are shown to the door, we are given a gift—a recycled Sprite bottle containing their precious homemade olive oil, emerald as a mossy stream. Sterling and Aleandro shake hands and then embrace with such force it almost makes me cry. Something powerful has taken place between them.

When we are back on the road and walking toward the abbey, Sterling is hyper. He tells me that the Calabreses heard through town gossip that Cecilia is missing.

"He gave us a lead where she might be. First and foremost, you don't have to come. I can handle it solo, spare you the upset."

"Whatever in hell it is you're talking about, I'm coming."

Olives, as Sterling well knows, are cured in sodium hydroxide. It reduces the bitterness, and if you soak them long enough, it will turn green olives black. He had a hunch they might be doing it the same way in Italy, and he was right. Aleandro has the pellets in his basement; he knows all about the chemical and who supplies it and where it's stored.

Another name for sodium hydroxide is lye.

At Sterling's empathetic prodding, Aleandro had disclosed that he, too, has a relative who is one of the "disappeared"—an uncle who also worked as an electrical inspector for the government. The uncle submitted a poor report on a water plant and did not come home from work one night. The police did nothing. Aleandro's family did nothing. They don't speak of it; five years later, they are still afraid.

All over the world, from Mexico to Albania, criminal networks dispose of victims using lye. It is a caustic metallic base used in manufacturing all kinds of corrosive products, like paint strippers. When pure pellets of sodium hydroxide are combined with water and heat, a reaction occurs that chews up the chemical bonds that normally keep tissues intact. The corpse dissolves into a pinkish liquid, occasionally leaving bone husks that are as fragile as cicada shells.

Aleandro had given Sterling directions to his own supplier of fertilizer and chemicals, including industrial lye. The company is called Spectra and is headquartered in Milan, but the local distributor operates out of a town nearby called Monte San Stefano.

MONTE SAN STEFANO, ITALY

26

MONTE SAN Stefano is an hour to the south—halfway to Rome. From the turnoff it is slow going on a two-lane road that coils through clay hills, only to discover that Monte San Stefano barely exists. There is a shoe outlet and a truffle museum, both closed for lunch. Inquiries at a gas station five kilometers past yield zero results, until the nice lady behind the counter asks to see the grimy paper on which Aleandro carefully printed the address, and recognizes the name of Marcello Falassi—a truck driver who makes deliveries for Spectra.

"She said he lives a couple of kilometers back that way," Sterling explains as we exit the store. "When we see a big white house, we turn left and keep going east."

"How far?"

"Until we come to an old barn. The turnout is across the road. We drive until we see a red fence, and there's the house."

I realize that Sterling had orchestrated the outing to Aleandro's farm not to indulge in nostalgia for growing olives in Texas, but because he believes Cecilia is already dead. That she was taken by the mob, shot within a couple of days, and her body has already been reduced to God knows what. The quicker we find the remains, the quicker we can track the bad guys.

Sterling insists it's a simple idea—deduction 101—to trace the supply route of the lye back to the mafiosi. Plausible, maybe; a long shot, definitely. In my opinion, we don't know enough to commit to chasing some delivery man all over Tuscany. As we get into the car, it is hard to stifle my impatience. I want to go back to Siena and investigate properly. Why am I listening to him? I am the trained Bureau specialist. If I don't actually say it, that is what I'm thinking, and at this moment I would be just as glad to drop the burden of Sterling's shell-shocked emotions, get back on the phone with my coolheaded FBI partner, Mike Donnato, and find Cecilia, unencumbered.

"Do you really think this is worth it?" I ask. "We're spending an entire day on a very shaky lead. The guy who drives a chemical truck? He's going to know where the bodies are buried? We should go back to Siena and nail that girl, Zabrina."

"The guy who drives a truck gets orders from somewhere." Sterling climbs behind the wheel.

"Yes, a manifest from an office in Milan—"

Sterling slams the door. "Stop nagging."

It stops me, all right. Like a bucket of ice water.

"We're arguing an investigative approach," I say unsteadily. "Back and forth. Your ideas, my ideas."

"I know what an argument is, honey."

"It's how we do it in the Bureau. Maximize the options."

"We do it the same way in my shop."

"Where? In a bunker in Iraq?"

I regret it immediately.

"I'm sorry," I say. "That was stupid. I didn't mean it."

He pulls over and stops.

"Up ahead, that's the big white house. That's the road where we turn. If you want to go back to Siena, we keep on going straight."

"I don't like the word *nagging*," I say quietly.

He exhales with exasperation. "What do you want me to do?"

"Talk to me like a professional. I'm talking to you like a professional—"

"You're gonna tell me how to talk, now?"

"I'm not taking orders from you."

"Nobody's giving orders. The FBI is playing you. Can't you see that? And meanwhile, the mafia has Cecilia."

"I see that."

"Seems to me, professionally speaking, whatever drug business your nephew or his father have been into is a sidebar. It might connect, might not. We tried following the investigator's report and ended up at an apartment with nobody home. With the kidnap, our objective has changed. First and foremost, we need to find Cecilia, dead or alive. This Marcello Falassi, who delivers the chemicals, he might know something about that, or lead us to someone who does."

Sterling is watching my face. He wants to know if I can really hear it. *Dead or alive. Alive or dead.*

"Make the turn to Falassi's place," I say.

He hesitates.

"I mean it. Go."

The road is a whispering tunnel of green. There are no other cars. We arrive at a crossroads, make a guess, and keep heading east, coming out to ripe farmland dotted with rolls of hay, and the low-pitched clanging of hundreds of tin bells. A herd of sheep is crossing, guided only by a white dog. Two by two, docile as a class of kindergartners, they go out one gate, across the asphalt, and into the neighboring field. The dog stands on a rise and barks, the sheep stream past, and the bells are like a living wall of sound. There are no humans in sight. Even when the herd has disappeared, the dog continues to bark at our car. As soon as we creep past, he goes.

It sobers me. Simple equations that I never really understood. Dogs and sheep. Farmland and sun. Build your fortress on the highest ground. Not for the first time since I've been in Italy, the external world—the wild-eyed horses in the Palio, this troubled man beside me in the car—seems extraordinarily vivid, while my own self feels distant from the experience, more and more transparent. Is that what a career in the black box of the Bureau does to you? Numbs the senses, as well as the soul?

Marcello Falassi lives in a powder-blue trailer on the dark side of the road, the only structure for several kilometers. We have seen many low-income houses cheerfully surrounded by sunflowers and artichoke plants, but this one has nothing to say for itself, except bales of wire in the front yard. I suppose nothing grows because of the damp, sunless location. But when we pass a dead dove splayed out on the walkway, I wonder if something else is at play.

Signora Falassi opens the door. She is a depressed-looking, spectacularly overweight person about fifty with a mane of artificially jet-black curls, wearing a pale lavender blouse and matching slacks. Her mouth pulls tight into a wary expression as she affirms that her husband is a driver for Spectra.

"Perchè lei vuole sapere?" Why do you want to know?

We stand on the steps looking earnest while Sterling explains in Italian that we are an American couple who just bought a farm in the area and were told Signore Falassi is the one to talk to about getting the chemicals we need to cure olives.

"Non è a casa. Guida la sua strada."

"Can you tell us where he is? Maybe we can catch him."

The woman says to follow her, but she can hardly walk, toddling slowly down a narrow hallway by hanging on to the walls. I glimpse a kitchen and an ancient *nonna* taking something out of the oven that smells of rancid lamb fat. A few steps farther, and we enter a tiny sloping room crammed with boxes of files. A camp bed is buried under stacks of newspapers and indistinguishable clothing. Hollowed out of this dark rat's nest is a corner desk with a laptop computer under a brilliant light.

Signora Falassi lowers herself to a wooden chair with a painful sigh.

"Sorry if we are bothering you," Sterling says in Italian.

She waves her hand. No bother. It's just her feet, and she lifts them up for our inspection—a pair of deformed stumps in rubber thongs. They look like pictures I have seen of leprosy. The toes curl sideways and the skin has erupted in permanent red welts.

Falassi's delivery schedule spurts out of the printer.

"She says he's making a drop at the feed store in San Piero," Sterling says. "It's close by; we can catch him."

"Ask how we get to San Piero," I say, not taking my eyes from the feet.

She begins to give directions, but it turns into a shouting match with the old lady—Falassi's mother, listening from the kitchen—who knows a better way to go. Not getting her point across, the *nonna* shuffles into the office, screeching and jabbing, while Sterling smiles and holds up his cell phone, indicating, *Thank you very much; we'll use the GPS.*

I don't think they understand, but they do calm down, and then a long exchange continues among the three of them in Italian. I can't stop staring at the old lady's feet. She, too, is wearing rubber thongs, and her welts go up to the ankles. It looks like both women have been burned by a caustic substance.

"**WHAT WAS** that all about?" I say when we are back in the car.

Sterling drives with an eye on the blinking GPS.

"They said there was an accident. The husband used to keep chemicals behind the house. The wife and mother are

out in the yard one day, and they notice their shoes are melting. There's a leak coming from one of the barrels. They didn't
even feel it at first. Corrosive substances dissolve the nerve
endings, along with the skin. That's the good news, I guess."

"Did Falassi want to do damage, or did he just screw up?"

"He screwed up. The wife says she has no use for him.
She's disabled now, stuck in the house with his mother, and
he's never home, yadda yadda yadda. But she got some money
out of Spectra after the accident, so she's going on a pilgrim-
age to Fatima."

"And never coming back?"

"The mother's going with her."

"Gotta love it."

We arrive at San Piero as the feed store is closing. The
entire town is closed for dinner and will reopen around eight
p.m. The manager says Falassi left a few minutes ago, but we
can catch him on the road, pointing the opposite way from
which we have come. The chemical delivery man does not
seem in a hurry to get home for that roast lamb dinner.

We jump back in the car and Sterling jams it. After several
tense, silent minutes of wondering if we are in fact going in
the right direction, we sight the silver Spectra van and slow
down to tourist speed, keeping a distance. He continues for
several kilometers and then turns off to the right.

We slide past and pull over. Sterling checks the GPS.

"Where does that road go?" I ask.

"Looks like it ends in the middle of a damn forest."

We swing around and make the turn onto a short dirt
spur—bumpy but passable. We take it slowly, stopping at
an iron gate about a hundred meters in. It's chain-locked to
vehicles, but obviously the van has just passed through. There
is no other way out and the tread marks are fresh. We leave
our car and hop over the gate. It is late in the day. Steamy
afternoon sun languishes in the high grass and dusty pines.

Not a motor, not a chirp, only ambient leafy rustling. We are definitely in the middle of a damn forest.

The road is old, maybe thousands of years old, worn into the landscape. The light beneath the canopy of needle clusters is wavering and soft. We trek along easily on well-used tracks. Between the tracks, tufts of lavender and daisies run wild. The air becomes lighter and perfumed—the trees break and we find ourselves in an enchanted valley, the kind of spot that calls out for habitation, with its own human-friendly microclimate sheltered by the hills. There is a long-neglected olive grove and the remains of a stream. A meadow of irises where two pure white Tuscan Chianina cows and a tawny calf are grazing.

The road takes a turn, past four worn gravestones, and goes downhill. The grassy median that grew between the tire tracks in the sun disappears as we enter thick oak woods. As in a fairy tale, the signs are warning us that we have crossed into an unfavorable realm. The foliage has grown spikes—juniper, gorse, and forbidding nettles. The air has cooled; motionless and buzzing with gnats. The tire tracks continue around what seems to be a hillock, but on second look we see that it's an old stone wall splattered with mustard-colored fungus and buried under eons of dead foliage.

"You know what this is?" Sterling says. "It's an ancient mill."

"Where?"

"There's the embankment. There's the dry streambed. Lord, that must be the millstone," he says of a round flint-colored boulder. "This is incredibly old." Sterling wipes the sweat above his lips with a bandanna.

"There's the van."

Spots of red and silver are shining through the brush. We climb across the streambed, cracking dead branches like rifle shots.

"He'll hear us."

"Better that he does," Sterling says.

We come to an old Tuscan-style house. The Spectra van is parked nearby. The house is nothing but a shell; a while ago there was a serious fire. The roof is half caved in and the wooden supports all charred. A caper bush has taken root in the walls and pried out the stones.

Sterling calls, "Signore Falassi?"

No answer. We walk to the other side of the ruins. A black and white Australian sheepdog trots around the corner and regards us with curious brown eyes. Sterling pets him and talks to him, and he follows us willingly, past a table and chair, a cache of gallon water bottles, burned tin cans, a tank of gas.

"There's your sodium hydroxide." Sterling points to bags of pellets like the ones we saw stacked in Aleandro's basement, piled against a prefab shack.

There is another structure, a small wooden water tower on stilts. I climb a walkway to a platform built around it. Meanwhile Sterling has found a chest containing goggles and gloves. He has noticed a hose leading from the gas tank to a circle of jets beneath the tower. Sticking his head under, he sees that the bottom is made of firebrick.

"Looks like they fire this thing up."

"Why would they?"

Now I'm on the platform, maybe ten feet off the ground. The dog is right behind me, nose in my butt. I find a tarp secured over the top of the tank with grommets. Just like your backyard hot tub. I open it and look inside. The wooden tower is lined with a steel vat that holds hundreds of gallons of sickly pink sludge, a living thing, a bubbling mix of water and lye that seems to have the power to suck you in. The chemical reaction caused by the jets below still radiates venomous heat, released when the top was lifted. There are teeth and a fragment of vertebrae floating in the strawberry-colored stew.

"What's the matter?" Sterling calls.

"Look at this."

Sterling lopes up the walkway and glances into the tank. Beside us the dog is barking frantically—not taking a breath—the same message over and over.

"That's our guy," I say.

"I'll talk to him," says Sterling, slowly making his way back down.

A stocky laborer wearing a filthy jumpsuit has stepped out of the woods. He has dark curly hair and a round, sooty face.

"Non muovere! Chi cazzo sono?" he shouts.

Sterling stops and speaks calmly in Italian.

"We are very sorry for the intrusion. We mean no harm."

The man raises a .45-caliber handgun and aims at Sterling's chest, continuing to yell that we have invaded his place.

"Tell him we got lost," I say. "We're American tourists—"

Sterling does. Falassi continues to rant. His face is red with sweat and fear. Sterling has been caught in the middle of the site with no options. An iron pry bar rests up against the shack, way out of reach.

"This is a suckface situation in hell," Sterling says.

Right next to me the dog is barking incessantly.

Falassi raises the gun with both hands and sights it.

I scoop up the dog under the belly and hold him over the tank.

"Tell him I'll kill his fucking dog."

The dog weighs fifty pounds and is struggling with all his might.

"Put the gun down or we'll dump your dog," Sterling shouts in Italian. "We'll throw him in! We'll do it, I promise you!"

The dog is whipping back and forth, all four legs cycling in midair. His body is warm, and I smell pine in his fur. I brace my back, but my fingers are slipping. He's strong, he's desperate, he licks my face, saying all he wants to do is to be let go. Another second and he'll worm out of my arms.

"Put the gun down!"

Falassi stares in disbelief, and then his peasant face goes dumb and grief-stricken.

"No!" he cries. *"Non farlo!"* Don't do it!

I grit my teeth, muscles aching, continuing to hold the squirming animal over the poisonous sludge.

"How long will it take for his body to dissolve? Ever do it while they're still alive? Put down the gun or the dog goes *now!*"

Falassi cries, *"Arete!"* and tosses the gun, sobbing, *"Per favore!"*

Sterling picks up the weapon.

"Good choice. Nobody gets hurt."

I put the dog down on the platform. Sterling tosses the gun into the tank, where it sinks with a caustic hiss. My legs are trembling.

"We are tourists," Sterling repeats as I climb off and we back away. "We made a mistake. And now we are going back to America. We are leaving."

Our goal is to get out of there with no further violence and no reason for pursuit. We keep murmuring how sorry we are as we slip past Falassi, who has become a tearful penitent, down on his knees in the resinous dust, begging the dog to come. Unfortunately, the dog wants to go with us. We have to speak harshly to him, and throw sticks, until he finally turns back.

27

"*IT ISN'T* her," Sterling keeps saying.

We run all the way back to the car, through the oak for-est and past the meadow. Sterling's shirt is soaked, but he is scarcely breathing hard. I am out of shape and tasting the exertion. When we finally stop, my whole body begins to quiver. I have to lean against the iron gate and force down the revulsion.

"How do you know it isn't her?"

"Those bones looked real old," he says.

"You don't *know* that! You don't know if they're human, or what human bones even look like when they've been in acid for who knows how long, and neither do I."

"I've seen it before," Sterling says somberly. "In mass graves in Rwanda."

"There's no comparison!"

"I know how you feel," he continues gently. "She's your sister."

"Don't be so condescending."

"What in hell are you talkin' about?"

Sterling takes a long look back down the empty road. I hear a sound like steel ball bearings rolling over each other and realize he is grinding his teeth.

"What if Falassi didn't buy our story?" I snap.

He starts shouting. "First of all, shut the fuck up! If it's all too much, go sit in the car."

He looks like a madman. The dirty bandanna, the sweat, the bristled jaw working, the bright eyes darting. He looks like a man who has in fact just parachuted in from a slaughter. But then it passes. I force myself to look at the treetops until my tears of shock and nausea are gone.

"Here's what we know," I say carefully. "The ruins in the forest are a crime scene. Whether it's her or not"—I can't say *Cecilia*—"the remains could provide evidence against the mob. We have to secure it. We have to take Falassi into custody. He is a witness and a potential informant. In the U.S., federal agents would be all over this within the hour. But here—who do we reach out to?"

Sterling wipes a palm across his forehead. He is past the episode. He does not apologize, which is not in his nature, either. Maybe he has not been aware of where he is or what he said. A few years ago I was involved in a shooting incident in Los Angeles. Afterward, I was told about things I had done of which I had no memory.

"Who does the crime scene belong to, legally?" he asks. "The tank, all of it?"

"The Italian authorities."

"Do we trust them?"

"No."

"What about the Americans?"

"You mean the FBI? I don't trust Rizzio, either. But it's my duty," I say, kicking at the dust. "I have to tell him what we found. Then it's his call to involve the Italians."

"How long will that take?"

"I don't know how much independence he has over here. If he's supposed to call headquarters before he takes a piss, it could be days."

Sterling takes out his cell phone. "I'll handle it."

"What are you doing?"

"Calling Chris."

The plan is for Sterling and Chris to stake out the witness, Falassi. They will secrete themselves at the mouth of the dirt road and follow him. According to the GPS, it is the only way out of the site. The long evening passes slowly, and there is no sign of Falassi. Chris arrives after dark with a trunk piled with sniper rifles, automatic weapons, and camouflage gear. In a country that bans guns, someone had to commit a crime in order to import all that firepower—hide it in a shipment or pay off a customs official.

"Do those weapons belong to Oryx?"

"Of course not. I tripped over 'em, taking out the trash."

I leave the surveillance to them and drive back to the abbey, where the embassy switchboard is able to put the call through to Dennis Rizzio at home. As expected, he says that with no jurisdiction, we are bound to turn the crime scene over to the provincial police. It is their responsibility to link the forensic evidence from the vat with the "disappeared." I explain to Rizzio that since the Commissario has already suppressed evidence during the attack on Giovanni, he might not be the best person to handle this important evidence.

"I'm in contact with the director of the crime lab in Rome. I'll make sure this stays on track," Dennis assures me.

Not at all assured, I leave a voice message for Mike Donnato at the Los Angeles field office.

I AM not surprised that Sterling and Chris have not returned by morning. Waiting until the Italian police show up to arrest Falassi could easily take all day. From the mirrored armoire in the sweet-pea bedroom I remove Cecilia's wrap skirt (*"When it is this hot, the only thing to wear is linen"*), holding it in my hands for a long time, studying the minute stitches along the hem, the hand-sewn buttonholes where the ties pass through, the weave of the oatmeal fabric.

The small arched window is filled with the light of daybreak. I stand there in my underwear and contemplate the vast breathing of everything outside that is alive, while, at the same time, aware of a chill penetrating the soles of my feet from the enduring cold of the inert clay tiles. In some deep place, I have begun to say my good-byes to Cecilia.

I had hoped, when this case began, to find what had been missing from my childhood in the insipid suburbs of Southern California, dominated by a grandfather too angry and narcissistic to even see me, except as an object of scorn. Even so, Cecilia was an unexpected discovery—driven, vibrant, brave, skilled at her profession, a little bit crazy—but fun. The rare kind of person who picks up the burdens; suddenly you don't have to carry responsibility for everything.

Maybe losing her before loving her is a blessing. Like a caustic substance, the kidnap case has seared those nerve endings away. I reflect on how much easier it is to play the role of law enforcer than that of sister. I don't know when the pain will start kicking in, but I'm certain Cecilia's loss will leave nothing of this venture into family; the tentative bonds with Giovanni, and certainly with Nicosa, will dissolve as inevitably as those fragments of life melting in a vat of acid.

As promised, Cecilia's skirt is cool and light. I wish my guilt in wearing it could be as weightless. Giovanni, eating breakfast in the kitchen, says Nicosa is working in his office.

"Where's his office?"

"In the tower. Top floor."

I was not even aware that the twelve-sided bell tower was used for living space. While a five-year-old could pick the lock on the main quarters, no high-tech toy has been unexploited to protect Nicosa's solitude. Entry is gained with fingerprint recognition or a special bypass code that appears on a screen when you identify yourself through the intercom. A second code is required to pass through the vestibule air lock, where cameras and motion sensors watch every move. An automated voice says in Italian that you have thirty seconds to step inside the glass elevator or an alarm will sound.

As you ascend, you are stunned to realize that you are passing through a vertical museum of Renaissance and pre-historic art. Inside the romantic tower is a secret, world-class private collection. Nicosa has created six stories of gallery space filled with artifacts, statuary, and paintings. There is one whole room of thirteenth-century Sienese Madonnas with gold-leaf haloes—all exactly alike, with the same swan-like faces and slanted eyes—and a steel vault that holds who knows what other priceless treasures.

When the elevator doors open at the top, you stumble into a circular space enclosed by twelve arched windows—three hundred and sixty degrees of mountains and sky. Looking out, you can see nothing in any direction but green fields, slanting olive groves, rustic stone houses, and cypress trees. Towns like balls of dust caught in the spires of distant hills.

Nicosa's desk is a curving command center of burnished cherrywood and chrome. There is a seating area of black leather couches, and, of course, a full kitchen, featuring a sleek top-of-the-line Nicosa Family espresso machine. With all those spouts and armatures, it looks like a robot from Mars, and probably costs as much as I make in a month. The refrigerator is stocked. Once you're up here with the falcons, why leave?

"I can see why you're not in the market for a new security system."

"Now you understand."

The coffee king sets down two small white cups, just as they should be, in their saucers, accompanied by a lemon twist. He is wearing jeans, sandals, and a short-sleeved sport shirt, but he hasn't shaved. The room is tempered by constant breezes crisscrossing between the windows with the hot breath of baked clay and pine.

"There is something you need to know," I tell him. "It may concern Cecilia."

"What is it?"

He sits on a curved leather chair that is as thin as a corn chip. His dark eyes are rheumy and distrustful. I wonder if seeing me in Cecilia's clothes is upsetting to him, but he doesn't seem to notice.

"Yesterday I was near Monte San Stefano with my friend, Sterling. We went down a road and found the ruins of an old mill. He's there now, guarding the site."

"That's a very old mill," Nicosa says.

"You know it?"

He nods. "The original foundation goes back to the Etruscan era. I have a clay pot from there."

"A man named Marcello Falassi has a place in the ruins. He's a deliveryman for the Spectra Chemical Company. We saw his van. He confronted us, and he was aggressive, but we were able to leave without incident. While we were there, we found a vat filled with lye. In the lye there were fragments of bones, possibly human. The provincial police are on the way."

"How do you know they were human? That's often the way farmers dispose of dead animals."

"It's also how the mafias dispose of victims."

Nicosa starts laughing.

"I didn't want to believe it, either," I add quickly. "And maybe it's not Cecilia; it could be another one of the disappeared—"

"Of course it isn't her!"

He stands up and his arms fly out in exasperation, and I think maybe he'll turn into a raven and fly out the tower window.

"Why come here and give me a heart attack?"

"Because you're her husband. You should know before the police get there."

Nicosa blows air through his teeth like the steam from the coffee-maker.

"Be calm."

"I am calm," Nicosa says, clenching his fists.

"How can you be so sure?"

"*Madonna!* You will never understand Italy. They want my *money.* They take my wife because they want my money! They don't want to kill her; they want to make an exchange. This country is *sick.* We are on the downturn and people are desperate. They take the money and give her back. Why? So they can kidnap her *again*! Because now they *know* you'll pay. You don't think it happens?"

Nicosa is on his feet, gesticulating against the sky, a grand performance—whether to convince himself or me, I can't tell.

"I'm afraid they didn't want Cecilia. I'm afraid they took the wrong person."

"What wrong person?"

"Do Cecilia and I look alike?"

"There is a definite resemblance."

"They wanted me, but they took Cecilia."

"What is this?" Nicosa's face squinches up with distaste. "They *don't* want my wife? They want an American?"

I tell him about the attack in London. That I witnessed a mob reprisal shooting outside a restaurant in South Kensington, that the killers got away with my picture on their cell phone, and that the word went out to the terrorist networks.

Someone in Siena thought he saw me, so they sent in their crack team of knuckleheads. Being knuckleheads from the south, they didn't recognize the biggest socialite in the north, Cecilia Nicosa, but the woman in church looked enough like the blurry image on the cell phone that they snatched her instead.

Nicosa isn't laughing now. He already sees the end of it. Or maybe my bleak expression worries him, because he folds back onto the leather chair and stares with mouth slack.

"But once they realize they have the wrong person—her instead of you—they'll still want ransom," he says weakly. "Why not? These people aren't stupid."

"Nicoli," I say gently, "are you aware that your wife has been paying *pizzo*?"

"Why would she do that?"

"To keep her clinics open."

"It doesn't make sense. If she's paying bribes, they would leave her alone."

I wait. "But you know she's been paying, don't you?"

"It's one of those things," he says finally. "Like a love affair. You wonder. You suspect. Words do not need to be said because they won't change the outcome."

"She takes a terrible risk by dealing with a criminal network."

"She is an independent woman. I can't speak for her."

"What about you? What is your involvement?"

"I pay *pizzo*, too."

"Is that all?"

"Yes, of course."

"Anything you can tell me will be in confidence. I'm only interested in getting Cecilia back."

"I have nothing to tell you. The question is, will they still ask for ransom money?"

"It depends on their motivation. If they are out for money,

yes. If it was their intention to kidnap an FBI agent, and they wound up with a do-gooding socialite…If they haven't already, they may just kill her."

My head is splitting. Vertigo from the sweeping view is getting to me, yet I can't help glancing out the tower openings, the way you're compelled to look at exactly what you do not want to see. The highway accident. The dead mouse in the shower.

He sees me looking unhappily out the window. "What is it?"

"The police."

Far away in the storybook countryside a white car with official markings can be seen gathering steam as it navigates the curving road leading up to the abbey.

"Why are they coming here?"

"They must have already been to the crime scene. I told the FBI legat in Rome about the remains. It was his obligation to inform the Italian police."

Nicosa stares wordlessly at the approaching unit.

"Do you want me to bring them up here?"

He snaps out of it. "Absolutely not!"

We take the elevator down.

When the police car slips into the courtyard of the abbey, Nicosa and I are already waiting on the front steps, side by side. I am dry-eyed but can't help fearing we are now into a murder investigation. Cecilia's skirt flutters around my knees. If Nicosa finds it at all painful to discover his wife's sister in her place beside him, he gives no sign. He has his game face on.

The driver gets out and opens the back door. The Commissario emerges. I had not expected he would show up himself, and from the curses streaming under Nicosa's breath, neither had he.

The chief of police draws his elongated body out of the

car and squares off against the opposition. He is wearing a funereal black suit and tie, putting Nicosa at a disadvantage, unshaven and in jeans. On the other hand, this is Nicosa's territory; his castle. The Commissario slips on sunglasses with a self-conscious flourish, peering around at the ruins of the thirteenth-century church and the stone façade of the family quarters. I find myself on Nicosa's side, hoping the grandeur of the abbey reminds the Commissario that he is nothing but a public servant; a commoner.

He comes toward us with that uneven stride. The two shake hands and greet each other formally. The meeting takes place at the wooden table beneath the loggia where I first saw Nicosa the day I arrived. I remember my nerves being on edge in anticipation of meeting Cecilia, and her husband's cool, impeccable sexuality. Now she has vanished, and he looks like a guilty man on the run; sleepless and defensive. The two men take wicker chairs. The accompanying officer waits by the car. I am dispatched to fetch water.

When I return with a bottle and glasses, the conversation is about Il Palio—polite enough, since both Torre and Oca were among the losers. By now I have picked up enough Italian to understand they agree that the judges were suckers of dicks. But when they turn to the business at hand, I request that they continue in English.

The Commissario looks at me with flat brown eyes.

"Your representative from the FBI, Signore Rizzio, was kind enough to call my office and share information about the discovery of remains near Monte San Stefano. We appreciate the cooperation of the Americans."

"Have you recovered the evidence?" I ask.

"Our team has just arrived."

"Are they human remains?"

"It's possible, but we won't know for certain until the lab report."

"Do we know how many bodies might have been dumped?"

"We will inform your office in Rome as soon as we have results."

"Thank you. As Inspector Martini explained, I am extremely concerned about my sister."

"I gave you my word that her case has the highest priority, which is one of the reasons I am here."

The Commissario turns to Nicosa. His moves are unhurried, forcing us to wait for his consideration. I can't believe Nicosa knows about Cecilia's affair with this charming operator. If so, there is no way he could remain civil.

"I am sorry that we need to discuss this," the Commissario says.

"Why? It is a gruesome thing, but it does not concern me."

"We believe otherwise."

"Really?"

"Perhaps. Would Signorina Grey mind describing the man who attacked her and her companion in the woods?"

"His name is Marcello Falassi, and he drives a van for the Spectra Chemical Company."

"A physical description, please?"

"Mid-forties, overweight, black hair, sloppy—"

The Commissario looks puzzled. "*Sciatto*," Nicosa translates.

"Low intelligence, probably psychopathic, lives with his wife and mother but his only attachment seems to be to a dog. A loyal soldier."

The Commissario nods. "We have been looking for this man. He is known as the Chef, Il Capocuòco, a notorious criminal hired by the mafias to dispose of their victims. Congratulations, Signorina Grey. You have made an important discovery that will lead to many convictions." He addresses Nicosa. "Is this someone you know?"

"No, I don't know him."

"Are you sure?"

"Yes. Why? Are you saying this thug took Cecilia?"

"I am curious, because Falassi is also the local distributor for Spectra, the manufacturer of fertilizer and industrial chemicals, which services most customers in the province, including you."

"For what?"

The Commissario swallows water and takes his time.

"Landscaping? Gardening? Processing coffee? Do you or your company buy chemicals from Spectra?"

"I don't know. I'd have to ask my production manager."

"Let me save you the trouble. We have already checked. The Nicosa Family company has an account with Spectra on average of two to three hundred euros per month."

"All right, then I guess we do."

"But you don't *know*? That is a significant amount of money."

"Not for us. I don't keep track of every supplier."

"And you've never met this man, Falassi?"

Nicosa rubs his temples. The darkness beneath his eyes grows deeper.

"What are you telling me? This driver comes here and sees my wife? Is he some maniac who is obsessed with women?"

The Commissario folds his hands. He wears a gold ring made from a Roman coin.

"How has your marriage been recently?"

"Fine."

"Have you and your wife been fighting?"

"Why is that your business?"

The Commissario answers Nicosa with blank button eyes: "Did you kill her?"

Nicosa returns the look with equanimity. "You are crazy."

"Did you get Falassi to dispose of the body? In the acid bath in the woods?"

Inch by inch, Nicosa's face goes scarlet.

I touch his wrist. "He's trying to provoke you."

He's trying to bury you.

Like any good cop, the Commissario waits patiently. For a moment, they stare each other down.

Nicosa breaks free of my touch and waves the chief off.

"Talk to my lawyers."

The Commissario gets up from the table. Ignoring his host, he turns to me.

"It is a pleasure, *signorina*." He shakes my hand with cold, bony fingers. "Call my office anytime."

Taking long halting steps, he walks toward the car. The driver comes to attention and opens the door.

DONNATO ASKS if there is a common denominator.

I am speaking to him in Los Angeles from my hideout in the far corner of the pool. Pine boughs sway above me, while he's looking out at a view of the bland cityscape that might as well be a painted backdrop; it never moves, never changes, only smolders.

"Common denominator between what?"

"Just doodling," he says. "Staring at the old yellow pad."

"What does the yellow pad say?"

"It says *coffee—vat—sister.* I've been thinking about what you're telling me. The vat of lye. Human remains. We're looking for your sister. She could be in there. She could not. It could be someone else they murdered. The Commissario makes a visit. Lays down the gauntlet to the coffee king. Nicosa is behaving—how?"

"Angry. Evasive."

"Evasive," echoes Donnato. I imagine him nodding, tasseled loafers up on the desk, toes ticking back and forth. "We ask, what is Nicosa hiding? Where is the mafia drug connection Rizzio keeps talking about?"

"I don't know, but the Commissario is trying to connect him to the chemical company that makes sodium hydroxide. It's called Spectra."

"Is lye used in manufacturing coffee?"

"Nicosa says no. But he does buy other stuff from Spectra."

"Is this Mr. Commissario actually trying to make the case that Nicosa adds sodium hydroxide to his regular order, and keeps it in the middle of a forest, on the off chance he might need it to get rid of his wife?"

"They're blood enemies. The Commissario is looking to destroy him. But Nicosa did know about the crime scene. He knows more than he's letting on," I say, feeling a flicker of excitement. "He knew it was the site of an ancient Etruscan mill."

"Twenty-five years in the FBI tells me your sister's disappearance has nothing to do with some ancient-ass old mill," Donnato says. "We have to take this in another direction."

"Where?"

"Follow the trail of the lye."

I can't bring myself to admit to him that's what Sterling said from the beginning.

THE SOUTH—LA FAMIGLIA

28

ZABRINA TURSI did the math. They had to get to Calabria before dark. The word was out; people would already be showing up. They had to leave right now.

Her current boyfriend, Yuri Kosta, was in the shower. There was no tub in the bathroom, just a showerhead and a drain. The tiny curtain was useless. The tile floor would flood, but nobody used the sponge mop Zabrina had stolen from the janitor to push the dirty water into the drain. She had obsessed about confronting her two roommates, but in the end she just gave up. The place smelled like a sewer. The toilet and sink were always damp with mildew. If you left something in there, like a towel, it would never dry. That's why they had clothes racks on the balcony, next to the rosemary plants, which were a gift from someone's deluded parents.

It was a nice building in a calm neighborhood outside the walls, as Sterling and I had discovered that blazing day when we attempted to find her, so nice that you had to be buzzed in. It rented monthly, mostly to students at the Università di Siena, but also to musicians who came for the jazz festival and even a few professors. It was a middle-class paradise. They had two bedrooms and only one other roommate, a thirty-two-year-old American named Simon Lawrence, who came from a wealthy family in Chicago and claimed to be studying to become the conductor of a symphony orchestra. He would walk around singing scores. Instead of a newspaper, he read music, and he was good on the guitar. They were all addicts. The place was dirty and the furniture dilapidated, but you would not have guessed it was a shooting gallery, where partygoers and white-collar professionals showed up for ten-euro hits, unless you caught sight, in the one-couch living room, of the odd metal cap containing remnants of blood, cocaine, and heroin.

The kitchen, though, was always tidy. If they got it together to prepare a meal, it would be the traditional pasta, *secondi*, and dessert, even though someone had to wash their meager collection of melamine dishes between each course, and they'd be crawling over each other in the hot, narrow space. The pale green tile wall was decorated with a calendar of naked women. Simon would tune the television on top of the refrigerator to the BBC. The sliding door to the balcony was an invitation to step outside and enjoy a smoke. The kitchen was the only sane room in the house.

Zabrina wiped the oilcloth on the kitchen table and checked the clock again. It was three minutes later. The shower was still going—just like their money, down the drain. They were two months behind on the rent and mooching off Simon's personal food cabinet. He was a nice guy, but he had a habit to support, and living in paradise isn't free. They were going to get kicked out, she knew it, but she couldn't deal with that right now. Right now they were broke and crashing.

Zabrina went into their bedroom, sat on the mattress on the floor, and fished a lipstick mirror from her bag. She was twenty, from Calabria—the child of an upholsterer and a seamstress—with a pug nose, light freckles, and dynamic black eyebrows. She'd come to Siena to get as far away as possible from the crime-ridden slums, but there was a weak place inside her that couldn't support the weight of freedom. She was a part-time student and waited tables at the Tuscan wine bar inside the fifteenth-century Medici fortress on the edge of town. She had chopped two-inch bangs across her forehead and put red streaks in her hair because, she said, her alter ego was the devil.

The girl lay on her stomach on the mattress and found her face in the tiny mirror, angling it to look at the good parts: the full lips and great eyebrows. With a little makeup, she could pass. The symptoms didn't show. Her skin wasn't even yellow. A couple of Valium would take care of the headache and the fiery abdominal pain until they got there.

Her cousin, Fat Pasquale, who ran things back home in Calabria, didn't like unhealthy *pòrci*—pigs. Human guinea pigs, that's what they called the addicts who showed up for free hits when raw powder came in and they were testing the cut. Not everybody was desperate enough to spring for the Russian roulette of trying out a new mix. Only the most extreme cases showed up, often from far distances. By the time they got there, they'd be so strung out all they could do was lie on the floor. Then the guy with the hands would make Fat Pasquale find a vein in their feet and do it, which could be dangerous. Even the big shot mafiosi were afraid of AIDS. You could accidently prick your finger and be dead. Also, *pòrci* didn't make great subjects if they were sick to begin with. The cut had to be good enough to beat the competition, but not so strong that it killed the buyer.

Yuri came into the bedroom—dark-skinned, emaciated, with dreadlocks caught up in a rubber band. He slipped on jeans and sat on the mattress beside Zabrina and lit a cigarette. They spoke in Italian although Yuri was half African, half Albanian, and had only been in Italy a year.

"I received a text from Fat Pasquale," Zabrina said. "He'll hook us up if we can get to Calabria tonight."

"*Sto da favola!*" said Yuri. "How? We don't have money."

Zabrina, lying prone, took a hit off the cigarette and demurely crossed her ankles in the air.

"Simon will lend us some for gas."

"He will want to go, too."

"Is he here?"

"No."

"Then too bad for him."

"If we take his money, he should get some."

"He's not here!" Zabrina yelled. "I'm not waiting for that bitch."

Yuri nodded, said, "Yeah, okay," and left the room.

Now that she had convinced him to go, Zabrina felt dragged-down and tired. She always came up with ideas—like the sponge mop in the bathroom—but as soon as she thought of something good, it seemed to disappear and ceased to matter. She felt scooped out and empty. That feeling that nobody cared. Calabria was far away. She blinked at her cell phone. It was eight minutes later than when she had checked the kitchen clock. Yuri came back with the keys and all the cash he could find in Simon's stash in the back of a drawer.

Zabrina hauled herself up and by sheer force of will against an unfathomable weight of sadness, buckled on the sandals with the silver death heads. You could only think six hours ahead.

29

LATER THAT afternoon, after the Commissario has left the abbey, Chris's black Fiat pulls up outside the gates, covered with dust from the surveillance of Marcello Falassi, aka Il Capocuòco, the Chef. Sterling, looking even thinner and scruffier with a day's growth of beard, gets out and crosses the courtyard, boot heels chipping at the gravel. I am still wearing my sister's linen skirt. The sensuous feel of it against my bare legs as I walk toward him makes me hope this unexpected shot of femininity will strike up the old spark in his eyes. He gives me an appreciative hug.

"How'd it go? What happened to Falassi?"

"Can't tell you."

"What do you mean, you can't tell me?"

"The Italian police got ahold of him. We were in position in the hide site, back up in the woods off the turnoff. At first light an unmarked car shows up, two plainclothes detectives get out. They busted through the iron fence and went on down the road that leads to the campsite. We figured our job was done. They were onto our man."

"They got there fast. I'm impressed. It was one in the morning by the time I spoke to the FBI legat in Rome. He must have gotten right to the Commissario. How did they get through the fence?"

"Bolt cutters."

I nod approvingly. "They came prepared. Did they take Falassi into custody?"

"Must have, because there's only one way in and one way out."

"You didn't stay to make sure? You didn't wait until you saw them bring him out in handcuffs and put him in the car?"

"Why risk getting made? By then it was full daylight."

"Are you kidding me?"

"No. No, ma'am." He takes my hand and kneads my knuckles, an overly bright expression in his eyes. "What's wrong?"

"You were supposed to stake out the witness."

"Babe, we did. We were there all night. You said we'd have to turn the evidence over to the Italian cops eventually. They were on it, so we took the opportunity to jack it out of there."

I relent. "Okay." My fingers yield in his. "Well, we had a hell of a morning." I detail the confrontation between Nicosa and the Commissario. "He was about to arrest Nicosa for murder right there."

"On what evidence?"

"Blood rivalry?"

"That ain't gonna fly."

"I guess the police are counting on what they find," I say. "In the vat."

My voice falters at the memory, and then it is as if I am right back on the platform, staring down at the unbearable pink human stew. Sterling feels it and his grip tightens. He pulls me toward his chest, a disquieting tremble in his arms. We cling together, my silent tears staining his shirt, but somehow it isn't me he's holding on to; his face is turned away, as if he's listening to something I can't hear.

"God have mercy," he whispers.

We step apart. I brush at my eyes. "Until proven otherwise, we have to keep going. We need to talk to that girl, Zabrina. See what she knows about Giovanni's drug contacts."

"Screw that," Sterling says. "It's not about Zabrina, it's the fact that nobody in your family knows what the other one's up to. Time to clue them in."

"Meaning what?"

"Where is Giovanni?"

"In church with his dad." I indicate the chapel on the property.

"Perfect."

I hurry after him. "Shouldn't we wait until he's stronger?"

"If he can go to school with his friends, he can answer a goddamn question."

The doors to the small abbey church are open. Peering inside is like looking at the world through a candle flame. The interior is suffused with a sensuous orange glow, warming the walls of pockmarked stone, laying a gloss over a floor of centuries-old aqua tile. Above the altar there is nothing but a simple wooden crucifix. Cecilia's touch is evident: the pews have been replaced by chairs slipcovered in peach damask and tied in back with bows, like dresses on rows of obedient churchwomen.

When we step inside, Nicosa and Giovanni are receiving communion from the Oca priest with the wire-rimmed glasses and dark hair. Otherwise the small space is empty. Afterward, the priest gathers father and son together and speaks earnestly. I wait uncomfortably, listening to the murmur of their voices, looking around and trying to spot the hand of the dead saint, but they must have it under lock and key. Growing up in Long Beach, California, I lived not far from a Catholic school, and once my friend Arlene and I dared to rap the golden knocker on the looming black-painted convent door. A nun opened it, with a stale white face and swirling batlike robes. Floating in the darkness high above was a round stained-glass window like the eye of God. Now, as then, I have the urge to flee. I tug at Sterling's belt, and we remove ourselves to a bench outside.

They emerge all together, Giovanni still leaning on a crutch, texting on his cell phone even before they are through the door. When everyone's hands have been solemnly shaken and the priest has gone, we come forward.

Nicosa eyes us warily. By now he knows we are not usually the bearers of good news.

I try to soften it. "Was it good to talk to the priest?"

"Where else can we turn? People are whispering about the awful thing in the woods. Giovanni keeps getting text messages and calls. *Is that your mom in there?* Disgusting."

Giovanni jerks his head away as Nicosa touches the boy on the chin.

"There is evil, but I want him to know there is also grace. There is hope. What did you think of what Padre Filippo said?"

Giovanni shrugs, and goes back to the screen.

"What did the Padre talk about?" Sterling asks.

Nicosa swipes at the cell phone. "Giovanni! Are you listening? Forget those people; they're only trying to make you feel bad."

"No, they're *not*. They're trying to *help*, and yes, I am listening."

"Answer him. What did Padre Filippo say?"

Giovanni recites in mocking singsong: "He talks about the Gospel of Luke. He tells us the parable of the shepherd who lost his sheep—as if I haven't heard it a million times—that the shepherd will go looking for 'the one' even if he has to leave 'the ninety-nine.'"

"What was his point?" Nicosa prods impatiently.

"That God will look for us if we're lost. Like right now,

Mama is lost, but God will find her. And we are supposed to pray the rosary. It makes no sense."

Nicosa rolls his eyes.

The phone in the house is ringing. Giovanni volunteers to answer, but Nicosa tells him to let it go. He is sick of gossipy *contrada* members and newspaper reporters begging for news of the kidnapping.

Sterling says, "Giovanni, we have to talk."

"I can't," says the boy. "I am meeting my friends."

The ringing inside the house stops.

"It's important."

"Your friends can wait. What is it?" asks Nicosa.

"There's a grocery bag in Cecilia's trunk," I say. "Would you mind getting it?"

Nicosa looks at Sterling and me, and there is acceptance in his eyes. We have peered into the simmering, pink pit of hell and now have reached the Day of Reckoning, the end of lies. He walks back toward her car as we three sit on a bench beneath the pines in an eddy of coolness and shade, watching Nicosa go to the green Alfa Romeo, disable the alarm, and open the trunk.

"What's he doing with my mother's car?" Giovanni asks.

I don't answer. Let him worry. Nicosa returns with the half-wrapped painting and the small bag of cocaine inside the grocery sack. He squeezes onto the bench and asks his son what he knows about this.

"What is it?"

"A painting by your English friend, Muriel Barrett. She left it for you at the Walkabout Pub."

Giovanni's eyes shift toward the canvas and away. "She did? Why?"

Nicosa looks at me. "You tell him."

"She had to make an emergency trip to London," I say flatly.

"This was inside the painting." Nicosa shows him the bag of cocaine.

The boy does not respond.

"What about it, kid?" Sterling asks.

"Non lo so."

"She left it for you."

"It has nothing to do with me. I don't know where that came from."

"I was there when Muriel Barrett gave it to the bartender," I say evenly. "She was all dressed up on her way to London. She gets out of the taxi and comes into the pub carrying this package. *She makes a point of it, of delivering this before she leaves the country.* Do you know what I'm saying? She says to Chris, 'It's a painting for Giovanni.' I say I'll give it to you. She's not happy, but the cab is waiting."

"She left you holding a bag of shit," Sterling tells the boy. "Any guesses why?"

Giovanni shrugs—an unconscious, on-the-spot admission of guilt.

"Here's what I think," Sterling says. "You, your mom, your dad—you don't know it, but you're all fighting the same enemy. Everything goes back to the mafias. That's why Ana and I think this"—he shakes the bag—"connects to why your mom disappeared."

Giovanni is jolted awake, cheeks red as a four-year-old's. "Where is Mama? What happened to her?"

"We can find your mom, if you tell us the truth."

"I thought you didn't know where she is."

"We have an idea. We need your help. Do you want to find your mom?"

"Okay. It's mine," the boy admits. "The shit is mine."

Nicosa runs his fingers over his eyes, picks up the tears that have gathered there, and seems to rub them into his face.

"Thank you," he says hoarsely. "Now you kill me. You put the nail right here."

Giovanni ignores the display. "You should talk. You are the biggest hypocrite," he murmurs. "Why should I tell the truth when all you do is lie?"

"I am the liar?" Nicosa cries. "You are the one we paid for to go to a psychiatrist and a drug counselor, who said you were clean."

"I don't use drugs, but nobody believes me," Giovanni says. "So I stopped trying to explain."

"We're listening," I say patiently. "This is your chance. Why did Muriel hide cocaine meant for you in a painting?"

"She was holding it for me."

"So you *are* selling?" Nicosa says.

"No, Papa. I do not sell; I do not use. I am a bank. I am a businessman, like you."

Nicosa growls, "Is that right?"

Sterling puts his hand out. "Let him speak."

"Everybody uses. It's not even about getting high anymore, it's just to do your stupid boring job and get through the day. The whole world is making money selling drugs, so why not Muriel, and other old people living on a pension?"

"*Mama mia*, you take their pension?"

"I make a smart investment for them. If you give me five hundred euros, I will invest it in the next drug lot and double your money in a month. The bank of cocaine," he adds with authority, "is a much better deal than a regular bank."

"You are the middleman," I say.

"*Cèrto.*"

"Who are your contacts?"

"They come up from the south."

"'Ndrangheta?" Nicosa flinches.

"What about the risk to the person who gives money?" I ask.

"No risk. Their hand is not dirty, and the profit is good. Sometimes the investors are asked to do a small favor, like hold the drugs, that's all."

It is now clear why Muriel left town. She knew the attack on Giovanni would lead the police toward mafia activity in Siena, possibly including the local branch of the bank of cocaine. I doubt very much that her partner had a recurrence of cancer. I expect Muriel and Sheila to be on the next plane to the Azores.

"Why did they beat you up, Giovanni?"

He clears his throat. "I am supposed to bring an amount every month, and I was behind. Muriel was my main customer, but she was drinking like a fish. She had no money to invest."

"You took the hit for her."

"I promise my customers to keep them out of it."

"Not only are you in danger of getting killed, but you are *helping* the mafias!" Nicosa cries. "You are giving them more money to buy more cocaine."

"That's the idea, Papa."

The phone inside the abbey starts to ring again.

Nicosa smashes the canvas across the bench, splintering glass and the wooden frame.

"Bitch! Fucking English bitch!"

"Hypocrite!" Giovanni shouts in return. "I only do exactly what you do! I learned from you!"

"This is not what I do!"

Giovanni screams at me. "Why did you tell him?"

"Because they tried to kill you, for God's sake! That's why Muriel split. She was afraid it would come back to her."

"You are not my aunt! If you were my real aunt, you would be on my side!"

"I *am* on your side."

"You're FBI, that's all you are!"

"Giovanni—"

"You and him together! Both liars and hypocrites!"

Grimacing with pain, he lopes across the courtyard on the crutch, slamming the kitchen door.

Nicosa is heaving. "That English bitch dragged him into it, you know that."

"I will make sure Muriel Barrett is picked up in London and interrogated."

Nicosa drops the wrecked painting at my feet. "Give her this."

The door opens and Giovanni appears, holding the phone.

"For Signorina Grey!" he sings out contemptuously.

Sterling says, "I need a drink."

When we get to the kitchen, whoever it was has already hung up. I ask if there's a way to see who called. Giovanni grabs the receiver and punches two digits. The screen says *Proibito*.

"What does that mean?"

" 'Prohibited.' You can't."

He turns away and opens the refrigerator and just stares into it. I'm thinking it was a blocked call from the American embassy about the recovered evidence from the vat. Nicosa enters the kitchen, turns on the taps, and sticks his head in the sink.

"There's nothing to eat," Giovanni observes.

Sterling ferrets out two beers. The phone rings again.

"Probably for me." I reach for it, but Nicosa, shaking water off his head like a lion, snatches it away.

"*Che vuole lei?*" he shouts angrily.

He listens. The person on the other end speaks swiftly and ends the call. Nicosa lowers the phone, strangely triumphant.

"You see? This is what I have been waiting for! What I have said all along. She's alive. These people have Cecilia."

"Mama is okay?"

"What did they say?" I urge. *"Exactly?"*

" 'We have your wife.' "

"Did they put her on the phone?" demands Sterling.

"No."

"Who are they?" Giovanni asks.

"Don't worry!" cries Nicosa, in a delirium. "They will call again."

"What do they want?"

"Two million euros."

Giovanni is wide-eyed. "Do we have that much money, Papa?"

Nicosa laughs exuberantly, drumming the boy's shoulders. "You see? Listen to the priest! God went looking. Your mother is alive!"

30

JUST AFTER dark, Zabrina and Yuri pass beneath the stone arch in the center of a dying coastal town in the province of Calabria—another set of stoplights in miles of unfinished shopping centers and buildings. Between getting lost, and pit stops due to stomach cramps, it has taken longer than they planned—almost nine hours on the motorbike—but by maintaining on Valium and caffeine, they keep pushing through the sweltering urban sprawl. The green hills of Tuscany don't even exist.

By the time they enter the narrow streets of the husk that is left of the old town center, Zabrina has collapsed against Yuri's back, crying softly from excruciating aches in her bones. She's crashing and can't hold on anymore. All he can do is shrug her off and keep going. He has the shakes too, and it's hard to follow her mumbled instructions to the massive public housing project called *la piccola città*, Little City. Because 'Ndrangheta is demanding higher fees for its contract to collect the garbage, household waste has been left in mountainous piles that block the streets, forcing them to keep making unexpected turns, getting more and more lost. Evening traffic comes to a standstill. Frustrated commuters are simply locking their cars, leaving them in the middle of the street, and going home. While they are stopped in a traffic jam, some skinny little jerk tries to rip Zabrina's bag right off the rack, but Yuri hits the gas, hops the curb, and drives thirty kilometers per hour on the sidewalk.

They find the road into the hills. When the anonymous concrete roofs of the housing project rise like a multistoried fortress, Zabrina remembers the crack house is in the middle sector, second floor, the corner apartment way at the end. The Little City is as spread out as a good-sized American shopping mall, over a thousand units in all. The sectors are connected by courtyards within courtyards, odd bridges and narrow walkways. Projecting from every wall is a slovenly jumble of tiny balconies, satellite dishes, networks of exposed electrical cables. The temperature is a hundred and eight degrees. There is not a breath of air, as if the entire community is being smothered under glass. Only the smallest children are wound up enough to play in this heat, kicking soccer balls in their underpants, or splashing in rubber pools while unemployed onlookers smoke cigarettes and soak their feet.

Neither the colliding tracks of blaring pop music nor the jarring reek of marijuana and roasting fish has any effect on the ragged, glassy-eyed junkies lounging on the peeling stairs below the corner apartment.

Fat Pasquale, Zabrina's cousin, is sitting on a chair, feet up on a cooler, listening to an iPod.

"Who's this guy?" he says by way of greeting, jerking a thumb at Yuri.

They are speaking in the dialect specific to Calabria.

"He's my boyfriend," Zabrina answers.

"You vouch for him?"

"I vouch for him."

Fat Pasquale opens the screen door. The kitchen is even hotter. The middle-aged woman with the black hair, now wearing an apron, sweat running down her temples, chops tomatoes at the sink.

"Maria Luisa gets a bigger allowance than me," she is saying.

"I know."

"Her husband was unlucky, that's all. He got in the way of a bullet. But my Peppino is a *capo*, who is in jail today because he is protecting all of you."

"I know."

The Puppet, wearing white trousers, a lizard belt, and an expensive linen shirt, is sitting at the kitchen table, legs crossed, relaxed. Before him is an array of bags of white powder, a digital scale, vials, and small spatulas used for paint, neatly lined up on butcher paper laid over the oilcloth. Disregarding the woman and her complaints, he gives instructions to his bodyguard, who is mixing the cut. That same guy was here last time; Zabrina recognizes the jade disk around his neck. She avoids looking at the boss's strange black wooden fingers, staring instead at the pattern of tulip tiles on the wall. *One tulip up. One tulip down.* The pain in her abdomen is unbearable.

"Three years in prison and sixteen months to go!" the woman goes on, shaking the knife at the Puppet. "You tell Don Toti I deserve a bigger allowance than Maria Luisa!"

The Puppet ignores this, peering closely at the powder dissolving in a small glass dish. He raises his prosthesis and motions to Yuri.

"You! Sit here."

Yuri slips into the chair, homing in on the ritual as the bodyguard loads the syringe.

"Who vouches for you?"

"Zabrina."

The Puppet's eyes rise to the girl waiting impatiently. Silently he nods, bestowing his approval on her guest.

"Where you from?" he asks the boy kindly.

Yuri stares hungrily, tightening a bandanna around his arm. "Albania," he replies.

The bodyguard passes the syringe to Yuri, who slips the needle into his vein.

"Are you listening to me?" demands the woman at the sink. "Will you talk to Don Toti?"

"Talk to him about what?"

The woman stares at the Puppet with stymied hate.

"Next," he says. "You, *signorina. Che bella!* I have seen you before. I would not forget such a beautiful face."

"Thank you," says Zabrina, but Yuri isn't standing up. *She needs her turn.* His torso contracts, like he's taking a very deep breath, then his eyes roll up, and he slumps sideways and falls out of the chair.

"Yuri!"

"What is this?" the Puppet inquires.

"I changed the cut," says the bodyguard. "Like you said."

"Too strong. Make it weaker."

The bodyguard goes back to the powder, ignoring the young man on the floor, who has gone into full-body convulsions.

Zabrina is on her knees, screaming, "Oh shit, oh shit, he's overdosing!"

"Get your boyfriend out of here."

"Help me. Do something! He's going to die."

"There is nothing I can do."

"Yes! Call a doctor. Get him to a hospital!"

She tries to drag Yuri's heavy body toward the door.

The woman, who has been watching all this with disgust, shakes her head and leaves the kitchen.

The Puppet looks at the watch strapped around the prosthesis. "Get them out of here."

The bodyguard sighs and calls, "Pasquale!" No answer. He gets up and opens the door.

"Pasquale isn't here. I don't know where he is."

"You're supposed to know!"

By opening the door, the bodyguard has allowed a score of skinny children in wet bathing suits to pour inside and rush to the refrigerator to shout for Kool-Aid. Seeing Yuri writhing on the floor causes them to stare, and then to all start shrieking at once—a chorus of high-pitched shrieking—some laughing, some shrieking just to shriek. Deep inside the apartment, there is banging.

"This place is a filthy zoo," says the Puppet. "Where is that witch? Where is the coffee?"

"What about him?" asks the bodyguard, pointing at Yuri.

"In five minutes he'll be dead," says the Puppet, and instructs the bodyguard to mix up another batch.

Zabrina is sobbing, trying to stop the convulsions by massaging Yuri's arms and legs. Meanwhile, looking as if she is doing nothing at all, the woman has meandered down the hall and unlocked the door to the bedroom.

"We need a doctor," she says. "A boy is overdosing."

Cecilia Maria Nicosa stumbles out, dressed in oversized men's sweatpants in the furnacelike heat, two thin ratty undershirts one over the other, to avoid indignity. Her auburn hair is piled up haphazardly. Once upon a time she had a pedicure. There are purple bruises down her arms and across the side of her face like the shadow of a hand.

"Where?" she croaks. She hasn't spoken out loud in days.

The woman points to the kitchen.

Cecilia moves unsteadily down the hall, enters the kitchen, and kneels by the boy.

"What is she doing here?" the Puppet demands. "She belongs inside!"

"You don't listen to me; I don't listen to you!" says the woman, and folds her fleshy arms.

Yuri is unresponsive. His breathing is rapid and he's sweating. Cecilia feels the pulse at his neck. His skin is burning hot.

"He's going into hyperthermia."

Zabrina raises wild eyes.

"What does that mean?"

"We have to lower his temperature, fast," says Cecilia. "We need to stop the spasms or he will have a heart attack. Get him in the bathtub and pour cold water over him and fill the tub with ice, if you have it." With their faces almost touching, Cecilia asks, "Do you have any Tylenol?"

"I have Valium," Zabrina says.

But Zabrina is not hearing the words, and Cecilia is barely aware of saying them, both shocked by recognition. Zabrina sees the lady's lip is swollen and a tooth is chipped. In the fever of withdrawal, she looks so deeply into the fierce eyes of the captive that she believes she can see the crystalline cells. The lady stares back intently. Detached from the cacophony of shrieking children and back-and-forth shouts between the woman and the Puppet, Cecilia and Zabrina realize that they know each other; they have met before, but where?

"Who are you?" whispers Zabrina.

Before Cecilia can answer, they are roughly jerked apart by the bodyguard and Fat Pasquale.

"Give him Valium!" Cecilia manages, before she is pushed back into the bedroom and the door is locked.

"What the hell is wrong with you?" the Puppet is shouting at the woman. "You listen in on every phone call; you know exactly what is going on with Nicoli Nicosa's wife. We are doing business here! I'm warning you, don't fuck with me!"

The woman turns her back.

"You!" she says to the children. "All of you! Help with this boy."

The kids and the woman drag Yuri's inert body to the bathroom and heave him into the tub, flooding it with cold water until his shorts float. One of them empties a tray of ice cubes.

"Isn't he going to take his clothes off?" asks a little child.

Inside the bedroom prison cell, Cecilia sinks onto the foam mattress, recalling where she saw the girl. She was a patient at the clinic. An intravenous drug abuser diagnosed with hepatitis C, an advanced disease that can be fatal. She tried to get her into treatment, but the girl never came back. And here she is, still shooting. At the thought of this, Cecilia springs up and pounds her fists against the wall. Of all the people in the world who might have recognized Cecilia, might have notified the police—who shows up to save the day but an addict. An ignorant, damaged, self-destructive, diseased addict.

In the bathroom, Yuri shivers violently as his eyes slowly open.

In the kitchen, Zabrina doesn't hesitate to sit in the chair. She gets her turn. The new cut has been adjusted by adding talcum powder. *One tulip up, one tulip down.*

31

I WON'T believe she is alive until I hear Cecilia's voice. While Nicosa goes off on a manic call to Sofri, instructing him to get the cash to pay the ransom *subito*, I am compartmentalizing the information we have, refusing to get keyed up. Somebody has to keep a clear head.

We can't miss the next opportunity to trace the calls.

"Nicoli? Can we use your office?"

"For what?"

"In the FBI, we have what we call a command post, the nerve center of a major case. I want to set one up in the bell tower. You already have the technology."

"Can I be there, too?" asks Giovanni.

"Come with me," I say, leading him from the kitchen to the entryway, where we can be alone. "Why should I trust you?"

He doesn't understand the question. "I'm worried about my mother."

"I hear that. It's a crisis now, but what about last week? Last year? All the time you've been running cocaine, putting your parents at risk?"

"I'm sorry. It's over."

"Just like that? Giovanni, you're a good kid, but you're all over the map. Smart in school, on the soccer team—but you still get sucked in. You don't like the way your father does business, do it differently. You're not him. You are not obligated to shoulder his mistakes. Make a statement—about who *you* are, not how pissed off you are at him. You need to figure out how you want to be in the world. I'm here if you want to talk."

"That's cool. Meanwhile, can I be in the command post?"

"No, you can't. I'm sorry, no minors."

"I'm sixteen!"

"In America, you'd be locked in a hotel room with a couple of agents, and the abbey would be under surveillance 24/7. If we had more manpower, that's exactly what we'd do."

"Why don't we?"

"Have the manpower? Because your father doesn't want to go to the police."

"Why can't I stay? What's safer than here?"

"You need looking after, and we have work to do."

" 'Looking after'? Are you serious?"

"Until you prove otherwise, yes."

We go back into the kitchen.

"Is there a responsible adult Giovanni can stay with?" I ask.

Nicosa says, "Padre Filippo."

Giovanni protests in rapid Italian.

"You have to be protected. That's the protocol," I say flatly.

Giovanni makes a face, grabs his keys and cell phone.

"You're not ready to drive."

"Are you serious?"

"Have a friend take you. Call when you get to the rectory."

"Thanks for trusting me," Giovanni replies sardonically, hopping out of the kitchen on his crutch.

The front door heaves shut. Nicosa smiles briefly with

something like gratitude. He believes that now he is in control: his wife has been kidnapped for ransom, a common crime he has the power to resolve, as long as we heed the kidnappers' warning and do not involve the police—and his rival, the chief.

"He accuses me of an act against God, against my *wife*?" Nicosa says of the Commissario as we ascend in the elevator. "He threatens to *arrest* me? Why? To prove Torre is great? I should have strangled him right there!" He points dramatically to the courtyard, a tiny puzzle piece below. "The police are lower than swine. They will never—never—come into this house."

I have to agree that right now it is better to leave them out of it. A kidnapping is unpredictable enough without an overlay of byzantine grudges and backstabbing disloyalties. I'd much rather deal with normal criminals. As the darkened floors of Renaissance art slip by, I tick off the tasks ahead: install phone taps to record and monitor calls. Establish communication with the kidnappers. Assign roles of negotiator and coach. Sterling has already been dispatched to Chris for the necessary equipment.

Trickier is Nicosa's insistence that we also do not inform Dennis Rizzio in Rome that contact has been made with the alleged kidnappers. He believes the situation is too porous. If they get a whiff of the authorities, they will kill her. I am not willing to take that risk. This is no time to get all bollixed up in Bureau procedure. When we have something solid, I will inform my boss.

We arrive at the top of the tower. Nicosa hops off the elevator, strutting around like a rooster in his airborne office, while I wonder what crazy arrogance had convinced me that we could pull this off on our own—and at what risk to my career at the Bureau?

The real command post in Los Angeles, created for response to terrorist attacks and natural disasters, is stocked with food and water. Okay, got that. There are dozens of TV monitors and laptops, to say nothing of hundreds of agents. I angle the flat-screen so it faces the empty leather couches, and make sure Nicosa's computer is online. Nice. Just like home. As for a timeline to keep track of unfolding events, instead of the familiar, low-tech roll of brown paper usually tacked across the wall, I lay pieces of printer pages edge to edge and secure them with cellophane tape, leaning back with a sigh. It's amazing what you can make out of desperation and a few ordinary household items.

The intercom buzzes and Sofri appears minutes later, carrying a small duffel. He gives Nicosa a strong embrace, patting him on the back.

"Did they call again?" Sofri asks.

"Not yet."

"Right now they're playing cat and mouse," I say.

"I have the money." Sofri takes off his blazer. Folding the sleeves precisely as a haberdasher, he lays it across the back of a chair. "What do we do, *topolina*?"

"We have to wait," Nicosa interrupts, before I can answer. "Exactly what I said in the beginning."

The intercom buzzes. They both jump.

It is Sterling.

When the glass elevator surfaces, it is filled with the alarming shape of a man dressed for war. Sterling, wearing boots, camos, and the black dragon T-shirt, brings soldierly weightiness into the room—the real possibility of someone getting killed. He shoulders the rucksack while carrying a sniper bag in one hand, a scuffed suitcase made of yellow plastic in the other. Nicosa and Sofri step away. This is not their movie.

"How are you all doin' today?" Sterling asks, setting the equipment down.

"*Adesso non lo so.*" Sofri chuckles. *Now I don't know.* "I think I felt better before you arrived."

On the other hand, I am feeling decidedly happier, now that Sterling's here. His presence conveys confidence in the mission. We're going to do this together. My mood of caution starts to lift, replaced by the adrenaline rush of engagement and the pleasure of knowing what needs to be done and finally getting down to it.

"This'll be good." I'm clearing space on the desk for the yellow suitcase.

"What is in there? A bomb?"

"An electroshock machine," Sofri quips. "In case we get a heart attack."

Sterling opens the case to reveal a mini switchboard with molded foam compartments for headsets and a tape recorder.

"It's to monitor the phone," he explains. "From now on, nobody talks to the kidnappers unless Ana or I am listening."

"Nicoli will be the primary contact," I say. "You're the one who speaks to the bad guys. Do you think you can do that?"

"Yes."

"We are going to insist they let you talk to Cecilia. Before any negotiation, before anything, you say, 'I want to hear her voice.'"

He snorts derisively. "You know how it is in the coffee business? Liars and thieves! The growers and the shippers and the kids who steal from the cash register. You don't think someone who deals with these people every day is not capable of saying, 'Let me talk to my wife'?"

I explain gently that sometimes it isn't words you hear. "Sometimes there are only screams. They could torture her to get to you."

Nicosa scratches at his head.

"I can do it," Sofri volunteers.

"You?" says Nicosa. "You're the one who will need the electroshock machine. No. It's me."

Sterling resumes: "Ana is the negotiator. She sits right next to you and tells you what to say."

"*Buona fortuna,*" murmurs Sofri.

"I'm writing you notes. You're repeating exactly what I write. Sofri, can you simultaneously translate, so we can hear you in our headphones?"

"I'll do my best."

"Sofri's listening in and translating. Nicosa's talking. Sterling's providing tactical support for how to recover the victim."

Sofri pats his forehead with a silk handkerchief. "*Mio Dio!*"

"Any other questions?"

"How long will this take?"

"No way to know," Sterling says. "Could be hours, could be days."

Nicosa's cell phone rings. We look up expectantly, but he waves us off—it's Giovanni, reporting that he has arrived at the rectory of Padre Filippo.

"You see? He is a good boy," Nicosa says, opening the refrigerator to a row of glistening wine bottles. "How about a drink?"

"We don't advise it, sir," Sterling says, expressionless.

Nicosa glowers. "Nobody made you *capo.*" But he closes the door.

BY FOUR in the afternoon, when the sun has probed each window on its way around the tower, we have turned on the TV and ended up watching *Die Hard* dubbed into Italian. Not really watching it, just someplace to put your eyeballs. There have been five other calls to the household throughout the day, all noted on the timeline, none relevant. The level of anxiety in the room is holding steady at 80 percent. The level of violence on the plasma screen is downright quaint.

It is comforting to watch actors destroy large amounts of phony glass. I wonder what it means to die, hard.

As much as I want to reclaim Sterling, even the slightest touch would be against the professional code of conduct we have tacitly agreed to follow as long as we are working the case. We make sure to sit apart; all of us are sprawled on the couches and leather chairs, with the paradoxical sense of a family held together by the suspension of time, like waiting for a baby to be born, or Thanksgiving dinner to be served.

Yet even across the room I feel it when Sterling's body stiffens. He jumps up, grabs the gun bag, and unzips a compartment that holds a Walther PPK/S 9mm and a cleaning kit. Sitting cross-legged on the rug in front of the TV, he fieldstrips the gun, removing the magazine and the front of the trigger guard.

Sofri and Nicosa watch, fascinated.

"What does a private security company do?" Sofri wonders.

"Whatever the customer wants. Bodyguard. Protect assets. Fight a war."

"Have you ever been hired on a kidnapping?"

Sterling works a soft brass brush over the residue on the outside of the barrel. "All the time."

"How do they usually end?"

"It all depends on patience, sir. Patience and negotiation. Mind if I have one of those?"

Sterling reaches for a bowl of chocolates.

"Sure, of course," says Nicosa, handing it over. "Can I get you something else? You didn't care for my food?"

"It looked great, but I'm not much hungry these days."

"He just came back from a mission," I explain. "Still adjusting to the concept of lunch."

"Really?" says Sofri, leaning forward, elbows on knees. "Can you tell us what the mission was?"

"All I can say is, I quit."

This is news to me. Anything he says would be news.

"Was it difficult?" Sofri asks.

Sterling doesn't answer. He's reassembling the Walther, pulling the slide back onto the barrel and checking the alignment.

Sofri and Nicosa watch every move.

"On this mission," Sofri continues, "was it too much fighting, people getting killed?"

"Is that why I quit, you mean?"

Sofri nods. "If I may ask."

Sterling finishes off with gun oil and a cloth. "We quit because they wouldn't give us holiday pay."

"Holiday pay?"

"That's right. Promised, wouldn't deliver, so we walked."

Nicosa laughs. "It's the same in every business!"

But I know that's not all. That's not why he showed up in my bedroom in the middle of the night, looking like a refugee, looking like something happened that was powerful enough to permanently take away his appetite.

The phone rings.

Everyone scurries into position. Sofri stumbles over a wire. We put on headphones and move to the desk, where four chairs are waiting. Sterling checks the tape recorder and gives the nod. Nicosa hits the phone.

"*Prègo.*"

The conversation takes place in Italian, with Sofri softly speaking English into our ears.

"Who are you?"

"We have your wife."

"I want to hear her voice," says Nicosa.

"Not possible."

"Why not? If she's alive, put her on the phone."

"We want the money."

"I have the money. But first I hear her speak."

"We want two million euros."

"I have it, believe me."

I write him a note. He hesitates, but I urge him on.

"Tell me where to meet," he reads.

They hang up. Nicosa rips off the headphones and kicks away from the desk.

"Could you get a trace?" I ask Sterling.

"Disposable cell phone."

"Don't worry," I tell Nicosa. "You did great."

"This is not going to work," he says angrily. "You, telling me what to say—they know something is wrong. It doesn't sound right."

Sofri intercedes. "You see, first you must talk to the right person. In Italy, the boss never speaks for himself. He is always one or two steps behind the one who is speaking"— which is exactly what Dennis Rizzio told me.

I nod. "I'm sure that with his connections, Nicoli could speak to whomever he pleases. Do you want to make a call?"

Nicosa shakes his head. "You must wait for the courtesy of *their* call."

We agree that next time Nicosa will ask for the boss, as well as insist that he hear Cecilia's voice. He jerks the refrigerator open and defiantly pours a long shot of vodka.

NIGHT PASSES in fits and starts. Some hours go quickly; sometimes the clock doesn't move. The TV stays on until Nicosa falls asleep on the couch with his mouth open, and then Sofri clicks it off and settles in one of the corn chip chairs, tipping it up like a recliner. The lights are low. Sounds are not lost way up here; crickets and the rustling of treetops blow in with the cold air. Sitting on the floor in an arc of moonlight, Sterling is fieldstripping and cleaning the Walther for the third or fourth time.

I settle beside him. "You're not eating, and you're not sleeping."

He doesn't answer.

"That's a very clean weapon. Cleanest I've ever seen."

He raises a warning finger. "Don't nag."

I watch him cleaning the gun. Meticulous. Obsessive.

"I've been there. That's all."

I went through it after the shooting incident—uncontrollable thoughts and some really bad insomnia. Like a vicious case of poison oak, it won't go away, and everything you do to calm it only makes it worse. Especially touching it.

Sterling's face is tight with concentration as his fingers rub the soft cloth back and forth. It seems as though he isn't going to answer, but then—

"Nobody knows what I see through those sights."

I put my arm around his shoulders. Massage the rigid muscles of his neck.

"It was a situation that gave us no way out," he says.

"I understand."

"No point in discussing it."

"Okay." I look over at the windows of black sky. "It's just that I miss you, baby. Sometimes it doesn't even seem like we're a couple anymore. I feel like you keep shutting me down. On the other hand, you came back from the mission to be with me. I guess. I'm confused. Why did you come back?"

"Chris said you were in trouble."

"Is that all?"

"I wouldn't be here if I didn't care."

His tone is flat.

"You'll neither confirm nor deny?" I say, playfully.

"Pitiful," he says of his own malfunctioning. "I know."

"No," I say. "It's just hard right now, for both of us."

"I hear you."

"Be in touch," I say.

He nods. I get up and lie on the other chair, adjusting it so my feet are in the air, like Sofri's, as if we are on an airplane flying over a blacked-out continent. Sterling continues to clean his gun. My mind drifts toward sleep, lulled by the sound of Nicosa's rhythmic breathing. A million images rush my mind at warp speed, and then I'm floating in a memory of being with Cecilia.

It was when I first arrived, and she had wished in some way to reveal herself to me, craving understanding beyond the wealthy circumstances of her life; she wanted me to know she was not happy in the austere halls of the abbey. So we went to the place in Siena that she said most moves her heart—and perhaps her husband's, too—a medieval hospital and orphanage called Santa Maria della Scala. In Los Angeles you take a person to Dodger Stadium; here you wind up staring at a 1440 fresco called *The Care and Healing of the Sick*.

"Contained in this picture are the reasons I wanted to become a doctor," she said. "But I am not that kind of doctor."

"Why not?"

"I became a doctor to serve," she said. "Like them."

"But you are. You're helping people."

"Not the way I want to be."

She held a yellow patent leather bag to the bosom of her black knit dress, clutching tightly, gazing with hunger at the painting that showed the huge vaulted room in which we were standing as it had been in the fifteenth century, when sick pilgrims and abandoned children were received by hospital friars, who had renounced the world and devoted themselves to service.

"Those were wealthy people, like us," Cecilia said, pointing to an attendant in a hospital tunic, washing the feet of a terrified young man with a grievous wound to the thigh. "But they became oblates, those who give everything they own to the hospital, including their labor, for life."

"What did they get in return?"

She smiled grimly. "Freedom?"

Now I know that she had been talking about the awful contradictions of her life: a rich, attractive husband who has other women; a murderous organization to which she is forced to pay money for the privilege of saving lives. The air in the empty ancient ward was still and smelled of polished wood. Quiet voices of tour guides speaking other languages could be heard from the galleries.

"Children were left here with notes that told their names, and who their parents were," Cecilia said. "So when times were better, they could be reunited with their families. They weren't just abandoned."

We stood together in front of the painting.

"When Papa used to talk about my relative, Ana, in America, I pictured you wearing a ruffled dress and patent leather shoes. I don't know where I got that, probably from a movie."

"I hated dresses until I was sixteen," I told her. "That was me, in shorts and flip-flops. I had to hose off the sand before they let me in the house."

"'California' always sounded magical," Cecilia said. "When I was in medical school, I tried to do my residency in California. The best facilities. The most exciting cities. It was an impossible dream. We are put in our lives and that's it."

When we could find no more messages in the mauve and ochre pigments, we were drawn to a tall grated window at the end of the hall, where a breeze coming in from the mountains brought with it the sound of birdsong and church bells, stirring the pigeon feathers caught outside in the terracotta brick.

"We used to have a beautiful bronze statue here, *Risen Christ* by Lorenzo Vecchietta, a Renaissance masterpiece, one of the great treasures of Siena. It looked so contemporary and alive. The expression of suffering was so aching, and the hand reaching out so soft and real—but it was stolen right out of the chapel of this hospital. Why do we agree to live like this?" Cecilia exclaimed in frustration.

Through the grated window was the city, colorless in the pressing heat of noon.

WHEN I awake in the chair, something is scrabbling around the edges of the tower. A blackbird has flown through an open window. We catch it in a wastebasket and let it go.

32

POWERED BY multiple shots of Nicosa Family espresso, we are at our stations by first light, but the next call doesn't come until three long hours later, at 9:10 a.m.

"Do you have the money?" asks the voice.

"I told you. Yes."

"Okay."

Silence.

"Okay what?" Our fearless leader cannot hide his impatience. "Do you realize you are speaking with Nicoli Nicosa?"

"Yes."

I pass a note. *Ask his name.*

"What is your name, *signore*?"

No answer.

"I need to know who I am talking to. It's only polite, wouldn't you agree?"

The man hangs up.

"Sounds nervous," Sterling says.

"Is that good?" asks Sofri.

In truth it's neither good nor bad, but worth noting on the timeline, which now shows two pieces of intel from the kidnappers in the last twenty-four hours. I am not surprised the night has passed unbroken by a call. Often the lowlifes are too drunk or stoned during those hours to do business.

We eat. We read the news online. Sterling, wearing just the camos, does his wake-up routine: one hundred crunches, one hundred push-ups, three minutes of shadow boxing. The next call comes within the hour.

"Imagine yourself in my position," Nicosa tells the kidnapper. "I am her husband. I want to know how my wife is. I want to hear her voice. Can't you put her on for just a minute?"

He is not used to commoners slamming the phone down.

"What the hell is going on? What kind of game do they think they are trying to play?"

"They don't even know," I tell him. "They're flying by the seat of their pants."

In the afternoon, because I am the girl, I go back to the main house for supplies. After the constant breezes through the tower, the courtyard feels like a suffocating sauna. I'm thinking we are in for a siege, and some food prep in the tower kitchen might be required. Stepping back out of the elevator, arms full of towels and toilet paper and carrying a bag of fruit, cans of tuna in olive oil, instant bean soup, and cold leftover pasta, I find the team in the middle of another call. Slipping on the headphones, I hear a different voice. This one is older, with nothing to prove.

"I have instructions," says the new voice.

Nicosa answers, "Tell me, please."

"We will return Signora Nicosa to you after you give us the money."

The mention of her name makes me hopeful. Not "the crazy bitch," not even "your wife." She is still a person to them.

"No police."

Nicosa agrees. "Absolutely not. You have my word."

There is the sound of whispered conversations on the kidnapper's side.

"The cash must be in euros."

"Agreed. Where do we meet?"

"We will tell you shortly. Take the Ferrari. Drive with Signorina Grey."

"Cecilia's sister?"

"Yes, her sister."

I bite my thumb.

You're doing great, Nicoli. Please don't blow it; just agree.

"Why Signorina Grey?"

"The American sister will bring the money. If not, no agreement."

I nod vigorously.

"Okay."

"You will listen on the cell phone for instructions where to meet. If we see that you are followed, we will kill Signora Nicosa immediately."

Nicosa swallows. "Understood. And we will meet my wife there? Where we bring the money?"

"She will be in another place. She will be unharmed. When we have the money, we will tell you where she is. We will call you in the car in five minutes."

"Now, please, can I hear her voice?"

Scuffling, soft breathing.

"Cecilia?"

"It's me."

The voice is timid and weak. But it is Cecilia.

The line goes dead, but I am fired up. We're closer than we've ever been. Sterling joins Nicosa where he's standing at a window, looking completely drained.

"I know you know that dude on the phone," Sterling says. "You were using the Italian informal form of address. Who is he?"

"Cosimo Umberto."

"The Puppet?"

Nicosa turns from the window and raises an ironic eyebrow. "You know him, too?"

"He is known to the Bureau," I say. "He's a powerful man, the head of a district of mafia families. Can we trust his promises?"

Sofri and Nicosa exchange glances. Sofri, stroking his mustache uneasily, finally gives the nod.

"Yes."

"He wants the money. And to prove to me he is the big guy, the *capomandamento*," explains Nicosa.

"You two have a history. We saw him outside Giovanni's hospital room."

Nicosa goes tight. "I told you before. He was paying his respects."

"And threatening you?"

"That's not important now."

Sterling pulls on the gulf-blue Oakleys and picks up the sniper bag. I'm opening the duffel and checking the cash.

Sterling's face bends close, and his voice is quiet. "Sure you want to do this?"

"Absolutely."

"You understand that you are possibly the target."

"I know. We should have a tac team, but there's no time to involve Rizzio."

"They figured out they've got your sister, but they still want you. They want it both ways—the money and you. Feels like a setup." Sterling shakes his head. "I don't like it."

"It depends on the drop," I tell him. "If it's a public place, and we think it's secure, we'll go with it. If not, we abort."

"Fair enough. I'll take Chris. We'll be in contact via cell phone hookup and visuals." Sterling's deep green eyes hold mine. "You won't see me, but I'll be there."

"Got it," I affirm, a host of implications squeezed into two quick words. Every time we part, it's an unknown.

Sofri and Nicosa, meanwhile, seem frozen in place. All of a sudden, the posturing has turned real. Sterling strides past them, smacking each one on the back, hard.

"Are we playing this?" he wants to know.

BUCKLED INTO the Ferrari and hurtling downhill, Nicosa says, "Tell me what bullshit is this, two different locations? You give them the money, but she's somewhere else?"

"It's not uncommon—it's called the double-drop. They think they can protect themselves that way, but once we make the exchange, Sterling and Chris will be on their tail, and then it's over. We'll get them. And Cecilia."

For the next forty-five minutes we follow orders on the cell phone that have us driving loops around Siena. It is a charade without logic, meant to ensure that we're not being followed, no doubt with mafia homies looking out along the way. The old woman with her feet up on a box, crocheting with a tiny needle. The waiter in an outdoor café, shredding cheese. The candle maker in the tourist shop window, folding curls of wax into a rose. Snitches, druggies, businesspeople, wannabes, killers—the whole network of cowed citizenry, keeping track of the red Ferrari. Inside the walls. Outside the walls. Sterling and Sofri are with Chris in the nondescript Fiat, listening to the instructions we are receiving, holding back at varying distances.

Daylight is still bright and scorching when the Puppet instructs us to park the car on Via di Pantaneto. Then I am to continue alone on foot.

"How will Signora Grey know your man?" Nicosa asks through the earpiece.

"By his colors," the creep replies.

Now we are back on familiar ground. The coded Sienese response. The maddening symbolism. By this time I realize, with some relief, that the ultimate destination, to which they have been steering us all along, is Il Campo, the huge crowded plaza where the Palio was held. They plan to pull off the exchange and blend into the crowd, while limiting our opportunities for pursuit. All right by me. The public venue is safer than an isolated meet.

I tell the team: "It's a go."

When we have parked the Ferrari, and I am buckling on the bulletproof vest that came out of Chris's trunk, Nicosa removes his sunglasses. His eyes are softened with emotion.

"Please, let me do this."

"Sorry. It's in my job description."

"It's my fault; I let Cecilia go—"

"You didn't. She was taken."

He stares, at a loss. "God protect you."

He kisses me rapidly on each cheek. I hoist the duffel with the money and the tracking device inside and get out of the car. I could not have been an FBI agent all these years without also asking the question that if Nicosa's ties to the mob are as real as Dennis Rizzio thinks they are, could he not, right now, be setting me up? And what if Sterling, for all his assurances of covering my back, is still not totally in his right mind? Trust whom? Where? Only the clear bright image of the victim's face before me keeps me walking straight ahead.

"I'm on Banchi di Sotto," I say into the microphone hidden in my hair. "Going into the Campo."

"Which entrance?" comes Sofri's voice.

Of course! There are eleven!

"Jesus, I don't know!"

"Which side of the Mangia Tower?"

"East. I *think* it's east."

"Is there a café that says Pizzicheria?" Sterling asks.

"Pizzi—what?"

"Tell us what you see."

"Okay, here's a street sign. I can't pronounce it—Mezzolom—?"

"Mezzolombardi-Rinaldi," Sofri says, and then he and Nicosa overlap. "She's at Palazzo Ragnoni."

"Gotcha!" Sterling says. He's in position somewhere, looking through the sniper rifle, and I am in his sights.

"Going to the fountain."

"Copy that."

Although it is barely five days since the Palio, you would never know the square had recently been filled to capacity with life-and-death drama, spectators clinging to every ledge. The track of special yellow earth has vanished without a trace. Where there had been horses crazy to run, jockeys beating one another, mad ecstasy, and underhanded deals on which the fate of the universe seemed to turn, now there are placid globs of tourists checking out café menus, and international students playing Frisbee. Only the *contrada* banners remain hanging from the palazzos for the second Palio race in August.

I sit on the edge of the Fonte Gaia, the Fountain of Joy, which was totally obscured by human bodies during Palio. How little I understood about Cecilia then, and about the entanglements of this family with the mafia beast, which has infiltrated this proud city through the sewers, despite *contrada* members patrolling every corner. Without moving my head, I scan for potential traps.

"All clear?" asks Sterling.

"So far."

I breathe the funky mist coming off the fountain. The she-wolf statue spits a docile stream as on this balmy evening the drama becomes much smaller than the grand pageantry of Palio, down to a subtle eye movement between an American woman perched on the stone and a balding Italian man wearing a white polo shirt and an Oca scarf coming toward her, who stops in the middle of the piazza, turns his back, and lights a cigarette.

"That's the contact, wearing green and white. The Oca colors."

Nicosa says something urgently into the earpiece, maybe Sofri does, too, but I don't hear them. I am in vapor lock, floating in a pool of now. I hoist the duffel and walk toward the man, who is standing alone, larger and more distinct than anything in the square. Objects become magnified and time slows down. I see the sunlight on the bald spot of his skull, reflecting hot as tin. I see the brown uniforms of a Boy Scout troop, and an orange Frisbee slicing by. The multi-colored *contrada* scarves flying from the tourist shack snap in a silent wind.

I hear the first rifle shot. You wouldn't hear it unless you were listening with extraordinary care. Not even the pigeons move. I don't stop walking. As far as I know, the gunfire does not concern me. Ten meters from the contact, though, there is a second blast. This one is heard by everybody. It echoes off the palazzos like the *mortaretto* cannon at the start of the race, sending tourists diving under tables and birds into the air. The balding man lighting the cigarette drops to the ground with sudden impact, as if he fell from the sky. A red micro-cloud of atomized blood and brain appears and vanishes.

I swerve slightly and keep on going, still carrying the duffel, through the first and second waves of panicked bystanders—not like during the riot after Palio, careening into one another's arms, laughing and crying, but a one-way, horror-driven stampede for all eleven exits, leaving the sprawling corpse in the Oca scarf in the center of the piazza, bleeding out on the sloping brick.

33

BACK IN the car, we are instantly surrounded by the clanging blare of ambulances and police.

"My God, what happened?" Nicosa says.

"Sterling took out the contact."

"*Why?*"

"I can't tell you right now, but I promise you, he had a reason."

"He's crazy! I knew it!"

"We're okay," I tell Nicosa soothingly. "Stay calm and just drive normally."

I have no idea what went down, except that I am still gripping the bag with two million euros, and the chance to recover Cecilia has vanished.

Everything was set. Why is Sterling taking shots at a kidnap exchange?

It takes thirty agonizing minutes to drive just a few blocks and make it outside the walls, during which there is no communication through the earpiece from anyone. My growing fear is that Sterling went on a rampage caused by post-traumatic combat stress. His behavior over the last few days could add up to that; with a loaded weapon in his hand, he might have snapped.

"We killed their man," Nicosa says. "They'll murder her. They'll murder all of us. My son, the whole family." He looks into the rearview mirror, swerving crazily across the highway. "They could be following us now."

"Nobody is following us."

"What went wrong?"

"We'll find out. Take a breath; you're doing great. Just get us to the abbey without running into a tree."

He is taking the hills at seventy kilometers per hour, churning up gravel like sparks. Still, by the time we roar through the gates, Chris's Fiat is already parked, and Sterling is in the kitchen, downing glasses of water, the sniper bag slung over a chair.

Barely through the door, Nicosa gasps, "What happened?"

"Took the shot," Sterling says. "Had to be done."

"You murder a man in the middle of Il Campo? We had an agreement with *Cosimo Umberto*! They promised to return my wife. Now there will be a massacre."

"They were lying. The plan was to draw Ana out. Get her out there in plain view. They had a sniper set up in a third-story window."

"How do you know?" Nicosa demands.

Sterling reiterates what he said to me: "Nobody sees what I see in that gun sight."

His face is tight; he's full of adrenaline after the kill.

"And what was that?" asks Nicosa, barely restrained.

Sterling crooks two fingers and jabs at his own eyes, indicating that this is what he saw:

"The eyes."

Nicosa doesn't understand. "Whose eyes?"

"The bald man in the Oca scarf. He should have had more faith in his own guy," Sterling says. "Instead, he looks up at the last minute, wanting to be sure everything's going according to plan. Big mistake. Because when you're looking through the magnifying scope of a Winchester 70, you can see something as small as the movement of an eye. I follow the eyes to where the subject's looking—a third-floor window, where a shooter is set up with a sniper rifle, tracking Ana across the piazza. In half a second, I'm on target and the threat is eliminated. Half a second later, the contact is down, too. The contact looked up at his own sniper," Sterling explains. "He was a trained assassin, aiming an incapacitation weapon at Ana. There was no other choice."

Nicosa slams a palm against the wall.

"Why is all this necessary?" he cries in anguish, while I picture a swarm of complications when the police examine the bodies—not the least of which will be the failure to inform my superior that I was involved in a ransom negotiation that went south. I'm feeling light-headed, not only because of recriminations at the Bureau, but because the hope of recovering the victim made me expose myself to the mafia's double cross.

"How is Sofri?" I ask hoarsely.

"When I left his apartment he was still pretty shaken up. Told him to go out and get a cup of coffee and make sure he's seen around the neighborhood."

"Mother of God," says Nicosa. "Were you inside Sofri's apartment?"

"Yes, sir."

"Did you shoot that gun out of his window?"

"It provided the clearest view of the piazza."

Nicosa smacks his own head. "Are you crazy?"

"Nobody saw, Nicoli. It's not like I was hangin' out the window like Billy the Kid."

"The only way to know where the shot came from would be sophisticated gunshot analysis," I say.

"You realize the Puppet will immediately murder Cecilia in retaliation," Nicosa says. "It's over. Everything is lost."

"I sincerely trust that is not the case. All I can tell you is they were prevented from killing Ana. That was my objective."

Nicosa has no idea how breathtaking that is, and what clear-sighted concentration is required. Half a second and on target—twice—at four hundred yards. Through all of this, Sterling has been watching me intently. It's like the light has come back to his eyes. *He saved my life.* Inside I'm crumbling, but—*code of conduct*—all I do is put my arm around his shoulders as he sits in the chair; he puts an arm around my waist. We pull each other close and tight. Nothing has ever felt so good. He's here. He's sane.

"Ah," says Nicosa, scrutinizing. "What is this?" He smiles. *"Lei due sono insieme."*

"What did he say?"

Sterling duly translates: "That the two of us are together."

Screw the code of conduct. I kiss the top of his sweaty, buzz-cut head.

But Nicosa has another question.

"Where is Giovanni?"

The last time Giovanni was in our hands was way back yesterday, when he said he had arrived at the priest's. Since then, we haven't heard a word. A call to Giovanni's cell goes to voice mail. A call to the rectory catches Padre Filippo by surprise. He never saw the kid. Never knew he was supposed to have arrived. Not for the first time, Giovanni flat-out lied to his dad. Now it is dark, the suspects know that two of their guys have been taken out, and Giovanni's absence seems a lot more worrisome than a rebellious sixteen-year-old out making trouble.

Nicosa's eyes are wide as he considers these alternatives. It must be like the primal terror of realizing you have lost your child in the supermarket aisle. He could be anywhere in the wide world.

"When your son's in trouble, where does he go?" Sterling asks calmly. "Who does he turn to? A girlfriend? A buddy?"

"The territory," says Nicosa.

He means the Oca district, specifically the Fontebranda fountain, around which information pivots like the wheeling doves. Of course Giovanni would go back to his childhood neighborhood, where the *contrada* protects its members. Where there are plenty of the bank of cocaine customers to drop in on, or drug contacts if reality gets too tough. On the other hand, anyone looking for the boy would go there, too.

Sterling says, "I'll find him."

"You'll never find him," Nicosa says. "Nobody of Oca will talk to you. I'd better go."

"Better if you and I stay here," I say. "In case the kidnappers call."

We agree Nicosa will alert the *contrada* members that Sterling will be pounding the streets. But none of us can go any farther without food. While juggling calls, Nicosa mixes up a quick omelet with potatoes, sausage, and basil while we put together bread, fresh hard goat cheese, prosciutto, and slices of melon. A double shot of the house espresso, and Sterling is fortified and out the door. I follow to the mailbox car, and we kiss in the balmy night. Up on my toes, I reach around his neck for more.

"Come back soon."

"I will."

And then he's gone. Nicosa appears in the kitchen doorway, looking in the frank courtyard light like he's aged twenty years since I first met him. He holds out his hand.

"Would you mind waiting with me?" he asks.

We choose the small room where the hospital bed used to be, since returned to normal, a landline phone in place, connected to the tape recorder in the tower. I've got a legal pad and the remote receiver from the kitchen. As soon as we settle onto the white couches, fatigue hits like an iron gong. Nicosa flicks on the TV, but within minutes we are both plummeting into deep unconsciousness.

In the dream, I am in a car driving at night. The headlights reveal empty fields. In the distance, there is a palazzo on a mountain—like the one we always pass on the way into Siena—a resort, with lighted umbrellas and molten golden light dripping down the furrows of the hill. The headlights illuminate the fields of sunflower faces weirdly, like inmates on stalks. On the horizon there is a fire.

The phone is ringing—not the landline, but my cell— buzzing in my breast pocket like a device to jump-start the heart. Jerking awake, I realize that in my sleep, I have been smelling smoke. At the same time, someone is pounding on the front door.

"I have Giovanni, but we can't get through," Sterling says over the cell. "He was in Oca, like we thought."

"Where are you now?"

"Bottom of the mountain."

"What time is it?"

"Two in the morning."

"What's going on?"

"The road up to the abbey is blocked."

Nicosa is snoring away. With the phone to my ear, I open the door and stand on the threshold. The neighbor, Aleandro, has run over from the olive farm, carrying a flashlight and shouting, *"C'è un fuoco!"*

"Aleandro is trying to say something," I tell Sterling. "What is *fuoco*?"

"Fire. There's been an accident," Sterling says. "Can't see it from here. There's an ambulance and a couple of fire trucks. Looks like a car caught on fire."

"I can see it from the house," I say, looking where Aleandro is pointing.

The sky is lit by flames, banging orange light off the low

cloud cover, under which you can see black smoke boiling up. I'm shivering in the chill as I recall images of California wildfires feeding on dry brush. Explosive fireballs that jump the road. Firefighters trapped with no way out.

"Are you in danger?" I ask Sterling.

"No; they've contained the fire around the car. Put Aleandro on. I'll tell him it's okay."

I hand the cell to the older man. He speaks in Italian to Sterling while nodding grimly. A fire let loose in these hills would be catastrophic. He gives me back the phone. I repeat *"Grazie!"* until our worthy neighbor waves good-bye and retreats into the night.

"How is it down there?" I ask Sterling.

"We'll just have to wait it out."

"How's Giovanni?"

"Just about like you'd expect. Aw, hell!" Sterling exclaims. "Here comes the coroner. Looks like there were fatalities. Go back to sleep, darlin'. This is going to take a while."

Two hours later, Sterling and Giovanni are permitted to drive past the site. Under lights set up by crime scene specialists, the smoking, blackened skeleton of Sofri's black Renault can be seen. As they pass, Sterling gently draws Giovanni close and turns the boy's head so he is prevented from viewing the corpse. They arrive at the abbey at the same time as the Oca priest, who had followed them up the hill. I open the door and stare at their bleak, heartbroken faces.

Sterling takes me in his arms. "They killed Sofri."

We all gather close, wondering what might be the kindest way to wake Nicosa from his sleep.

34

WHEN WE push through the wooden doors of the *questura*, every detective and file clerk looks up, as if they had been waiting for us to appear. Even spookier is the universal expression of pity in their eyes, tracking as we follow Inspector Martini through the bullpen. Not sympathy. Pity. The odd looks cause my skin to prickle; once again, I'm a clueless outsider. Nicosa, wearing a coal-black suit, skin as transparent as skim milk, is stopped at every desk for a handshake or a glancing hug. Deferentially, I wait a pace or two behind, feet planted and hands clasped in the rest position, as if I were a Secret Service agent protecting the president.

Inspector Martini guides us up a marble staircase with a peculiar bad smell that leads to the executive offices on the second floor, steering us through a jumble of cubbyholes with scummy windows that obscure what could be a spectacular view of the main cathedral in the Piazza del Duomo. Instead, everybody's face is turned toward a computer screen. At the far end of the room, a pair of mahogany doors with brass knobs opens to the private office of Commissario Dottore Enrico Salvi.

Once more I am impressed with how thin he is for a man with such a heavy-duty job: how narrow the shoulders, how feminine the waist becomes when you have to cinch a belt that tightly. The white collar of an impeccably pressed blue-striped shirt frames a bony face that is shaped like a violin, all cheekbones and hollow eyes. The man is underweight, possibly ill, but remarkably lithe as he slips out from behind the desk, extending a manicured hand.

"My deepest sympathies. This is a terrible situation."

"We are grateful for your attention," Nicosa replies.

Inspector Martini slides two packs of cigarettes across the varnished surface of the desk, and the Commissario accepts them off her fingertips without a glance. She excuses herself and backs out, closing the double doors like an obedient servant.

"Sofri was an exceptional man. He will be missed. How well did you get to know him, Agent Grey?"

"Unfortunately, I didn't know him very long, but in the time that I did he became like an uncle to me. That's why I'm here. It's not just official business."

The chief gives a little shrug. Official. Unofficial. Depends which side of the page is up.

"How can I help?"

Nicosa and I exchange a look. By prearrangement, he nods at me to go ahead.

"Commissario, with respect, when my sister, Cecilia Nicosa, went missing, we were told there weren't enough police officers in Siena to investigate because of Palio. You promised to help, but we have seen nothing, except some unfounded threats by you against my brother-in-law. We presented you with evidence of human remains in a vat of lye. Have they been analyzed?"

"A team from Rome is working on it."

"Cecilia is *still* missing, and you have another Palio coming up in August. Last night a man very close to the Nicosas was killed. The violence here is out of control."

"I am sorry you have that impression, Agent Grey. This kind of atrocity does not happen in Siena. This is a calm city. We do not even allow cars in the heart of the downtown. In ten years of working here, I have had twelve bank robberies and six murders—three of them in the last twenty-four hours, coincidentally since you arrived. You have heard that two men were shot to death in Il Campo?"

"Yes," answers Nicosa.

"How do you plan to investigate these murders?" I continue briskly. "As well as the kidnapping of my sister and the attack on her son?"

The Commissario's slender shoulders seem to sink even farther under such heavy burdens.

"I am nothing but a high civil servant," he apologizes. "I am in charge of immigration, passports, and weapons licenses—which is all that is generally called for. But as I said, the police in Rome are of the top-notch."

"Then let me suggest that we bring in Rome right now, with the assistance of the FBI. We have the expertise and the manpower. Why not?"

"I am sorry, *signorina*. That is impossible." He raises his eyebrows for emphasis. "It would not help to get your sister back."

He reclines in the chair. The chair is blue. The carpet is blue, just like in the Bureau. I guess blue is the international color of law enforcement and its consequent evasions. Beside me, Nicosa is tense and staring straight ahead. I can feel the storm gathering and try to head it off.

"You work immigration. Does that mean terrorism?" The chief does not reply. "I'm trying to get a picture of what happened to Sofri. Cars don't just spontaneously catch on fire."

The long fingers in the white cuffs come together, signaling that we are about to be granted crucial, top secret information.

"There is a mosque in a neighboring city that is receiving high attention," he allows.

"Is that relevant to this investigation?"

"I don't think so."

"Then you're saying the fire bombing of Sofri's car was *not* an act of terrorism meant to destabilize the city before the next Palio, or something like that?"

"Unlikely."

"Do you have any suspects at all?"

"Nothing I can discuss."

"Please. We are both professionals."

The Commissario briefly shuts his eyes as if avoiding a painful thought.

Like a thunderclap, Nicosa shouts, *"Al diavolo questo!"*

"We don't know," the Commissario says calmingly. "But we will find out."

"When? How? What is your plan?"

He leans forward, bringing his skull face toward us. On the wall behind him are photographs of his children, and the usual certificates in gilded frames. His tone takes on elegiac solemnity.

"Signore Nicosa, I must tell you, the coroner's report is grim."

"A man of seventy-one is burned to death in his car. How much worse can it be?"

"The fire didn't kill him, *signore*. First, he was beheaded."

The pitiful looks we received from the cops downstairs are now understandable. They already knew what we were about to hear.

I briefly touch Nicosa's hand. He is wordlessly gripping the chair.

"Then it's clear. Sofri was killed by the mafia."

The Commissario nods. "It is a mafia-style killing, meant to convey a message." His flat brown eyes slide toward

Nicosa. "As to the meaning of that message, we should properly ask the victim's business partner."

"Sofri was never involved in anything illegal," Nicosa replies, tight-lipped.

"...Although," the Commissario continues as if Nicosa hadn't spoken, "given the timing, it may have had something to do with the killings in the Piazza del Campo."

I force myself to exhale and relax, hoping Nicosa gets the cue and doesn't broadcast with telltale body language that we were right in the middle of it. The Commissario may be a high bureaucrat, but he has no doubt been trained to recognize the stiff posture and rapid blinking of a guilty man.

"What do you mean?" I ask.

"There were two male victims. One was shot in the middle of the square, right in front of a group of Boy Scouts, the other through the window of a third-story apartment."

"What is the connection between the victims?"

He doesn't bite. "We are investigating."

As if the body in the apartment wasn't found beside a sniper rifle. As if the bald one lighting a cigarette wasn't instantly identified by police sources as a mafia operative.

"I mean," I say naïvely, "what is the connection of these victims to *Sofri*?"

"In both homicides, the bullets were fired from Sofri's apartment. And he was killed hours later."

Nicosa manages to ask, "How do you know where the bullets were fired?"

"The ballistics report. We have reconstructed the path and speed of the bullets. In fact, we *have* the bullets. You see, we are just as good as the Americans."

He smiles smugly, and I realize he's been playing us all along, only to get to this point.

I return the smile and ask, "Are you seriously suggesting

that Sofri, a seventy-one-year-old scientist with no history of violence, was capable of firing a high-powered weapon from his own window in broad daylight, with a hundred percent accuracy?"

"We don't know who fired the gun, but we are certain as to where the shots came from. Our theory is that the mafia murdered Sofri and set fire to his car in retaliation for the deaths of those two men. That's all I can say at this time, and I have probably said too much."

"Have you given this to the press?"

"Not everything. I reserved it for your ears only."

"We appreciate your candor," I assure him.

He nods curtly. Nicosa stands.

"What about my wife?"

"I have pulled in extra officers and assigned every available detective to the case. Our department is under a microscope—the case is all over the Internet, those sick websites that love the misfortunes of famous people."

"And what progress have you made, with all this police work?"

A pause. "We're doing the best we can."

"*Non fare sopra te stesso,*" Nicosa says.

The Commissario fixes him with an impassive stare.

"Again, my sympathies for the tragic loss of your friend."

Going down the marble staircase with the bad smell, I ask Nicosa what he said to the chief of police.

"I suggested that he not get above himself. People who get above themselves are generally brought down."

"Damn right. Talk about arrogant. You were good," I tell my brother-in-law. "Didn't let on, didn't give an inch."

We scramble down a few more steps and then Nicosa stops. Taking hold of the flaking metal banister, he bends his head, and weeps. Watching from the bottom of the stairs, Inspector Martini waits respectfully.

. . .

WHEN WE return to the abbey, Nicosa goes straight up to his tower. Giovanni is once again gone. He slept past noon, Sterling says, and then the same kid who took him to school showed up and they left.

"How was he about Sofri?"

"Badly shaken. But he won't talk about it. When we rolled past the roadblock, he put his hood over his head and just kind of zipped up."

"Did he say anything at all?"

"He said, 'This is crazy.'"

"What was he doing when you found him yesterday?"

"Like his dad said, he went back to the old neighborhood. He was in the *contrada* headquarters, eating soup."

"Eating soup?"

"They have a kitchen set up. I guess there's always a mama or two around."

"Well that's okay, then," I say.

"Wish I could say that's true. When I found him, he was high as a kite."

"That's disappointing. My talk with him had no effect."

"When you were sixteen, did you have a clue?"

I take off the worn-out courthouse heels I wore to see the Commissario, letting them drop one by one to the floor.

"I don't know what I'm doing here. We might as well go home."

Sterling looks at me with clear eyes. "You understand there's not a real good chance of rescuing Giovanni from himself."

"I'm not going to let him just go down."

"Poor ole Ana. The Invasion of Normandy, all by her own self."

"Leave me alone."

"Aw, come on."

Sterling is lying across the sweet-pea bed with his hands behind his head, wearing nothing but undershorts. The heat of the afternoon funnels through the small arched window like a flamethrower.

"Come on, now." He pats the sheets. "Come on over here."

This is a welcome change. I take off my skirt and flop beside him in just my camisole and bikini. Sterling slips an arm under my neck, and I roll against his shoulder, finally safe in protected territory. We are quiet. I breathe the living smell of his body.

"Sterling, the Commissario is dirty."

"All right."

"You knew that?"

He shrugs. "What'd he do?"

"He gave himself away. In the meeting with Nicosa. He's telling us Sofri was killed in retaliation for the mafia bozos being shot from his window. But the only way you could know that is from the ballistics report. And the ballistics report hasn't been released. Not even internally."

"Are you sure?"

"Inspector Martini told me. I saw her in the police station on the way out. I asked if she'd seen the ballistics report on the shootings in the Campo, and she was surprised, said nobody has, the lab is days away from even letting the detectives know the results. The only one with access to a preliminary finding is the Commissario."

Sterling thinks about it. "He saw the report that said the shots came from Sofri's apartment, makes a call, and sets him up for a retaliation kill. Because the Commissario is a *cominato*. A made man."

"That's why he won't involve the FBI or Rome," I say.

"He's trying to contain it."

"Two mafia guys are killed in his piazza. On his watch. He's responsible. They own him. Everybody is owned by somebody around here. Half the time they themselves don't even know who. Look at it! Giovanni's a soldier in the bank of cocaine. Cecilia pays bribes. Everyone in this family is owned. And here I come, like you say, the Normandy invasion, waving the flag of liberation. What a joke."

"Let's go after the bastard," Sterling says. "Let's take him down."

"With what proof? We have no evidence to tie him to the mafias."

We stare up at the beamed ceiling.

Sterling says, "I really miss baseball. I bet it's the All-Star Game."

I laugh out loud and snuggle close. His fingers begin tracing circles on my back and are just finding their way under the silk strap of the camisole when my U.S. cell phone goes off. The screen says Los Angeles.

"It's Mike Donnato."

"What is it with that guy?" Sterling mutters.

"Mike? You're on speaker."

"Hi, guys. I thought you'd want to know."

"We always want to know." I smile over at Sterling, who rolls his eyes.

"I've got something on Spectra."

"The chemical company?"

"Yes," says Donnato. "Where Nicosa's company has an account. I've been looking for a common denominator between Nicosa, sodium hydroxide, and your sister."

"We know Cecilia's remains aren't in the tank of lye," I say. "She's been kidnapped, and we have proof of life." I fill him in on the ransom call, and Sofri's murder in retribution for the shootings in the piazza.

When I am finished, Donnato tells us what *he's* got.

"Remember I said to follow the lye? I put Spectra into my computer," he says. "I typed in 'Spectra Chemical Company,' and 'under surveillance' comes up, entered by an agent in Pittsburgh, meaning the Bureau is already onto them. I pull up what the case agent wrote. He's been monitoring a 'Ndrangheta connection that moves cocaine concealed in bulk cargo on container ships from Colombia through Naples to Pittsburgh—then from Kentucky to Ohio and on to Chicago."

"Is this container ship connected to anything else?"

"That's what I'm onto," Donnato says. "I'm going to our Field Intelligence Group and checking with other agency partners in the intelligence community."

"Good to spread the net."

"I'm hoping that DEA or ATF has more information on Spectra, how it connects to the drug route to Chicago, and if Nicosa is somewhere in the mix. I'll see what I can weave together."

By the time we hang up, Sterling has left the bed and pulled on jeans.

"Let's go find your nephew," he says. "I don't like leaving an open fire unattended."

WE FIND Giovanni in plain sight, sitting on the steps of the Fontebranda fountain in the Oca district. Silken green and white crowned goose banners still festoon the alleyways, perennially jammed with a slow-moving river of tourists. A duo of street guitarists competes with radios and the waves of sound pouring into the heads of every teenager through an ear bud of some kind. They all have something in their mouths as well—baby pacifiers from the Palio, a cigarette, or someone else's tongue. Giovanni is sitting thigh to thigh with a slightly older girl who sports choppy bangs and streaks of crimson in her black hair. She is inordinately thin, with a devil tattoo crawling up one leg toward the crotch of a torn miniskirt. I recognize her as the waitress from the photos taken by the detective who trailed Giovanni to her apartment.

"I want you to meet Zabrina," Giovanni says. "She has something to say." He nudges her. *"È giusto. Andare avanti."*

The girl raises heavy-lidded eyes. Her movements are dreamy to the point of narcolepsy. We wait until even Sterling can't wait anymore.

"You have something to tell us, darlin'?"

"I know where Giovanni's mother is. I saw her."

35

FOR FIFTY euros and a gelato she agrees to come with us, moving out of the range of eyes and ears in the Oca district, staying with the crowds, through the clogged commercial center, past McDonald's and the post office, to the flat residential neighborhoods as they steadily grow darker, streetlights dimmer and more sparse. The closer we get to the edge of the city, the quicker we pick up the pace, Giovanni keeping up with the crutch.

Explaining that her boyfriend, Yuri, has just moved out, Zabrina nestles seductively between Giovanni and Sterling, filling out the image of the vamp she cultivates—ripped leggings under the miniskirt, big gold-tone earrings, and multiple strands of plastic beads. Her lips are matte red, her eyes rimmed with black, the pupils enlarged. She tramples along in silver heels like some kind of gypsy rock star.

Sterling steers us toward the bus station. The kiosk is closed, but one bus is lighted and idling near a concrete island, exactly where I had landed from Rome. In the distance the wine bar in the Medici fortress where Zabrina and Giovanni met is still lighted and alive. Sterling and I don't have to speak to confirm the intuition both of us have had since leaving Oca: that we are being followed.

Sterling orders the kids to get on the bus.

Giovanni objects. "You have to buy a ticket."

"Then buy the tickets."

"To where?"

"Doesn't matter where. Just do it, fast."

And Giovanni does. When we first met, at this spot, he was late. Irresponsible, even spoiled. The difference is that at that time he had still been whole—he could take for granted his mother's steady presence, that his parents would be the center of his world forever. Picking up his American aunt had been just one of his many important obligations, including a flurry of calls to his customers in the bank of cocaine, the moment we got into the car. He bounded like a retriever then, never out of breath. Now he is willing to take orders, careful not to twist the leg or tweak the arm as he turns from an automated ticket machine. There is no way back to being that uninjured sixteen-year-old.

"Where do we go?" Zabrina asks as we hustle up the groaning steps of the bus.

"Just for a ride," I assure her.

"Where?"

"Monteriggioni," Giovanni answers. "Not far."

"Why?" she asks, showing a suspicious streak that we will have to negotiate.

"Do you have other plans?" Sterling wonders, keeping her moving toward the rear.

She blinks at him with her kohl-rimmed eyes. "What kind of plans?"

Although we are the only passengers, the four of us have squeezed into the very last row, where we can see anyone who comes on board. The doors close and the bus moves out. You can feel the heat of the engine through the seats. Already Zabrina has a crush on Sterling, and it is easy to see why. He is the type of man who looks great even in yellow LED transit lighting, while everyone else appears tubercular. At ten-thirty p.m., on a local bus to nowhere, he is alert and protective, his eyes ceaselessly scanning the darkened countryside—which must appear to a young excitable girl as sexy indifference.

Mind you, if she were an asset we were working through the Bureau, things would be entirely different. We would still be back at the field office, filling out permission forms, and no encounter would have taken place without a remote team recording every word. But here in the back of the bus, there are no rules. We can get information out of Zabrina by any means.

"Why you kidnap me? I think maybe I should be scared."

"You are free to go, any time."

"In the nowhere? In the night?" she says haughtily. "What is that?"

"We need for you to tell us exactly where you saw Signora Nicosa," Sterling says nicely. "And we don't want anyone else to hear."

"Oh, sure."

Giovanni assures her this is true.

"I want a cigarette."

"You can't smoke on the bus."

"Who cares?"

"It will draw attention."

She stands, swaying with the movement. "I get off."

"Why are you such a bitch all of a sudden?" Giovanni snaps. "You're the one who came looking for me."

Hanging on to a strap, Zabrina bends over in pain. A tremor passes through her body.

"I am scared." She catches her breath. "I am looking for Giovanni and everyone knows I am—*una straniera*."

"A stranger," Giovanni explains. "When she entered the Oca district and was asking for me, naturally people are suspicious."

This is a surprise. "I thought *he* was looking for *you*."

"No, no," says Zabrina. "We don't really know each other. I search to speak to Giovanni, to tell him where his mother is. Because I hear his name from..."

"Around," Giovanni interjects, as if we couldn't guess it was through other druggies in the *contrada*.

"You went looking for him?"

"That's a dangerous game so close to Palio," Sterling drawls.

"Is why I scared."

She fidgets with her earrings. Sterling eases her into a seat and she sits with obvious relief. But the effort to speak English is too hard, and she begs Giovanni to translate.

"I am from Calabria," she continues emotionally in Italian. "The poorest place in Italy. It is not like the north. The countryside is not like here. There it is very rocky and hard to grow things. The mafias—Camorra and 'Ndrangheta—they are a way of life. No family is untouched, and don't get me wrong, the women are just as bad. They will be on the cell phone warning their sons what's going on in the village or if someone has a grudge against them—because they are proud of their sons, they help them climb the ladder. Everyone sees people murdered in the streets, even little children. You can't get out.

"It sucks for everyone. But if you're poor, what do you do? My mother used to sew. She made lace and towels and things like that. It brought in a little money. In Calabria, the way to make money is drugs. You sell a little, you do a little. Then you become a courier. My mother was a courier. Yes, of course I am angry. She was a middle-aged woman taking drugs into the United States. I wish she'd been caught because now she is dead—one of those murdered in the street. A guy goes by on a motorbike and *poom poom poom*, at the market, in front of everyone. There were protests at the funeral and everyone got upset. A mother! It was in the news.

"I know I'm addicted. We're all addicts—my friends, my old boyfriend, Yuri. We know we're all going to die. I knew from the time I was born I was going to suffer. I tried to leave and come to a beautiful place like Siena, but it is my fate to suffer, like the women in Calabria. Sometimes they marry you off, and then the husbands leave. My father drove a truck all over Europe. He was never home. My mother raised six children alone. When I saw that lady...Giovanni's mother...I recognized her. She was the doctor in Siena who said I have to stop taking drugs because already, at this moment, I have hepatitis."

"You have hepatitis?" Surprised, Giovanni asks in English.

She pats his hand. "Don't worry, I am fine." Continuing in Italian, she says, "I went to Calabria to get high. Big deal. If you get there right after a new shipment comes in, the stuff is good, and my cousin, Fat Pasquale, takes care of me. This time, we went there to get high and Yuri almost died. Because that sick freak with the hands like Frankenstein made it too strong. He couldn't give a shit. You are just a sack of weeds to them. And I saw this poor lady—I am sorry to tell you because she is your sister and Giovanni's mother—well, she looked very bad."

I press my lips and turn to Giovanni.

"The man she describes is called the Puppet. His real name is Cosimo Umberto, and he's a well-known mafioso. He lost his hands in a bomb explosion and now he wears prostheses. Ring a bell?"

Giovanni shakes his head.

"He's pretty hard to miss. When you were in the hospital, your mother and I saw this creep, right outside your room."

"Why would he be outside my room?"

"You tell me."

"I don't know anything that happened in the hospital. I was in a coma, remember?"

The bus is slowing down. A shuttered convenience store swings into view.

"This is Monteriggioni," Giovanni says with more enthusiasm than you'd expect for a deserted bus stop. "From here it goes straight to Poggibonsi. Do you want to go there?"

Satisfied that if someone was following us they aren't anymore, Sterling says we don't need to go any farther. Monteriggioni is another, smaller walled fortress town, a mini-satellite built for the defense of medieval Siena. We get off the bus outside the gates and see that in the piazza they are having a festival. A kiddie carnival has been set up in front of the old stone church. Although it is close to midnight, the rides are still going. Giovanni says the bus back to Siena won't come for an hour, so we buy sodas and tufts of fried dough and sit on a wall.

The wind is humid and cold. The misty lights against the flat storefronts remind me of the outdoor dinner party in the ruins of the church at the abbey when I first arrived— white tables, white roses, the Nicosas' flashy friends. All of that has vanished with Cecilia. Under tender little strings of lights, sleeping children are carried by their young fathers, leaves blow across the piazza, and the black sky presses in. The moment is surreal.

"Will you help us?" Sterling asks the girl.

"Yes; I'll do anything. I don't care what happens. I hate that man with the terrible hands. He didn't care if Yuri died on the kitchen floor. I'll shoot him myself."

"We don't want you to do that," Sterling says. "But can you draw a picture of the apartment complex?"

"I'm a bad artist."

"Just a sketch."

Sterling takes out a memo pad and pen he keeps in the pocket of his cargo pants. Zabrina puts down the tiny mirror she is using to reapply the bloodred lipstick. Beneath the studded jacket she wears a black shirt with extra-long sleeves that have holes for the thumbs, like leggings for your hands. The sleeves make it awkward to hold the pen; childlike, she clutches it and scratches out the rectangles of the Little City.

"Now show me the apartment."

She makes an X.

"You're doin' real good." He flips the page. "Give me a layout inside the apartment. Every window and door you remember."

A picture emerges of Cecilia's prison.

"Here is where you come in. This is the kitchen," Zabrina says.

"Where does that hallway go?"

"*Sinistra.* Going left. Next to it, the bathroom."

"Where do they keep Dr. Nicosa?"

"It must be here, in the back."

I get up and pace, while Sterling runs the interrogation and Giovanni throws in a few words of translation. The three of them huddled on the wall in the foggy nighttime chill, creating the outlines of a hostage rescue plan, could almost look like an investigative team.

"A shipment comes in, and the druggies show up for a free fix. How do they know?"

"They receive a text message," Zabrina says.

"Who sends it?"

"For me, it is my cousin, Fat Pasquale."

"You're from Calabria, so you have cousins there. Family."

"That is correct."

"They know you."

"They don't live there. In Little City. But Fat Pasquale knows me."

"What happens when you bring your boyfriend, Yuri?"

"Yuri comes with me, so it is fine."

"You vouch for him and it's okay?"

"Yes."

"Have you ever brought anyone else?"

"Once, a girl. She paid for the gas."

"And Fat Pasquale had no problem with that? If you vouch for someone, in they go. No questions asked."

She shrugs. "Why not?"

We see the lights of the oncoming bus split horizontally in the mist.

"Do they check for weapons?" I ask. "Before you go inside?"

"Not me," says Zabrina. "Because I am family."

We are not the only ones on the ride back to Siena. It turns out a group of English tourists has come over to Monteriggioni for the little festival. They ask how we liked it, and we say fine. Zabrina falls asleep next to Sterling with his arm around her shoulders.

36

WE INTERCEPT Nicosa at his morning swim. Despite the alluring nothingness of sunlight on clear water, the pool holds no appeal. Sterling and I are ready to engage; our minds are working twenty-four, forty-eight hours ahead.

"We know where your wife is and how to get her out. But you need to hire professionals," Sterling says. "You need us."

"Who?" asks Nicosa, toweling off. "You and the bartender?"

"No, sir. Oryx, the security outfit we work for. Chris and I could not execute an operation this size alone."

"What size operation are you talking about?"

"There are a couple of ways to go, but each one involves manpower and hardware. It'll be expensive."

"I've been there before, in El Salvador."

"This will be kinda different from protecting coffee beans."

Nicosa, wary of a sell job, lights a cigarette and moves toward the pool house—more like a CEO considering coffee futures than a desperate husband.

"Why can't you just go in and get her out?"

"Think of it this way," Sterling explains. "You know the Taliban?"

"Not personally."

"You know how they operate in Afghanistan. Without

mercy, trust me. Rescuing your wife being held captive in Little City by 'Ndrangheta is like trying to spring someone from a Taliban prison compound."

"Sorry, I don't see the connection."

"You have to get inside an armed fortress protected by a close-knit, fanatical local population," I explain. "And then you have to get her *and* your operatives safely out."

"Sir?" Sterling looks straight into Nicosa's eyes. "Please believe me—this is not the time to fuck around."

"Just because you *tell* me you can do it, why should I put my faith in you?"

I am losing patience. "We got a lucky break with Zabrina. We knew Cecilia is alive, but now we know exactly where she is being held."

"As of the time Zabrina saw her in Calabria," Sterling reminds us. "This thing is like rotten meat. Each day that goes by, it becomes more spoiled. You keep letting time run on, and we can't guarantee you'll even recognize your wife when we bring her back. That's the truth as I've seen it."

Sterling's candid delivery finally gets to Nicosa. He slips on a white terry robe, takes a quick hit off the cigarette, and decides.

"Let's go upstairs," he says.

THE DEEP voice coming from the speakers in the twelve-sided tower belongs to "Atlas," the handle for the crafty boss at Oryx whom I have never met. I picture him in a fake wood-paneled office in their covert warehouse outside Heathrow Airport, but he could be anywhere in the world. The theatrical Welsh accent is the same as when he called to offer Sterling the mission that took him out of London—although, come to think of it, Atlas could be putting on the persona to disguise his identity. They love pulling that crap.

It doesn't matter. At the end of the day, Nicosa is buying the services of a private army that will materialize at the right time and in the right place, with extreme prejudice.

"Not only does 'Ndrangheta have an infinite number of boy lookouts, but also, quite frankly, their best defense is the fact that they have your wife entombed inside a living maze of a thousand civilian apartments," Atlas intones. "Negotiation has failed. Despite all this endless macho posturing, there is a point when the bad guys actually do become fatigued, and then the application of force is a reasonable alternative."

"That's what I have been saying." Nicosa, still wearing the robe, says in the direction of the speakerphone. "Go in and get her out."

"We could go full-on tactical," Atlas agrees. "Would you like to know what that would look like?"

"I'd like to know what I'm buying, yes."

"Understood. We would execute before first light, when the suspects are asleep or drugged out, or at best, generally unfocused. Using the advantage of surprise, we quickly defeat their lookouts, move in fast and locate the victim. In and out in less than two minutes."

"Killing everyone who gets in your way?"

"There will be casualties. Not ours."

"You sound very certain."

"I am certain, Mr. Nicosa."

"How do you know Cecilia won't be—*Come si dice?*—"

"Collateral damage? Has Sterling told you about his experience and training?"

"No, sir," Sterling answers.

He is sitting ramrod straight beside me on the leather couch, both of us looking FBI-ish and military in boots and jeans. Outside it is another summer day in Tuscany.

Atlas invites him to explain.

"In Delta Force," Sterling says, "we have a training exercise

they call the shoot house. The walls are made of ballistic material that will stop bullets, and they can be moved around so
the configuration changes every time out. On initiation there
would be a flash-bang—that's a little bomb that gives off noise
and smoke to distract the suspects. Then a team of three or
four will enter, and it's their job to take out the targets. The targets are paper cutouts of men, like shooting targets, okay? So
they rush the door and take up positions, making sure they're
not crossing fields of fire. The first guy in is always right. You
follow his lead—go where he's not. There can be no missed
shots," Sterling adds. "All bullets accounted for."

Nicosa is unimpressed. "So? Target practice with paper
dummies."

"There is a bit of a complication. There's always one living
body in the shoot house, and you never know where he will
be. Maybe sitting there on the couch. That's your victim, the
one you're *not* supposed to kill. First out, it's the unit commander, then we all trade off with our teammates—being the
one sitting on the couch, live ammunition whizzing past your
head. It's like if Ana and I burst in here and you're at that
desk, and we let loose busting out those windows with real
bullets. And you just sit there. That's how much you have to
trust your buddies. It's the point of the exercise, really."

For the first time since I've known him, Nicosa is struck
silent.

After a moment Atlas says, "All right?"

Nicosa shakes his head and shouts at the speakerphone.

"No! It's not all right! Shooting crazy guns with my wife
on the couch!"

Atlas's voice is bemused. "I thought not. Would you care
to hear another alternative?" He waits and continues. "The
most reliable way to rescue your wife would be to use human
intel."

"No guns?"

"Yes, guns."

"They still ain't gonna just hand her over," Sterling says.

"It means getting tactical assets *inside* the apartment," I explain. "Without using deadly force. We enter the apartment, locate the room where Cecilia is being held, and use force *if necessary* to get her out."

"How do you get those soldiers, fighters, whatever they are, inside the apartment with nobody seeing?"

"Because they don't *look* like soldiers," Sterling says. "They look a hundred percent like drug addicts. They'll be posing as friends of the little girl, Zabrina—the one who came lookin' for Giovanni. She vouches for them. They get in."

"Will she do this?" Nicosa wonders.

"Zabrina has something special we can use to our advantage—a deep abiding hatred toward the Puppet for using her boyfriend as a test dummy. He gave the kid a high dose of heroin that almost killed him," I say. "Cecilia saved her boyfriend's life."

"You're willing to use this girl, just like that?"

"She knows the risks. She's from the south, she understands revenge, and she wants it. My company believes infiltration by our operatives with her help is the best course," Atlas says.

"Do it."

"Good. The mission must be completed within the next thirty hours," Atlas adds. "Before your wife is moved to another location."

"Just one question," Nicosa says. "How *do* you plan to get Cecilia out?"

"No worries. That's why you hire Oryx," Atlas tells him. "Peace of mind."

THE ORYX team assembled outside London, secreted in a nondescript industrial building near the airport. Because they are often hired to get people out of impossible situations—reporters held by North Korea, or a Red Cross ship hijacked by pirates off the coast of Somalia—there are many hostage rescue scenarios in the Oryx playbook to which they can quickly turn.

The accuracy of Zabrina's drawing could not be trusted; they needed to update schematics of Little City, particularly the roofs. For this, they used Google Earth, and from there worked with an engineer, using the overhead views to computer-generate three-dimensional drawings of the buildings.

The housing project had been built according to low-cost government standards, each pod exactly alike. They first considered the vast underground basement as an escape route for Cecilia and their operatives, but Sterling, who would be the strategic commander, did not like the possibility of being trapped. The answer to Nicosa's question—once we were in, how would we get Cecilia out?—became a point of heated argument until a compromise was reached. There would be a diversion, and the victim would be removed to a point of safety hundreds of miles away.

Inside the hangar, the layout of the apartment had been hastily constructed. They rehearsed the breech. They knew where the front door was, how it opened to the kitchen, and the hallway that led to the back bedrooms. If they determined that Cecilia was not on the premises, they would abort. Atlas called the abbey early on the morning the team was to leave for Italy. All that remained was for Nicosa to wire the money, and we were good to go.

37

MOMENTS AFTER getting the green light, I hurry from the sweet-pea bedroom, down the marble steps, and run smack into Dennis Rizzio.

He eyes the rucksack and field boots. "Slow down, Ana. Where're you off to?"

"Dennis! What are you doing here?"

We face each other in a cube of morning light between the stairs and the main quarters. Dennis, large enough to block the sun, is wearing a somber blue suit and not about to give way. Behind him lies the steamy flower garden, and farther back, in the hot gravel courtyard, four American FBI agents standing at the ready beside two idling black sedans.

"I'm looking for your brother-in-law. Is he on the property?"

"What's going on?"

"I have a warrant for his arrest."

"What for?"

"We've obtained new evidence—enough to charge him with smuggling cocaine into the United States."

"How did this happen?"

"Well, we had a little excitement in the port of Pittsburgh. The Bureau's had a vessel owned by the Spectra Chemical

Company under surveillance for some time. Spectra, we discovered, is part of a layered business syndicate going back to 'Ndrangheta, which uses the vessel to conceal drugs in bulk cargo. But it didn't come together until Special Agent Mike Donnato in the L.A. field office put the cargo in the ship next to your brother-in-law. Based on that, he initiated a joint task force request by DEA and the FBI for Customs to do a red alert inspection.

"A Coast Guard cutter went out to escort the Spectra ship, but it ignored repeated orders to stop. The Guard sent a helicopter. The Spectra ship reversed direction. The chopper followed in pursuit, and the bozos started throwing stuff overboard. Ultimately the Coast Guard removed eight people off the ship and seized 4,558 pounds of cocaine with a street value of $61 million. The cocaine was tucked away inside sacks of coffee. It's Nicosa's coffee."

Nicoli Nicosa will be arrested, today or tomorrow; it hardly matters when. Foremost on my mind right now is that every minute going by is making me later to meet Sterling and Chris at the Walkabout Pub. The strategic clock to recover Cecilia is ticking. We can't afford a celebrity takedown right now, involving lawyers and the press.

"Can you delay the warrant?"

"Gee, honey, I don't think so. There's a steady stream of coke flowing from Colombia to Naples to the Midwest—and we'd kind of like it to stop."

I keep striding toward Giovanni's car, fast-forwarding every angle I can think of to *deflect this now*, and coming up blank.

"Good morning," I say to the American agents.

"Good morning, ma'am," one answers, politely blocking the path. "Do you mind holding up a minute?"

"Sure. Not at all."

I turn back. Dennis is waiting in a patch of shade with a disapproving look.

"Who are you trying to kid?" he says.

Unshouldering the rucksack, I let it drop to the ground.

"I've been briefed by Mike Donnato on the task force with DEA concerning smuggling routes through the port of Pittsburgh," I say. "I didn't think it would unwind this quickly."

"It's not a good play for you to try to protect Nicosa," Dennis advises.

"That's not it. We found his wife. She's alive."

"Thank God!" Dennis says with genuine relief. "That's great! Really good news. Where?"

"Captive in a 'Ndrangheta stronghold in Calabria."

"That's where you're going—with the unauthorized use of force?"

"This operation has nothing to do with us. Nicosa hired Oryx, the private military company, to get her out."

"Well, he can afford it."

"We have good intel. We've got a source who—"

Dennis holds up a palm. "Don't say another word."

"We've exhausted every resource. Negotiation failed. We can't go to the police. The Bureau's hands are tied—"

Dennis displays *two* palms. "I can't hear this, *please!*"

"Sorry."

"The timing is rotten," he says, removing folded documents from a coat pocket. "But the evidence is solid. The cocaine was buried inside bulk quantities of raw coffee beans with the generic label Bravo Beans, traveling on board a container ship owned by the Spectra Chemical Company. Special Agent Mike Donnato requested that the DNA of Bravo Beans be tested by Quantico, and they found a match to an arabica variety only grown by Nicosa's company. Bravo Beans is a front, but a sophisticated one. They had all the right bills of lading, invoices, layers of falsification, everything."

"And the scientific evidence is conclusive?"

"You're asking the right person," he says self-mockingly. "In seventh-grade science we had to make DNA out of Life Savers. My mom did it for me." He glances at the documents. "There's something called 'class III chitinase LR-7, signal peptidase complex subunit SPD35.' I believe it's a gene that makes it possible for the coffee plant to pollinate a couple of times a year, so that it produces more coffee. It's a biologically engineered gene unique to this particular brand. They created a new plant. Nicoli Nicosa was responsible."

Nicosa has appeared in the doorway. Despite the pressed white shirt and tailored trousers, he looks like hell, deprived of sleep and racked with anxiety.

"That's a lie. I had nothing to do with it."

"Let's just take it easy, Mr. Nicosa," Dennis advises.

"My late partner, Sofri, is the one who created that gene. He was the first to crack the genome of the coffee plant. He deserves the credit."

"He can have all the credit in the world," Dennis says.

"Are you here, like Il Commissario, to accuse me of murdering my wife? If so, I can assure you, because I heard her voice on the phone, you will not find her in a barrel full of lye."

"Glad to hear it," says Dennis. "But the lab in Rome hasn't gotten started on that yet. They're not even in possession of the evidence."

"Why not? The provincial police secured the site."

"Between Siena and Rome there are a million footsteps. My name is Dennis Rizzio, FBI legal attaché," he goes on, crisply offering Nicosa the papers. "Sir, on behalf of the U.S. government, I have a warrant for your arrest. As a federal officer, I have jurisdiction when it comes to crimes committed in the United States, and in this case the charge is smuggling cocaine into the cities of Pittsburgh, Columbus, and Chicago."

Nicosa glances at the papers. "Come in from the sun," he suggests.

Dennis needs to pat Nicosa down, and I advise my brother-in-law to accede. This accomplished, we follow him into the kitchen. In synch with Dennis now, I place myself between the suspect and any potential weapons of heavy pots or knives. Glancing at the clock, I see that I am now seventeen minutes behind schedule.

Nicosa offers a cold drink.

Dennis isn't playing. "Thank you, no. Best you should call your lawyer and get your affairs together here, in case things are delayed while you're in custody in Rome, as they surely will be."

Giovanni comes into the kitchen, free of the crutch, walking just on the soft cast.

"Why are you going to Rome, Papa?"

"This man is from the FBI. He needs to talk to me."

"About what? Why did he say you are in custody?"

I warn him, "Giovanni, this is not for you."

"He's innocent," cries the boy.

"Go upstairs. Go see your friends," Nicosa says tiredly.

"He doesn't do anything bad!"

Dennis says, "You're a good kid, standing up for your dad. But this is out of your arena. *Partirlo solo e lasciarlo va.*"

"I know he doesn't. I saw."

"You saw what?"

My cell phone is vibrating. "That's Sterling. He's waiting in Siena. Nicoli, please, just go with Agent Rizzio now."

"When the man they call the Puppet came into my room," Giovanni says.

Nicosa gives a cry of pain. "*Basta! Chiudere tu ora!*"

"In the hospital," Giovanni insists. "I heard everything."

"How is that possible? You were in a coma."

"I was coming out of it. I could see and hear. I saw what happened, Papa."

Looking back, I realize he is talking about the twenty

minutes or so when Cecilia and I were in the basement, eating potato chips and garlic mayonnaise. The nurse saw the first signs of returning consciousness and tried to call, but there was no cell reception in the basement.

"Tell them what kind of man you are," Giovanni says to his father in English.

Nicosa begs, "Please!" and gropes for a jacket lying across a chair. "I am ready to go."

"No! Don't arrest him! Listen. This freak came into my room. I could see him. I could smell him. My father was there. He told my father that if he did not cooperate, even worse things would happen. My father said, *Non lo farò! Non mai di nuovo!*"

"Why did he say that? What did he promise never to do again, Giovanni?" Dennis asks.

"Because they beat me up and he didn't want it to happen again. Because of drugs I fall down in the shower...I am almost killed in the street...I almost die from drugs, and so he refused." He looks at his father, tears streaming freely down reddened cheeks. "He refused! I never told anyone what I heard," he whispers. "I swear."

"That's enough," Nicosa says quietly.

"No, Papa. Tell them what happened."

"Right in my own kitchen, I am crucified. My blood is on the walls!"

"Tell them."

"It is revolting."

Dennis says, "There's nothing you can say we haven't heard before."

"I apologize to this man," Nicosa admits through gritted teeth. "I show respect. But still I say that I want nothing more to do with this business of cocaine because I see what it has done to my son. For his sake, I have to stop the whole thing.

All of it. Cosimo Umberto accepts this. He understands a father protects his son. And then he asks that I show proper repentance. To 'Ndrangheta, you see. For this, he urinates into a plastic cup and tells me to get on my knees and drink."

Giovanni clenches his fists. "But he refuses! My father refuses!"

"If I drank, it would mean nothing. If I didn't drink, it would be the same result. There was no way out. They were never going to let me or my family go. Things were good for them, using my coffee shipments. I had agreed to that under force of threat. And on top of it, I paid *pizzo* for the privilege! They wanted everything to stay the same. When I refused, Cosimo Umberto left the hospital room. I thought I had prevailed. But then they took Cecilia. Still, I was arrogant. I believed we could get her back by the usual means...until they murdered Sofri. Then I saw that I had lost everything. Things will go on as they are. I am sorry, Giovanni. Sorry you have me as your father."

Nicosa takes the boy into his arms. Giovanni sobs against his shoulder.

"I thought you didn't love me."

Nicosa's fingers grip his son's hair. "What insanity is that?"

Ruthless and lawless as the mafias are, in a weird way, they are the only ones to depend on in a world of betrayals. I am sorry—sorrier and sadder than I can express at that moment in the abbey kitchen—that Cecilia, her husband, and their son became so isolated and distrustful, they turned to the enemy instead of to each other. That's the insanity.

"I thought they took Mama for a hostage because if they took me, you would not pay the ransom."

"I love you." Nicosa rocks him. *"Ti voglio bène, ti voglio bène, non era mai qualunque domanda."* He looks over the boy's head at Dennis. "Now you see my humiliation."

"Dennis?" I say. "Can we talk?"

We walk outside to the courtyard.

"We need time. We're on the verge of getting Cecilia back. Can you keep Nicosa under house arrest? Thirty-six hours is all I ask."

Rizzio scans the open gate and unprotected boundaries of the abbey.

"Security will be a bitch."

"Put him in the tower."

Dennis smiles at the thought. "You know this whole thing started because of an egg fight?"

"You lost me."

"The massacre in London. Your photo popping up on the bad guys' network. Even your sister's abduction. I'm serious, there was an egg fight in Calabria between two clans of 'Ndrangheta—the Ippolitos and the Barbettis—that has resulted in over a dozen murders that we know of."

"How does it tie in to London?"

"It was a birthday party for the Ippolito family. That's why they targeted the restaurant. We traced the cell phone calls to the shooters from Calabria. The calls originated from leaders of the Barbetti clan in a town called San Luca, where family feuds go on for decades. This one started out at one of these little carnivals, with kids throwing eggs. The enemy comes back throwing fireworks. Now two young men are dead, and the revenge killings commence—over twenty years and three countries, including a shoot-out in Germany where four people are killed. The Ippolitos left to escape the warfare, but it followed them to London."

"Who tipped off the Barbettis?"

"We think it was Martin Barbetti, the owner of the restaurant," Dennis says, a pained expression crossing his face.

"But?"

"But we can't find him. He disappeared."

Poor fawning, obedient Martin. He will never be found, unless someone initiates a sweep of the English countryside for tanks of lye. I pick up my rucksack with a questioning look at the FBI legat.

"Tell me when it's over," Dennis says. "Just don't get caught."

38

SOMEWHERE ON the southern coast of France, a Volkswagen hatchback is stolen. Later that night it will arrive in Siena, driven by a young Serbian woman operative whose combat name is Delilah.

Over the next few hours, the Oryx team will continue to infiltrate Italy, entering the country by different routes. This is to avoid being tagged by the mafia rats who have day jobs as customs agents. As a further precaution, the team will never be together at the same time and place. Being former military, they are trained in exactitude; once the whistle blows, it is as if their body clocks are locked into synch. At 11:48 p.m., when Delilah makes initial contact with Zabrina at the wine bar, the former Special Forces explosives expert, combat name Ripper, who lent us the flat in London, is touching down at Reggio di Calabria airport, at the very tip of the mainland.

The trickiest part was finding an operative who could pose as a drug addict friend of Zabrina's. Atlas decided she should be young and female, and came up with the Serbian woman who stole the Volkswagen, who has been through so many wars she can sleep during a gun battle. Her task is to have Zabrina vouch for her so that she can gain entry to the apartment. Once inside, she will locate Cecilia and transmit that information to Sterling, who will oversee the operation from a mobile command center.

Zabrina is the wild card, as Delilah discovered the first time they met, at the wine bar in the Medici fortress. We needed them to be seen together by witnesses who could verify that the two are tight. When Delilah showed up she said in English, "I just got in from Florence," and Zabrina responded correctly: "I love Florence." While she poured wine, Delilah chilled at the bar. Later, they danced with some Brits who were high on amphetamines, boasting about having dropped "the world's strongest legal party pill." The club lights flashed, music pounded, and Zabrina disappeared with the English boys. Delilah spent the night in the Volkswagen, searching for her new best friend, who had ended up in Quinciano, eighteen kilometers away. The pills *were* legal in England—if you happened to be a veterinarian. They contained an anti-worming drug used on animals.

"Blew my head off," Zabrina explained.

We wanted to believe Zabrina was trainable. She seemed to enjoy playacting; it appealed to her exaggerated sense of self. We ran through techniques I learned at the FBI Academy—role-plays, in which Sterling was the Puppet. When he grabbed her forcefully, shouting, "Who is this new little piggy, and why should I let her in?" Zabrina forgot it was an exercise and started to cry. Another time she wanted to know when we would give her a gun. Wasn't she supposed to shoot the Puppet?

Sterling reported to Atlas that the girl was too unstable to carry a mission in which the lives of both the victim and Oryx employees were at risk. We considered ditching the entire approach and going back to all-out tactical, but then her cousin, Fat Pasquale, texted to say a new shipment of cocaine was in. The timing was right. Atlas decided we were "green to go," but insisted that we stick to the plan and play it inside the apartment. If we tried an assault in the tightly packed complex, we could not contain the danger to civilians. He assigned Chris as backup firepower. Working with a stopwatch, we calculated that all we needed from Zabrina was thirty seconds of rationality.

From that time on, Delilah stuck close—did not even allow Zabrina to go to the bathroom alone—and kept her clean and sober, except for a couple of Percodan for abdominal pain, until they got into the Volkswagen for the drive to Calabria. I hopped a commercial flight to Reggio di Calabria. Sterling and Chris had already left Siena in the mobile command unit—a van outfitted with tactical video allowing them to see several actions taking place at once; a Cougarnet communication system working on an encrypted FM signal; weapons; cash; phony passports; changes of clothes; ammunition; medical pack.

IMMEDIATELY ON arrival there is an obstacle. When Zabrina and Delilah, covertly trailed by Chris, reach Little City and cross the bridge to the far sector, they are stopped by a rambunctious block party taking place in the courtyard between two divisions of the housing unit. Several hundred people in undershirts, shorts, housedresses, and bathing suits are carrying on—grilling food, drinking, dancing, and fighting. Children are running wild. When Zabrina and Deliah appear, a silent alarm seems to ripple through the population; heads turn and eyes slide their way as they continue to the apartment.

Little kids scramble over junkies stoned out on the steps; an encouraging sign that it is business as usual, until they discover that Fat Pasquale isn't there. At the store? Out murdering someone? Who knows? Lounging on the folding chair, keeping watch over who is permitted to enter the

pharmaceutical lab, is a different obese guy, wearing a bandanna around his head and slicing a cantaloupe into quarters
on top of a cooler with a very big knife. Zabrina explains in
southern dialect that she is Fat Pasquale's cousin. He looks
at Delilah—big-boned, big-chested. Sunglasses perched on
a baseball cap; bushy black ponytail. Fake plastic Louis Vuit-
ton rucksack. Almond eyes. Inviting smile. Skintight jeans.

"Who is this?"

"A friend from the university."

"You vouch for her?"

"I vouch for her."

Without getting up, a wedge of cantaloupe stuck in his
mouth like an obscene grin, he sticks a foot out and pries the
door open with dirty toes.

"Bullrider, we're at yellow," Delilah murmurs into the
transmitter under the cap, meaning they're at the last position
of cover and concealment. The last point at which they could
still turn around and nobody would know they were here.

THE KITCHEN may be exactly as Zabrina described it—the
tulip tiles, the sink where the woman chopped tomatoes—
but the Puppet is not at the table. Instead there is another
joker fooling with the white powder and syringes, and a
terrified *porcino* who gets up and runs. The dealer reaches
for a shotgun propped against a chair. Delilah assassinates
him with a single shot from a silencer-equipped Beretta. She
draws a weapon from a hidden compartment in the rucksack,
pulling on infrared goggles, moving down the hall, trusting
that Chris, thirty seconds behind them, has taken out the
guy with the cantaloupe.

Just like in the shoot house, the first one in is always right.
Delilah, in the lead, saves the *porcino*'s life by shoving him
into the bathroom and shouting for him to get down and

shut up. Then she is at the locked bedroom door, behind which the infrared image shows a human figure.

"Bullrider, I see the hostage!" Delilah says. "What is the order?"

"Move to green and execute," Sterling answers from the command unit in the van.

Chris sets a charge and they blow the door to Cecilia's room.

Sterling, parked a block from Little City, copies Delilah's report that they have breeched, and conveys the order to execute to two other operatives who are stationed in a warehouse several miles away, where a light helicopter has been standing off—the team having agreed at the training run in England that airlifting the victim to safety was the best way to get her out. The warehouse doors open, and the little bird rolls out on skids, rotors already turning. Within fifteen seconds it is airborne.

At the same time, Ripper, who has been enjoying a *panino* in a café across from the van, leaves the table and ambles toward an alley, where he punches a number on a cell phone. As he passes, a small box clamped to a gas line fizzles and explodes with an unremarkable *pop*.

Delilah and Chris rush the bedroom, finding Cecilia curled up in a corner, shivering like a dog, her arms covering her head. They pull her to her feet and say the prearranged words:

"Nicoli Nicosa sent us. We're going to get you out."

Cecilia's face screws up and she makes sounds. She is trying to cooperate but can hardly walk. Chris lifts her onto his shoulder.

"We're in control of the hostage and coming out," Delilah reports as they exit the front door of the apartment.

Here there was always a problem. We could figure no way *out* of the apartment except the way they came *in*—but there would be no time to check whether the planned escape route was clear. Despite our misgivings, that job had to be done by Zabrina. As soon as Chris defeated the lookouts, she was to exit the apartment, turn right, enter a dead-end hallway, and open the door to the roof.

Chris and Delilah get through the front door of the apartment with twenty seconds to make it to the point of contact with the helicopter—past tenants and junkies potentially clogging the second-floor walkway. But these people have witnessed too many mafia shootings to hang around and gawk. When they see the man with the bloody melon rind smile slumped in the chair, and hear sirens from the gas explosion, they scatter.

Farther down, Zabrina is faithfully at her post, holding the door to the roof. Chris lopes up the steps with Cecilia draped around his neck in a fireman's carry. All three break out of the stairwell to the roof and open sky as the helicopter appears and stabilizes.

Chris lowers Cecilia to her feet. In the whirlwind of debris she sees the figure of Zabrina in the midst of the pandemonium—a hopeless drug addict, who somehow, impossibly, miraculously, came back to this hellhole to save her.

An operative is lowered on a rope. There is a harness at the end. Cecilia sags against Delilah as they force her legs into the straps.

"Her too!" she murmurs.

Zabrina, stunned by the noise and impact, tries to hold her long hair back from whipping painfully across her eyes. Voiceless in the earsplitting drone, Cecilia struggles and reaches toward the girl.

"Take her! She's coming, too!"

Chris shouts, "Don't worry, we'll take care of her."

They muscle Cecilia into the harness and buckle it. The operative places his body over hers.

"No! Wait!"

"You're safe! I've got you!" he shouts as the chopper lifts and banks away with the two of them still dangling.

Zabrina watches as they're dragged across the sky. Delilah remembers her wide-eyed stare of awe, met by Cecilia's downward look of anguish. Without hesitating, the two Oryx operatives were already securing a rope to an iron stanchion they'd identified on Google Earth, and tossed it over the side of the roof. It will be easy to rappel down and become lost in the confusion created by the gas line explosion. Delilah is already over the top. Chris is calling to Zabrina to get her ass over there, when the roof door bangs open and Fat Pasquale lumbers out, followed by a dozen half-grown boys who spring ahead like wolves.

"*Vieni qui!*" Chris yells at Zabrina. "Now!"

Slowly Zabrina hooks her hair behind her ears with a dreamy gaze, as if it were a summer night and she was standing at a fountain with her friends.

"*Now*, you stupid bitch!"

"I will be okay," she says with a soft wave of the hand. "I am family."

One quiver of hesitation and Chris would have gone back, but she emphatically turns from the route of escape. She makes her choice. He disappears over the edge. One jerk from below and the rope is unloosed and drops to the street.

The helicopter is gone, and with it, the wind, the whole episode. Heat rises off the tarred rooftop. The sky is bleached white, empty. Fat Pasquale keeps coming, weapon sighted. Zabrina fingers the plastic bags of powder she snatched off the kitchen table, safe inside her pockets. She gives an innocent shrug, as if she, too, is a victim in this, but he keeps on coming, up to point-blank range, until he is close enough for her to see the ripples in his sweat-soaked forehead, and look into the cold eyes of her cousin.

Zabrina smiles and says, "It's me."

39

WHEN I arrive at the airport in Reggio di Calabria, the last stop on the mainland of Italy, I am met by a barrel-chested, forty-year-old Englishman wearing sailor's whites. He has a wind-burned face and sun-bleached red hair going up his arms. We drive urgently, almost wordlessly, to the harbor. Once we had identified ourselves as Oryx, there was little interest on either side in getting-to-know-you. The only thing that matters is the clock.

There is plenty of action at the terminal where hydrofoils and ferries make the twenty-minute crossing to the island of Sicily. It being the high season, the ferries run 24/7. This is good, as the plan is to blend in with the boat traffic. At a private marina farther up the seaside promenade, we board the *Miramare*, a seventy-foot megayacht chosen by Atlas for its speed and large rear deck—a good target for a helicopter put-down. There are two other Oryx people as crew, a full-scale operating room with an Italian surgeon and a nurse, a one-hundred-horsepower tender in case of the need for evasive action, and a cache of arms. It takes forty minutes to clear the harbor and another hour to reach cruising distance from the coast. Once the navigation system confirms that we are at the coordinates, the skipper cuts the engines and we put out fishing lines, like any well-heeled party on holiday. Moments later, we receive the radio message from Sterling that the helicopter is on its way.

LATER, FROM the vantage point of a weathered redwood deck on the California coast, it will strike me that these events could never have taken place on our side of the world, not in the easygoing Pacific Ocean—lazy, and flat as a sheet. Not in America, where everything is known. I was something of a baffled passenger on that mystery cruise, just as I had often been mystified by the secrets of Siena. Now, standing on the rear deck of the *Miramare*, feeling the vibration of the motors and staring at the foamy wake as it fans out and is lost, I try to make the pieces of this voyage fit, but ultimately, there is no rational explanation for why, at any minute, a woman who was a stranger, and is now my sister, will come out of the sky at the end of a rope.

But rational things are not what make you cry, and I begin to cry even before the helicopter appears; in fact, as soon as Sterling radios that Cecilia is on the way. Not from the release of emotion even hardened agents feel when a victim is returned to safety—the abducted child back in the arms of the mom—but a calm, almost imperceptible letting go.

When I left my grandfather Poppy's house to go to college, I had been conditioned to expect that being cared for would always come with a side dish of punishment. One day a pair of new sneakers would appear under the bed, and the next day he would open the door and hit me across the face because I had kissed a boy. Forever after, I wrapped myself in isolation to avoid being smacked. I didn't know the sentence was of my own making, and that it could be absolved as quietly as a bird flying off a branch.

On the yacht there is nothing but action and noise—slicing

rotors, whipping water, angling for position, and radio squawks—but inside me a tranquil space has opened. The side doors of the chopper slide apart and human faces peer out: Cecilia and the other operative, whose body protects hers as they are lowered to the deck. She is hanging limp, and for a gut-squeezing second I think she is dead, but when the crew unbuckles the harness she stands on her own. The operative is winched back up, the helicopter angles away, and Cecilia and I are safe in each other's arms. The wind mixes our tears and tangles up our hair. I allow my sister into my heart.

The engines catch and the huge vessel kicks up speed, rock-solid and comforting. The nurse and doctor help Cecilia slowly down a flight of polished teakwood steps to a living room suite with enormous windows looking out at the bright green ocean, and a white sectional couch thirty feet long.

Stripped of the helmet and rescue gear, she is almost unrecognizable, as if she's been in a horrendous car accident. Her face is swollen in uneven contusions. She is filthy, emaciated, with an ugly gap in her front teeth, her lips caked and peeling. The muscles in her arms have atrophied, and everywhere her skin is splotched and bruised. They take her vital signs and say her blood pressure is high and she is dehydrated.

"We've got her! She's here!" I tell Nicosa, and put Cecilia on the phone.

"Sto bène. Ti amo. Com'è Giovanni?"

She speaks in hushed Italian. Nicosa is confined to the abbey under house arrest, but Giovanni is waiting in the small coastal town of Agropoli, where a launch will take him out to the yacht. Cecilia is only able to speak to her husband in two-word sentences. She has no tears, maybe none left.

I sit beside her on the couch while the nurse administers an IV.

Cecilia puts a hand on mine. It sits there, light as a sparrow.

"They left the girl behind."

"Zabrina?"

"Is that her name?" she murmurs tiredly.

The doctor prepares a syringe and injects it into the IV line. Clear liquid moves through the tube into her bloodstream.

"She's my patient, and she's very ill," Cecilia says, before the dark.

CHRIS REPEATED the code words to Atlas in London: "It's been sorted. We've given them the good news." After setting off the diversionary explosion on the gas line, Ripper, in cleanup position, moving in the opposite direction of the confused crowds, gained entry to the rearmost courtyard of the Little City, where the crack house was situated, and climbed the steps to the roof. There he saw the body of Zabrina Tursi, shot in the chest at close range. Fat Pasquale, balancing heavily on one knee, was attempting to recover the bags of cocaine from her pockets when Ripper took him out with an easy head shot. He lined the pack of boy-criminals who were loyal to Fat Pasquale up against a wall, and made them wait there in the sun while he disappeared down the steps and locked the door to the roof, abandoning them to the buzzing corpses.

40

AT FIRST the families come respectfully to the *questura*. In the cool of the morning, the olive farmer Aleandro, whose uncle had also vanished, meets with thirty others on the steps of the shambling building. Middle-aged, dressed in casual summer clothes, they might have been mistaken for a neighborhood coalition lobbying for more streetlights, except there is something profoundly cohesive about that group—solemn determination on their faces, as opposed to the mixed bag of international tourists mindlessly wandering the sunlit passage between the modern world and the commanding black-and-white medieval cathedral looming in the Piazza del Duomo ahead. The tourists are expecting to be entertained by whatever tale history wants to tell. The families of the "disappeared," who have come to see the Commissario, have abandoned their illusions.

Rumors of human remains found in a tank of lye in the woods have been around for days, but Sofri's grotesque murder, which carries the stamp of the mafias, stirs fear and disgust in a town where, despite the divisions of the *contrade*, much of the population still believed they were free of the influence of criminal networks. Maybe it's also the nature of a fortress town, where, as Giovanni said, anyone outside the walls is viewed as an enemy, but these few dozen citizens have taken an unprecedented step: to come forward after years of silence to look for answers to the whereabouts of missing loved ones who have gone white shotgun as a result of mafia incursion into the north.

The Commissario receives the families with cordiality. They crowd into his private office and stand humbly on the clean blue carpeting before the authority of flags and certificates. The slim, superior chief of police expresses empathy for their suffering, and then shares some vital information not yet available to the public. The forensic laboratory in Rome, he reports, has determined that the contents in the tank were not human after all, but rather the remains of cows, like the white Chianina cows we had seen on the road to Falassi's dump site. Disappointed, they have to acknowledge it is common practice for farmers to dispose of the bodies of animals by dissolving them in lye. They accept the Commissario's condolences for their collective losses, and his wish that they might find some comfort in this news.

CECILIA TELLS the press that during the ordeal it was her Catholic faith that kept her alive. She now counts eating good food and sleeping in a bed as great blessings. She talks about the power of God's grace to restore her to her family, and how the upcoming August Palio will bring renewal to the troubled people of Siena.

But after the euphoria comes depression. She is confused about hours and dates. She has an overwhelming fear of going into the city, specifically to the church of Santa Maria di Provenzano where she was snatched—chloroformed, in the traditional way of kidnappings—and quickly carried out, like another fainting victim, to the ambulance that abducted her to Calabria. The offer of a visit to the Oca district, once a haven of security, triggers a panic attack because she insists, irrationally, that we will have to pass that church.

Imprisonment in Calabria has made her panicky inside rooms. Either she shuts down or paces, repeating, "I have to take a walk. I have to get out of here."

She only feels good when she can see the horizon. She takes long walks, past ordinary households and blazing fields of broom and red poppies, observing like a visitor the way people in this part of the world spend their time—tending to aviaries, constructing stone walls. Often I am with her. Sometimes we sleep outside on the chaises by the pool, like schoolgirls on a sleepover. Our pace is gentle; our talk is about small things: chores that need to be done to keep the abbey running and supplied with food and clean laundry. We assume the comfortable roles of providing for men, as if they need more care in the aftermath than we do. But always, underneath, is the deep tone of parting—just when we have begun.

DENNIS RIZZIO rolls in like a tank, using every threat of prosecution in the legal arsenal to put the squeeze play on Nicosa. He finally agrees to provide information on 'Ndrangheta's drug routes into the United States in exchange for immunity on the cocaine smuggling charges. In the court of Rizzio, Nicosa's defiance of the Puppet in Giovanni's hospital room on behalf of his son was an act of renunciation that absolved him of moral sin. It is win-win for Rizzio. Tasked to infiltrate the mafias, he busted their trade network and came up with a four-star informant. To his credit, the big guy made a big point with SAC Robert Galloway of my role. By the time I receive the call from Donnato that they need my deposition in the conspiracy trial of former FBI deputy director Peter Abbott, I am ready to go home.

STERLING AND I say our good-byes to Chris at the Walk-about, with a toast to Muriel Barrett in absentia. Metropolitan Police Inspector Reilly picked her up at her partner Sheila's cottage in Surrey, and mediated a deal between the British anti-mafia task force and the Italian authorities in which the "sodden old cow," as Chris put it, would cooperate in providing information on 'Ndrangheta's bank of cocaine. Muriel will not be prosecuted in Italy as long as she never returns to that country. Banishment somehow seems an appropriate punishment for a crime that happened in a medieval town. The worst part is that her cloud paintings will most likely end up for sale beside the stale cakes in the deranged landlady's half-dark *mercato*.

When the bar is littered with empty shot glasses and drained pints, a text comes in on my cell with a link to photographs. The source is *Proibito*. Untraceable. The photographs show Falassi's dump site, where we discovered the vat of lye. Instead of an orderly crime scene, marked with tape, tents set up to protect the evidence, and someone standing guard, everything has been torched. Nothing is left of the water tower, the shack, and the half-burned house but piles of charred timber and curled metal. A deliberately set circle of fire has reduced every bit of organic matter to charcoal.

The human remains are lost, never to be identified. Whatever evidence the Chef might have left that could lead to his bosses—records of payment, bank statements or weapons—is gone. Every trace of Falassi's crimes has been systematically eradicated.

Chris, Sterling, and I huddle around the tiny screen.

"Who did this? The police or the mafias?"

"Flip a coin."

"How long ago?"

"Hard to tell. We could go down there..."

"Something still might be recoverable."

"I'm gonna bet," Sterling says, "that no bone fragments, nothing from the vat, ever made it to the lab in Rome. The story that it was animal remains is a flat-out lie."

Chris leans on the bar. "Whoever did this had knowledge, access, and means. So did whoever sent Ana the pictures. Who do you think that could be?"

I have been balancing the cell phone in my palm as if the weight of it could give me the answer.

"Let me take a shot."

I punch in a number. Inspector Martini answers. Her voice is noncommittal.

"Are you at work?" I ask.

"Yes."

"Just wanted you to know I'm going home soon."

"Oh," she says. "That's too bad. I hope you enjoyed your time in Italy."

"It's hard to leave such a beautiful country. But luckily I have pictures to remind me."

"I'm glad you will go with good memories," she replies.

"Thanks for all your help. Kisses to your daughter."

"*Prègo.*"

The two men are watching as I click off the phone.

"It was her. Martini sent the photos. She must have been at the site with the police when they 'found out' it was torched."

Chris and Sterling nod, not at all surprised.

"I knew the Commissario was dirty," I say. "Now he's succeeded in obliterating the entire investigation. Not only has he wiped out the evidence, but also he's got Falassi, the only witness, and he could be dead by now, who knows?"

"He doesn't have Falassi, love," says Chris. "We do."

. . .

INSTEAD OF heading through the gates of the abbey, we continue a hundred yards up the road and turn into Aleandro and Antonella's driveway.

"What are we doing here?" I ask.

"The witness is inside," Sterling says.

"Falassi?"

"Uh-huh."

"The whole time? After you told me he was taken into custody by the provincial police?"

"Yup."

"Why didn't you tell me the truth?"

"You had no need to know."

"No need to know?"

I stifle the exasperation as Sterling removes three handguns from the trunk of Chris's Fiat and hands one to me. We go up to the front door of the red-tile-roofed house. It is late and we awaken Aleandro, who appears wearing pajama bottoms and a T-shirt. They exchange words in Italian, and we go down to the basement.

The room has a shiny new deadlock. Aleandro opens the door and turns on the light. We enter with weapons drawn. Inside it is stifling. There are no windows and nothing in the room but the canister where the olive oil is stored, a chair, and a cot, where Marcello Falassi is sleeping naked.

He does not offer any resistance.

"Che ora è?" he asks.

Aleandro tells him it is time. When he puts on jeans and a maroon rayon shirt, he no longer looks like a brute who drives a truck and disposes of bodies, who turns his house into a toxic dump where his wife and mother limp around in the chemical waste of his crimes. All cleaned up—shaved, hair cut short—he looks like a witness, and that is what he will be.

When we had returned to Siena after discovering the vat of lye, between the time I made contact with Dennis Rizzio and when he notified the provincial police, Sterling and Chris had gone back to the campsite to stake out Falassi. Not trusting anyone, even me, they had taken Falassi prisoner for his own protection. While I was slavishly operating within protocol, Sterling was executing the independent covert action necessary to prevent the one link we had to the mafias' chain of command from escaping, or being compromised by corrupt authorities.

Sterling and Chris had brought Falassi to Aleandro, whose anger at the disappearance of his uncle had been so palpable when we sat at the dining room table. For many years, Aleandro had been waiting for a better day, when the politics were right, to expose the lot of them. He promised Sterling he would hide the witness until the time came to present him to the world. Falassi agreed to become *pentito*— a penitent who confesses and is therefore forgiven by the Catholic state. For this he would recount everything he had witnessed. The bodies that were brought to be disintegrated. The ones who brought them. And those in charge.

"You were playing me," I tell Sterling as we handcuff the witness and march him to the car.

"Protecting assets."

"Chris knew."

"Course he knew. He was there."

"You trust him, but not me?"

"This ain't about that," Sterling says.

"What'd you think? I'd leak it to the FBI?"

Sterling stops and turns toward me in the chilly night.

"I was protecting you from being put in a compromising position."

"I would not have told Rizzio if it compromised the mission. There's a lot of things I don't tell him, but I tell you everything."

"Okay!" says Sterling, raising his hands in defense.

We put Falassi in the backseat with Chris. We get into the car.

"You know exactly what I'm saying." I slam the door.

"Kittens!" scolds Chris. "Play nicely. There's a witness here."

I doubt Falassi is interested in anything except hiding from the mafias for the rest of his life. He agreed to testify that he had taken care of Aleandro's uncle's body, and to state that it was the Commissario who gave the order for arrest and disposal. I am hopeful that the momentum of his confessions will encourage Inspector Martini to come forward and identify the Commissario as the one who ordered his police goons to torch the campsite.

I noticed that the only other object in Falassi's basement room was a Bible.

A FEW days later Sterling gets the call from Oryx. A Russian billionaire is arriving in London and needs body-guarding for his family. I am surprised when he asks me to partner up.

"It's an easy gig," Sterling promises. "We pose as a couple of American tourists. Follow the Russian's wife and kidniks to Harrods. Keep an eye out while they're having tea. No worries, Atlas will hire you on a freelance basis. Make some bucks before heading back to L.A. How about it?"

If Sterling is trying to make it right after hiding Falassi from me, this isn't cutting it. I want no part of the old lady hooch, nor am I up for wrangling over the same old issues. After being immersed in the mysteries of Siena, I want something shiny and concrete, like a brand-new apartment that smells of fresh paint, with appliances wrapped in plastic and pristine walls in which nobody has set a nail.

"Appreciate the offer, but I need to get home," I tell him.

"Sure thing," he says. "I'll call when I'm back in the States." But when we kiss good-bye in the courtyard, with Chris waiting to drive him to the airport in Rome, I honestly don't know if we will see each other again. Cecilia is waiting sympathetically in the doorway when I hurriedly turn back to the abbey. I don't want to see Sterling walk away, carrying the black rucksack, once again.

JUST BEFORE the August Palio, Siena is swollen with visitors, and the sound of the *tamburino* mixes with human voices—not singing songs, but shouting for justice. When the story breaks that anti-mafia prosecutors have a witness willing to admit that he has been responsible for the disposal of hundreds of bodies killed by the mafias, the thirty or so polite citizens who had turned up in the Commissario's office and were offered the opportunity to drink his piss, swell to a huge crowd of families and anti-mafia reformers demanding answers.

Siena becomes the scene of a parade considerably less charming than drummers in medieval costumes. Angry marchers pack the narrow streets—many of them young people, as well as relatives carrying snapshots of those who have been taken. They line up outside the *questura* in the sad hope that Falassi can identify the faces of the loved ones he cremated in acid. Their signs read, ANTI-RACKET and ADDIO, PIZZO (GOOD-BYE, PIZZO), and REFUSO! International TV crews follow. One of the speakers is Nicoli Nicosa:

"The government can no longer silence what cannot be

silenced," he says into the cameras. "We have a witness to these diabolical acts. They cannot be hidden any longer."

The marchers pour into Il Campo, where the police have mobilized. I stay on the periphery, a bystander, nothing more. Now it is up to the Italian prosecutors. I do not envy the job of diffusing the turbulent emotions of the marchers—thousands of them, from all over Italy. If the Commissario were not already in custody, the mob would tear him limb from limb. An older woman, well-dressed, wearing a suit and large sunglasses, passes close enough for me to see the photo she is carrying of a smiling young man wearing an earring. Over the picture she wrote in English, "Please help me find him."

ON MY last night at the abbey, we make El Salvadoran *pupusas*. It is the kind of time-consuming dish for which you need the hands-on help of a sister. You have to make cornmeal dough from scratch, pork and potato filling, and a topping of marinated carrots and cabbage. I know I will never make it again, unless I make it with Cecilia.

"Nicoli cooked for us while you were gone."

"He's a good cook."

We are both wearing aprons, flattening balls of dough into circles with our palms.

"I think you're wrong about Nicoli," I tell Cecilia. "He was desperate when you went missing."

"I know."

"I don't think you do."

"And I think you're wrong about Sterling."

"That's another case entirely," I say lightly. "Nicoli was lost without you."

"He spent a lot of money and went through a lot of stress," she acknowledges.

"Jesus, Cecilia, it's not like he was buying a car! I can tell you, he was tortured to his soul."

She just laughs.

"You don't believe he's capable of really loving you?"

"What did he say?" she asks curiously.

"He said, 'I love my wife.' He would have done anything to get you back. He would have walked into the line of fire."

"I'm glad," she intones like a sleepwalker. "Don't put too much filling in."

My yellow stuffed half moons looked like Play-Doh time in kindergarten.

"Cecilia!" I want to shake her. "Your husband loves you! You have to believe me."

"Like you believe me when I say our father loved *you*?"

"It's hard when there's no empirical evidence."

"There is evidence." She points with a wooden spoon. "In your heart."

"Really? Our father was murdered. I'll never know how he felt about me. But your husband is here, every day."

She sighs. "Something like this goes so deep, it changes the way you look at life. You never feel right. It never goes away."

"Are you still talking about the other woman?"

"Not only her. I have lost my belief," she says.

We grill the *pupusas*. The cabbage goes on top. Giovanni and Nicosa come into the kitchen and we eat the *pupusas* hot with glasses of Pinot Bianco. Giovanni tells me he has decided to put off going to the university for another year.

"Are you sure?" I ask. We are driving back from Siena in the mailbox car, dispatched by Cecilia to get honey and pears for dessert.

"I don't want to leave my mom."

"That's very thoughtful, but I don't think she would want you to miss out on a whole year of school."

"It's okay; I don't really know what I want to do."

"What are you thinking about doing?"

"You're going to laugh."

"Make me."

"FBI. You're laughing."

"It's a *good* laugh," I say. "But in order to apply, you have to be a naturalized citizen."

"I'll move to America."

"The FBI requires you to have a college degree."

He thinks about it.

"I can do that," he says.

Already I am missing the combative teenager; it is bittersweet to see that he is growing up, deferential to his mom and peaceable with his dad. I don't tell Giovanni about the sacrifice Zabrina Tursi made. At least I can preserve that much of his innocence.

Nicosa still refuses Rizzio's insistence that the family relocate in exchange for his testimony.

"**YOU CAN'T** stay here," I tell Cecilia after the honey and pears, when we take our evening walk. "The family is marked."

"As I said, it's a war. You adjust."

"You people are targets! They'll get you at a traffic light, Cecilia! They killed seven people in England over an egg fight in Calabria! Why are you so stubborn?"

"My husband will never leave Siena. His blood is here. His work is here. He won't give in. For better or worse, I am with him. Isn't that what you wanted?"

"Your husband is behaving like a horse's ass." I stop and grip her shoulders. I look into her troubled eyes. "You're my sister. I love you. I can't just leave you in harm's way."

"I love you, too," she answers with resignation, and kisses me tenderly on both cheeks.

THE FOLLOWING day I fly back to Los Angeles. Cecilia and I do not speak of her marriage again. Nor do I bring up her affair with the Commissario. There are some things even sisters shouldn't ask.

SAN LUIS OBISBO, CALIFORNIA

EPILOGUE

ON MY first day back at the Los Angeles field office, SAC Robert Galloway calls me into his office.

"I brought you a souvenir." I unfold a green and white square depicting the crowned white Noble Goose.

"What is that?"

I try to explain the *contrada* system. "It's a scarf for Oca, the Goose."

Galloway removes an unlit cigar from his mouth and squints at the silk.

"Is that supposed to be me?" he asks suspiciously.

"Why?" I say. "Because it's wearing a crown?"

"I thought you were making a joke."

"It's not a joke! It's the symbol of the fighting spirit of the people of Oca."

Galloway says, "A goose?"

"Ever tangle with one?"

Galloway folds the scarf and puts it with his collection of law enforcement oddities, including a bear trap used to catch escaped cons in the Oklahoma territories and a miniature guillotine.

"I owe you an 'attaboy,' Ana. The intel from Nicoli Nicosa on trafficking from Italy is good. FBI HQ is *ecstatic*," he says with the deadpan irony I have learned to appreciate.

"Glad it's working out."

"Headquarters is talking about a two-year undercover operation spread over four states to bust the mafia's drug route."

"Great. I'm on it."

"You're done with this one. The lawyers want your body," Galloway says. "They need to prep you on the deposition for the Peter Abbott case."

"I know—it's already on my calendar. Is that why you called me in?"

"No," he says. "It's something else."

His tone is serious and I think, *Good. A new case.*

"I understand you came into an inheritance in Italy," he says.

"Yes, but it wasn't much."

"Whatever it was, you still have to declare it to the Bureau. Any undisclosed income has to be reported. Here are the forms," he says, and damn if they're not right there, waiting on his desk.

"**HOW'S IT** going?" asks Mike Donnato when I join him at the coffee machine.

"Another day at the office," I say, dropping the forms into the wastebasket.

"Want some?" He holds up a blackened glass pot.

"No, thanks. I've been ruined by coffee in Italy. Especially the Nicosa brand. They really invented a tasty bean."

"They never invented any bean."

"What are you talking about? The Nicosa bean that broke the case? The DNA specific to their coffee? Sofri, rest in peace, cracked the coffee genome and created a new plant."

"He's not the one who cracked it."

"Yes, he was."

"No, he wasn't. I came across that particular factoid researching the case. The Brazilians are the ones who decoded the coffee genome."

"Then how did Nicosa get ahold of it?"

"Sofri sold it to your brother-in-law for a share in half the company."

"How did Sofri get it?"

"How do you think?"

It takes me half a second. "Sofri stole it from the Brazilians."

Donnato gave me that world-weary look that says, *Welcome back.*

IF YOU move the chairs into the far corner of the deck, you get a slice of the Pacific Ocean through the roofs and telephone poles sloping down to a private beach just north of Santa Barbara, where I'm house-sitting for an old college friend. Her dad had the foresight to be a professor at UCSB back in the seventies, and to buy this modest stucco family home, which now would sell for a gazillion dollars. It's worth the commute to work, while I'm still looking for that dream apartment.

Sterling promised to call when he came back from Europe, but he never did. Instead, he just shows up.

"I'm at the L.A. airport," he says in the middle of a Sunday afternoon. "Where are you?"

I explain the situation, and he is there in two and a half hours.

"Where's your pack?" I say when he comes up the driveway.

"In the rental car."

"Planning to stay?"

"Thought I might."

"Good, because I have everything we need."

"What would that be?" he asks, with a light kiss on the lips.

"Fresh sea bass and a grill?"

I don't ask where he's been or where he is headed. From his restlessness it is a given that he is on a job. We are half-way through a pitcher of margaritas, but it is still almost like a first date. The needle is hovering at "Maybe." We could push through the charged, heavy air that still seems to sepa-rate us, or we could let it go. I've had time to obsess over whether I love him, and decided that I do. But you can love a lot of people and still let them go.

There is a large envelope on the patio table. I put a rock on top to keep it from lifting off in the sea breeze. Sterling notices that the stamps are from El Salvador.

"What's all this?"

"A letter from Cecilia. They moved down there, the whole family."

"They left Siena?"

"It wasn't safe."

"No kidding."

"The abbey is going to become one of those historic five-star hotels."

"I wouldn't know about those."

"Me either, but that's what Cecilia said. She was going to just take Giovanni, but Nicoli decided to go. And she decided that she wanted him to come."

He perches on the wooden arm of the Adirondack chair, where I am minding my own business, looking at the view.

"You can read it," I say. "Go ahead."

Sterling draws out the letter and a smaller envelope that is sealed.

"When were you planning to open this?"

"When I'm ready."

He fingers the envelope. "Any clue as to what's inside?"

"It's a picture that Cecilia wants me to have."

"What's the problem?"

"When I open it, I know what I'll see. My father."

He downs the margarita and pours another.

"No time like the present," he says.

"Except the past."

He gives me a reproving look. I grimace and open the envelope. Inside is a color print that has turned yellow and magenta with age. It shows a squarely built, dark-skinned young man in his twenties standing on a rise over a newly plowed field. In the background is jungle. His black hair is slicked back and he holds a straw hat. He is looking out of frame with an expression of calm anticipation, as if everything—the harvest, the rest of his life—is before him.

Sterling puts his arm around me, and looks over my shoulder at the photograph of my father.

"First time you've ever seen him, huh?"

"I was too young to remember."

I never imagined him that youthful. His face is untroubled and confident. For a long time we don't say anything.

"I see the resemblance," Sterling says. "You never found out what happened to him, did you?"

"I know that he was murdered, and they never found the body. Like the 'disappeared.'"

I lower the photo and notice that Sterling has been stroking my neck.

"Are you feeling me?"

"Yes, babe. I'm very glad you're here."

I put my hand over his hand.

"You know, all the time we were in Italy, whenever you'd touch me, I couldn't feel it," he says. "I mean, literally, I was numb."

I look into his face, surprised. "I guess you were still getting used to buildings that didn't have bomb craters in them."

He pulls back. "Should we take a walk on the beach?"

It is close to sundown and the air is chilly. We throw sweatshirts over our bathing suits. You have to go down a long flight of redwood steps, and then there is a tiny cove the other houses share, with big charcoal gray carved-out volcanic cliffs on either side; if you go around them you would be on a wide state beach. A steady gust is coming off the ocean and everything seems to be in motion—seagulls, waves, pelicans, sailboats way out. We walk along the wet sand, mirrored with flocks of long-legged pipers needling for crabs.

"What happened was, they changed the rules of engagement," Sterling says.

"This was after London?"

"When I left you back in London, yeah. The mission was in Pakistan. We paid the right people and crossed the border to Afghanistan. The target was a senior Hamas commander who was supplying guns to the militants. He was responsible for a lot of deaths, not only in Gaza. As you know, it's hard to get close to these guys, so they have a new policy—like with all these predator drones now, they're willing to accept a certain number of civilian casualties. I'm a sniper. It ain't how I was trained. For me, you sit in a hole for three days and surgically remove the bad guy. I was very vocal about the changes, but they overrode me. The client was just going to go ahead with it, knowing there could be other deaths, including family members. It became a numbers game. Like seven people is acceptable, but not eight.

"The way we pulled it off, we put a bomb in his cell phone. We switched out his phone and planted a small explosive charge in one exactly like it—had the same wear and feel as the old one. We were in a hide site in the desert. He showed up on the road driving his Land Rover. We called, he answered the phone. Our interpreter confirmed his identity: 'Is this Colonel So-and-So?' He said yes. We tapped in a code on the keypad, and it sent a signal and blew his head off. Surgical strike and no collateral damage. Mission accomplished. I should have felt good, right? Except the Hamas commander was also a dad, and he got his head blown off in front of his wife and kids, who were also in the car."

I suck in brackish air. "Doesn't quite sit right, does it?"

"I never used to have a problem. This time I didn't feel justified. I just felt dirty."

"Quit."

"And do what?"

"Go back to horses?"

We have been walking in surf up to our ankles. The damp salt wind keeps pushing, wrapping itself around our legs and insistently through our hair, as if nuzzling us to pay attention. The light is holding strong. Against the tide we walk into the water, finding ourselves waist-deep in a forest of rust-colored kelp, the soup of life. No longer resisting loneliness, I fold into his arms. My fingers dig into his flesh with desperation. He never flinches. He never once lets go. Halfway hidden, he pulls off my bikini bottom, and I wrap my legs around his hips, and the swells lift us together.

IN SIENA, Italy, a miracle occurs. The 1476 bronze sculpture of *Risen Christ* by Lorenzo Vecchietta, a Renaissance masterpiece that disappeared from the Santa Maria della Scala orphanage chapel four years earlier, is anonymously returned to the high altar. Experts believe it was stolen on behalf of a wealthy collector who kept it in a vault in his private museum, because it reappeared in perfect condition—the face of suffering, the right hand reaching out in forgiveness—as luminous and powerful as ever. No explanation was given for this apparent change of heart.

CRIME & GUILT

BY FERDINAND VON SCHIRACH

By turns witty and sorrowful, unflinchingly brutal and heartbreaking, the deeply affecting, quietly unnerving cases presented in *Crime and Guilt* are remarkable examples of minimal prose that is as mesmerizing as it is affecting. In "Fähner," a small-town physician and avid gardener betrays little emotion when he takes an ax to his wife's head, an act that shocks the locals but provides a long-awaited reprieve for the good doctor. In the startling story "Love," a young man's infatuation with his girlfriend takes a grisly turn when he comes to grips with his unconventional—and uncontrollable—impulses to truly know a woman. Attempting to hurdle through a midlife crisis, a housewife staves off depression with the rush she derives from the act of stealing in "Desire." And in "Snow," an old man whose home is used as a way station for a heroin ring agrees to protect the identity of the lead drug runner, who nonetheless receives his comeuppance.

Crime Stories

ALSO AVAILABLE
Blind Man's Alley by Justin Peacock
Dead Line by Stella Rimington
The Garden of Betrayal by Lee Vance
Layover in Dubai by Dan Fesperman

POCKET BLACK LIZARD
Available wherever books are sold.
www.randomhouse.com

THICK AS THIEVES

BY PETER SPIEGELMAN

Ex-CIA man Carr is on the other side of the law these days as the de facto leader of an elite band of thieves. If they can pull off an international robbery, they'll be set for life. But the higher the stakes, the greater the paranoia, and this crew's fears are about to explode. Their old boss, who set up this job, has been murdered. They're paying big, in more ways than one, for some badly inaccurate intel. And the one person in the gang Carr trusted most seems to be following her own, new agenda. Terrifically suspenseful and psychologically complex, *Thick as Thieves* is a hair-raising ride through the sleek, rarefied world of white-collar crime.

Thriller

BLACKJACK

BY ANDREW VACHSS

A savage murderer is leaving a trail of eviscerated bodies all over the world. Despite knowing the Cross team as ultimate mercenaries, a shadowy team of government operatives hires them to track and capture—but not kill—this elusive hunter. When a pattern is finally deduced in the seemingly random strikes, the Cross crew devises an elaborate plan that will put their leader directly into the creature's path. Andrew Vachss's first Cross novel mixes a murder-for-hire story with a horror novel in this mind bending, spine-tingling new thriller.

Thriller

ACKNOWLEDGMENTS

I must first acknowledge the work of others that has informed this journey. Roberto Saviano's *Gomorrah*, a first-person account of organized crime in Naples for which he is still at this time forced to live in hiding, was inspirational, along with *McMafia* by Misha Glenny. To understand the meaning of the Palio, *La Terra in Piazza* by Alan Dundes and Alessandro Falassi was an essential text, and *Palio, The Race of the Soul* by Mauro Civai and Enrico Toti was an insightful tribute.

White Shotgun would not have come into being without the generous assistance of many international law enforcement professionals. In Los Angeles: FBI Supervisory Special Agent Pam Graham and Special Agent George Carr, Principal Firearms Instructor for Los Angeles, as well as Assistant Director in Charge Steve Martinez and Supervisory Special Agent Mary B. Prang—with thanks for the privilege of attending the FBI Citizens Academy. In Washington, D.C.: Rex Tomb, Unit Chief, retired, and FBI Public Affairs Office and Public Affairs Specialist Philip Edney. In Rome: FBI Legat Leo Taddeo. In Siena: Commissario Dottore Andrea Arcamone and Barbara Poazzolti of the provincial police, who were extraordinarily welcoming and patient.

I am obliged to those who unstintingly shared their expertise. Michael Grunberg and Tim Collins provided crucial background on private military operatives. Dr. William Skinner was an indispensable medical adviser. Jesse Sweeney at Caffé Umbria coffee roasting company in Seattle, Washington, kindly provided a spur-of-the-moment tour. Ines Cortez graciously described her experiences growing up in El Salvador.

The enduring love of my husband, Douglas Brayfield, and daughter, Emma, allowed me to stay sane during the roller coaster of writing a novel. While our son, Benjamin, was living in Italy, he suggested that a crime taking place during Palio might make an intriguing thriller. He has continued to be an invaluable webmaster and photographer throughout this project.

On the home front at Alfred A. Knopf, I owe a huge debt to production editor Maria Massey and her crack crew, Maralee Youngs and Elizabeth Schraft, for meticulous reading; Paul Bogaards, Nicholas Latimer, and Pam Henstell for getting the word out; Anne-Lise Spitzer for state-of-the-art marketing; and Diana Coglianese for editorial support. I would like to offer profound gratitude to Sonny Mehta for his brilliant leadership, and to express special appreciation to Edward Kastenmeier, executive editor at Vintage Books, for gracing the manuscript with his keen attention.

Thank you to my friends at CAA, and to my longtime literary agent, Molly Friedrich, whose many gifts hardly fit in the four words of the dedication. She is unstoppable when it comes to excellence in publishing—a passionate advocate for both authors and readers.